D1632022

THE TRAVELLERS' LIBRARY

*

MASTRO-DON GESUALDO

A complete list of all volumes now ready will be found at
the end of this volume

MASTRO-DON GESUALDO

by

GIOVANNI VERGA

Translated by

D. H. LAWRENCE

LONDON
JONATHAN CAPE 30 BEDFORD SQUARE

FIRST PUBLISHED 1925
RE-ISSUED IN THE TRAVELLERS' LIBRARY 1928

INTRODUCTION

Giovanni Verga was born in the year 1840, and he died at the beginning of 1922, so that he is almost as much of a contemporary as Thomas Hardy. He seems more remote, because he left off writing many years before he died. He was a Sicilian from one of the lonely little townships in the south of the island, where his family were provincial gentlefolk. But he spent a good deal of his youth in Catania, the city on the sea, under Etna, and then he went to Naples, the metropolis; for Sicily was still part of the Bourbon kingdom of Naples.

As a young man he lived for a time in Milan and Florence, the intellectual centres, leading a more or less fashionable life and also practising journalism. A real provincial, he felt that the great world must be conquered, that it must hold some vital secret. He was apparently a great beau, and had a series of more or less distinguished love affairs, like an Alfred de Vigny or a Maupassant. In his early novels we see him in this phase. *Tigre Reale*, one of his most popular novels, is the story of a young Italian's love for a fascinating but very enigmatical (no longer so enigmatical) Russian countess of great wealth, married, but living in distinguished isolation alone in Florence. The enigmatical lady is, however, consumptive, and the end, in Sicily, is truly horrible, in the morbid and deathly tone of some of Matilde Serao's novels. The southerners seem to go that way, macabre. Yet in Verga the savage, manly tone comes through the morbidity, and we feel how he must have loathed the humiliation of fashionable life and fashionable love affairs. He kept it up, however, till after forty, then he retired back to his own Sicily, and shut himself up away from the world. He lived in aristocratic isolation for almost another forty years, and died in Catania, almost forgotten. He was a rather short, broad-shouldered man with a big red moustache.

It was after he had left the fashionable world that he wrote his best work. And this is no longer Italian, but Sicilian. In his Italian style, he manages to get the rhythm of colloquial Sicilian, and Italy no longer exists. Now Verga turns to the peasants of his boyhood, and it is they who fill his soul. It is their lives that matter.

There are three books of Sicilian sketches and short stories, very brilliant, and drenched with the atmosphere of Sicily. They are *Cavalleria Rusticana*, *Novelle Rusticane*, and *Vagabondaggio*. They open out another world at once, the southern, sun-beaten island whose every outline is like pure memory. Then there is a small novel about a girl who is condemned to a convent: *Storia di una Capinera*. And finally, there are the two great novels, *I Malavoglia* and *Mastro-don Gesualdo*. The sketches in *Cavalleria Rusticana* had already established Verga's fame. But it was *I Malavoglia* that was hailed as a masterpiece, in Paris as well as in Italy. It was translated into French by Jose-Maria de Heredia, and after that, into English by an American lady. The English translation, which weakens the book very much, came out in America in the nineties, under the title *The House by the Medlar Tree*, and can still be procured.

Speaking, in conversation, the other day about

INTRODUCTION

Giovanni Verga, in Rome, one of the most brilliant young Italian literary men said: There is Verga, ah yes! *Some* of his things! But a thing like the *Storia di una Capinera*, now, that is ridiculous. — And it was so obvious, the young man thought all Verga a little ridiculous. Because Verga *doesn't* write about lunatics and maniacs, like Pirandello, therefore he is ridiculous. It is the attitude of the smart young. They find Tolstoi ridiculous, George Eliot ridiculous, everybody ridiculous who is not "disillusioned."

The *Story of a Blackcap* is indeed sentimental and overloaded with emotion. But so is Dickens' *Christmas Carol*, or *Silas Marner*. They do not therefore become ridiculous.

It is a fault in Verga, partly owing to the way he had lived his life, and partly owing to the general tendency of all European literature of the eighteen-sixties and thereabouts, to pour too much emotion, and especially too much pity, over the humble poor. Verga's novel *I Malavoglia* is really spoilt by this, and by his exaggeration of the tragic fate of his humble fisherfolk. But then it is characteristic of the southerner, that when he has an emotion he has it wholesale. And the tragic fate of the humble poor was the stunt of that day. *Les Misérables* stands as the great monument to this stunt. The poor have lately gone rather out of favour, so Hugo stands at a rather low figure, and Verga hardly exists. But when we have got over our reaction against the pity-the-poor stunt, we shall see that there is a good deal of fun in Hugo, and that *I Malavoglia* is really a very great picture of Sicilian sea-coast life, far more human and *valid* than Victor Hugo's picture of Paris.

The trouble with the Italians is, they do tend to take

over other people's stunts and exaggerate them. Even when they invent a stunt of their own, for some mysterious reason it *seems* second-hand. Victor Hugo's pity-the-poor was a real gallic gesture. Verga's pity-the-poor is just a bit too much of a good thing, and it doesn't seem to come *quite* spontaneously from him. He had been inoculated. Or he had reacted.

In his last novel, *Mastro-don Gesualdo*, Verga has slackened off in his pity-the-poor. But he is still a realist, in the grim Flaubertian sense of the word. A realism which, as every one now knows, has no more to do with reality than romanticism has. Realism is just one of the arbitrary views man takes of man. It sees us all as little ant-like creatures toiling against the odds of circumstance, and doomed to misery. It is a kind of aeroplane view. It became the popular outlook, and so to-day we actually are, millions of us, little ant-like creatures toiling against the odds of circumstance, and doomed to misery; until we take a different view of ourselves. For man always becomes what he passionately thinks he is; since he is capable of becoming almost anything.

Mastro-don Gesualdo is a great realistic novel of Sicily, as *Madame Bovary* is a great realistic novel of France. They both suffer from the defects of the realistic method. I think the inherent flaw in *Madame Bovary* — though I hate talking about flaws in great books; but the charge is really against the realistic method — is that individuals like Emma and Charles Bovary are too insignificant to carry the full weight of Gustave Flaubert's profound sense of tragedy; or, if you will, of tragic futility. Emma and Charles Bovary are two ordinary persons, chosen because they *are* ordinary. But Flaubert is by no means an ordinary person. Yet he insists on pouring his own deep and bitter tragic consciousness into the little skins of the country doctor and his dissatisfied wife. The result is a certain discrepancy, even a certain dishonesty in the attempt to be too honest. By choosing *ordinary* people as the vehicles of an extraordinarily passionate feeling of bitterness, Flaubert loads the dice, and wins by a trick which is sure to be found out against him.

Because a great soul like Flaubert's has a pure satisfaction and joy in its own consciousness, even if the consciousness be only of ultimate tragedy or misery. But the very fact of being so marvellously and vividly *aware*, awake, as Flaubert's soul was, is in itself a refutation of the all-is-misery doctrine. Since the human soul has supreme joy in true, vivid consciousness. And Flaubert's soul has this joy. But Emma Bovary's soul does not, poor thing, because she was deliberately chosen because her soul was ordinary. So Flaubert cheats us a little, in his doctrine, if not in his art. And his art is biased by his doctrine as much as any artist's is.

The same is true of *Mastro-don Gesualdo*. Gesualdo is a peasant's son, who becomes rich in his own tiny town through his own force and sagacity. He is allowed the old heroic qualities of force and sagacity. Even Emma Bovary has a certain extraordinary female energy of restlessness and unsatisfied desire. So that both Flaubert and Verga allow their heroes something of the hero, after all. The one thing they deny them is the consciousness of heroic effort.

Now Flaubert and Verga alike were aware of their own heroic effort to be truthful, to show things as they are. It was the heroic impulse which made them write their great books. Yet they deny to their protagonists

any inkling of the heroic effort. It is in this sense that
Emma Bovary and Gesualdo Motta are "ordinary."
Ordinary people don't have much sense of heroic effort
in life; and by the heroic effort we mean that instinc-
tive fighting for more life to come into being, which is
a basic impulse in more men than we like to admit;
women too. Or it used to be. The discrediting of the
heroic effort has almost extinguished that effort in
the young, hence the appalling "flatness" of their lives.
It is the parents' fault. Life without the heroic effort,
and without *belief* in the subtle, life-long validity of the
heroic impulse, is just stale, flat and unprofitable. As
the great realistic novels will show you.

Gesualdo Motta has the makings of a hero. Verga
had to grant him something. I think it is in *Novelle
Rusticane* that we find the long sketch or story of the
little fat peasant who has become enormously rich by
grinding his labourers and bleeding the Barons. It is
a marvellous story, reeling with the hot atmosphere
of Sicily, and the ironic fatalism of the Sicilians. And
that little fat peasant must have been an actual man
whom Verga knew – Verga wasn't good at inventing,
he always had to have a core of actuality – and who
served as the idea-germ for Gesualdo. But Gesualdo
is much more attractive, much nearer the true hero.
In fact, with all his energy and sagacity *and* his natural
humaneness, we don't see how Gesualdo quite escaped
the heroic consciousness. The original little peasant,
the prototype, was a mere frog, a grabber and nothing
else. He had none of Gesualdo's large humaneness.
So that Verga brings Gesualdo much nearer to the
hero, yet denies him still any spark of the heroic consciousness, any spark of awareness of a greater impulse
within him. Men naturally have this spark, if they are

the tiniest bit uncommon. The curious thing is, the moment you deny the spark, it dies, and then the heroic impulse dies with it.

It is probably true that, since the extinction of the pagan gods, the countries of the Mediterranean have never been aware of the heroic impulse in themselves, and so it has died down very low, in them. In Sicily, even now, and in the remoter Italian villages, there is what we call a low level of life, appalling. Just a squalid, unimaginative, heavy, petty-fogging, grubby sort of existence, without light or flame. It is the absence of the heroic awareness, the heroic hope.

The northerners have got over the death of the old Homeric idea of the hero, by making the hero self-conscious, and a hero by virtue of suffering and awareness of suffering. The Sicilians may have little spasms of this sort of heroic feeling, but it never lasts. It is not natural to them.

The Russians carry us to great lengths of introspective heroism. They escape the non-heroic dilemma of our age by making every man his own introspective hero. The merest scrub of a pickpocket is so phenomenally aware of his own soul, that we are made to bow down before the imaginary coruscations of suffering and sympathy that go on inside him. So is Russian literature.

Of course, your soul will coruscate with suffering and sympathy, if you think it does: since the soul is capable of anything, and is no doubt full of unimaginable coruscations which far-off future civilizations will wake up to. So far, we have only lately wakened up to the sympathy-suffering coruscation, so we are full of it. And that is why the Russians are so popular. No matter how much of a shabby little slut you may be, you can learn from Dostoevsky and Tchekov that you have got the most tender, unique soul on earth, coruscating with sufferings and impossible sympathies. And so you may be most vastly important to yourself, introspectively. Outwardly, you will say: Of course I'm an ordinary person, like everybody else. — But your very saying it will prove that you think the opposite: namely, that everybody on earth is ordinary, *except* yourself.

This is our northern way of heroism, up to date. The Sicilian hasn't yet got there. Perhaps he never will. Certainly he was nowhere near it in Gesualdo Motta's day, the mediæval Sicilian day of the middle of the last century, before Italy existed, and Sicily was still part of the Bourbon kingdom of Naples, and about as remote as the kingdom of Dahomey.

The Sicilian has no soul, except that funny little naked man who hops on hot bricks, in purgatory, and howls to be prayed out into paradise; and is in some mysterious way an *alter ego*, my me beyond the grave. This is the catholic soul, and there is nothing to do about it but to pay, and get it prayed into paradise.

For the rest, in our sense of the word, the Sicilian doesn't have any soul. He can't be introspective, because his consciousness, so to speak, doesn't have any inside to it. He can't look inside himself, because he is, as it were, solid. When Gesualdo is tormented by mean people, atrociously, all he says is: I've got bitter in my mouth. — And when he is dying, and has some awful tumour inside, he says: It is all the bitterness I have known, swelled up inside me. — That is all: a physical fact! Think what even Dmitri Karamazov would have made of it! And Dmitri Karamazov doesn't go half the lengths of the other Russian soul-twisters. Neither is he half the man Gesualdo is, although he may be much more "interesting," if you like soul-twisters.

In *Mastro-don Gesualdo* you have, in a sense, the same sort of tragedy as in the Russians, yet anything more un-Russian could not be imagined. Un-Russian almost as Homer. But Verga will have gods neither above nor below.

The Sicilians to-day are supposed to be the nearest descendants of the classic Greeks, and the nearest thing to the classic Greeks in life and nature. And perhaps it is true. Like the classic Greeks, the Sicilians have no insides, introspectively speaking. But, alas, outside they have no busy gods. It is their great loss. Because Jesus is to them only a wonder-man who was killed by foreigners and villains, and who will help you to get out of Hell, perhaps.

In the true sense of the word, the Sicily of Gesualdo is drearily godless. It needs the bright and busy gods outside. The inside gods, gods who have to be inside a man's soul, are distasteful to people who live in the sun. Once you get to Ceylon, you see that even Buddha is purely an outside god, purely objective to the natives. They have no conception of his being inside themselves.

It was the same with the Greeks, it is the same to-day with the Sicilians. They aren't *capable* of introspection and the inner Jesus. They leave it all to us and the Russians.

Save that he has no bright outside gods, Gesualdo is very like an old Greek: the same energy and quickness of response, the same vivid movement, the same ambition and real passion for wealth, the same easy conscience, the same queer openness, without ever really openly committing himself, and the same ancient astuteness. He is prouder, more fearless, more frank, yet more subtle than an Italian; more on his own. He is like a Greek or a traditional Englishman, in the way he just goes ahead by himself. And in that, he is Sicilian, not Italian.

And he is Greek above all, in having no inside, in the Russian sense of the word.

The tragedy is, he has no heroic gods or goddesses to fix his imagination. He has nothing, not even a country. Even his Greek ambitious desire to come out splendidly, with a final splendid look of the thing and a splendid final ring of words, turns bitter. The Sicilian aristocracy was an infinitely more paltry thing than Gesualdo himself.

It is the tragedy of a man who is forced to be ordinary, because all visions have been taken away from him. It is useless to say he should have had the northern inwardness and the Russianizing outlet. You might as well say the tall and reckless asphodel of Magna Græcia should learn to be a snowdrop. "I'll learn you to be a toad!"

But a book exists by virtue of the vividness, the aliveness and powerful pulsing of its life-portrayal, and not by virtue of the pretty or unpretty things it portrays. *Mastro-don Gesualdo* is a great undying book, one of the great novels of Europe. If you cannot read it because it is *à terre*, and has neither nervous uplift nor nervous hysteria, you condemn yourself.

As a picture of Sicily in the middle of the last century, it is marvellous. But it is a picture done from the inside. There are no picture-postcard effects. The thing is a heavy, earth-adhering organic whole. There is nothing showy.

Sicily in the middle of the last century was an incredibly poor, lost, backward country. Spaniards, Bour-

bons, one after the other they had killed the life in her.
The Thousand and Garibaldi had not risen over the
horizon, neither had the great emigration to America
begun, nor the great return, with dollars and a newish
outlook. The mass of the people were poorer even
than the poor Irish of the same period, and save for
climate, their conditions were worse. There were some
great and wealthy landlords, dukes and barons still.
But they lived in Naples, or in Palermo at the nearest.
In the country, there were no roads at all for wheeled
vehicles, consequently no carts, nothing but donkeys
and pack-mules on the trails, or a sick person in a mule
litter, or armed men on horseback, or men on donkeys.
The life was mediæval as in Russia. But whereas the
Russia of 1850 is a vast flat country with a most pic-
turesque life of nobles and serfs and soldiers, open and
changeful, Sicily is a most beautiful country, but hilly,
steep, shut-off, and abandoned, and the life is, or was,
grimly unpicturesque in its dead monotony. The great
nobles shunned the country, as in Ireland. And the
people were sunk in bigotry, suspicion, and gloom.
The life of the villages and small towns was of an
incredible spiteful meanness, as life always is when
there is not enough change and fresh air; and the conditions were sordid, dirty, as they always are when the
human spirits sink below a certain level. It is not in
such places that one looks for passion and colour. The
passion and colour in Verga's stories come in the villages near the east coast, where there is change since
Ulysses sailed that way. Inland, in the isolation, the
lid is on, and the intense watchful malice of neighbours
is infinitely worse than any police system, infinitely
more killing to the soul and the passionate body.

The picture is a bitter and depressing one, while ever

we stay in the dense and smelly little streets. Verga wrote what he knew and felt. But when we pass from the habitations of sordid man, into the light and marvellous open country, then we feel at once the undying beauty of Sicily and the Greek world, a morning beauty, that has something miraculous in it, of purple anemones and cyclamens, and sumach and olive trees, and the place where Persephone came above-world, bringing back spring.

And we must remember that eight-tenths of the population of Sicily is maritime or agricultural, always has been, and therefore practically the whole day-life of the people passes in the open, in the splendour of the sun and the landscape, and the delicious, elemental aloneness of the old world. This is a great *unconscious* compensation. But what a compensation, after all! — even if you don't know you've got it; as even Verga doesn't quite. But he puts it in, all the same, and you can't read *Mastro-don Gesualdo* without feeling the marvellous glow and glamour of Sicily, and the people throbbing inside the glow and the glamour like motes in a sunbeam. Out of doors, in a world like that, what is misery, after all! The great freshness keeps the men still fresh. It is the women in the dens of houses who deteriorate most.

And perhaps it is because the outside world is so lovely, that men in the Greek regions have never become introspective. They have not been driven to *that* form of compensation. With them, life pulses outwards, and the positive reality is outside. There is no turning inwards. So man becomes purely objective. And this is what makes the Greeks so difficult to understand: even Socrates. We don't understand him. We just translate him into another thing, our own thing.

He is so peculiarly *objective* even in his attitude to the soul, that we could never get him if we didn't translate him into something else, and thus "make him our own."

And the glorious objectivity of the old Greek world still persists, old and blind now, among the southern Mediterranean peoples. It is this decayed objectivity, not even touched by mediæval mysticism, which makes a man like Gesualdo so simple, and yet so incomprehensible to us. We are apt to see him as just meaningless, just stupidly and meaninglessly getting rich, merely acquisitive. Yet, at the same time, we see him so patient with his family, with the tisical Bianca, with his daughter, so humane, and yet so desperately enduring. In affairs, he has an unerring instinct, and he is a superb fighter. Yet in life, he seems to do the wrong thing every time. It is as if, in his life, he has no driving motive at all.

He should, of course, by every standard we know, have married Diodata. Bodily, she was the woman he turned to. She bore him sons. Yet he married her to one of his own hired men, to clear the way for his, Gesualdo's, marriage with the noble but merely pathetic Bianca Trao. And after he was married to Bianca, who was too weak for him, he still went back to Diodata, and paid her husband to accommodate him. And it never occurs to him to have any of this on his conscience. Diodata has his sons in her house, but Gesualdo, who has only one daughter by the frail Bianca, never seems to interest himself in his boys at all. There is the most amazing absence of a certain range of feeling in the man, especially feeling about himself. It is as if he had no inside. And yet we see that he most emphatically has. He has a warm and

attractive presence. And he suffers bitterly, bitterly.
Yet he blindly brings most of his sufferings on himself,
by doing the wrong things to himself.

The idea of living for love is just entirely unknown
to him, unknown as if it were a new German invention.
So is the idea of living for sex. In that respect, woman
is just the female of the species to him, as if he were a
horse, that jumps in heat, and forgets. He never
really thinks about women. Life means something else
to him.

But what? What? It is so hard to see. Does he
just want to *get on*, in our sense of the word? No, not
even that. He has not the faintest desire to be mayor,
or podesta, or that sort of thing. But he does make a
duchess of his daughter. Yes, Mastro-don Gesualdo's
daughter is a duchess of very aristocratic rank.

And what then? Gesualdo realizes soon enough that
she is not happy. And now he is an elderly, dying man,
and the impetuosity of his manhood is sinking, he
begins to wonder what he should have done. What was
it all about?

What *did* life mean to him, when he was in the
impetuous tide of his manhood? What was he uncon-
sciously driving at? Just blindly at nothing? Was that
why he put aside Diodata, and brought on himself all
that avalanche of spite, by marrying Bianca? Not that
his marriage was a failure. Bianca was his wife, and he
was unfailingly kind to her, fond of her, her death was
bitter to him. Not being under the tyrannical sway of
the idea of "love," he could be fond of his wife, and
he could be fond of Diodata, and he needn't get into
a stew about any of them.

But what was he under the sway of? What was he
blindly driving at? We ask, and we realize at last that

it was the old Greek impulse towards splendour and self-enhancement. Not ambition, in our sense of the word, but something more personal, more individual. That which swayed Achilles and swayed Pericles and Alcibiades: the passionate desire for individual splendour. We now call it vanity. But in the countries of the sun, where the whole outdoors consists in the splendour of the sun, it is a real thing to men, to try to make themselves splendid and like suns.

Gesualdo was blindly repeating, in his own confused way, the magnificent old gesture. But ours is not the age for splendour. We have changed all that. So Gesualdo's life amounts to nothing. Yet not, as far as I can see, to any less than the lives of the "humble" Russians. At least he lived his life. If he thought too little about it, he helps to counterbalance all those people who think too much. Because he never has any "profound" talk, he is not less a man than Myshkin or a Karamazov. He is possibly not more a man, either. But to me he is less distasteful. And because his life all ends in a mistake, he is not therefore any more meaningless than Tolstoy himself. And because he simply has no idea whatsoever of "salvation," whether his own or anybody else's, he is not therefore a fool. Any more than Hector and Achilles were fools; for neither of them had any idea of salvation.

The last forlorn remnant of the Greeks, blindly but brightly seeking for splendour and self-enhancement, instead of salvation, and choosing to surge blindly on, instead of retiring inside himself to twist his soul into knots, Gesualdo still has a lovable glow in his body, the very reverse of the cold marsh-gleam of Myshkin. His life ends in a tumour of bitterness. But it was a life, and I would rather have lived it than the life of

INTRODUCTION

Tolstoy's Pierre, or the life of any Dostoevskian hero. It was not Gesualdo's fault that the bright objective gods are dead, killed by envy and spite. It was not his fault that there was no real splendour left in our world for him to choose, once he had the means.

D. H. Lawrence.

BIOGRAPHICAL NOTE.

GIOVANNI VERGA was born in Catania, the sea-coast city of East Sicily, in 1840, and died in the same town in January 1922. The family, however, owned lands at Vizzini, in Southern Sicily, and here Verga spent much of his time, his youth, and again periods in the second half of his life. In or around Vizzini is laid the scene of *Mastro-don Gesualdo*.

As a young man, Verga lived in Milan and Florence, writing novels and doing some journalism. To this period belong *Eva*, *Tigre Reale*, *Eros*, his more vulgarly-popular novels. In 1880 he returned finally to Sicily, and began his best work, when he was forty years old.

He contemplated writing a series of novels about *I Vinti* (the Defeated), in the manner of Hugo or Zola. In 1881 Treves of Milan published the first book of this series: *I Malavoglia*. It is a long novel about the "defeat" of a poor fisher family on the sea-coast near Catania. It was hailed as a masterpiece in Italy and Paris. The second novel of the series is *Mastro-don Gesualdo*, rising in the social scale, but still "defeat." It was published in 1888. From that time till his death, apparently, Verga worked in fits at the manuscript of the third novel of the "defeated" series: *La Duchessa di Leyra*. He never finished it, probably because he had lost all sympathy with the aristocracy of his day, and what he wrote of it has never been published.

The more serious Italian critics regard Verga as the

best Italian novelist after *Manzoni*, and *I Malavoglia* as the best Italian novel after *I Promessi Sposi*. The Italians, however, do not read Verga, and the world knows him as the librettist of the rather trivial opera: *Cavalleria Rusticana*. So much for the world.

Verga wrote Italian, not Sicilian dialect. But he deliberately made his style, "unliterary," trying to give it the impulsive, non-logical, broken rhythm of peasant speech.

The story of *Mastro-don Gesualdo* opens about 1820, twenty years before Verga's own birth. The revolution is the premature revolution of 1821, the year of Isabella's birth. The epidemic of cholera is the famous calamity of 1837, three years before Verga's own birth.

The title *Mastro-don* is an irony in itself. *Mastro*, which is the same as *Maestro*, is addressed to any adult workman or craftsman. A peasant is addressed as *Compare*, the same as the French *Compère*. A gentleman is *Don*. *Mastro-don*, then, is jeering: *Sir-workman!* But *Don* is also applied by the peasants half ironically to footmen, barbers, sexton, anyone who doesn't really work.

BIBLIOGRAPHY

Storia di Una Capinera.   (Milan) 1871.
Eva—1873.
Tigre Reale—1873.
Nedda, a Sicilian Sketch.   1874.
Eros. 1875.
Vita dei Campi (Cavalleria Rusticana)—Sketches
and Stories. 1880.
I Malavoglia—1881.
Il Marito di Elena—1881.
Novelle Rusticane—Sketches of Sicily.   1883.
Vagabondaggio—Stories and Sketches of Sicily.
Il Capitano d'Arce.
Mastro-don Gesualdo. 1888.

PRINCIPAL CHARACTERS

Gesualdo Motta—called Mastro-don Gesualdo.
Nunzio Motta, his father, called Master Nunzio.
Santo Motta, his brother.
Speranza, his sister, married to
Fortunato Burgio, called Farmer Burgio.
Don Diego Trao.
Don Ferdinando, his brother.
Donna Bianca Trao, his sister.

Relatives of the Traos

Donna Marianna Sganci, also called Donna Mari-annina, a rich aunt.
Donna Sara, or Sarina, Cirmena: Aunt Cirmena: a poor aunt.
Aunt Macri—moderately rich.
Donna Agrippina Macri—her daughter.
Baroness Rubiera—Aunt Rubiera.
Baron Nini Rubiera, her son; cousin of Bianca. Called Don Nini, or the young baron.
Marchese Alfonso Limoli, knight of Malta, Bianca's uncle.
Baron Mendola and his old mother.
Baron Zacco, called cousin Zacco; his wife and daughters, Donna Lavinia and Donna Marietta.
Donna Giuseppina Alosi, a rich widow.

Other Gentry

Don Filippo Margarone, chief man in the village.
Donna Bellonia, his wife.

Donna Fifi, Donna Giovannina, Donna Mita, his daughters.

Nicolino, his son.

The Captain's lady: Donna Carolina.

The Civic Captain, her husband, responsible for order in the village.

Cavaliere Peperito, a poor gentleman.

Canali, an official of the Town Hall.

Arch-priest Bugno.

Canon-priest Lupi.

Lawyer Neri.

Doctor Tavuso.

Bomma, the druggist.

Poor People

Don Liccio Papa—police sergeant.

Don Luca, the sexton.

Grazia, his wife.

Don Giuseppe Barabba, footman to Aunt Sganci.

Pirtuso, middle-man, corn-broker.

Master Titta, the barber.

Signora Aglae.

Ciolla—lounger, scribe, spy, agitator.

Peasants

Diodata.

Nani l'Orbo, Brasi Camauro, Nardo the laborer, Uncle Carmine the keeper: workmen of Mastro-don Gesualdo.

Pelagutti, Neighbour Cosimo, etc.

CONTENTS

CONTENTS

MASTRO-DON GESUALDO

FIRST PART

I

They were ringing sunrise mass at San Giovanni; but the village still slept heavily, because for three days it had been raining, and on the plough-land you sank half up to your knees. All of a sudden, upon the silence, there was an uproar, the shrill bell of Sant' Agata ringing for help, doors and windows banged open, people running out in their shirts, crying: "Earthquake!—Saint Gregory the Great!"

It was still dark. Far off, in the wide, dark expanse of the Alia, blinked only a light from the charcoal burners, and more to the left the morning star, over a big low cloud that cut across the dawn of the long tableland of the Paradiso. From all the open country came a lugubrious howling of dogs. And suddenly, out of the lower quarter struck up the heavy sound of the big bell of San Giovanni, giving the alarm as well; then the cracked bell of San Vito; then another from the mother church, further off; then the one from Sant' Agata which seemed to fall right on the heads of the inhabitants of the little square. One after the other the bells of the monasteries had also aroused: the College, Santa Maria, San Sebastiano, Santa Teresa; a general clanging which ran frightened over the roofs, in the darkness.

"No! No! It's a fire! . . . Fire in the Trao house! . . . Saint John the Baptist!"

3

The men came running, shouting, with their trousers in their hands. The women put a light in the windows; all the village, on the hillside, swarming with lights, as if it were the Good Friday eve, when they ring the second hour of the night; something to make your hair stand on end, if you saw it from a distance.

"Don Diego! Don Ferdinando!—" you could hear them shouting at the bottom of the square, and somebody banging at the entrance door with a stone.

Out of the street up from the big square, and from the other alleys, people arrived continually; a continual clatter of heavy boots on the cobblestones; from time to time a name called from the distance; and always that insistent banging at the big entrance door at the bottom of Sant' Agata Square, and that voice calling:

"Don Diego! Don Ferdinando! Are you all dead?"

From the house of the Traos, above the dilapidated cornice, you could now actually see in the paling dawn globes of dense smoke billowing up, sprinkled with sparks. And a ruddy reflection, showered down from above, lit up the anxious faces of the neighbours gathered in front of the battered door, their noses in the air. All at once you heard a window rattle, and a shrill voice crying from above:

"Help!—Thieves!—Christians, help!"

"The fire! Your house is on fire! Open the door, Don Ferdinando!"

"Diego! Diego!"

From behind the frantic face of Don Ferdinando Trao now appeared at the window the dirty nightcap and the flying grey hair of Don Diego. And then the hoarse consumptive voice also shrieking:

"Help!—Thieves in the house! Help!"

"What thieves? Why, what would they want up there?" jeered somebody out of the crowd.

"Bianca! Bianca! Help! Help!"

At that weary moment Nanni l'Orbo appeared, swearing he had seen the thieves, in the Traos' house.

—"With my own eyes! One of them trying to escape out of Donna Bianca's window, and he had to climb in again, seeing the people coming!"

"The mansion is burning, do you understand! All the neighbourhood will be in flames. And I've got my house next here, by God!" began to shout Mastro-don Gesualdo Motta. The others, however, pushing and prising at the doorway, succeeded in penetrating into the courtyard, one after the other, and the grass in there half up to their knees, shouting, brawling, armed with buckets, with pitchers full of water, neighbour Cosimo with the wood-axe; Don Luca the sexton wanting to ring the bells once more, to call to arms; Pelagatti as he was when he ran up at the first alarm, with his rusty pistol which he had rushed to fish out from under the straw.

From the courtyard the fire was not yet to be seen. Only, from time to time, as the wind blew from the northwest, great waves of smoke rose up, passing away behind the dry-stone wall of the little, shut-in garden, between the branches of the flowering almond trees. Under the lean-to shed was piled the chopped firewood; and at the far end, right against the house of the neighbour Motta, was more, heavier timber, flooring planks, rotten joists, a mill-post which they had never been able to sell.

"Worse than tinder, look you!" exclaimed Mastro-don Gesualdo. "Stuff to set fire to all the neighbourhood!—Saints and blessings!—And so they put it against my wall; because *they've* got nothing to lose, saints and blessings!——"

At the top of the stairway, Don Ferdinando, bundled in an old greatcoat, his head tied up in a rag of a kerchief, unshaven for eight days, rolling his greyish eyes, which looked like a madman's in that parchment face of an asthmatic subject, kept on repeating like a duck:

"Quick! Up here! Quick! Up here!"

But nobody dared risk himself on the shaky stairs. A perfect hole that house; the walls broken, corroded, the plaster fallen; cracks which ran from the eaves right to the ground; the windows off their hinges and without glass; the worn-out coat-of-arms, battered at the corners, hung from a rusty hook over the door. Mastro-don Gesualdo wanted first of all to pitch out all that wood piled up in the courtyard, throw it into the square.

"It would take a month," replied Pelagatti, who stood there yawning, his pistol in his hand.

"Saints and blessings! Piled against my wall!— Will you hear, or won't you?"

Giacalone said, "Better knock down the shed"; Don Luca the sexton assured them that for the moment there was no danger; a tower of Babel!

Also other neighbours had come running. Santo Motta with his hands in his pockets, his face jovial, always ready with a joke. Speranza, his sister, green with bile, pressing her flabby breast in her baby's mouth, spitting poison against the Traos.—"My sirs!—just look!—We've got our stores next here!—" And she turned on her husband Burgio, who was there in his shirtsleeves: "*You* don't say anything! You stand there like an owl! What have you come for then?"

Mastro-don Gesualdo was the first to dash yelling up the stairs. The others behind like so many lions through the dark, empty rooms. At every step an army of rats scaring the people. "Look out! Look out! The garret is coming in!—" Nanni l'Orbo, who had still got that fellow at the window on his mind, shouting every time: "There he is! There he is!—" And in the library, which was falling to pieces, he was within a hair's breadth of massacring the sexton with Pelagatti's pistol. Always in the darkness you could hear the hoarse voice of Don Ferdinando calling: "Bianca! Bianca!" And Don Diego was knocking and storming at a door, catching everybody by the coat as they passed and screeching the same: "Bianca! My sister!"

"What are you playing at?" replied Mastro-don Gesualdo, red as a tomato, ripping himself free. "I've got my house next door here, see? The whole street is going in a blaze."

There was a wild running in the big dismantled old house: women carrying water; children running about rowdily in all the confusion, as if it was a feast; inquisitive creatures who wandered round open-mouthed, tearing the rags of stuff which still hung from the walls, touching the carvings of the door-frames, shouting so as to hear the echo of the big empty rooms, lifting their nose in the air to look at the gilding of the mouldings and at the family portraits; all these smoky Traos who seemed to peel their eyes, seeing such a mob in their home. A come-and-go that made the floors dance.

"There you are! There you are! At this minute

the roof is going!" jeered Santo Motta, tramping
about in the water; wells of water at every stride,
between the displaced tiles or the missing tiles of the
floor. Don Diego and Don Ferdinando, shoved about,
dazed, upset in the midst of the crowd which ransacked
every corner of misery in their house, continued to cry:
"Bianca! My sister!"

"Your house is on fire, do you know?" Santo Motta
shouted in their ears. "It'll be a fine flare-up, with all
this old stuff!"

"Over here! Over here!" a voice was heard from
the alley. "The fire is upstairs in the kitchen."

Master Nunzio, the father of Gesualdo, clambering up a ladder, was making signs in the air, from the
roof of his own house, there opposite. Giacalone had
fastened a pulley to the rail of the balcony to draw up
water from the Motta's cistern. Master Cosimo, the
joiner, mounted on the eaves, was giving furious blows
with his axe at the skylight.

"No! No!" they shouted from below. "If you
give the fire air, the whole mansion will go in a
minute."

Don Diego then struck his forehead with his hand,
stammering: "The family papers! The papers of the
law-suit!"

And Don Ferdinando went running off, clutching his
hair in his hands, shouting also.

At the windows, at the balcony, as the wind blew,
whirlwinds of thick smoke billowed in, making Don
Diego cough as he kept on crying outside the door:
"Bianca! The fire!"

Mastro-don Gesualdo, who had rushed furiously up
by the kitchen stairs, came back blinded with smoke,

pale as death, his eyes almost out of their sockets, half
suffocated:

"Saints and blessings!—You can't get from this side.
. . . I am ruined!"

The others shouted all together, each one saying his
say; a row enough to daze you: "Chuck the tiles
down!—Lean the ladder against the chimney flue!—"
Master Nunzio, standing on the roof of his own
house, capered like one obsessed. Don Luca, the sexton, had now really run to hitch himself on to the bells.
The people in the piazza thick as flies. From the corridor mistress Speranza succeeded in making herself
heard, raucous with screaming, tearing the clothes off
the backs of people to make way for herself, her nails
unsheathed like a cat and scum at her mouth: "From
the staircase down there, at the end of the corridor!"
—Everybody ran there, leaving Don Diego to call at
his sister's door: "Bianca! Bianca!" A confused noise
was heard behind that door; a wild running as of folks
who have lost their head. Then the sound of a chair
thrown over. Nanni l'Orbo began to shout again from
the bottom of the corridor: "There he is! There he
is!" And the explosion of Pelagatti's pistol sounded
like a cannon going off.

"The authorities! Hey, here are the police!" came
the voice of Santo Motta shouting from the courtyard.

Then the door opened unexpectedly, and Donna
Bianca appeared, her dress not fastened, pale as death,
waving her hands convulsively, without offering a
word, fixing on her brother her eyes mad with terror
and with anguish. All at once she dropped on to her
knees, clutching the doorpost, stammering:

"Kill me, Don Diego!—Kill me then! But don't
let anybody come in here."

What happened then, behind that door which Don
Diego had shut again, pushing his sister back into her
little room, no one ever knew. Only his voice was
heard, a voice of desperate anguish, stammering:

"You? . . . You here?"

Came running the Captain, the fiscal attorney, all
the authorities. Don Liccio Papa, the chief of the
police, crying from a distance, brandishing his unsheathed sabre:

"Wait! Wait! Stop! Stop!"—and the Captain
with his stick: "Make way! Make way! Make way
behind him, fatigued like Don Liccio, beating his way
for the Law!"—The fiscal attorney gave orders to
have the door beaten down. "Don Diego! Donna
Bianca! Open! What has happened?"

Don Diego appeared, having aged ten years in a
minute, embarrassed, rolling his eyes, with a terrible
vision in the depths of his grey pupils, a cold sweat on
his brow, his voice choked with an immense grief:

"Nothing!— My   sister!— Frightened!— Nobody
must come in!"

Pelagatti furious with Nanni l'Orbo:

"A nice thing he made me do!—As near as nothing
I was to murdering Neighbour Santo!"

Then the Captain gave him a dressing down:

"With firearms, eh!—What are you playing at!—
You beast, for you are one!"

"Oh, Captain, sir, I thought it was the robber, down
there in the dark. I saw him with my own eyes!"

"Shut up! Shut up! You drunken lout!" chimed
in the fiscal attorney. "Anyhow, let's go and see the
fire."

And now, in the corridor, on the stairs to the
kitchen-garden, everybody carrying water. Neighbour

Cosimo had climbed on to the roof and was hacking away at the cross-beams with his hatchet. From every side they showered tiles, stones, broken pots on the smoking ceiling. Burgio, on the ladder, firing shots upwards, and Pelagatti, on the other side, ambushed beside the chimney-flue, loading and discharging his pistol mercilessly. Don Luca ringing the bells full clang; the crowd in the square yelling and gesticulating; all the neighbours at their windows. The Margarones stood on their terrace above the roofs opposite, to look on, the daughters with their hair still in curl papers; Don Filippo giving advice from the distance, directing the operations of those who were busy extinguishing the fire, with his malacca cane. Don Ferdinando, returning at that moment with his arms full of old papers, bumped his nose against Giacalone, who was running in the dark passage.

"Beg pardon, Don Ferdinando. I'm just going to fetch the doctor for your honour's sister."

"Fetch Doctor Tavuso!" screamed Aunt Macrì after him; she being a relation poor as they were themselves. She had been the first to come rushing. "Near here, at Bomma's pharmacy."

Bianca had gone into convulsions: a terrible attack; four people couldn't hold her down on the bed. Don Diego, also beside himself, was trying to drive the people back, with his bony, trembling hands.

"No!—It's nothing!—Leave her alone!"

The Captain began to land out right and left with his stick, hitting at haphazard the neighbours who crowded inquisitively round the door.

"What are you looking at?—What do you want?— Clear out!—Good-for-nothings, vagabonds! You, Don Liccio Papa, keep guard at the street-door."

Baron Mendola came a moment later, for the look of the thing, and Dame Sarina Cirmena poking her nose in everywhere; and the canon-priest Lupi, sent by the Baroness Rubiera. Aunt Sganci and the other relatives sent servants to enquire about their niece. Don Diego, hardly able to stand on his feet, put his head out of the door and replied to everyone:

"She is a little better!—She is quieter!—She wants to be left alone."

"Eh! Eh!" murmured the canon-priest, shaking his head and looking around the squalid walls of the drawing-room. "I remember how it used to be! Where are the riches of the house of Trao gone!"

The Baron also shook his head, stroking the bristles of his stiff-bearded chin with his hairy hand. Aunt Cirmena let out:

"They are mad! Ought to be in a madhouse, the pair of them! Don Ferdinando always was wanting . . . and Don Diego—you remember? When Aunt Sganci had got him that job in the mills?—No-thank-you!—a Trao couldn't take a wage!—Charity, yes, they can take that!"

"Oh! Oh!" interrupted the canon-priest, with the malice laughing in his little rat's eyes, but shutting tight his flexible lips.

"Yes indeed! What else would you call it? All the relations crying out about what they have to send at Easter and at Christmas, wine, oil, cheese—corn as well. . . . And the girl is absolutely dressed in what her Aunt Rubiera gives her."

"Eh! Eh!" The canon-priest, with an incredulous smile, kept nudging first Dame Sarina and then the Baron, who for his part bent his head and continued to scratch his chin discreetly, pretending to look this way and that, as if to say:

"Eh! Eh!—so it seems to me!"

At that moment appeared Doctor Tavuso, in a hurry, with his hat on his head. Saluting nobody, he went into the sick chamber.

A little while after he came out again shrugging his shoulders, swelling out his throat, accompanied by Don Ferdinando, who looked so thin he was like an old stick. Aunt Macrì and the canon-priest Lupi ran round the doctor. Aunt Cirmena wanted to know everything and fixed you in the face with her two round spectacles worse than the fiscal attorney.

"Eh? What is it? —Do you know? They talk about nerves nowadays—fashionable to have nerves. They send for you for every trifle—as if they could afford to pay for doctor's visits!—" replied Tavuso churlishly. And then, fixing Donna Sarina back again with his eyeglasses:

"Do you want me to tell you? Girls when they get to a certain age ought to be married!"

And he turned aside hawking loudly, coughing, and spitting. The relations looked from one to the other. The canon-priest, to appear discreet, began to turn it off with Baron Mendola, giving him snuff and making chatter, and spitting all over the place, wanting to ferret out what was happening behind that closed door, compressing his parched lips as if he was swallowing every moment.

"Yes, of course!—She was frightened!—They'd made her think there were thieves in the house!—poor Donna Bianca!—So young too!—and so delicate!"

"Hark here, Cousin!" said Donna Sarina, drawing

Dame Macrì aside. Don Ferdinando, crazy-like, wanted to get near to hear as well.

"Just a minute!—What manners!" cried Aunt Cirmena to him. "I've just got a word to say to your aunt!—you go and get a glass of water for Bianca, it will do her good——"

Santo Motta came climbing down from overhead, rubbing his hands with a smiling air.

"The kitchen's absolutely ruined! There isn't place to cook an egg in! It'll have to be built all afresh."

As nobody took any notice, he stared first one and then the other in the face, with his foolish smile.

The canon-priest Lupi, to get rid of him, said at last:

"All right! All right! We'll think of that later."

Baron Mendola, when Santo Motto had gone, burst out at last:

"Think of that later! If there'll be any money to think of it with! I've always told them—Sell half the house, cousin—even one or two rooms—something to be going on with!—But oh dear no!—Sell the house of the Traos?—They'd rather fasten up the doors of the rooms as they fall into ruin, and make shift in the ones that are left.—And that's what they'll do with the kitchen—They'll cook their eggs here in the drawing-room—when they've got any to cook. Sell a room or two!—Not for the world—and they couldn't if they wanted to—! The room of the archives?—where all the family papers are!—The room with the balcony on to the square?—and nowhere to stand and look when the Corpus Domini procession passes!—The cuckoo chamber?—For they've got a room for the cuckoo-clock, and all, if you please!—"

And the baron, having let off that little tirade,

departed leaving them all fit to split themselves with laughter.

Donna Sarina, before leaving, knocked once more at her niece's door, to ask how she was. Don Diego opened slightly and put his nose through the crack, repeating from his cardboard face:

"Better! She is quieter! She wants to be left alone."

"Poor Diego!" sighed Aunt Macrì. Dame Cirmena took a few steps across the antechamber, out of hearing of Don Ferdinando, who was coming to shut the door, and added:

"I've known it for quite a bit now. . . . You remember the evening of the Immaculate Conception, when there was such a fall of snow? I saw the young Baron Rubiera going down the alley two strides from here—muffled up like a thief——"

The canon-priest Lupi, as he crossed the courtyard, lifting his cassock above his thick boots in all the weeds, turned round to the dilapidated house to see if they could hear him, and then, in front of the street door, looking uneasily this way and that, he concluded:

"You heard what Doctor Tavuso said? We can speak, because we are all intimate friends and relations —Girls when they get to a certain age ought to be married!"

In the square, as the folks saw Don Diego Trao going by in his greasy hat and the long coat he wore on state occasions, it was quite an event.

"It takes a fire to bring you out of the house."

His cousin Zacco wanted also to take him to the "Café of the Gentry."

"Tell us about it. Say how it all was——"

The poor wretch excused himself as best he might; besides, he wasn't a member; poor, yes, but the Traos had never taken their hats off to anybody. He went the longer way round in order to avoid Bomma's pharmacy, where Doctor Tavuso sat installed all day long; but climbing up Conduit Street, creeping under the wall, he stumbled against that tongue-wagger Ciolla, who was always on the lookout for a scandal.

"Nice day, nice day, Don Diego! You are going to your cousin Rubiera?"

Don Diego went red. It seemed to him that everybody read his secret in his face. He turned back, hesitating, cautious, before entering the alley, afraid that Ciolla was hovering to spy on him. By good luck the latter had stopped to talk with the canon-priest Lupi, and was giving shouts of laughter, to which the canon-priest replied by twisting his mouth also to a laugh, discreetly.

Baroness Rubiera was having the corn winnowed. Don Diego saw her passing before the door of the storage barn in a cloud of chaff, bare-armed, her cotton skirt hitched up on her hips, her hair all dusty in spite

of the kerchief which she had pulled forward over her
nose like a little house-roof. She was wrangling with
that thief of a middleman, Pirtuso, who wanted to rob
her of her corn by paying her two groats less per
measure; red in the face, flourishing her hairy arms,
her stomach heaving:

"Have you no conscience, you Jew?"

Then, as she saw Don Diego, she turned, smiling:

"How do you do, Cousin Trao? What brings you
this way, then?"

"I came specially, Cousin—" and Don Diego,
choked with the dust, began to cough.

"Get out of it! Get out of it! Away from here,
Cousin. You're not used to it," interrupted the
Baroness. "Look at the things I have to do! Eh, but
what a face you've got, good gracious me! The fright
you had last night, eh?"

From the trapdoor, at the top of the wooden steps,
appeared two clumsy shoes and coarse blue stockings,
and the high voice of a girl saying:

"My lady, here they are!"

"The young Baron has come back?"

"I can hear *Marchese* barking down below."

"All right, I'm coming. Well then, what about the
corn, Master Lio?"

Pirtuso had remained squatted on the bushel-
measure, peacefully, as if to say that the corn was no
matter to him, looking indifferently here and there at
the strange things in this storage barn, which itself was
vast as a church. Once upon a time, in the days of the
Rubiera's splendour, it had been the theatre also.
Even now you could see the vaulting painted with
nude women, and with columns like a chapel; the large
family box opposite, with rags of stuff dangling from

the parapet; a carved, broken-down big bedstead in a
corner; some leather seats stripped to make shoes; a
saddle of dusty velvet astraddle on the beam of a
loom; sieves of every size hung around; heaps of
stakes and brooms; a sedan-chair shoved under the
stairs that went up to the family box, the Rubiera
coat-of-arms on its little door, and an ancient lantern
standing on its little roof, like a crown. Giacalone
and Vito Orlando, in the midst of heaps of wheat
as high as mountains, shook themselves round
about the immense sieves as if possessed, all sweaty
and white with dust, singing in cadence; while Ger-
bino, the boy, heaped up the grain continually with
the broom.

"In my days, your ladyship, I have seen comedy
played in this barn," replied Pirtuso, to evade the
question.

"I know! I know! That's how the Rubieras wasted
what they'd got.—And now do you want to go on with
business?—Are you taking the corn, or aren't you?"

"I've told you: at three guineas and a quarter."

"No, upon my conscience, I can't do it. Already I
lose fourpence a measure."

"Good-day to your ladyship."

"Come now, Master Lio, since that her ladyship has
spoken," added Giacalone, making the sieve dance all
the time. The middleman took up his bushel-measure
and went his way without replying.

"At three and three shillings. Do you take it?"

"Good-day to you! Good-day to you!"

But she, out of the tail of her eye, perceived that the
middleman had stopped to talk with the canon-priest,
who, rid at last of Ciolla, was coming up the narrow

street. Reassured therefore, she turned to her cousin Trao to speak of something else.

"I was just thinking about you, cousin. I want to send a bit of this corn across to your house.—No, no, don't mention it.—We are relations. A good harvest should bless everybody. Then the Lord helps us!—You've had your house on fire, what? God save us! They tell me Bianca is still half dead with fright. I couldn't leave things, here—you must excuse me."

"Yes—I came on purpose—I want to speak to you."

"Speak up, then—But wait a minute;—while you're out there, just look if Pirtuso is coming back—So, without letting him see you———"

"He's a jackass!" put in Vito Orlando, wagging himself all the time about the sieve. "I know Master Lio. He's a jackass! He won't come back."

But at that moment entered the canon-priest Lupi, smiling with that nice amiable face which put everybody into harmony, and behind him the middleman with the bushel in his hand.

"Deo gratias! Deo gratias! Shall we bring it off, this marriage, my lady?"

As he perceived Don Diego Trao, who was holding himself humbly aside, the canon-priest suddenly changed tone and manner, with his lips narrowed, pretending to hold himself aside also, out of discretion, all intent on settling the negotiations about the wheat.

But they had to harangue a little longer. Master Lio now raved and carried on as if they wanted to rob the money out of his pocket. The Baroness, however, with an indifferent air, turning her back on him and calling towards the trapdoor:

"Rosaria! Rosaria!"

"Now drop it!" exclaimed the canon-priest at last,

clapping Master Lio on the shoulder with his big hand.
"I know whom you are buying for. It's for Mastro-
don Gesualdo."

"No, it isn't. Mastro-don Gesualdo has got nothing to do with it!" the agent began to shout. "This
isn't in Mastro-don Gesualdo's line."

But finally, as they agreed about the price, Pirtuso
grew calm. The canon-priest added:

"You be quiet, everything is in Mastro-don Gesualdo's line, if there's anything to be made by it."

Pirtuso, who had seen Giacalone's side-wink, went
up to him to tell him to his nose what he thought of
him.

"Don't you eat bread yourself? Can't you keep
quiet in other people's business, can't you?—"

The Baroness, from her corner, while the middleman had his back turned, winked also at the canon-
priest Lupi, as if to say, as for the price, it wasn't bad.

"Yes, yes," replied the priest, *sotto voce*. "Baron
Zacco is going to sell for less. However, Mastro-don
Gesualdo knows nothing of it so far."

"Ah, so he's taking up corn-dealing, Mastro-don
Gesualdo! Isn't he a builder any longer, then?"

"He does a bit of everything, that demon. They
even say he wants to come in at the auction of the
taxes on the lands."

Then the Baroness opened her eyes.

"Cousin Zacco's lands? The communal taxes which
have descended for fifty years from father to son!—
Why, it's real roguery!"

"I won't say it isn't! I won't say it isn't! Nowadays there's no respect for anybody. Nowadays it's
whoever has got the money is in the right."

Then they turned to Don Diego with great emphasis, abusing the new times:

"To-day there's no other God! You can be a gentleman—or a girl born of a good family! But if you've got no fortune!—Whereas one who has sprung from nothing—like Mastro-don Gesualdo, for example—!"

The canon-priest took up the conversation, pretending to be mysterious, talking in a low tone with the Baroness and Don Diego Trao, spitting first to one side then to the other:

"Ah, but he's got his head screwed on the right way, has Mastro-don Gesualdo! He'll get rich, I tell you. He'd be an excellent husband for a respectable girl—and there are plenty such, with not much dowry to them."

This time Master Lio was really going:

"Well then, your ladyship, I can come and load the corn?"

The Baroness, again in a good humour, replied:

"Yes. But you know what it says in the taverns— 'Here you eat and here you drink; but bring the money with you.'"

"On the spot and cash down, your ladyship. Thank the Lord, you will see we are punctual."

"I told you so!" exclaimed Giacalone, gasping over his sieve. "It's Mastro-don Gesualdo."

The canon-priest exchanged another look with the Baroness, and after Pirtuso had gone, he said to her:

"Do you know what I was thinking? Your ladyship might come in at the auction, along with some other party. I would stand by you."

"No, no; I've got too many irons in the fire! Besides, I shouldn't like to do anything against Cousin Zacco. Because you know—we're all in the same

world—we have to look to one another sometimes,
for a hand's turn."

"Yes, I know—but let somebody else take the lead:
Mastro-don Gesualdo Motta for example. He's got
a nice bit of capital, that I know for certain—Your
ladyship would give the credit of your name. We
might make a company of it, between the three of
us——"

Then, thinking that Don Diego Trao was listening
to their plans, as he stood waiting there for the moment when he could speak with his cousin Rubiera,
folded round in his great-coat, and having quite other
matters on his mind, poor creature the canon-priest
suddenly changed the thread of the discourse:

"Eh, eh, the things that this barn has seen! I remember when I was little hearing Marchese Limòli
recite *Adelaïde and Comingio* with Madame Margarone, good soul, the mother of Don Filippo, she
who went to spend her last days on the Salonia property: *Adelaïde! where art thou?*—The scene in the
Carthusian monastery—You should have seen it!—
everybody wiping their eyes! Till Don Alessandro
Spina could bear it no longer, and began shouting:
Tell him it's you, then! and something else a bit
stronger than that he said to her, as well. Afterwards
there was all that about the shot that was fired at the
Marchese Limòli as he was taking a stroll, after
supper; and Don Nicola Margarone carrying his
wife away into the country and not letting her see
another soul while she lived. Now they are both
resting together, husband and wife, in the Church of
the Rosary, peace be to their souls."

The Baroness kept nodding acquiescence, giving a

sweep with the broom from time to time, to separate
the corn from the husks.

"And that's how families went to ruin. If I hadn't
been here, in the house of the Rubieras—! You see
what would have been left of all their grandeurs!
Well, I've got no pride and conceit, thank Goodness!
I've kept as my father and mother made me—country
folks, folks who built up their house with their own
hands, instead of ruining it!—and it's because of them
that there's still substance in the Rubiera storebarn,
instead of feasts and theatre-shows———"

At that moment arrived the driver with the loaded
mules.

"Rosaria! Rosaria!" the Baroness began to shout
again towards the wooden steps.

At last from the trapdoor appeared the clumsy
shoes and blue stockings, then the monkey face of the
servant, dirty, unkempt, with her fingers always in her
hair.

"Don Ninì was not at the Vignazza," she said
calmly. "Alessi has come back with the dog, but the
young master wasn't there."

"Oh, Holy Virgin!" the mistress began to scream,
losing a bit of her flaming colour. "Oh, Holiest Mary!
Wherever can he be? What has happened to my
boy?"

Hearing this Don Diego went red and white in
turns. His face looked as if he would say: "Open,
earth, and swallow me!" He coughed, looked for his
handkerchief in his hat, opened his mouth to speak;
then turned away again, wiping the sweat from his
brow. The canon-priest hastened to reply, looking
stealthily at Don Diego.

"He must have gone somewhere else. . . . When

you go out shooting, there's no telling where you get to."

"All the vices of his father, rest his soul. Shooting, gaming, pastimes, that's all he thinks of—and never telling me, either. Just you think of it, to-night, when the bells rang for the fire, I went to look for him in his room, and he isn't to be found! But he shall hear about it—! Yes, he shall hear about it!"

The canon-priest tried to cut her short, uneasy, a silly smile on his face, as if *he* wasn't going to say anything.

"Eh, eh, Baroness!—your son isn't a boy any longer. He's twenty-six years old."

"He can be a hundred if he likes!—But until he marries, you understand!—and even after!"

"Your ladyship, where have we to unload the mules?" said Rosaria, scratching her head.

"I'm coming. I'm coming. We'll go this way. You two can go out through the courtyard, when we've finished."

She bolted Giacalone and Vito Orlando in the barn, and went towards the big door.

The house of the Baroness was vast, added together by bits and pieces, according as her parents had ousted one by one the various proprietors, until they had installed themselves at last with their daughter in the mansion of the Rubieras, and joined in everything common: roofs high and low; windows of every size, here and there, as it happened; the great door of the nobles set in the middle of a lot of hovel-fronts. The building occupied almost the whole length of the street. The Baroness, talking in a low voice with the canon-priest Lupi, had almost forgotten her cousin, who

came after step by step. But when they came to the
great door, the canon-priest drew prudently back.

"Another time. I'll come again. Now your cousin
wants to speak with you. You go through with your
own business, Don Diego."

"Ah, excuse me, Cousin. Come in. Do come in."

Immediately inside the immense dark entrance, that
was flanked with little low doors iron-studded like those
of a prison, you felt yourself in a rich house; a mouldy
smell of oil and cheese catching you in the throat; then
a smell of mustiness and of wine-cellar. From beyond
the wide-open rail-gates of this cellar, as if from the
depths of a cavern, came the laughter of Alessi and the
servant girl who were filling little barrels, and the
feeble glimmer of a light that stood on the great cask.

"Rosaria! Rosaria!" the Baroness began shouting
once more. Then she turned to her cousin. "You've
always got to be lifting your voice to that blessed girl;
because when you've got men to look after it's a serious
matter! However, she is faithful, and one must have
patience. What am I to do?—A house full of stuff
as mine is!"

Further on, in the court that was like a farm-yard,
peopled with hens and ducks and turkeys which
crowded clucking round the mistress, the mustiness
changed into a smell of manure and abundant litter.
Two or three mules, from the long row under the
shed, stretched their necks braying; pigeons swept in
clouds from the roofs; a sheep-dog, fierce, began to
bark, rattling his chain; even some rabbits pricked
their uneasy ears, from the mysterious shadow of the
woodshed. And the Baroness, in the midst of all
these blessings, said to her cousin:

"I want to send a pair of pigeons, for Bianca——"

The poor wretch coughed, and blew his nose, but couldn't find a word of answer. At last, after a labyrinth of passages and stairways, after going through dark chambers full of all sorts of stuff, heaps of beans and of barley in various divisions, farming implements, linen-chests, they arrived in the Baroness' bedroom, which was whitewashed, with the big marriage-bed remaining just the same, after twenty years of widowhood, from the sprig of consecrated olive at the foot of the crucifix, to the husband's gun by the bed-head.

Cousin Rubiera had begun complaining about her son again: "His father all over again, rest his soul! Never giving a thought in the world to his mother's concerns, or to his own interests——"

Seeing her cousin Trao nailed in the doorway, shrunken inside his greatcoat, she put him a chair:

"Come in! Come in, Cousin Trao."

The poor thing let himself sink on to the chair, as if his legs were broken, sweating like Jesus in the Garden; then he took off his greasy old hat, wiping his forehead with his kerchief.

"You've got something to say to me, Cousin? What is it then, tell me."

He clasped his hands tightly, inside his hat, and stammered hoarsely, his lips livid and trembling, his moist, miserable eyes avoiding the eyes of his cousin:

"Yes, ma'am. . . . I want to speak to you. . . ."

She, from the start, seeing him with such a face, thought he had come to ask for a loan of money. It would have been the first time, that is true: they were too proud, the Trao cousins; a bit of a present now and then, to help them to struggle along—wine, oil, cheese—yes, that they would accept from their rich

relatives; from her, from Cousin Sganci, from Baron
Mendola; but they'd never held their hand out. Nevertheless, necessity makes you bend your head at last even
to something else. The instinct of caution which was in
her blood froze for a moment her benevolent smile.
And then she thought of the fire they'd had, and of
Bianca's illness—and she was a kind woman at the
bottom—Don Diego had really a pitiable face. She
moved her chair nearer to his, to give him courage,
and added:

"Say what it is then, say what it is, Cousin.—Whatever we *can* do—you know—since we're relations.
The times aren't very promising—but what little we
can do—It's not a great deal—but the bit I *can* do—
between cousins—Tell me then."

But he couldn't, no! his throat was so tight, his
mouth bitter, as he lifted his eyes to her time after
time, opening his lips without uttering a sound. At
last he got out his handkerchief again to wipe his forehead, and passed it over his parched lips, stammering:

"A misfortune has happened! A great misfortune!"

The Baroness was afraid she'd let herself go too
far. In her eyes, which quickly avoided the tearful
looks of her cousin, began to flash the lightings of a
peasant's uneasiness when he fears for his property.

"What is it? What is it?"

"Your son is so rich!—And my sister, no, she
isn't——"

At these words Cousin Rubiera opened her eyes, her
face all at once set in the mask of her parents, lined
with that churlish mistrust of the peasants who had
given her the blood in her veins and their house which
they had put together bit by bit with their own hands.

"But explain yourself, cousin. You know I've got a lot to do——"

But instead of explaining himself Don Diego burst into tears like a boy, hiding his parchment face in his cotton handkerchief, his back bent and shaken with sobs, repeating:

"Bianca, my sister!—A great disaster has happened to my poor sister!—oh, Cousin Rubiera—you are a mother yourself——!"

And now his cousin had also quite another face on her; her lips tight so as not to let her patience escape, and a deep fold in the middle of her forehead; the fold of people who have stood in sun and wet to get what they have got—and who have to defend it now they've got it. In a flash came back to her all the things she had taken no notice of in the great rush of her affairs: a hint that Cousin Macrì had dropped; the gossip which Don Luca, the sexton, went scattering around; certain of her son's subterfuges. All at once she felt her mouth also as bitter as gall.

"I don't know, Cousin—" she answered him, short and dry. "I don't know what this has got to do with me——"

Don Diego remained for a time hunting for his words, looking fixedly into her eyes that expressed so many things, looking through his tears of shame and grief, and then hid his face again between his hands accompanying with his head his voice which could hardly come out of his throat.

"Yes! Yes! Your son Nini!"

This time the Baroness couldn't find her words, her eyes, bolting out of her big apoplectic face, fixed on her cousin Trao as if she wanted to devour him; then she sprang to her feet like a young thing of twenty, and threw open the window, screaming in fury:

"Rosaria! Alessi! Come here!"

"For pity's sake! For pity's sake!" pleaded Don Diego with clasped hands, running after her. "Don't make a scandal, for pity's sake!" And he could say no more, suffocated with coughing, pressing his chest.

But his cousin, beside herself, took no more notice of him. It was like an earthquake in the house; the cackling of the fowls, the loud barking of the dog, the clattering shoes of Alessi and Rosaria who came running to break their necks, dishevelled, spent, their eyes lowered.

"Where is my son, I ask you? What did they say to you at the Vignazza? Speak, you clown!"

Alessi, balancing himself first on one foot, then on the other, stammering, looking uneasily here and there, repeated continually the same thing:

"The young Baron wasn't at the Vignassa. He had left the dog there, *Marchese,* the evening before, and had gone away.—On foot, yes, my lady. That's what the farm-bailiff told me."

The servant girl, tidying herself on the sly, her head ducked, said that when the young baron was going out shooting early in the morning, he generally went out by the little door of the stable, so as not to wake anybody:

"The key? I don't know. He threatened to break my bones—It's not my fault, my lady."

Her ladyship seemed as if she was having a fit. Then they took themselves off, the pair of them, quiet as mice. On the stairs you heard their thick boots again clattering down at full speed, one after the other.

Don Diego, a corpse by now, his handkerchief over

his mouth to stifle his coughing, kept on stammering suffocated and meaningless words.

"He was there—behind that door! He'd better have killed me right out—when he pointed his pistol at my breast—at me!—his pistol at my breast, Cousin Rubiera!"

The baroness wiped her lips, bitter as gall, with her cotton handkerchief.

"No!—That I never expected!—Tell the truth, cousin Don Diego, that I haven't deserved it!—I have always treated you as blood relations.—And that creeping cat of a Bianca whom I've had here for whole days at a time—like a daughter———"

"Leave her alone, Cousin Rubiera," broke in Don Diego, with a flicker of the old blood of the Traos in his cheek.

"Yes, yes, my word, leave her alone! As for my own son, I'll look after him, don't you make any mistake. He's going to do what *I* bid him, is my young lord.—Villain! Murderer! He'll be the death of me———"

And her tears rose. Don Diego, abashed, didn't dare to raise his eyes. He was seeing, implacably, Ciolla, Bomma's pharmacy, the ironic grins of the neighbours, the gossip of village wives, and also, insistent and painful, the sharp vision of his own house, where a man had been let in at night: the old house which he seemed to feel shuddering still in every stone at the echo of those thievish steps; and Bianca, his sister, his own child, his own blood, had lied to him, had absolutely refused to say a word, in the shadow of that man who had come to commit such a mortal outrage against the house of Trao; her poor, delicate, fragile body in the arms of a stranger! The tears came bitter and hot down his own wasted cheeks, as he hid them between his hands.

The Baroness, at last, dried her eyes and sighed, turning to the crucifix:

"God's will be done! You as well, Cousin Trao, must be feeling bitter. But what then! It's our look-out, who have the weight of the house already on our shoulders!—God knows I've laboured my skin into leather, from morning till night! I've taken the bread from between my teeth for the sake of the property!—And now all at once an affair like this comes down on you!—But this is the last that my young lord is going to do to me!—I will set it right, don't you fret. When all's said and done he's not a child!—I'll marry him according to my own liking!—The chain round his neck, that's what he wants! But you, if I may tell you, you ought to have kept your eyes open, Cousin Trao! —I'm not talking about Don Ferdinando, who is dull-witted, poor thing, even if he is the first-born;—but you who have more sense—and aren't a child either! You ought to have taken care—! When you've got a girl in the house!—Man is a hunter, and you know it. —You ought to have taken care of your sister, you ought—or she should have taken care of herself—. You could almost say, really, it's her own fault!— Who knows what she had in mind? to become Baroness Rubiera, as leave as not——"

Cousin Trao went red and white in the same moment.

"My lady,—we are poor—it's true— But as far as birth goes——"

"Eh, my dear fellow, birth!—ancestors—all very fine—I don't say it isn't.—But the ancestors who made my son a baron—do you want to know who they were?

Those who hoed the ground!—In the sweat of their brow, do you realise?—They didn't slave themselves to death so that their possessions should fall into the hands of just anybody—do you understand?—"

Just then somebody knocked at the street-door with the heavy iron knocker, so that it resounded through the house, and the cackling of the poultry and the barking of the dog started once more. While the Baroness went to the window to see who it was, Rosaria shouted from the courtyard:

"It's the agent—about the corn———"

"I'm coming, I'm coming—" the Baroness went on grumbling, turning to take the key of the granary from its nail.—"See what it means to make fourpence a measure with Pirtuso and all the rest. If I've worked all my life, and taken the very bread out of my mouth for love of the house, I intend my daughter-in-law to have a dowry to bring along with her, I do———"

Don Diego, scrambling as fast as he could after his Cousin Rubiera, through the passages and chambers full of stuff, replied:

"My sister isn't rich—Cousin Rubiera. She hasn't got the dowry she should have—We'll give her the house and everything—We'll strip ourselves for her —Ferdinando and I———"

"You heard what I told you!—Mind, there's a broken step—I want my son to marry a good dowry. I'm the mistress, I made him a baron. *He* hasn't got the property together! Come in, come in, Master Lio. There, through the wooden wicket. It is open."

"But your son knew that my sister isn't rich—" argued poor Don Diego, who could not find in his heart to go, though Cousin Rubiera had so much to do.

Then at last she turned like a fighting-cock, with her
fists on her hips, at the top of the stairs:

"I'll look after my son myself, I tell you again.
You look after your sister!—Man is a hunter!—I
shall send him away from this! I'll lock him up! I'll
sink him! He shan't come back to this village till he's
married!—with the chain round his neck!—I tell you!
My cross that he is!—my ruin!"

Then, moved to compassion by the mute despair of
the poor wretch, who could hardly stand, she added,
coming downstairs a step at a time:

"And for all that, mind you, Don Diego, I'll do what
I can for Bianca, I will—I'm a mother myself!—and
a Christian!—But just think what a thorn I must have
here inside me—!"

"Your ladyship, he says that the grain isn't full
weight," shouted Alessi from the door of the store-
barn.

"What! what does he say?—The weight now, is it?
—Drawing back as usual!—to beat me down again!"

And the Baroness set off like a fury. For a while
a great shouting was heard from the depths of the
store-house: they sounded as if they were tearing one
another by the hair. Pirtuso screamed worse than a
lamb in the hands of the butcher; Giacalone and Vito
Orlando yelled as well, to bring them to an agreement,
and the Baroness, beside herself, said her say in very
highly-coloured language. Then seeing her Cousin
Trao going by with his tail between his legs, his head
sunk in his shoulders, staggering, she stopped him in
the doorway, changing in a breath her face and her
manner:

"Listen, listen—we'll settle this business between
us.—When all's said and done, what does it amount

to?—Nothing that's any harm, I'll be bound. A God-fearing girl!—The thing will rest between you and me—we'll settle it between us—. I'll help you all I can, Don Diego—I am a mother—and a Christian—We'll marry her to a gentleman."

Don Diego shook his head bitterly, overcome, staggering like a drunken man in his walk.

"Yes—yes! We'll find her a gentleman.—I'll help you all I can. Patience!—I will make a sacrifice——"

At these words he stopped, his eyes dilated, all trembling.

"You!—Cousin Rubiera! No! No!—That can't be!"

At that moment the corn-dealer came out of the barn, white with wheat-dust, hard, right to his beard which blackened his face even when he was newly shaved; his eyes as grey as two silver coins, under his brows that were knitted with continual standing in the sun and the wind of the open country.

"Kiss your hand, your ladyship."

"What! You're going and leaving it? What now? Don't you like the corn?"

The other shook his head in negation, in the same way as Don Diego Trao, who was going off hugging the wall and continuing to shake his head as if he had had a stroke, stumbling in the stones at every stride.

"What do you mean?" the Baroness went on bawling. "It's a finished bargain——"

"What about the earnest-money, your ladyship?"

"No, there's no earnest-money; but there's your given word——"

"In that case, kiss your ladyship's hand."

And he went off, obstinate as a mule. The Baroness, enraged, screamed after him:

"It's a dirty, mean trick, and just like you!—A pretence for breaking off the bargain—worthy of that Mastro-don Gesualdo who sends you—now that he's repented——"

Giacalone and Vito Orlando also ran after him, in a frenzy to make him hear reason. But Pirtuso continued his way, without replying at all, saying to Don Diego, who took no heed:

"The Baroness may well talk—as if she wouldn't have done the same herself! Now that Baron Zacco has begun to sell at a lower figure! Labourer or Baroness, it's the earnest-money that counts. Aren't I right, your honour?"

III

Madame Sganci had her house full of people, come to see the procession of the patron saint: there were lights even on the staircase: and the five balconies sent fire and flame down on to the square that was black with onlookers; Don Giuseppe Barabba in full livery and cotton gloves, announcing the visitors.

"Mastro-don Gesualdo," he bawled suddenly, poking his towsled head through the gilded folding doors. "Must I let him in, ma'am?"

There was the fine flower of the nobility present: the arch-priest Bugno, glossy in black satin; Madame Giuseppina Alòsi, loaded with jewels; the Marchese Limòli, with face and periwig of the last century.

Madame Sganci, caught like that in front of all the company, couldn't contain herself.

"What a fool! A fool you are! You say Don Gesualdo Motta, you fool!" Thus Mastro-don Gesualdo made his entry into the society of the big-wigs of the village, newly-shaven, dressed in fine cloth, his new hat gleaming between his hands that were burnt with lime.

"Come forward, come forward, Don Gesualdo," shrilled the Marchese Limòli in his sharp, piercing voice. "Don't be afraid."

Mastro-don Gesualdo, however, still hesitated a little, intimidated, in the middle of that big salon hung with yellow damask, under the eyes of all those Sganci forefathers who looked at him askance from the portraits around the walls.

The mistress of the house encouraged him.

"Here! Here! Here's a place for you too, Don Gesualdo."

It was precisely the balcony on the alley, looking squinting on to the square, for the second-grade guests and the poor relations: Dame Clara Macrì, so humble and so shabby that she seemed like a servant; her daughter, Mistress Agrippina, a *house-nun,* a girl with such a moustache, and a pimpled brown face like a begging friar, and two eyes black as sin which roved round among the men. In the first row Cousin Don Ferdinando, more inquisitive than a child, who had pushed himself forward with elbow-thrusts, and was stretching his neck out of his black cravat to look toward the Great Square, like a tortoise, with his grey, rolling eyes, his sooty, pointed chin, his long, quivering Trao nose, his queue curving in like the tail of a dog on his greasy collar that came up to his hairy ears; and his sister, Donna Bianca, poked away behind him, her shoulders rather bent, her breast thin and flat, her hair smooth, her face meagre and washed-out, dressed in flannelette in the midst of all her fine relatives.

Her Aunt Sganci continued:

"Come here, Don Gesualdo. I've kept a place for you. Here, with my nephew and niece."

Bianca drew back, timidly. Don Ferdinando, afraid he was going to be disturbed, turned his head for a moment scowling, and Mastro-don Gesualdo came on to the balcony stumbling, stammering, overwhelming himself with excuses. He remained there, behind the backs of those who stood in front of him, lifting his head at every rocket that went up from the square, in order to give himself a less embarrassed appearance.

"Excuse me! Excuse me!" puffed Donna Agrippina

then, curling her nose, making herself way with her
ponderous hips, disdainfully straightening her white
kerchief on her enormous bosom; and she joined the
company wherein was her Aunt Cirmena with other
ladies, there on the great balcony, amid a great fluster
and murmur, everybody turning to look towards the
alley-balcony, away at the bottom of the salon.

"They put him next to me—right beside me, you
know!—Fairly indecent!"

"Ah, is he the fiancé?" asked Donna Giuseppina
Alòsi in an undertone, her little eyes smiling in the
middle of her calm full-moon face.

"Hush! Hush! I'm going to see—" said Dame
Cirmena, and she crossed the drawing-room—like a
sea of light in her yellow satin—to sniff what they
were plotting on the alley-balcony. There everybody
seemed on thorns: Aunt Macrì pretending to gaze into
the square, Bianca quiet in a corner, turning her head
from side to side without saying a word.

"You're enjoying yourselves here, eh? You're having a good time, Bianca?"

Don Ferdinando turned his head, annoyed: then
seeing Cousin Cirmena he grumbled:

"Ah—Donna Sarina—good evening! good evening!" And he turned away again. Bianca lifted her
sweet, humble eyes to her aunt without replying: Dame
Macrì stifled a discreet smile.

Dame Cirmena went on at once, looking in the
direction of Don Gesualdo:

"Isn't it hot here, my word! One is suffocated!
There are too many people, this time. Cousin Sganci
has invited all the town."

Mastro-don Gesualdo made as if to draw aside.

"No, no, don't disturb yourself, my good man.—
Just listen, Cousin Macrì——"

"Ma'am! Ma'am!" roared Don Guiseppe Barabba
at that moment, making signs to his mistress.

"No," she replied. "Let the procession pass first."

Marchese Limòli caught her by the dress as she was
passing:

"Cousin! Cousin! Set me at rest: what are you
concocting with Mastro-don Gesualdo?"

"I was expecting *you*—sharp tongue?" muttered
Dame Sganci; and there she left him, without more
ado; he grinning after her between his bare gums,
sunk in his arm-chair like a malicious mummy.

At this juncture entered the lawyer Neri, little, bald,
rotund, a veritable peg-top, with petulant belly, noisy
laugh, and a strident way of talking like a shrill pulley-
wheel.

"Donna Mariannina!—Ladies and gentlemen!—
But what a lot of people! And what a lot of beauty!"

Then, having descried Mastro-don Gesualdo also
present in great style, he pretended to lean forward as
if he needed to see better, couldn't believe his eyes,
lifting his brows, shading his eyes with his hand; he
crossed himself, and rushed in fury towards the great
balcony, plunging into the crowd, using his elbows,
stuttering:

"This is the limit!—As true as God's in heaven—!"

Donna Giuseppina Alòsi instinctively put her hand
up to her jewels; and the Captain's lady, who since she
had no jewels to flaunt made a display of other riches,
feeling somebody suddenly fumbling in her shoulders,
turned like a viper.

"Beg pardon! Beg pardon!" stammered the lawyer. "I was looking for Baron Zacco."

From the street of San Sebastian, above the roofs, you could see a glow of fire drawing towards the square, and fireworks leaping out of it from time to time; it was moving before the statue of the saint, with a shouting of the villagers rising like a tempest.

"The procession! The procession!" squealed the children pressed against the balustrade. The others squeezed forward; but the procession did not yet appear. Cavaliere Peperito, who was devouring the jewels of Donna Giuseppina Alòsi with his eyes—his eyes like a famished wolf's, in his thin face that was dense up to the eyes with a bluish beard—seized the opportunity to breathe once more into her ear:

"You look like a girl, Donna Giuseppina; on my word of honour!"

"Be still, wicked creature!" replied the widow. "Turn yourself to the patron saint who is just coming."

"Yes, yes, if he'll give me grace——"

From the arm-chair in which Marchese Limòli was huddled, came at that moment his cracked thin voice:

"Say what you like, yes, say what you like! I'm deaf, I am! and you know it——"

Baron Zacco, red as a red pepper, re-entered from the balcony without bothering about the saint, holding forth to the lawyer Neri:

"It's all the canon-priest Lupi's doing!—Now they set Mastro-don Gesualdo between my feet as well, to bid at the auction of the communal lands!—But they shan't get them from me!—not even if I have to sell Fontanarossa, you see!—Lands which have been in my family for forty years!——"

All at once under the balcony the band burst out in a furious double-quick march, hurling themselves into the square along with a great wave of people that seemed almost menacing. The Captain's lady drew back, curling her nose.

"What a smell of one's fellow-men rises from down there!"

"Isn't it!" Baron Zacco went on exclaiming—"Land which I pay a guinea and a half a furlong for already! And he thinks it isn't much!"

Lawyer Neri, not anxious to let anybody know his affairs, turned to the Captain's lady, who was in such a low dress that she was really indecent: pretending she got her gowns from Palermo. At the moment she was flirting in the middle of a group of young fellows.

"Mistress Captain! Mistress Captain! That's how you rob the saint of his honours! Everybody turns their back on him!"

"How stupid they are, all these people!" replied the Captain's lady, fairly beside herself with bliss. "I'm going over to the marchese, he's got more sense than you here."

"Oh, no! Oh, no! Dear lady—!"

The marchese, his eyes awake now, kept putting his nose close to her, sniffing her scent of bergamot, till she had to defend herself with her fan, though the little old man persisted and persisted.

"No! No! Let me attend to my devotions!"

The arch-priest took snuff, blew his nose, coughed, and at last rose and made as if to leave, his cheeks puffing;—his cheeks shining, his gown shining, and his big ring shining, although spiteful tongues said it wasn't real; while the marchese cried behind him:

"Don Calogero! Don Calogero! I mean to say, what the devil!—At my age!——"

And hardly had the laughter at the marchese's sally

died down, than Donna Giuseppina Alòsi was heard
saying in confidence to her cavaliere :

"—Quite as if I was free, don't you see! The two
eldest at the Mary College; the boy at the seminary;
only the youngest, Sarino, at home, and he's not as
high as this fan. And then my children are all pro-
vided for, by their father—rest his soul————"

Donna Sarina returned to the big balcony, gossiping
in a low tone with Cousin Macrì, giving little shakes
of her head and little smiles, as if to say :

"For all that, I don't understand the mystery that
Cousin Sganci is preparing—We're relations of Bianca
as well, when all's said and done!"

"Is it he?—him there?" Donna Giuseppina began
asking again, with the same malicious little smile as
before.

Dame Cirmena nodded, pressing her thin lips
and turning her eyes elsewhere, being mysterious herself also. But at last she couldn't contain herself any
longer :

"They do things underhand—as if it was really
shady. They know well enough that they're doing a
dirty business.—But folks aren't such fools that they
don't know;—Canon-priest Lupi has been on the move
about it for a month—back and forth between the
Sgancis and the Rubieras————"

"You don't tell me!" exclaimed Peperito. "A Trao
marrying Mastro-don Gesualdo! No, don't tell me
such a thing!—When I see an illustrious family like
that come down so low, it gives me a pain in my
stomach, on my word of honour it does!"

And he turned aside blowing his nose like a trom-
bone in his dirty handkerchief, shaking with indigna-
tion through all his poverty-stricken person, after

having darted a look full of eloquence at Donna Giuseppina.

"Who do you expect to marry her?—without a dowry!" retorted Dame Cirmena at the cavaliere, who was already some distance off. "And then after what's happened!——"

"Well, anyhow she'll put herself right in the sight of God," observed Aunt Macrì in a low voice.

Her own daughter, who was listening and saying nothing, staring everybody who spoke in the face, with her big ardent eyes, now shook her tunic, as if she were afraid of dirtying it among so much nastiness, and murmured in her man's voice, with thick disdainful lips on which one seemed to see the black hairs trembling, turning towards the glow of the procession, that drew nearer over the roofs of the street, like the glow of a fire:

"Patron Saint! Oh thou preserve me!"

"Yes, this is the consequence.—I don't know what the girl had got into her head.—Upset the family and all the relations!—Cousin Sganci has done well to try and mend matters—I won't say she hasn't. But she ought to have spoken to us, whether or not, for we're relations of Bianca's as much as she is.—Instead of doing things on the sly—I'll wager even Don Ferdinando doesn't know a thing."

"But the other brother—Don Diego, what does he say?"

"Ah, Don Diego!—He'll be rummaging among his old papers—The papers of the law-suit. He thinks of nothing else.—He believes he'll get rich with the law-suit!—You see, he hasn't set foot out of the house, even for the festival!—Then perhaps he's ashamed to show himself among people. . . . They're all like that, the Traos are—Stupid they are!—People who'll be found dead in their beds one fine day, rather than open their mouths for——"

"The canon-priest, no!" the notary was saying as he came towards the balcony, talking in an undertone with Baron Zacco. "The Baroness more likely—if he offers her a profit.—She hasn't any scruples, she hasn't! —I'm not afraid of the canon-priest"—And then all smiles to the ladies:

"Ah—Donna Clara!—The lovely nun you have in your house. One of God's blessings, upon my word!"

—"Eh, marchese? Eh? Who would have foretold, in your days?—that you would come to look on at the procession of the Patron Saint shoulder to shoulder with Mastro-don Gesualdo, in the Sganci house?" resumed Baron Zacco, who was always chewing over the same thing, and couldn't get it down, looking here and there with the devil in his eyes, winking at the women to make them laugh.

The marchese, impenetrable, only replied:

"Eh, eh, my dear baron! Eh, eh!"

"Do you know how much Mastro-don Gesualdo has made in the mill factory?" put in the lawyer in a half-voice, mysterious-seeming. "A nice sum! I tell you! —He's lifted himself up from nothing—I can remember when he was a navvy, with stones on his shoulder —yes, my sirs! Mastro Nunzio hadn't the wherewithal to pay for the kindling to burn the lime in his kiln—. Now he's got the contract for the bridge at Fiumegrande!—His son laid down the guarantee money, all in four-shilling pieces, one on top of the other—— He's got his finger in every pie in the parish— They say he wants to go in for land-speculating as well—The more you eat the more you want—He's

got a rare appetite—and a fine set of teeth, I tell you
—If they let him go on as he is doing, in a very little
while you'll be able to say that Mastro-don Gesualdo
is boss of the place!"

At that the marchese raised his little monkey head
for an instant; but then he shrugged his shoulders,
and replied with that same cutting little smile:

"As far as I'm concerned—it doesn't matter to me.
I am on the shelf anyhow."

"Boss!—boss!—when all these are dead who were
born before him!—and better than him!—I will sell
Fontanarossa; but Mastro-don Gesualdo shan't take
the communal lands from me. Neither by himself, nor
with Baroness Rubiera to help him!"

"What is it?—what is it?" interrupted the lawyer,
running to the balcony to avoid the discourse, because
the baron couldn't restrain himself and shouted too
loud.

Down below in the square, in front of the Sganci
door, there was a commotion, light-coloured dresses in
the middle of the crowd, caps flying in the air, and
somebody or other cudgelling his way, aiming his blows
straight and crooked, through the throng. Then immediately after appeared Don Giuseppe Barabba in
the doorway of the anteroom, his hands in the air,
strangled with respect.

"Ma'am! Ma'am!"

It was the whole Margarone family this time:
Donna Fifì, otherwise Donna Giovannina, Donna
Mita, Mama Margarone, Donna Bellonia, of the
Brancalani of Piertraperzia, her very self, suffocating
in a corsage of green velvet, purple in the face, smiling;
and in the rear Papa Margarone, dignified, swelling
out his cheeks, leaning on his malacca cane with the

gold knob, without turning his head in the least, holding by the hand the youngest of the Margarones, Nicolino, who was squealing and dragging his feet because they wouldn't let him see the saint in the square. His papa, brandishing the malacca cane, wanted to teach him how to behave.

"What, now?" smiled the marchese mockingly, to calm him.—"To-day, when it's high holiday? Nay, leave the poor child alone, Don Filippo."

Don Filippo left him alone, confining himself to hurling now and again some look of authority at the boy who took not the slightest notice. Meanwhile the others made a fuss of the Margarone ladies.

"Donna Bellonia! Donna Fifì!—What a pleasure, this evening!"

Also Don Giuseppe Barabba, in his usual fashion, exerting himself to death carrying more chairs and snuffing the wicks of the lights. Then from the balcony he began sending telegraphic messages down to somebody in the square below, shouting to make himself heard above the great hubbub of the crowd:

"Baron! Your lordship! Baron!"

Then he ran to his mistress, triumphantly:

"Ma'am! Ma'am! Here he is, he's coming! Here's Don Ninì!"

Donna Giuseppina Alòsi sketched a small smile in answer to the nudge which Baron Zacco gave her. The Captain's lady, however, stretched herself above her corsage,—so that her fine, bare shoulders heaved themselves out of her puffed sleeves.

"Stupid creature! A nice way to do it! What's all this row about? That's the style you announce anybody!"

Don Giuseppe took himself off, grumbling.

But at that point entered Don Ninì Rubiera, a tall, stout young fellow almost too big to go through the doorway, red and white complexion, curly hair, and with rather sleepy eyes that simply turned the heads of the girls:—Donna Giovannina Margarone, also a fine piece of goods, tightly laced like her mother, became red as a poppy seeing the young baron enter. But the mamma pushed her eldest girl forward, Donna Fifì, dried up and yellow with long celibacy, all hairs, with certain front teeth that looked as if they wanted to snatch a husband on the wing; loaded up with ribbons, trinkets, frills like a rare bird.

"Fifì spied you first in all that crowd!—*What* a crowd, upon my word! My husband had to use his stick to get us through it. Really a fine festival! Fifì said in a moment: 'There's the young Baron Rubiera, near the band-stand'——"

Don Ninì looked uneasily round. All at once discovering his cousin Bianca stowed away in a corner of the balcony over the alley, her face deadly pale, he started, lost for a moment his fine florid colouring, and replied stammering:

"Yes, ma-am!—in fact—I am on the committee——"

"Bravo! bravo! A grand festival, indeed it is! You know how to do things well, that you do!—And your mother, Don Ninì?—"

"Quick! Quick!" cried Aunt Sganci from the balcony. "Here's the saint!"

Marchese Limòli, afraid of the damp of the evening, had caught Mamma Margarone by her dress of green satin and was playing the libertine:

"There's no hurry! There's no hurry! The saint comes again every year. Come here, Donna Bellonia!

Let us leave room for the children, we who have seen
so many festivals!"

And he continued mumbling smutty jokes into the
ear that seemed to blush with shame; hugely diverted
by the serious face which Don Filippo was making
above his satin cravat; while the Captain's lady, to
show that she knew her way about in such talk, laughed
like a mad-woman, leaning forward every moment, and
retiring behind her fan, to hide her white teeth, her
white bosom, all those charms the effect of which
she was studying out of the corner of her eye,
whilst pretending to be angry when the marchese took
some excessive liberty—now that they were alone, as
he said, with his satyr's toothless grin.

"Mita! Mita!" called Mamma Margarone at last.

"No! no! Don't forsake me, Donna Bellonia!—
Don't leave me alone with Madame la Capitaine—at
my age!—Donna Mita knows how she must behave.
She is as big and tall as her two sisters put together;
but she knows what she's got to do, that child does,
not to get in the light of the other two."

Lawyer Neri, who through his profession knew all
the business of the town and wasn't backward in what
he said, asked Madame Margarone:

"Now then, when are we ging to eat that bridal
cake, for Donna Fifi's wedding?"

Don Filippo coughed loudly. Donna Bellonia replied that so far it was only gossip; people talked
because they knew that Don Nini was rather assiduous
in his attentions to her daughter.

"Nothing serious. Nothing positive——"

But you could see that she wanted very much not to
be believed. Marchese Limòli as usual found the right
word:

"Till the relations have agreed about the dowry, nobody has any business to talk in public."

Don Filippo nodded assent, and Donna Bellonia, seeing her husband's approval, went so far as to say:

"Yes, that's true."

"They will make a fine couple," put in the Captain's lady graciously.

Cavaliere Peperito, rather than stand any longer with his mouth open like a looney in the middle of the group where Donna Giuseppina had planted him, in order to attract less attention, suddenly burst out:

"But, Baroness Rubiera hasn't come!—How is it the baroness hasn't come to her cousin Sganci's?"

There was a moment's silence. Baron Zacco alone, like a real country-bumpkin, in order to give vent to some of the bile he'd got inside him, took the pains to reply in a loud voice, as if everybody were deaf:

"She is ill!—She's got a headache!—" And at the same time he shook his head, to say no! it was not so. Then, standing in the middle of an audience, in a lower voice, but with a flaming face:

"She sent Mastro-don Gesualdo in her place!—her future partner!—Yes, indeed!—Didn't you know? They're going to take the lease of the communal lands —that we've had for forty years—all the Zaccos, from father to son!—A piece of roguery!—A scheme between the three of them: Father, son, and holy ghost! The Baroness daren't look me in the face after the lovely game they want to play on me—I don't mean to say she's stopped at home so as not to meet me— The devil!—Everybody is after his own ends—To-day it's money before blood-relationship—I don't give much for ours, anyway—We know what stock Baroness Rubiera comes from!—So naturally she follows her own interests—Yes, you bet your life! I have it from people who are actually in the know!—The canon-priest puts them up to it: Mastro-don Gesualdo lays out the capital, and the Baroness gives—a rosy nothing—the support of her name!—But we'll see which is worth more, their side or mine!—Yes, we'll see!—And so, to try it on, they push Mastro-don Gesualdo forward—see him there, in the balcony with the Traos?—"

"Bianca! Bianca!" called Marchese Limòli.

"Did you want me, uncle?"

"Yes, come here."

"What a charming creature!" observed the Captain's lady, to flatter the marchese, while the girl was crossing the salon, timid, in her flannelette dress and her humble and embarrassed air of a poor young woman.

"Yes," replied the marchese. "She is of good family."

"Here it comes! Here it comes!" came the cry at that moment from those who were looking out. "Here's the saint!"

Peperito caught the word as it flew, and plunged headlong into the crowd behind Madame Alòsi. The Captain's lady rose on tiptoe; the lawyer, gallant, proposed to lift her up in his arms. Donna Bellonia ran to her motherly duties, beside her own offspring; and her husband contented himself with mounting on a chair, to look.

"What are you doing there with Mastro-don Gesualdo?" muttered the marchese now that he was left alone with his niece.

Bianca fixed her big, gentle blue eyes on her uncle

for a moment, those eyes that were her only real beauty in her worn, thin Trao face, and replied:

"But—my Aunt put him there——"

"Come here. Come here. I'll find you a place myself."

All at once the square seemed to flare up in a vast flame, on which were printed the windows of the houses, the cornices of the roofs, the long balustraded balcony of the Town Hall, swarming with people. In the doorways of the balconies the heads of the guests clustered together, black upon that fiery background; and in the middle one, the angular figure of Donna Fifì Margarone, surprised by that light, looked greener than usual, her surly face trying to appear moved with emotion, her flat bosom panting like a pair of bellows, her eyes dazed behind the cloud of smoke, only her teeth remaining ferocious; almost abandoning herself against the shoulder of the young Baron Rubiera, who looked violet-coloured in that glare of light, stuck between her and Donna Giovannina; while Mita stretched wide her childish eyes, because she couldn't see, and Nicolino went pinching the legs of people, so that he could get his head through and work himself forward.

"What's the matter?—don't you feel well?" said the marchese, seeing his niece so pale.

"It's nothing—It's the smoke which hurts me— Don't say anything, uncle! Don't disturb anybody!"

From time to time she pressed her imitation-cambric handkerchief, embroidered by herself, on her lips, and coughed, slowly, slowly, bending her head down; her flannelette frock made folds on her thin shoulders. She said nothing, but stood and looked at the fire-works, with her face sharp and thin, as if stretched towards the corner of the mouth, where were two painful folds; her eyes wide-staring and gleaming, almost wet. Only the hand which leaned on the back of the chair trembled a little, while the other, which hung at her side, opened and shut mechanically; thin convulsed white hands.

"Viva the Patron Saint! Viva Saint Gregory the Great!"—In the crowd below in the square was the canon-priest Lupi, howling like one possessed, in the thick of the peasants, and gesticulating towards the balconies of the Sganci mansion, his face upturned, calling at the top of his voice to his acquaintances:

"Donna Marianna?—Eh?—Eh?—Baron Rubiera ought to be pleased!—Baron? Don Ninì?—are you satisfied?—How d'ye do, Don Gesualdo? Bravo! bravo! There you are!"

Then he ran up as fast as he could, fairly bursting himself, red in the face, out of breath, his cassock tucked up, his mantle and his three-cornered hat under his arm, his hands filthy with powder, bathed in sweat:

"What a festival, eh, Signora Sganci?"—then he called Don Giuseppe Barabba to bring him a glass of water.—"I'm dying of thirst, Donna Marianna! What splendid fireworks, eh? About two thousand squibs! I've lighted above two hundred with my own hands. Look what hands, marchese!—Ah, you are here, Don Gesualdo! Good! Good! Don Giuseppe? Who knows where that old stupid of a Don Giuseppe has got to?"

Don Giuseppe had gone up to the attic, to see the fireworks from the roof window, at the risk of coming a cropper into the square below. He appeared at last, with the glass of water, himself covered with dust and cobwebs, after his mistress and the canon-priest Lupi had shouted themselves hoarse for him through all the rooms.

The canon-priest Lupi, making himself at home in the house, also gave him the length of his tongue. Then, turning towards Mastro-don Gesualdo with a beaming face:

"Bravo, bravo, Don Gesualdo! I'm as pleased as punch to see you here. Madame Sganci said to me a while back: 'Next year I want Don Gesualdo to come to my house, to see the procession.'"

Marchese Limòli, who had gracefully saluted the Patron Saint as he passed, bowing over the back of the chair, now drew himself erect with a grimace.

"Ahee! Ahee!—By God's will this one also has passed by. If you live the year through you see all the feasts."

"But you never expected to see what you've seen this time," jeered Baron Zacco, indicating Mastro-don Gesualdo.—"No! no! I remember him carrying stones—and his shoulders in rags!—on the building-scaffoldings, this dear friend, whom we've got here to-day as one of us—!"

The mistress of the house, however, was all courtesy for Mastro-don Gesualdo. Now that the saint was in her own street it seemed as if the feast was for him: Donna Marianna talking to him of this and that, the canon-priest Lupi clapping him on the shoulder; Dame Macrì who had even given up her place to him; Don Filippo Margarone also letting drop from the height of his cravat such compliments as these, for him:

"Noble birth is an accident, it's not a virtue!—To rise up from nothing, that's the real merit!—The first mill you contracted to build—what?—with money you borrowed at twenty per cent."

"Yes, sir," replied Don Gesualdo quietly. "I didn't sleep a wink, those nights."

The archpriest Bugno, jealous of the nice words wasted on somebody else, after all the crackers that had gone off, all the shouting, all the uproar that he thought really was dedicated somewhat to himself, as head of the church, now managed to get a little group round himself as well, talking of the merits of the Patron Saint:

"A great saint—and a big fine image!—The foreigners came on purpose to see it—Some Englishmen, it had come out afterwards, would have paid its weight in gold, to take it away with them to put among their idols over there—"

The marchese, who was ready to burst with laughing, interrupted him at last:

"What rubbish!—Who's been stuffing you up, Don Calogero! The statue is papier-mâché—a hideous thing! The rats have made their nest inside it—The jewels?—Eh! Eh! They wouldn't make even me rich, I'm telling you! Coloured glass—like a good many others you see!—A carnival-doll!—What? What d'ye say?—Yes, a sacrilege! The fellow who made that saint ought to be sent to the devil—I'm not speaking of the saint in Paradise—I know, that's another matter—Faith is enough.—I am a Christian myself, I am—what the deuce!—and I pride myself on it—"

The Captain's lady affected to stare pointedly at the necklace of Donna Giuseppina Alòsi, at the same time as she rebuked the marchese:

"Libertine—! Libertine—!——"

Peperito had stopped his ears. The archpriest Bugno started all over again:

A work of art, that statue!—The King, God keep him, wanted to sell it at the time of the war with the Jacobins!—A saint that works miracles!—"

"What's the latest, Don Gesualdo?" cried the marchese, in his little cracked voice, fed up, turning his back on the archpriest.—"There's something in the wind?"

Baron Zacco began to laugh loudly, his eyes bolting out of his head; but the other, a bit dazed by the crowd round him, did not answer.

"Oh, you can tell it to me," continued the malicious little old man. "You needn't be afraid that I shall enter into competition."

Even those to whom it didn't matter were amused by this squibbing. As for Baron Zacco, you can imagine what he was like.

"Eh!—Eh!—marchese!—You won't compete, you won't?—Eh!—Eh!"

Mastro-don Gesualdo threw a glance over all these laughing people, and replied quietly:

"What about it, marchese?—Everybody does what he can for himself—"

"Do it then, do it, my dear fellow. As for me, I've nothing to worry about."

Don Giuseppe Barabba came up on tiptoe to his mistress, and said in her ear, with great mystery:

"Am I to bring the ices, now the procession has gone by?"

"A minute, just a minute!" interrupted the canon-priest Lupi. "Let me wash my hands."

"If I don't bring them quick," added the servant, "they'll be nothing but soup. It's a good while since

Giacinto sent them, and they were all soft even then."

"All right, all right—Bianca?"

"Aunt?"

"Be so good as to help me a bit, will you?"

Through the wide-open double doors entered after a few moments Don Giuseppe and Master Titta, the barber who attended to the household, carrying two large silver trays, that dripped; and they began to make the round of the guests, step by step, like another procession the two of them. First the archpriest, Donna Giuseppina Alòsi, the Captain's lady, the guests of most importance. The canon-priest Lupi nudged the barber, who was passing before Mastro-don Gesualdo without stopping.

"How am I to know? There are new ones now!—" grumbled Master Titta.

The Margarone boy put his finger into everything. "Uncle?"

"No, thank you, Bianca, my dear—I've got a cough —I'm an invalid—like your brother."

"Donna Bellonia, there, on the balcony!" suggested Aunt Sganci, who was also slaving to serve her guests.

After the first general movement, a manœuvring of chairs to escape the rain of syrup, there followed a few moments of pensiveness, a discreet clicking of little plates, a circumspect and silent working of spoons, as if it was a solemn ceremony. Donna Mita Margarone, greedy, without lifting her nose from her plate. Barabba and Master Titta, having put the trays aside, wiped away their sweat with cotton handkerchiefs.

The young Baron Rubiera, who was talking in a corner of the balcony nose to nose with Donna Fifì, looking into her eyes, eyes that were melting like the ice-cream, started violently seeing his cousin appear, and went a little pale. Donna Bellonia took the little plate from Bianca's hands, bowing awkwardly.

"How kind of you!—really too kind,'too kind!"

Her daughter pretended to realise only at that moment that her friend was there.

"Oh, Bianca!—is it you?—how nice to see you! They told me you were ill—"

"Yes—a little.—Now I'm better."

"Yes, one can see—You're looking well—that's a sweet dress, simple!—but so becoming!"

Donna Fifì bent forward pretending to look at the stuff, but really to make the topazes which she wore at her neck glitter. Bianca replied, colouring:

"It is flannelette—a present from Aunt—"

"Ah!—Ah!"

The young baron, who was on thorns, proposed that they should go back into the salon.

"It's beginning to be damp—we shall catch a chill or something."

"Yes!—Fifì! Fifì!" said Madame Margarone.

Donna Fifì had to follow her mother, with a feeble walk which seemed to her very sentimental, her little head drooping a trifle sideways to her shoulder, her eyelids fluttering, hurt by the stronger light on her eyes that were languid as if they were sleepy.

Bianca put her hand on the arm of her cousin, who was also decamping from the balcony, gently, like a caress, like a prayer: she was trembling all over, her voice was suffocated in her throat:

"Ninì!—listen, Ninì!—be so kind to me!—Only just a word!—I came on purpose—If I don't speak to you here it is all over with me—all over with me!—"

"Be careful!—there are so many people!" ex-claimed her cousin in an undertone, looking this way and that to escape her with his eyes. But she fixed her beautiful, pleading eyes on him, with great dis-couragement, a great and painful abandon in all her person, in her pale, worn-out face, in her humble bearing, in her inert arms which she lifted desolate.

"What do you say to me, Ninì?—What do you tell me to do?—See—I am in your arms—like the Mater Dolorosa!"

He began to beat his fists on his head, moved, with his heart swelling also, taking care not to make a noise, and watching that nobody was coming on to the bal-cony. Bianca caught his hand.

"You are right!—we are two lost creatures. My mother doesn't leave me free even to blow my own nose! You see, you see?—You think I don't think of you? You believe I don't think?—At night—I never close my eyes! I'm a poor unlucky fellow! And people think me happy and contented."

He looked down into the square that was empty now, to avoid the desperate eyes of his cousin, which went to his heart; and his own eyes were also wet.

"Do you see?" he added. "I wish I was a poor devil—like Santo Motta down there! In the tavern of Pecu-Pecu. Poor and contented—"

"My aunt doesn't want it—?"

"No, she doesn't want it!—What can I do?—She is the mistress!"

From the salon was heard the voice of Baron Zacco, disputing angrily; and then in the moments when he was silent, the chitter-chatter of the ladies, like a twittering of sparrows, with the piercing laugh of the Captain's lady shrilling out like a piccolo.

"You must confess everything to my aunt—"

Don Ninì stretched his neck towards the doorway of the balcony, cautiously. Then he replied, lowering his voice still more:

"Your brother has told her—There was the deuce to pay! Didn't you know?"

Don Giuseppe Barabba came on to the balcony carrying a little plate on each hand.

"Donna Bianca, your aunt says—before it's all gone——"

"Thank you. Put it there, on the flower-pot."

"Better eat it quick, Donna Bianca. There's hardly a bit left."

Don Ninì then put his nose into his plate, pretending not to heed anything else:

"Don't you want any?"

She did not reply. After a while, when the servant had gone, came her dull voice again:

"Is it true that you're getting married?"

"I?"

"Yes, you—to Fifì Margarone—"

"It isn't true—who told you such a thing?"

"Everybody says so—"

"Not by my wish—It's my mother who's got this into her head. You as well—they say they want to marry you to Don Gesualdo Motta."

"I?"

"Yes, everybody says so—Aunt—my mother even—"

Donna Giuseppina Alòsi put her head into the balcony for an instant, as if looking for somebody; then seeing the two young people, she turned back at once into the salon.

"You see? You see?" he said. "Everybody's got

their eye on us!—Take your ice-cream—for my sake—
and for all the people who are watching. Everybody's
got their eye on us!"

She took from his hands, gently, the little plate
which she had had put on the pot of carnations; but
she trembled so much that once or twice was heard the
tinkling of her spoon knocking against her glass.

Barabba came running immediately, saying:

"Here I am! Here I am!"

"Just a moment! Just a moment still, Don Giuseppe."

The young baron would have paid money out of his
own pocket to keep Barabba on the balcony.

"How does the festival suit you, Don Giuseppe?"

"Why how would you expect, your lordship? Everything on my shoulders!—the house to put in order, the
loose covers to take off, the lights to prepare—Donna
Bianca here, I must say, gave me a hand. Master
Titta was only fetched for the waiting. And then
to-morrow I've got to start again sweeping and putting
the chair-covers on again—"

Don Giuseppe went off grumbling with the two
empty glasses. From the drawing-room came the
sound of a general laugh, after something that the
lawyer Neri had said, something which you couldn't
hear very well because when lawyer Neri had something smutty to say he lowered his voice.

"Let us go in as well," said the young baron. "To
prevent them suspecting."

Bianca, however, did not move. She was weeping
softly, in the shadow; and from time to time you saw
her white handkerchief lifted to her eyes.

"There you are!—It's you who set folks talking!"
broke forth her cousin, who was on thorns.

"What do you care?" she replied. "What do you care?—Now!"

"Yes! Yes!—Do you think I'm not fond of you?"

A dissolution, an endless bitterness came up from the wide black expanse of the Alia, away beyond, beyond the houses of the Barresi; and from the vines and olives of Giolio, which you could still dimly make out, across the street of the Rosary, that swarmed with lights; and from the long tableland of Casalgilardo, interrupted by the high corner of the College; and from the deep sky, sewn with stars—one of which, brighter than the rest, far down, seemed to be watching, cold, sad, solitary. The noise of the feast faded and died in the distance, towards San Vito. A desolate silence fell little by little, a silence that wrung the heart. Bianca was erect against the wall, motionless; her livid face and hands seemed to waver in the uncertain gleam which rose from the stall of the man who sold almond toffee. Her cousin was leaning on the balustrade, pretending to watch attentively the man who was going round putting out the illuminations in the deserted square, and the lad of the man in charge of the decorations, who was running up and down the band-stand, like a black tom-cat, pulling out nails, hammering, throwing down the festoons and garlands of paper. The rockets that still went off from time to time, far away, behind the black mass of the Town-Hall, the hammering of the decorator, the fewer cries, tired and drunken; all seemed extinguished in the vast lonely countryside. Together with the acrid odour of gunpowder, dissipating now, came a sweet scent of carnations; some people passed singing; a burst of chatter and laughing was heard from the salon, near

to them, in the laceration of that last, wordless farewell.

In the luminous doorway of the balcony passed a
lean shadow, and was heard the little cough of Marchese Limòli.

"Eh, eh, children!—blessings on you!—I have come
to see the festival—now it's gone by. Bianca, my niece
—take care that the evening air doesn't do you harm."

"No, uncle," she replied in her dull voice. "One is
suffocated inside there."

"Patience! You've always got to have patience, in
this world. Better sweat than cough—You, Nini,
you see that the Margarone ladies are leaving—"

"I'm going, uncle."

"Go on then, go, even if you see nothing but teeth!
I wouldn't like to tackle them, for my part. And
it's a fact I'm not a shy bird, either. What the deuce
possesses your mother to make you marry those
teeth?"

"Ah—uncle—"

"You are a fool! You ought to let her play the
devil and all, as much as she likes and pleases, your
mother!—You're her only son!—Who's she got to
leave her property to, then, when she dies?"

"Eh—in twenty years' time!—You can starve to
death before then! My mother is stronger than you
or me, and she can hang on for another thirty years!"

"That's a fact," said the marchese. "Your mother
wouldn't be very well pleased to hear her years grudged
her.—But it's her own fault."

"Ah, uncle—believe me, it's an awful hole!"

"Keep calm! Keep calm! Console yourself with
thinking of somebody who is left worse off than you—"

The Captain's lady presented herself, quick, uneasy, looking smiling up and down the street.

"My husband?—Isn't he coming yet?"

"The saint hasn't got back yet," replied Don Ninì. "You'll hear the big bell of San Giovanni as soon as he gets to the church and joins the other procession."

However, people began to leave the Sganci house. Cavaliere Peperito was the first to be seen going out of the door, and disappearing behind the corner of Bomma's pharmacy. A moment later issued the lantern belonging to Donna Giuseppina Alòsi, who crossed the square, that was dirty with burnt paper, and beanshells, and nutshells, on tiptoe, holding her skirt over her arm, making her way up the Rosary; and immediately after, from the pharmacy emerged the shadow of Peperito once more, going off in pursuit, stealthily, keeping under the wall. The Captain's lady gave a dry little laugh, and young Baron Rubiera added:

"Yes, it's him!—Peperito!—as sure as heaven!"

The marquis took his niece's arm and re-entered the room with her. At that moment Mastro-don Gesualdo, standing near the balcony, was talking with the canon-priest Lupi, the latter perorating hotly, *sotto voce,* with an air of mystery, pressing closer and closer, as if he wanted to get into the other man's pocket, with his ferret's face; the former serious, with his chin in his hand, not saying a word, only nodding his head from time to time.

"Exactly like a government minister," jeered Baron Zacco.

The canon-priest ended up with an emphatic handshake, throwing a look at the baron, who pretended not to notice, red as a cock. The mistress of the house was bringing the ladies' mantles and hats, while all the

Margarones with their scuffle were turning the house upside-down, getting ready.

"Well—Bianca!—I thought you'd already gone!" exclaimed Donna Fifì with her fanged smile.

Bianca only replied with a surprised-seeming look. She was so overcome and suffering; while her cousin was making a great flurry among the mantles and the bonnets, his head dropped.

"One moment! One moment!" exclaimed Don Filippo, raising his free arm, while on the other he held the sleeping Nicolino.

An uproar was heard in the Square; screams in the distance; people were running towards San Giovanni, and the big bell was ringing unceasingly, down there.

The Captain's lady came in from the balcony stopping her ears with her beautiful white hands, screaming in falsetto:

"My husband!—They are fighting—!"

And she collapsed on the sofa, her eyes closed. The ladies all began to shout at once; the mistress of the house called to Barabba to go down and bolt the big door; while Donna Bellonia shoved her children in a herd into Donna Mariannina's room, and the Marchese Limòli slapped the hands of the Captain's lady with sharp little blows. Lawyer Neri proposed to unlace her bodice.

"What do you mean?" said she, springing to her feet in a fury at this. "What do you take me for, Mr. Jackass?"

The Captain arrived at that moment, followed by Don Liccio Papa, who was simply tearing himself to shreds in the antechamber, giving an account of what had happened,—a hundred people wouldn't have been able to suppress him.

"The same story every year," said monsieur the Captain, after he had pulled himself together, emptying a glass of water in one breath.—"The devotees of San Giovanni setting the big bell going a quarter of an hour too soon!—Their dodges!—And the San Vito-ites of course won't stand it—Fighting like fiends with cudgels they were!"

"The same tale every year!" repeated the canon-priest Lupi.—"Swinish behaviour! And the authorities do nothing to prevent it—"

The Captain, in the middle of the room, stretching his finger at the speaker, snorted at last:

"Hark at him!—Why don't you go yourself then? For two pins they'd have started on me!—Your husband has been in danger of his life, Donna Carolina—"

The Captain's lady clasped her hands, tightening her mouth to cry:

"Oh, heaven above! Oh, Holiest Mother of Peril!"

"Yes, you're in a sad way!" muttered the lawyer Neri, turning in her direction. "You're in a sad way! —if you expect your husband to risk his skin to make you a widow!"

Don Ninì Rubiera, looking for his hat, ran against his cousin, who followed him like a ghost, broken, stumbling at every step.

"Be careful!" he said to her. "Be careful!—They're watching us!—There's Don Gesualdo there—!"

"Bianca! Bianca! The mantles of these ladies!" called Aunt Sganci from the bedroom where the whole swarm of the Margarones was stuck.

The girl rummaged among the heap of cloaks, with trembling hands. Her cousin was so upset that, for his part, he kept on wandering round looking for his hat

"Why look, I've got it on! I don't know what I'm doing!"

He looked round like a robber, while everybody was hunting their things in the lobby, and then he drew her aside towards the door.

"Listen—for God's love!—be careful!—Nobody knows anything—Your brother won't have told—And I haven't—You know I've cared more for you than for my own soul!"

She didn't answer a word, only her eyes spoke, and they said many things.

"Don't look at me with that face, Bianca!—no!—don't look at me like that—I shall betray myself, I shall—"

Donna Fifì came out with her mantle and bonnet, stiff, her lips as tight as if they'd been stitched together; and as her sister, a jolly creature, ran to kiss Bianca, she called her away with her irritable voice:

"Giovannina! Come along! Come along!"

"She's not so bad, this one," muttered the young baron. "But her sister is a punishment from God."

Aunt Sganci, accompanying the Margarones to the door, said to Mastro-don Gesualdo, who was simply overdoing himself in bows on the landing, at the risk of going head foremost down the stairs:

"Don Gesualdo—be so kind. Go with my nephew and niece, the Traos. You are neighbours as it is— Don Ferdinando doesn't see well at night."

"Hark at that! Hark at that!" said the canon-priest to him.

Zacco couldn't rest; he pretended to look for the torch-lamp in the chest in the antechamber, to give it to Mastro-don Gesualdo to carry.

"Since he's got to accompany Donna Bianca—one

of the Traos—It would never have entered his head
that he could receive such an honour—Mastro-don
Gesualdo!"

However, the latter couldn't hear, because he was
waiting in the square, talking with the canon-priest.
Only Don Liccio Papa, who brought up the rear with
his sabre fastened to his shoulder-belt, began to laugh:

"Ah! ah!"

"What is it?" asked the Captain, who was giving
his arm to his bundled-up wife. "What is it, an in-
subordination?"

"Nothing," replied the marchese. "Baron Zacco
baying the moon."

Then, as he descended the stairs along with Bianca,
leaning on his little cane, he said in her ear:

"Listen!—To-day the world belongs to those who
have money—All the others are bursting with envy.
If the baron had a daughter to marry, he'd give her
to Mastro-don Gesualdo!—I'm an old man, and I
know what poverty is; and I'm telling you."

"Eh? What did you say?—" Don Ferdinando
wanted to know, as he came carefully wandering behind, counting the flag-stones.

"Nothing.—We were saying what a fine night,
Cousin Trao!"

The other looked up into the air and repeated like
a parrot:

"A fine night! A fine night!"

Don Gesualdo was waiting there before the door,
together with the canon-priest Lupi, who was talking
into his face, *sotto voce:*

"Eh? Eh? Don Gesualdo? What do you think?—"

The other nodded and stroked his hard-bearded chin
with his coarse hand.

"A pearl! a girl who doesn't know a thing beyond home and church!—Careful!—she'll cost you nothing —She's not used to spending in her own home, that's certain! But of good family!—She'll bring lustre into your house!—You'll be marrying into all the nobility. —Did you see, eh, this evening?—what a fuss they made of you?—Your business will go full sail—That affair of the communal lands as well.—It's better to have the support of all the big guns—"

Don Gesualdo did not reply at once, lost in thought, his head dropped, following in the tread of Donna Bianca as she took her way up the steps of Sant'Agata, together with her uncle the marchese and her brother Don Ferdinando.

"Yes!—Yes!—I won't say no—But it needs thinking about—a serious matter. I'm afraid of launching into something a bit too big, my dear Canon. She's a lady, when all's said and done—Then I've got so many things to get into shape before I can decide—Everybody knows his own troubles—Better sleep on it. Night brings counsel, my dear Canon."

Bianca, who was walking with a tight heart, listening to the indifferent small-talk of her uncle, beside her silent, emaciated brother, heard those last words.

Night brings counsel. The dark, desolate night in her wretched little room. The night which carried away the last sounds of the festival, the last light, the last hope—Like the vision of him who went away with another woman, without turning, without speaking, without replying to her who called to him from the bottom of her heart, with a moan, with a sick lament, burying her face in her pillow wet with hot and silent tears.

IV

While the brick-layers were still sheltering from the downpour in the oil-press of Giolio, that was big as a church, playing pitch-penny, entered the boy who kept guard at the door, chewing a piece of bread and shouting with his mouth full:

"The master! There's the master!"

Behind him appeared Mastro-don Gesualdo, sopping wet, dragging after him the mule that was shaking its ears.

"Splendid!—That's just what I like!—Enjoy yourselves!—Go on, your pay continues just the same!—Body of——! Blood of——!"

Agostino, the foreman, gesticulating, muttering, standing in the doorway to look at the still clouded sky, with unseeing eye, at last managed to answer:

"Well, what do you want us to do? All get wet through?—It's this minute stopped tumbling down—Are we christians or pigs?——If I catch my death my mother won't make another Agostino, she won't!"

"Yes! Yes! Right you are!—I'm the fool, I am!—I've got a thick skin!—I did well to send my brother here to look after my interests!—It looks like it!—Spends his time also gambling, praise Heaven!"

Santo, who had remained open-mouthed, squatting beside the hollow in which were the halfpennies, rose to his feet covered with confusion, scratching his head.

Gesualdo, while the others went back to work, mum

and meagre, set to to measure the piece of new wall
with the rod; he clambered up the rung-ladder; he felt
the weight of the sacks of lime, raising them from the
ground:

"Blood of Judas!—The way I'm robbed of my
money!—All the lot of them of one mind to ruin me!
—Two days for three yards of wall? I shall make a
fine profit on this contract!—The bags of lime half
empty! Neli! Neli! Where's that son of a bad
woman, who brought this lime?—And that chalk will
go down to powder, eh?—that chalk?—Haven't you
the conscience of a christian?—God of Paradise!—
Even the rain at my expense!—I've got the sheaves
out yet on the threshing-floor!—Couldn't you fix up
the mill-stone while it was raining?—Now then! At
it! the mill-stone! I'll give you a hand, seeing I'm
here—"

Santo wanted to make a bit of a fire to dry the wet
clothes on his brother's back.

"That doesn't matter," replied Gesualdo. "I've
dried plenty of water off my back!—If I'd been like
you I should be carrying mortar on my shoulders yet!
—You remember?—And you wouldn't be here playing
pitch-penny."

Grumbling, going about to prepare the lever, the
wedges, the props, he turned round to throw his
brother a look.

"Plague it!" exclaimed Santo. "Always the same
old story!"

And he went to the doorway scowling, folding his
arms and looking here and there. The labourers hesitated, walking round the enormous stone; the oldest,
master Cola, with his chin in his hand, shook his head,
dripping with perspiration, looking at the millstone

as if it were an enemy. At last he pronounced that they were too few to raise it on to the platform.

"If the lever slips, God deliver us!—Who's going to go underneath to change the wedges?—I'm not, as sure as God's above!—If the lever slips!—my mother won't make another Master Cola Ventura!—Eh! eh! —We want more man-power—a crane!—or tie a pulley-wheel up there to the beam of the roof—then a quoin-wedge underneath—you see, your honour, to turn the quoin-wedges you can stand at one side and there's no danger—"

"Bravo!—now you'll be master-mason to me! Give me the bar!—I'm not frightened! While we stand cackling time is flying. The day goes by all the same, eh?—As if my money was robbed from me!—Heave! —on that side!—Don't bother about me, I've got a tough skin!—Ready!—heave!—Jesus with us!—Mary be praised!—a bit more!—Look out! Look out!—Ah, Mariano! Saints and devils, you're killing me!— Heave!—Viva Maria!—For your life! for your life! —Heave!—What are you doing, fool, that side there? —Heave!—it's coming! We've done it!—again!— on that side!—Don't be frightened that father will die—Heave!—Heave!—if the lever slips!—again!— if I'd cherished my own skin—again!—as my brother Santo does his—saints and devils!—saints and devils, look out!—I should be carrying mortar on my shoulder at this minute.—Want—now then! now!—want brings the wolf—again!—heave!—wolf out of the wood!— See my brother Santo standing watching?—If it wasn't for me he would be under—under the mill-stone—instead of me—and not scratching himself—raising the mill-stone—and the house—All on my shoulders!— Ah! thank God!"

D

At last, assured, the mill-stone on the platform, he went and sat down on a stone, exhausted, still trembling with the beating of his heart, wiping his sweat with his cotton handkerchief.

"See how you dry yourself from the rain? Water inside and water out!"

Santo proposed to pass round the bottle.

"Eh?—because you're so tired?—to dry your sweat, you?—You go to the pump—outside the door here."

The weather had improved. A ray of sun came in through the doorway that opened on to the country, which now seemed to spread smiling, with the village on the elevation in the distance glittering its windows.

"Sharp, sharp, boys! on to the scaffolds, come on! Let us earn ourselves a full day's wage—Put yourselves a bit in the shoes of your master who pays you! —I risk my neck in this contract!—I'm losing already, true as God's above!—Agostino, let me ask you!— keep a sharp eye!—A kind word and a sharp eye!— Master Cola, you're the master-mason!—who taught you to hold a putlock?—Be damned to you! Mariano, give me that putlock up here, on the scaffold—Haven't you got eyes, what the devil!—The plaster cracking and coming off!—And I've got to hear what the architect will have to say, plague on the lot of you!—When the lad comes again with the lime, just give him what he deserves, the son of a bad woman!—just tell that Neli that I'm in the trade myself!—That we'll talk about it again on Saturday, at pay time!"

He had an eye for everything, going round this and that, turning over the heaps of roof-tiles and of floor-tiles, testing the material, lifting his head to observe the work done, shading his eyes with his hand in the strong sun that was shining.

"Santo! Santo! Bring me the mule here—At least do so much for your brother!"

Agostino wanted to keep him to eat a mouthful, since it was almost mid-day, and a scorching sun, enough to make you ill crossing the open country at that hour.

"No, no, I must get to Camemi—it takes two hours—I've a lot more to do! If the sun is hot, all the better! I shall be dry by the time I get to Camemi —Get on, now, boys! Remember I'm always there on top of you, like the presence of God! You'll see me appear when you're least expecting me! I've worked at this job myself, and so I know if you've kept going or if you haven't—"

However, he was departing. Santo ran after him, stroking the neck of the mule, and holding him the stirrup. When at last he saw him mount without taking any notice, he stood in the middle of the road scratching his ear:

"Is that how you leave me?—without even asking me if I want anything?"

"Yes, yes, I know. You've played away the money you had on Monday. I know. I know!—here's the change. And amuse yourself at pitch-penny, since there's me when it comes to paying—the debtor of all the lot!"

Growling still, he went off at the ambling pace of his mule, under the burning sun; a sun which split the stones now, and made the stubble crackle as if it was catching fire. At the gully between the two mountains he seemed to enter into a furnace; and the village on top of the heights, hanging above the precipices, scattered between enormous rocks, mined with caverns which made it seem suspended in the air, blackish, rusted, appeared abandoned, without a shadow, with all the windows wide open in the heat, like so many black holes, the crosses of the church-towers trembling in the sun-dark air. The very mule panted, covered with sweat, climbing the steep road. A poor old man whom they met, laden with sheaves, done-for, began to murmur:

"Oh, where are you going, your honour, at this hour of the day! You've got so much money, yet you give your soul to the devil!"

He arrived at the village as it was striking mid-day, while everybody was scuffling indoors as if there was a thunder-storm. From the Rosary street came the canon-priest Lupi, heated, with his three-cornered hat on the back of his neck, breathing heavily:

"Ah, ah, Don Gesualdo!—you're going to eat a mouthful?—Not me, worse luck for me! I've not had a bite this day—I'm going to celebrate holy mass——mid-day mass!—One of Monsignore's caprices!"

"I came up to the village on purpose for you!—Gave myself all that trouble!—Hot, eh?—well, one can wipe one's sweat on one's handkerchief.—I'm afraid they'll play me some trick or other, about that contract for the village road, your reverence. You, your honour, you make yourself felt in the place—have you thought about it? I know I'm obliged to you as it is—"

"Why, what are you talking about?—Between ourselves; I'm seeing to it.—But that other affair now, what are we going to do about that?—have you thought about it? What answer do you give me?"

Don Gesualdo had brought his mule to a walking pace, keeping alongside the priest. He sat bent in the saddle, somewhat overcome by the great sun.

"What affair?" he answered. "I've got so many!
—Of what affair are you speaking, your honour?"

"Ah! Ah! that's how you feel about it,—is it?
Excuse me—excuse me, I'm sure—"

The canon-priest immediately changed the subject,
as if it was a matter of no importance to him either;
he talked about that other affair of the communal
lands, that they would have to come to a conclusion
with the Baroness Rubiera:"

"There's something else fresh. Lawyer Neri has
joined with Zacco. I'm afraid that—"

Don Gesualdo now dismounted from the mule,
anxious, drawing along with the reins the creature
behind him, as he paced slowly with the canon-priest,
all ears, his head bent and his chin in his hand.

"I'm afraid they'll win over the baroness!—I saw
the baron confabbing with that clown of a Don Ninì,—
last evening, behind the College. He pretended to
go into the pharmacy so that I shouldn't notice. You
follow?—a serious matter!—about five hundred acres
of land——"

Don Gesualdo got excited too; his eyes, already
kindled by the heat, shone in this conversation. He
was afraid of the intrigues of his adversaries, all big
guns who had a say in matters! The canon-priest on
the contrary was getting more and more chilly, knitting his brows unpleasantly, shrugging his shoulders,
staring straight at the other man from time to time,
and nodding his head up and down, as if to tell him
he was an ass.

"That's why I was speaking!—But you want to take
it like that!—Excuse me, excuse me, I'm sure!—I
wanted to get you the support of family relations
that count in this place—the first nobility. But

you make out as if you weren't concerned. All right, excuse me, I'm sure!—Also I've got to give Madame Sganci an answer, who's taken so much pains in the matter—Excuse me, it's just a mucked-up business——"

"Ah, you're talking about that affair of the marriage?"

This time the canon-priest pretended not to hear him.

"Ah, here's your brother-in-law! How do you do, farmer Fortunato?"

Burgio had a face as long as a fiddle, scowling, with all the sulks in the world in his fat-jowled visage.

"I saw you coming up, brother-in-law. I've been waiting for you there at the outlook place. Do you know the latest? Hardly fifteen pecks the beans came to. Not even pay expenses, as God's above!—I came especially to tell you——"

"Thank you very kindly! Thank you very much! Now what do you want of me? I told you, when you wanted to take that field!—only good for thorn-bushes!—Always must follow his own notions, and never right once, the blessed fellow!" replied Gesualdo angrily.

"Very well, you're right. I'll give up the field. I don't want it any more. What else have you got against me?"

"You don't want it?—Your lease lasts two years yet!—Who do you think is going to take it?—It isn't everybody that's such a looney!"

The canon-priest, seeing that this wasn't going to end, turned away:

"Good-day to you! Don Luca the sexton is waiting for me—he's fasting like me till this moment!"

And he took the steps up to the high part of the village.

Then Don Gesualdo, infuriated, began to speak his mind to his brother-in-law.

"And you came on purpose to tell me this nice piece of news?—while I was busy talking about my own affairs—just when I was at the very most important point? You've spoilt me a bit of business I was just settling!—The fine way you manage things!—Who do you think is going to take that field?"

Farmer Fortunato kept on saying behind his brother-in-law:

"If we look round—we shall find somebody to take it—The ground is already fallow and right for next year—it costs me the eyes out of my head—Your sister plays the devil in the house—she gives me no peace!—You know what a God's-curse she is, your sister!"

"It costs you, it costs you!—I know who it costs!" snarled Gesualdo, without turning round. "All these fine undertakings fall back on my shoulders."

Burgio took offence at these words:

"What do you mean? Explain yourself, brother-in-law!—I work on my own account, I do! I don't ride on anybody's shoulders."

"Yes, yes, all right; it's come to this now, that I must beg and pray of you, has it? As if I hadn't got the responsibility of your field—as if I wasn't the guarantee——"

So growling the pair of them they went to look for Pirtuso, who was at the Fosso, away towards San Giovanni. Master Lio was eating a few broad beans, with the door pushed to.

"Come in, come in, Don Gesualdo. How are you,

your honour! Anything I can do for you? Won't you come in?" Then as he heard of the field that Burgio wanted to ladle on to somebody else, he changed his jolly face to a gloomy one, scratching his head. "Eh! Eh! The field of Purgatory? It's a hard matter! Nobody wants it even for goat grazing."

Burgio worked himself up in its praise, good river-plain soil, deep soil, which had given nearly thirty pecks of beans this year only, fallow ready prepared for next year! His brother-in-law cut him short, like one who has many more irons in the fire, and no time to waste.

"In short, Master Lio, I want to get rid of it. Do the best you can—with prudence!"

"That's what I call talking," replied Pirtuso. "Your honour knows how to speak."—And now he winked with his sunken eye, a malicious little smile wandering through the wrinkles of his hairy, dirty chin.

On the sun-stricken street, deserted at that hour, a peasant stood waiting, with a handkerchief tied under his chin, his hands in his pockets, yellow and trembling with malaria. Obsequious, forcing a sad smile, making as if he wanted to get behind his cap which he held below the handkerchief:

"God keep you, your honour Don Gesualdo—I knew your mule. As I was looking for you, your honour! What shall we do about those two-or-three olive-trees at Giolio? I haven't got the money to have them gathered—You see what a state I'm in?—five months of ague, yes your honour, God preserve your honour! I'm nothing but skin and bone—no bread by day and no light by night—but we've got to bear it! But the expense of having the olives gathered, I can't

pay it—indeed I can't!—If you would, your honour—
do a work of charity, your honour——"

"Eh! Eh! Money is scarce for everybody, father.
Why have you put the cart before the horse?—When
you aren't able to—All of you alike! You'd take on
a whole estate if you were let do it. We'll see. I'm
not saying I won't. It depends on if we agree——"

And he let fall the smallest possible offer, continuing
on his way without turning round. The other kept
up for a time his lamentations, running behind, calling
God and the saints to witness, whimpering, swearing,
and finally accepting, consoling himself all at once,
changing his tone and his manner.

"Neighbour Lio, did you hear? A settled business!
A good stroke for Don Gesualdo—never mind!—but
it's settled! As for me, it's the same as if we'd been
to the lawyer!"—And he turned back, his hands in
his pockets.

"Listen here, Master Lio," said Gesualdo, drawing
Pirtuso aside. Burgio withdrew discreetly with the
mule, knowing that the soul of business is secrecy, while
his brother-in-law told the agent to buy beasts of burden for him, as many as were obtainable, at the current
price. Burgio only heard Master Lio replying with a
laugh that stretched his mouth to his ears:

"Ah! Ah!—you're a devil!—You must have had
a talk with the devil! You know what you must buy
and sell a week beforehand. All right, we're one about
it. I'll go back now. I've got those few beans waiting for me."

Burgio could hardly stand, he was so hungry, and
began to grumble when his brother-in-law wanted to
call at the post.—"Always mysteries—underhand
dodges!——"

Don Gesualdo returned full of content, reading a letter covered with scrawls and sealed with bread-crumb.

"You see the devil that whispers in my ear! Eh? He's given me good news, and I must go back to Master Lio."

"I know nothing. My father never taught me to do such things," replied Burgio grumbling. "I do as my father did before me. Won't you come and eat a bit of something at home—I can hardly stand, as true as I'm here."

"No, I can't; I haven't time. I've got to call at Camemi before I go to the Canziria. I've got twenty men there working at the road—the sheaves out in the threshing yard—I can't——"

And he went off in the great sun, drawing the weary mule behind him.

It was as if he would suffocate in that gully of Petraio. The naked rocks seemed red-hot. Not a scrap of shade, not a scrap of green, hill upon hill, piled on one another, bare, scorched, stony, scattered with rare, poor-looking olive-trees and dusty cactuses, the plain under Budarturo like a waste burnt by the sun, the mountains dim in the heat-darkened air, in the background. Some crows rose cawing from a piece of carrion that stank in the ditch, puffs of sirocco-wind burnt his face and stopped his breath; a maddening thirst, the sun beating on his head as if it were the hammering of his men working on the Camemi road. When he got there on the contrary he found them every one stretched out in the ditch-hollow, here and there, their faces covered with flies and their arms extended. Only one old man was breaking stones, sitting on the ground under a battered umbrella, his bare chest the colour of copper sprinkled with white hairs, his arms wasted, his shins white with dust, as was his face which looked like a mask, only the eyes burning in the midst of so much dustiness.

"Well done! Well done! I like that! Fortune comes while you sleep—I've come to bring it to you! And so the day goes by!—How many yards of road-bed to-day; let us see?—Nothing but three yards! —And that's why you have to be resting now? You must be tired, blood of Judas!—A fine look-out for me!—I ruin myself to keep you lot sleeping and rest-ing!—Body of—! Blood of——!"

Seeing him with that inflamed, burnt face, white with dust only in the eye-sockets and on the hairs; his eyes like those of the fever-stricken, and his lips thin and pale; no one dared answer. The hammering started again in the wide silent valley-space, in the dust which rose upon the bronzed flesh of the men, and on the fluttering rags, together with a dry gasp-ing that accompanied every stroke. The crows passed again cawing in the implacable heavens. And the old man lifted his dusty face to look at them, with his in-flamed eyes, as if he knew what they wanted and was expecting them.

So that when at last Gesualdo arrived at Can-ziria, it was about two hours after dark. The great door in the wall that surrounded the farm-place was open. Diodata was waiting, nodding on the door-step. Farmer Carmine, the keeper of the estate, was stretched out on the threshing floor, with his gun be-tween his legs; Brasi Camauro and Nanni l'Orbo were gone off somewhere or other, like dogs do at night when they scent a bitch in the neighbourhood; and the farm-dogs alone welcomed the master, barking round the establishment.

"Ehee?—nobody there?—Things without a soul to look after them, if I'm not here!"

Diodata, wakened unawares, went feeling for a light, still stupid with sleep. Uncle Carmine, rubbing his eyes, his mouth contracted with yawns, was making excuses.

"Ah!—God be praised! You sleeping away in one corner, Diodata in another, in the dark.—What were you doing in the dark?—expecting somebody?—Brasi Camauro or Nanni l'Orbo?——"

The girl took the onslaught with drooping head, quickly lighting the fire, while her master continued to hold forth, outside there in the dark, as he examined the oxen tied to the poles inside the yard. The keeper went behind him silent and soft-foot, to reply on occasion:

"Yessir, Redroan is a bit better; I gave him dog's-grass to clear his blood. Now Whitey is bothering me—We s'll have to change the pasturage—all the cattle. The evil eye, yessir! I say that somebody has been here who has the evil eye!—I've even sowed Saint John's seed in the pasture—The sheep are all right, thank God—and the harvest also. Nanni l'Orbo?—Gone down to Passanitello, hanging round the skirts of that witch. One day or another he'll come home with his legs broken, as true as God's above!—and Brasi Camauro as well, for the sake of a handful of nothing——"

Diodata called from the door that it was ready.

"If there's nothing else you want me to do, your honour, I'll go and lay me down a minute——"

By God's grace at last, after a fast of twenty-four hours, Don Gesualdo could come to table, and sit facing the door, with his shirt-sleeves rolled back above the elbow, his feet eased in a pair of old slippers that were a blessing in themselves. The girl had prepared him a pottage of fresh broad-beans with an onion in, four new-laid eggs, and two tomatoes which she had gone and plucked behind the house, feeling for them in the dark. The eggs frizzled in the earthenware casserole, the full flask of wine was in front of him; through the open door came a fresh little wind that was a pleasure to feel, bringing the sound of the trilling of the cicalas and the scent of the sheaves on the yard floor:—his own harvest there under his eyes, his mule feeding greedily at the barley rick, poor beast—a sheaf at every tug! Down the slope beyond, from time to time, was heard the tinkling of the sheep-bells in the enclosure; and then the oxen lying about the yard, tied to the mangers full of hay, lifted their heavy heads, breathing heavily, and you saw a glinting of their sleepy eyes, like a train of fireflies passing.

Putting down the flask Gesualdo gave a heavy sigh, and leaned his elbows on the table.

"You're not eating?—what's amiss wi' thee?"

Diodata was quiet in a corner, seated on a little barrel, and at these words there came into her eyes the smile of a caressed dog.

"Aren't you hungry? Eat something, eat——"

She put the dish on her knees, and crossed herself before beginning, then said:

"God be with your honour!"

She ate slowly and quietly, bending over her dish and drooping her head. She had a mass of soft fine hair, in spite of the frosts and the cutting wind of the mountains; rich people's hair, and chestnut-brown eyes, like her hair, timid and sweet; caressing, beautiful eyes of a patient dog, that forced you to like her, just as all her pleading face did. A face over which had passed toil and hunger, blows, and brutal caresses; wearing it, furrowing it, consuming it; leaving upon it the parchedness of the dog-days, the precocious wrinkles of the days without bread, the livid look of weary nights—only the eyes still young, with livid rings round them. Seated crouched like that, she looked just a young girl, her bosom thin and agile, the nape of her neck showing the white skin where the sun had not burnt it. Her hands, thin and blackened, were small; poor hands for her hard tasks.

"Eat it up, then, eat it up. I'm sure thou'rt tired."

She smiled, so content, without lifting her eyes. Her master also handed her the wine-flask.

"Here you are, drink, don't be backward——!"

Diodata, still a little hesitating, wiped her mouth on the back of her hand, and drank out of the flask, throwing back her head. The wine, warm and generous, could be seen going down her amber-coloured throat almost at every swallow; her bosom still young and firm seemed to swell. Then her master began to laugh.

"Bravo, bravo! You know how to play the trumpet, right enough!"

She also smiled, wiping her mouth again with the back of her hand, blushing deeply.

"Best of health to your honour!"

He went out to take the air. He sat down on one of the sheaves near the door, his back against the wall, his hands hanging between his knees. The moon must have been already high, behind the mountain towards Francoforte. All the plain of Passanitello, at the mouth of the valley, was lit up with a gleam like dawn. Little by little, with the spreading of that gleam, even in the river-hollow the sheaves began to show, gathered into heaps like so many stones in rows. Other dark objects moved across the slope, and as the wind travelled there came the heavy, distant sound of the cattle-bells, as the beasts went down slowly, easily towards the torrent. From time to time however came a puff of fresher wind from the west, and all down the valley was heard the rustling of still-standing crops. In the yard the high rick, still dark, seemed crowned with silver, and in the shadow you could distinguish dimly other sheaves in heaps; other cattle were chewing the cud; another long stripe of silver came upon the roof-ridge of the store barn, which loomed immense in the dark.

"Eh? Diodata? Are you asleep, you doze-owl?"

"No your honour, no!"

She appeared all dishevelled, forcing open her sleepy eyes. She began to sweep in front of the door with her hands, throwing aside the litter, going on all fours, rubbing her eyes from time to time not to let herself be overcome by sleep, her chin lax, her legs listless.

"You were asleep!—I told thee thou wert asleep!"

And he fetched her a slap on the head by way of caress. For his part he wasn't sleepy. He felt his heart expand. Pleasant memories came back to him. He had carried stones, before he built that store-barn! And he'd gone days without bread, before owning all these worldly possessions.—A boy—he seemed to go back again to the time when he carried lime from his father's kiln, at Donferante! How many times had he travelled the Licodia road, behind the donkeys that fell down on the way and died sometimes under their load! How he had cried, and called on saints and christians for help! Then Master Nunzio played

the deprofundis on his back, with the rope of the
very donkey.—He was ten or twelve groats out of
pocket for every ass that went and died, poor man!—
Burdened with a family! Santo who made him gnaw
himself for rage even then; Speranza who began to
want a husband; his mother with fever thirteen months
in the year!—More thrashings than bread!—Then
when Mascalise, his uncle, took him with him as a
labourer, to seek for fortune—His father was against
it, for he'd got his own pride even he, always been
his own master, at the kiln, and it simply made him
smart to see his own flesh and blood working at somebody else's bidding.—It took him seven years to forgive him, and that was only when Gesualdo was able
to make his first contract on his own account—
for the olive-mill of Molinazzo. About two
hundred loads of lime that went from the kiln at
Master Nunzio's own price—and Speranza's dowry
as well, because the girl couldn't stop at home any
longer—And the disputes when he began to speculate
in agriculture!—Master Nunzio wouldn't have anything to do with it.—He said it wasn't the trade he
was born to—"Stick to what you can do—"—But then,
when his son took him to see the land he had bought,
at this very place, Canziria, he was never tired of
measuring it up and down, poor old man, with long
strides, as if he had the surveyor's rods in his legs.—
And he began to give orders "—you must do this and
you must do that—" to show his authority and not
confess that his son might have a sharper head than
his own.—The mother didn't live to see it, poor thing.
She died telling them all to be good to Santo, who
had always been the favourite, and Speranza burdened
with a family as she herself had been—a baby every

year—All on Gesualdo's shoulders, since he earned
for the lot. He had earned some money, my word!
He had got property! He had gone through hard
days and sleepless nights! For twenty years he had
never once gone to bed without looking at the sky to
see what the weather would be.—How many prayers,
and of the sort that must reach to heaven, for rain
and for fine weather!—How many irons in the fire!
how many thoughts, how many anxieties, how much
weariness! The working of the land, the disposing
of the produce, the risk of the land taken on lease,
the speculations of his brother-in-law Burgio who never
made a success of anything and left all the damage
in Gesualdo's hands!—Master Nunzio who insisted
on risking his son's money in contracts of his own
undertaking, to show he was master in his own house!
—Always on the go, always striving, always on his
feet, here and there, in sun and wind and rain, his
head heavy with thoughts, his heart big with anxiety,
his bones broken with weariness; snatching a couple of
hours of sleep when he could get it, and where he could
get it, in a corner of the stable, behind a hedge, in
the yard, with stones under his back; eating a piece
of hard black bread when he could catch it, on the
mule's pack-saddle, in the shadow of an olive-tree, on
the side of a ditch, in the malarial places amid a swarm
of mosquitoes.—No holidays, no Sundays, never a
merry laugh, everybody wanting something from him,
his time, his work, or his money; never an hour like
those of his brother Santo, regaling himself in full
swing in the tavern!—at home always the surly face
of Speranza, or the complaints of his brother-in-law,
or the howling of the children!—the quarrels between
the lot of them, when affairs did not go well.—Forced

to protect his own property against them all, to look after his own interests.—In the village not one who wasn't his enemy, or his dangerous and feared ally.— Always having to hide the fever of money-making, or the blow of a piece of bad news, or the rush of satisfaction in success; always to have his face shut, his eye vigilant, his mouth serious! The everyday cunning, the twists and turns even to say "how do you do!"; the uneasy hand-shakes, with the ear alert; the fight with false smiles, or with faces red with rage, spitting slaver and threats—the nights always worried, the morrow always heavy with hope or with fear——

"You've had to work as well, among your master's things. You've got a broad back too, haven't you! —poor Diodata!"

She, seeing he was speaking to her again, came to him quite pleased, nestling at his feet, on a stone, her face white with the moon, her chin on her knees, crouching over her elbows. Then passed the tinkling of cattle bells, the slow, heavy trampling of the beasts across the expanse, as they went down to the stream, the voices of the herdsmen driving them, voices which carried a long way in the sonorous air. The moon, coming down now even into the yard, printed black shadows in a cold dawn-light; showing the wandering shadow of the watch-dogs, who had smelt the cattle; the inert mass of the farm-keeper, stretched out on his face.

"Nanni l'Orbo, eh?—or Brasi Camauro? Which of the two of them is your boy?" resumed Don Gesualdo, who was in a joking vein.

Diodata smiled: "No your honour!—nobody!"

But her master took pleasure in teasing her:

"Yes, yes!—One or the other—or both of them

at once! I shall find out. I shall catch you in the valley with them, one of these times!"

She smiled always in the same way, with that sweet, content smile, at the jests of her master, which seemed to light up her face, refined now in the soft glow; her eyes like two stars; her beautiful hair slipped down on her neck; her mouth somewhat large and swollen, but young and fresh.

Her master continued to look at her thus for a moment, smiling to himself, and he gave her another affectionate slap.

"This is no goods for that rascal of a Brasi Camauro, neither for Nanni l'Orbo! no!"

"Oh Jesu-maria!"—she exclaimed, crossing herself.

"I know, I know. I only say it to tease thee, silly!"

He was silent for a while, then he added:

"Thou'rt a good lass!—good and true! and careful with thy master's things thou'st always been."

"My master has given me bread," she replied simply. "I should be a bad one if——"

"I know! I know!—poor lass!—that's why I'm fond of thee!"

Little by little, seated in the coolness, after supper, in the beautiful moonlight, he let himself drift into tender memories.

"Poor Diodata—Thou'st had a hard time as well!—We've seen some bad days!—Always on the look-out, like thy master!—Always with thy hands full—doing something! Always keeping an eye on my things! Faithful as a dog!—It's taken something, I tell thee, to get this property together——"

He was silent for a moment, softened. Then, after a bit, he began again, changing his tone:

"Do you know? They want me to take a wife."

The girl did not answer; he, not heeding, continued:

"To have someone behind me. Make a connection with the big-wigs of the place. Without them you can do nothing! They want to make me one of the family—so that I shall have the family support, do you see?—So as not to have everybody against me, in time of need—Eh? what do you think?"

She was still silent for a moment, her face in her hands. Then she replied in a tone of voice that turned even his blood:

"Your honour is the master——"

"I know it, I know it—I'm only talking now for the sake of talking—because thou'rt fond of me. I'm not thinking of it yet awhile. But one day or the other I shall have to give in, I suppose—Who have I worked and starved for, then?—I've got no children——"

Then he saw her face, bent down to earth, very white and wet with tears.

"What art crying for, silly?"

"Nothing, your honour!—So!—Don't take any notice."

"What had ta got in thy head, tell me."

"Nothing, nothing, Don Gesualdo."

"Saints and blessings! Saints and blessings!" he began to shout, fuming round the yard. The farm-keeper lifted his sleepy head at the noise, and asked:

"What's amiss?—Has the mule got loose?—Shall I get up?"

"No, no, go to sleep, Uncle Carmine."

Diodata went after him inch by inch, with her voice humble and submissive:

"Why are you in a rage, your honour?—What have I said?"

"I'm in a rage with my fate!—Nothing but miseries

and trials everywhere—wherever I go! Even you, now!—with your snivelling! Fool! Do you think I'd ever leave you on the street—without help?"

"No your honour.—It wasn't for myself—I was thinking of those poor innocents——"

"This now!—What's it to do with you? That's how the world is!—Besides there's the parish to look after them. The parish can keep them at its own expense—with everybody's money! I pay as well! I know every time I go to the rate-collector's."

He scratched his head a moment, then resumed:

"Hark ye, everybody comes into this world with his own star. You, for example, have you had any father or mother to help you? You came into the world by yourself, as God sends the grass and the plants which nobody has sown. You've come into the world as your name says—Diodata—God-given! Which means from nobody!—And yet maybe you're the daughter of a baron, and your brothers now are eating fowl and pigeons! The Lord is for everybody! You've found food to eat like everybody else!—And all my property?—did my parents give it to me, maybe? Didn't I make myself what I am, by myself? Everybody has his own destiny!—I've got my own share, thank God, and my brother has got nothing——"

So he went on grumbling, up and down the yard, back and forth before the door. Then seeing that the maiden was still crying, very softly so as not to annoy him, he came back and sat down beside her again, kind once more.

"What dost want?—A man can't always do what he likes. I'm no longer free—as I was when I was a poor devil with nothing. Now I've so much property

to leave behind—I can't go and pick up my heirs in
the street—or in the foundlings' homes. It comes to
this, that the children I shall have when I'm married,
if God helps me, will be born under a lucky star!——"

"Your honour is the master."

He thought about it a bit, because that talk had
stung him worse than a wasp, and he repeated again:

"Look at you—you've never had father nor mother.
And yet what do you lack, eh?"

"Nothing, thanks to God."

"There's the Lord for everybody. I shan't leave
you on the street, I tell you!—My conscience won't
let me. I shall find you a husband."

"Oh—as for me, Don Gesualdo!"

"Yes, yes, you'll have to be married! You're young,
you can't stop as you are—I shan't leave you without
support. I shall find you a decent young fellow, a
respectable man. Nanni l'Orbo now! I'll give you a
dowry——"

"The Lord reward you——"

"I'm a christian! I'm an honest man!—And you
deserve it. Where would you end, else?—I'll think of
everything, I will. I've got so many thoughts in my
head!—this among others! You know I like you. I'll
find you a husband right away. You are young—a
pretty lass—Yes, yes, pretty you are!—let me speak,
I know! And a gentle nature, too!—blood of a
baron, for sure."

Now he took another tone with her, with a sly laugh
and his hands tingling. He pressed her chin with two
fingers, lifting by force her face that she would keep
drooped to hide her tears.

"Anyhow it's nothing but words in the wind as yet.—
I care for thee as I care for nobody else—there

then!—That's what we'll think of now, silly!—silly that thou art!"

As he saw that she kept on crying, obstinately, he burst out swearing again, like an enraged calf.

"Saints and blessings! A cursed lot!—Always miseries and snivellings!——"

V

Masi, the lad, came to wake Don Gesualdo before dawn, with a voice that froze the blood in your veins.

"Get up, your honour; there's the workman from Fiumegrande come to speak to you at once!"

"From Fiumegrande?—at this hour?"

Mastro-don Gesualdo went feeling for his clothes, in the dark, still almost asleep, with his head all in a muddle. Suddenly he shouted:

"The bridge!—Something must have gone wrong!"

Downstairs in the stable he found the workman seated on the bench, sopping wet, trying to dry his few rags at a straw fire. The moment he saw the master he began to whimper afresh:

"The bridge!—Master Nunzio, your father, said it was time to take down the timber work!—Nardo is lost under it."

There was a turmoil in all the house. Speranza, the sister, rushing downstairs while her husband was pulling on his trousers; Santo, still half drunk, falling down the ladder-way from the trap-door, howling as if he was being murdered. The workman began again to every new arrival:

"The bridge!—The timber-work!—Master Nunzio says it was the bad weather."

Don Gesualdo strode up and down the stable, pale, without saving a word, without taking notice of anybody, waiting for them to saddle him the mule which, also frightened, was kicking, and Masi in the con-

fusion couldn't get the pack-saddle on him. At a certain point he struck his fists on his face, the eyes almost
starting out of his head.

"When? Holy God!—Have you never finished,
plague on you!"

"It's your own fault! I told you! They aren't
jobs for us to take on," yelled his sister in her night-
dress, her hair all on end, an absolute fury. Master
Fortunato, calmer, agreed with his wife, nodding his
head in silence, seated on a bench, like a mill-crank.

"You don't say anything! You sit there like a
looney!"

Now Speranza inveighed against her husband.

"When it's a question of helping you, who are his
brother-in-law right enough!—and saddled with a
swarm of children!—then the difficulties crop up!—
no money!—all the money lost in that accursed
bridge!"

At first Gesualdo turned on her like a viper, foam
at his mouth. Then he swallowed his bile, and began
to hum a tune as he fastened the mule's head-harness;
a cheerfulness which devoured his own liver. He
crossed himself, put his foot on the stirrup; then once
mounted, so that his head almost touched the roof,
he spat out his say before going:

"Yes, you're right! Your husband has done some
beautiful business for me! The seed that we threw
away at Donninga!—The vineyard that he planted for
me where even stuff for goats won't grow!—A smart
chap your husband!—When it comes to, I pay for
your speculations out of my pocket! But I'm sick of it,
see, sick of bearing the burden! When the donkey's
tired he lays him down in the middle of the road and
he goes no further———"

And he spurred the mule, that was still restive; his sister yelling after him, from the stable doorway, as long as the mule's shoes were heard upon the cobble-stones of the little street, in the dark. The workman set off running behind, out of breath, limping; but his master, whose head was going like a mill, did not heed him. Only when they had come to the Carmine fields he turned his head hearing the noise of foot-steps in the mud, and made him get up behind. The boy, his voice broken by the trotting of the mule, re-peated continually the same thing:

"Master Nunzio said it was time to take down the timber-work. It had stopped raining since mid-day— No, your honour, said Master Nardo: let us leave it till to-morrow—Then Master Nunzio said: You talk like that to handle another day's pay—But I was cook-ing the soup for the men then—From the mountain came the shout: The flood! Christians! And while Nardo was just untying the last rope——"

Gesualdo, his face to the wind, whipped by the squall, spurred the mule all the time with his heel, with-out opening his mouth.

"Eh?—What did you say, Don Gesualdo? You didn't answer?"

"Doesn't your tongue ever drop out?" replied the master finally.

It began to dawn before they got to the Torretta. A peasant whom they met driving forward his mule, getting the downpour through his calico jacket, his kerchief tied round his head and his hands in his pockets, wanted to say something; he made a sign towards down there, towards the river, while the wind carried off his voice. Further on a little old woman huddled under a carob-tree began to shout:

"You can't pass, no!—The river!—Look out!——"

In the distance, in the mist of river and rain, you could dimly make out an enormous pile of ruin, like a hill fallen into the river, and on the pillar which still remained standing, lost in the fume of the low sky, something black which moved, arms making signals from the distance. The river, all around the pieces of débris, overflowed in large muddy pools. Further down, men in a row, up to their knees in water, bent forward all together and pulled, with an *Oooh!* which sounded like a lament.

"No! No!" yelled the brick-layers, holding back Don Gesualdo by the arm. "Do you want to drown yourself, your honour?"

He did not reply, up to the knees in mud, going up and down the water-corroded bank, his hair flying in the wind. From the top of the pillar Master Nunzio shouted something at him; shouts which the squall tore away from his mouth and ripped to pieces in the distance.

"What are you doing up there now?—Crying for the dead?—Drop it, leave it alone!" replied Don Gesualdo from the bank. But the noise of the water devoured even his furious words. The old man up there in the mist always made signs of No! pig-headed. Other folk from the far shore, under big, oiled umbrellas, called without making themselves heard, pointing to where the men were hauling, salvaging beams of wood. According to the wind, however, came voices from above, from whence the current flowed, voices that seemed to fall from the sky, desperate cries, and the sounding of a raucous horn.

Gesualdo, bent under the downpour, floundering on the bank, helped to salvage the timbers of the bridge-scaffolding which the furious current was churning and smashing.

"Here!—Holy God!—can't you see it's taking those there?"

Then he staggered and all but went under into the spumy swirl which rushed round him.

"What the devil! Do you want to make an end of yourself?" yelled the foreman, seizing him by the collar. "You nearly dragged me to perdition as well."

He, pale as death, his eyes starting out of his head, his hair on end, almost foaming at the mouth, replied:

"Let me sink then! It's no matter to you!—You talk like that because you haven't got your own blood squandered in that water!—Let me die!"

Master Nunzio, seeing him raving in that fashion, his own son, wanted to throw himself headlong down right into the flood.

"Not to hear him any more!—Now he'll tell me it's all my fault!—You'll see!—I'm not free to lift a finger in my own house!—I'm master to be made game of— So it's better to end it straight off!"—And he kept trying the water with his foot!

"Hark here!" interrupted his son in a dull voice. "Leave me alone, you! I've let you do as you liked. You wanted to take on the contract for the bridge— so as not to stand idle. See how it's turned out!—And we've got to start all over again, if we're not going to lose the deposit money.—You could have stopped at home in ease and quiet. What was amiss with that? Then leave me alone. Anyhow you haven't lost anything——"

"Ah, I haven't lost anything!—I knew well enough you'd throw that up at me—at your father!—I don't count for anything, I don't!—I made you what you

are!—As if I wasn't the head of the house!—as if I
didn't know my own business!———"

"Ah—your business?—what have you got the lime-
kiln for?—and even that I've had to buy back for
you twice! You think yourself an engineer!—This is
the sort of thing that you know how to do!"

Master Nunzio looked at his son infuriated, gesticulating, moving his lips without being able to utter
a word, glaring round again to look for the best place
to go and drown himself, and at last he complained:

"What do you want to keep me back for then?—
Why don't you let me throw myself in the river?
—why don't you?"

Gesualdo began to tear his hair, to bite his arms, to
spit into the sky. Then he planted himself desperately
in front of the old man, shaking his clasped hands in
his face:

"For the love of God!—by the soul of my mother!
—with this half a brick that's fallen on my neck—
don't you know I'm in no mood for fooling now!"

The foreman interfered to calm him.

"Well, what's done is done. You won't alter
anything with talk. Better come and dry yourselves, both of you, for you're going to catch your
death into the bargain, soaked as you are."

They had lighted a big fire of canes and broken
wood, in the barn. Pieces of beams on which were
still stuck the pictures of the saints who should protect
the bridge, bless its soul! Master Nunzio, who was
even losing his religion in that misfortune, spat on
them once or twice, his face dark. Everybody was
weeping and wiping their eyes with the smoke, while
they were drying their wet clothes. In a corner under
the broken, tiled roof lay Nardo, the workman

who had broken his leg, sweating and writhing. He wanted also to put a good word in, between the rage of father and son.

"I've got the worse of it," he lamented. "Now I shall be a cripple and not able to earn my bread."

One of his companions, seeing he couldn't move, heaped him a bit of straw under his head. Master Nunzio, in the doorway, his fists raised to heaven, vented fire and flame.

"Judas Iscariot! Blessed devil! It needed this blow from God, at this point, that it did!——"

Everybody said what he had to say. Neighbours, come to see, travellers who wanted to cross the river and were waiting, under cover, with their back to the fire.

"Well done you! You've managed rarely! All that money gone! And parish money!—Now who knows how long we shall have to wait before we see another bridge—What was it made of, do you reckon, cheese?"

"What, this lot now!—You come at the right moment!—Do you want me to bring down God and the saints from above?" bawled Master Nunzio.

Gesualdo did not say a word, his face the colour of earth, seated on a stone with his hands hanging between his thighs. And then he turned on the lad:

"Look at that swine! Left the mule standing out there for me, in this weather! Miserable brat! Enemy of your own master!"

"Don't take it too hard, your honour!" whimpered Nardo from his corner. "So long as you're alive and well, the rest is nothing."

Gesualdo looked at him furiously.

"He speaks well, he does—who's got nothing to lose!"

"No, no, your honour!—Don't talk like that, God will punish you!"

Master Nunzio, leaning against the door-post, had been chewing his own thoughts between his toothless gums for some time. At last he spat it out, turning unexpectedly on his son:

"And do you know what I've got to tell you? That I don't want anything more to do with this miserable bridge!—Let us rather make a mill out of the material we manage to rescue. Something really safe——"

"Now another one!" Gesualdo sprang up. "Are you really out of your mind? And the deposit-money? Are we to lose that as well? If I left things to you!—When I started building mills, I had to hear that it was ruin. Now that you've made up your mind they're all right, don't want to do anything else—as if all the village had nothing to do but grind their bones night and day, and mine to start with!—holy God above!"

The quarrel started afresh. Master Nunzio squealing and lamenting that he wasn't respected.

"You see I'm nothing but a puppet?—a clown!—the head of the house—my sirs?—What do you think!——"

Gesualdo, to make an end of it, jumped on his mule again, green with bile, and went off while the water tumbled down from heaven as the Lord sent it, his head between his shoulders, wet to the bone, his heart inside him blacker than the dark sky before his eyes; the village also grey and wretched in the rain, up there on the top of the hill, the ringing of mid-day coming in waves, carried by the wind, and losing itself in the distance.

Those who met him, knowing of the misfortune, drew aside and forgot to greet him. He looked askance, crookedly, and muttered to himself from time to time:

"I'm not down yet! My name's Mastro-don Gesualdo!—As long as I can stand I know how to help myself!"

Only one poor devil who was going the same way offered to take him under his umbrella. He replied:

"It needs something else besides an umbrella, my dear chap. Don't you worry, I'm not afraid of water and hail, I'm not."

It was past mid-day when he got to the village. The canon-priest Lupi had just lain down, at that very minute, after dinner.

"I'm coming, I'm coming, Don Gesualdo!" he shouted from the window, hearing somebody call him.

One of the villagers passing just then on his own business, seeing him so wet, streaming water like an umbrella, said:

"Eh, Don Gesualdo?—what a misfortune!"

He, as hard as a stone, with a bitter smile on his flexible pale lips, replied:

"Eh, things will happen. If you go out in the rain you'll get wet, and if you travel on horseback you'll have a fall. But since nobody's met their death, everything can be mended."

The majority gave him a wide berth, only turning round inquisitively when they had got by. At last the canon-priest appeared in his little porch, buttoning his cassock.

"Eh? Eh? Don Gesualdo!—There you are!— there you are!"

Don Gesualdo had made his face as cheerful as he

could, considering the malignant fever he had in his belly.

"Yessir, here I am!" he replied with a smile that he tried to spread over all his dark face. "Here I am, at your disposal. Yours to command. However, tell the truth, you talk with the devil, don't you?"

The canon-priest pretended not to understand.

"Why?—About the bridge? No, on my faith! I'm sorry enough!"

"No, no—I'm not talking about the bridge! But let us go up, your honour. We can't say what we've got to say here in the street."

The bed was still unmade in the canon-priest's room; all round the walls a fair number of little cages where the canon-priest, a great hunter with the fowling net, kept his little decoy birds; an enormous black crucifix facing the door, and underneath it the box of the confraternity, like a coffin, in which were the securities of money lent on loan; images of saints here and there, stuck on the wall with holy wafers, dirtied by the birds; and a smell enough to kill you, what with all those creatures.

Don Gesualdo began at once to give vent to all his troubles; his father who insisted on going his own way to show he was still head of the house, after having dissipated the patrimony—He'd had to buy him back the lime-kilns twice! And yet he kept on making these messes! And if he himself said one word, when he was forced to open his veins and bleed more blood to pay again, then his father screamed that no respect was paid him. His sister and her husband fleecing him on the other side. A fool, that brother-in-law Burgio!—a fool, and presumptuous! And who paid every time?—he, Gesualdo!—His brother Santo eating and drinking at his expense and doing nothing from morning till night:

"And with my money, you understand, your honour?—with my blood! I don't know what it costs me. When I left my father with his lime-kiln in ruin, so that he didn't know even how to feed the four pack-donkeys, and I went with nothing but my shirt on my back—and a pair of breeches that didn't hold together enough for decency's sake—without shoes on my feet, yessir, the first trowel I needed for starting as a brick-layer, my uncle Mascalise had to lend it to me—And my father carrying on because I left the trade I was brought up to—And then, when I took the first piece of work on contract—he shouted that it was the down-fall of everything! I have had some courage, Canon! And I know what it costs me! All the fruits of my own sweat, is everything I've got!—And when I see them chucking it away for me, one this way and the other that!—why, your honour, what do you think?— blood rebels against it!—I've kept silent till now to have a bit of peace in the family—to eat a mouthful of bread in holy quiet, when I come home tired. But now I've done. Even a donkey when he's done up lies down in the middle of the road and won't go any further. You don't know what a trial my sister Speranza is!— I want to have done with her! Everybody for his own home. Aren't I right, Canon?"

The canon-priest, however, was attending to his decoy-birds.

"If you don't listen to what I say, your honour, it's no use my talking."

"Yes, yes, I'm listening. What the deuce!—it doesn't take a Saint Augustine to know what you mean!—The upshot of it all is that you want to save the deposit-money, isn't that it?—to have some help from the commune?"

"Yessir—the deposit-money——"

Then Gesualdo fixed his penetrating grey eyes on him, and continued:

"There's something else as well. I told you I wanted to have a house of my own—a home for myself—if I can find a wife to suit me. But if you're not listening to what I say, your honour, then it's no good. Or if you pretend you don't understand. You remember?—that talk we had on the evening of the festival of the Patron Saint?—But you make a face as if you didn't understand why I've come here to you —when I said to you the very first thing—I said to you: 'Here I am—at your disposal'——"

"Ah! Ah!" replied the canon-priest, lifting his head like an ass that jerks the halter. Then he left off the careful dusting of his three-cornered hat, and fixed on the other his eyes of a man who isn't going to be put in a sack.

"Listen, Don Gesualdo—this is not the way to come and talk to me now, in this fashion! It means that you don't know your friends from your enemies, dear Lord! I'm glad you've made up your mind that the advice I gave you then was pure gold! A pearl of a maiden, used to every privation, whom you'll have altogether at your bidding, and of a first-class family into the bargain!—who'll connect you in relationship with all the big guns in the place!—You see now what a help it would be to you? You would have on your side the sworn councillors and all the lot. And for that other business of the communal lands as well, if you want to come in along with us——"

"Yessir—" replied Gesualdo vaguely. "One might do a lot of things.—We could talk about it——"

"We've got to speak plainly, my friend. Do you take me for a child? One hand washes the other. Serve me, as I serve thee, says the Holy Ghost, indeed. You, dear Don Gesualdo, have the fault of thinking that everybody else is a bigger simpleton than you are. First you pretend you don't grasp, you're deaf in that ear, and then, in case of need, when the house comes down on top of you, you run to me with a face like that——"

"It'll be the heat—it'll be all these birds—" stammered the other, a little bit out of countenance. "I'd like to see you in my shoes, Canon!" he exclaimed at length.

"In your shoes?—certainly—I put myself in them! I want to make you see and make up your mind whether I'm on your side or not! Here I am with you. Let us think of this affair of the bridge first—to save the deposit-money—with a subsidy from the commune. We'll go at this minute to the Captain—and to the Sworn Councillors who won't be against you. Pity Baron Zacco already suspects that affair of the communal lands!—Let me think——"

While he finished tying his mantle round his neck he continued collecting his ideas, frowning, looking here and there on the ground.

"That's it! I'll go first to Madam Sganci!—no! no! I'll say nothing to her as yet! just a vague hint—to put her on the track. Enough for me that Donna Marianna writes two lines to the Captain. As for Baroness Rubiera, I can sleep between two pillows—I promise me she's as good as if she was your own self.—But let us be sure of what we're doing, see!——"

And the canon-priest widened his eyes. Don Gesualdo stretching his hand towards the crucifix.

"No, I mean for the other affair, the communal lands. I don't want us to play at empty-the-barrel between ourselves, dear Don Gesualdo."

The latter wanted to stretch out his hand again, but the canon-priest had already slipped through the door.

"You wait for me downstairs, at the street door. One moment, I'll be back at once."

He returned, rubbing his hands:

"I told you. Donna Marianna simply can't contain herself, because of that niece of hers. You'll make a famous job of it."

They were hardly out of the house when they ran into laywer Neri, who was going to open his office. He made a face of condolence for Don Gesualdo.

"A nasty business, what?—I'm sorry." But one could see that underneath he was exulting.

The canon-priest, to stop him, made reply:

"No great matter. The devil's not so black as he's painted. We shall make it right.—We've already saved the materials——"

Afterwards, when they had gone on, the lawyer, with the key in the key-hole, looked back still laughing, and the canon-priest whispered in Mastro-don Gesualdo's ear:

"You don't know the face you make, my dear fellow."

"I?"

"Yes. You're not aware of it, but it's there! If you make a face like that everybody will put their feet on you and walk over you!—You don't go to ask a

favour with a face like that—Wait for me here; I'll
go up for a moment to Cavaliere Peperito. He's a
fool; but they've made him a councillor."

The canon-priest had hardly gone up the broken
staircase with the plaster falling, than the cavaliere
arrived from his vegetable plot, mounted on an emaciated ass, with a saddlebag full of beans behind. Don
Gesualdo, to make a good impression, helped him to
unload the beans, and to tie the ass to the manger, be-
neath the curve of the stairway; but the cavaliere
seemed rather annoyed at being caught in that pickle,
all muddy, in his torn country clothes.

"We shan't do anything there," said the canon-
priest returning after a little while. "He's a fool!
He fancies himself a real cavalier—He must have
something against you. We'll have to find Ciolla?—
Hallo?—Ciolla? I'm asking you, Ciolla! Do you
know if Don Filippo is at home? Have you seen him
go out?"

Ciolla winked with his one eye, twisting his paralysed mouth again.

"No. Canali is still there, at Bomma's, waiting to
go with him to his sister-in-law's, the wax-chandler's,
you know. It's their after-dinner walk—to amuse
themselves with her behind the goods-shelves. What's
the news, Don Gesualdo? Are you going to bless the
bridge, along with the canon-priest?"

Don Gesualdo turned on him now, taking the stuffing out of him, to some tune.

"You'd got that bridge on your chest, had you?—
As if _you'd_ had to spend out of _your_ pocket!——"

The canon-priest drew him away by the arm:

"Come on, come on! Do you think you can stop
every idle rascal's mouth?"

Going up the street where the Margarones lived they met the Marchese Limòli, who was taking his usual afternoon walk from the Rosary to Santa Maria di Gesù, alone as ever, with his red umbrella under his arm. He took off his hat ceremoniously, and the canon-priest, just as he was returning the salute, had an inspiration:

"Wait, wait a moment!"

A little later he came back to Don Gesualdo with quite another face:

"A great fellow that marchese! Poor as Job, but he's one that's got a voice in the Chapter. They stick to one another, the whole bunch!—a good word, on occasion!—among themselves they can't say no to one another. They'd let him die of hunger, but they couldn't deny him a favour."

Don Filippo was still at home, busy ruling lines on a sheet of paper for Nicolino's A. B. C.:

"What good wind blows you in?——"

Then seeing Don Gesualdo enter behind the canon-priest, he dropped his spectacles on to his nose again.

"I'm so busy!—Ah, yes!—the deposit-money?—You want the commune to help you to get it back? You want some assistance to help you start the work again? —We'll see—we'll consider it—You've made a mess of this blessed bridge the first time, what?—A serious thing. I don't know what it amounts to actually—I've not enquired. It's some time now since I had anything to do with these things. I'm so awfully busy!—I haven't time to blow my nose. Well, we'll see—we'll consider it——"

At that point entered Canali, coming to look for Margarone and surprised at not having seen him at the usual hour. He knew about the bridge, of course,

and seemed to enjoy immensely dragging out his con-
dolences—the poison running under his yellow face:

"Oh dear! Oh dear, Don Gesualdo!—A large undertaking!—That's a blow to knock you over!—
You've got too many irons in the fire, you have!"

Don Filippo, now he'd got support, also started on
him:

"You must take your stride according to your legs,
my dear man!—You want to pull the heavens down
with your hands!—You mustn't get it into your head
that you can get the start of the whole place——"

Then Don Gesualdo lost patience. He got straight
up, red as a cock, and opened his mouth to let go. But
the canon-priest covered the mouth with his hand:

"Be quiet! Let me talk! Listen here, Don Filippo!"

He drew him by the coat-tails into the ante-chamber.
After a while they returned arm in arm, Don Filippo
changed into a piece of sugar towards Mastro-don
Gesualdo, opening his great ox-eyes at him as if he
saw him now for the first time.

"We'll see!—As for me,—whatever I can do.—I
have put in a word for you, dear Don Gesualdo——"

Don Gesualdo, descending the stairs, growled
again:

"Why have I got them all against me?—I do nobody any harm—I only look after my own affairs——"

"Eh, dear Don Gesualdo!" exclaimed the canon-
priest at length. "Your affairs are daggers drawn
with the affairs of the rest of them, what the deuce!—
Of course, they've got to go for you. Amongst
themselves they're hand in glove with one another—
they're all relations. You're the outsider—you're the
enemy, what the deuce!"

The canon-priest stopped on his two feet, in the

middle of the small square, right in front of the high, black, dilapidated mansion of the Traos, and looked fixedly at Don Gesualdo with his sharp little rat's eyes that seemed to want to pierce into him like two needles, his knife-blade face averting itself furtively from everything.

"Don't you see?—when you've come into this camp as one of them—That's the dowry Donna Bianca will bring you!—It's good money for a man like you, with a hand in so many affairs——"

Mastro-don Gesualdo began to stroke his chin again, as if he was making a bargain with some one more cunning than himself; he looked at the mansion; then he looked at the canon-priest, and replied:

"But the earnest-money handed over, eh Canon? I want to see first how her relations take it."

"They'll take it open-armed!—I'm telling you!— You just consider that the river will build you the bridge up again better than before, and go and sleep on it."

In the little alley just by, near his own house, he found Diodata waiting for him with her cloak over her head, huddled under the arch of the terrace, since they wouldn't have her in the house, particularly Speranza, who tolerated her only in the country for heavy work. The moment she saw her master the girl began again to weep and lament, as if the bridge had fallen on top of her.

"Don Gesualdo, what a calamity! I'd rather have been drowned myself!—I came to see you, your honour—what with this thorn you must have in your heart!"

"Look at this now! What have you come for?— And you're wet through!—look!—just on purpose to come snivelling at me. As if I hadn't enough of my own troubles! And now where do you think you're going at this hour?"

He made her go in the stable. In moving away from the wall she left a pool of water behind, there in front of the door where she had been waiting for him. As for him, he felt his bones also were broken. To add to it all his sister received him like a dog.

"So you've come back from the fair? You see the fine profit this time, do you?"

Then she turned like a viper on her husband, black, thin as a nail, with her eyes like coals and her mouth as wide open as if she wanted to devour folks:

"You say nothing!—Doesn't your blood boil?"

Burgio, more peaceable, tried to clear out, lifting his big shoulders, lowering his big ox-head.

"There you are!—Nobody gives a thought to the troubles that fall on us!—Only I have to devour my spleen!"

Her brother, Gesualdo, his mouth bitter, kept chiming:

"Shut it up, Speranza. Leave me alone, I've got enough without your preaching!"

"You don't want to hear my preaching? You don't want me to say a word! And all that money lost!—Don't you have to earn your money, you?"

He, to escape that wasp, went hunting in the kitchen for something to put between his teeth, after such a day. He rummaged in the bread-bin. Speranza followed him all the time, like the curse of God.

"Going on at this rate there'll soon be no bread in the bin, no, there won't!—nor bread-bin neither, there won't!—The house will go straight to the devil."

Santo, who came back famishing from lounging all

day in the square, finding the fire out went into a rage, like a real animal. The children screeching; all the neighbours at their windows to enjoy the scene; till at last Gesualdo lost patience:

"Do you know what I've got to tell you?—that you're driving me to something you'll be sorry for! I've promised it you often enough!—now I'll do it and have done, as sure as God's above! When the ass can stand no more he lays him down, and good-night to the rest of you."

And he took himself off into the stable, while Speranza screamed after him:

"Going off, are you? after that Diodata? Do you think I haven't seen her? Half the day she's been waiting for you, the brazen hussy!——"

He slammed the door. At first he wouldn't even eat, fasting as he was for twenty-four hours, with his belly full of vexations. Diodata went to buy him bread and slices of sausage, wet to the bone like him, her throat dry. There on the bench in the stable in front of a fire of litter they could at least swallow in peace a bit of nourishment.

"D'you like it, this lovely life, eh? Dost like it?" he asked, chewing like two mill-stones, still angry.

She watched him eating, her face red with the flame, and said yes, if he wanted her to, with a contented smile now. The day ended serene. There was a glimpse of sun, which spread gold on the cornice of the Trao mansion, across the way, and Donna Bianca hanging out a bit of old worn washing, on the terrace where she couldn't be seen from the square, with her fine, delicate hands and her figure which seemed taller and slimmer in that shabby dress, as she rose on tip-toe to reach up to the string stretched from wall to wall.

"You see the one they want me to marry?" said he. "A Trao!—and a good housewife too!—they said the truth there."

He sat watching, thoughtful, chewing slowly, slowly. Diodata looked as well, saying nothing, her heart swelling. The goats passed bleating down the alley. Donna Bianca, as if she felt those eyes fixed on her, at length turned her pale, agitated face towards them and drew brusquely back.

"She's lighting the lamp now," continued Don Gesualdo. "She does everything in the house herself. Eh, eh—there isn't much to tire herself with, in that house!—I like her because she's used to trouble, and I should have her at my bidding. Say then, what do you think of it?"

Diodata turned away, going to the end of the stable to give a handful of fresh corn to the mule, then she replied after a moment, in a hoarse voice:

"Your honour is the master."

"That's true—But see now!—what a silly! You must be hungry yourself—Eat, eat, poor lass. Don't think only of the mule."

VI

Don Luca, the sexton, was putting out the candles of the high altar one by one, with a tuft of grass tied on the end of a cane, keeping his eye at the same time on a bunch of young rascals who came running into the church every now and then, at that hot hour when the place was almost deserted, pursued by abuse from the sexton. Donna Bianca Trao, kneeling before the confessional, bent her head humbly; mumbling subdued words that seemed like sighs. From the confession-box came the placid reply of a voice that insinuated itself like a caress, relieving the anguish, calming the scruples, pardoning errors, making a dim opening into the future, into the unknown, like a new life, a new blue sky. A ray of sun escaped from the curtains up above, and made the wounds of Saint Agatha, on the high altar, bloom again almost like two big roses in her breast. Then the penitent raised herself again eagerly, glowing with consolation, cleaving avidly to the ledge of the confessional, her voice more fervent, leaning her forehead on her crossed hands, to let herself be penetrated by that sweetness. There rose a buzzing of sleepy flies, an odour of incense and of melted wax, a heavy torpor, and as if a weariness of the place and the hour. An old woman waited crouched on the steps of the altar, like a dirty mantle on top of a bundle of washing, and when she got up, muttering, Don Luca pounced on her:

"Nice manners! Don't you see there's a lady before you at the confessional?—and hers aren't the few bits of gossip which are all you have to bring to the tribunal of repentance!—family matters, bless you!— important affairs!"

In the shadow of the confessional gleamed a white hand making the sign of the cross, and Donna Bianca rose at last, staggering, closed in her cloak right down to her feet, her face shining with a sweet serenity. Don Luca, seeing that the old woman couldn't make up her mind to go, touched her little cape with his cane. "Hey! Hey! Aunt Filomena?—It's late to-day, late. It's just going to ring mid-day, and the confessor must go to his dinner."

The old woman lifted her head stupefied, he had to repeat the same thing to her, two or three times, obstinate, childish as she was.

"I tell you, I'm going to shut the church. You can go now, mother. To-day?—no, you can't!—Father Angelo is threshing at Passo di Cava. Work-days, good soul!——"

In the long run he managed to send her away, mumbling, dragging her slippers. Then, while the priest was slipping through the sacristy door, Don Luca had to chase away those brats, overturning benches and chairs, pretending to seize the censer.

"Out with you! Out with you! Go and play in the square."

At the same time he passed and repassed near Donna Bianca who was kneeling, praying before the chapel of the Sacrament, that blazed with gold and bright colours enough to blind you, coughing, hawking, stopping to blow his nose, grumbling:

"Not even in church!—one can't have peace to make one's orations!"

Donna Bianca rose to her feet, crossing herself, her

lips still full of ave-marias. The sexton addressed
her point-blank, while she was withdrawing to leave
the church.

"Are you content, my lady? A holy man, Father
Angelino! He confesses well, eh? He has left you
content?"

She nodded assent, smiling briefly, slackening her
pace out of courtesy.

"A good man! a sensible man! Now he *can* give
you a bit of good advice . . . better than your brother
Don Ferdinando—or Don Diego either, yes!"

He looked around with cat's eyes used to seeing in
the dark of the church, then glanced up the tower
stairs, and added in a low voice, changing his tone, with
a great air of mystery:

"Do you know what answer they've given to Don
Gesualdo Motto? He sent to make the formal proposal of marriage, yesterday afternoon, by the canon-
priest Lupi——"

Bianca blushed without raising her head. The sexton who was looking into her lowered eyes as he followed her step by step, continued more loudly:

"They told him no—just exactly as I say it now.
The canon-priest simply turned to salt!—Nobody
would have expected that answer, would they, now?—
the canon-priest, Donna Marianna, as well as your aunt
the Baroness, who had all been at ever so much
trouble!—It would have moved that there Christ
made of wood, it would indeed! Nobody would ever
have believed he was so hard, that Don Diego, your
brother; such a nice, humble gentleman you fairly felt
you could go to him to confess!—I'm not speaking of
Don Ferdinando, who is worse than a child, poor
thing——"

He had succeeded in stopping Donna Bianca, planting himself in front of her, his eyes shining, his face excited, lowering his voice again as he made her a decisive confidence:

"Don Gesualdo seemed crazy!—They say he can't get over it! That he'll be ill of it, as sure as God's above. I went to see him at Canziria. He was threshing the corn—Don Gesualdo, is this the way to take it, now?—You'll kill yourself, your honour!—Leave me alone, dear Don Luca, I know it!—ever since the canon-priest brought him that beautiful answer!—He looked really ill and a hundred years old!—His beard growing—He doesn't sleep nor eat any more——"

At that moment they heard footsteps of some clerical person. Don Luca raised his voice immediately, as if he was speaking to somebody deaf:

"Father Angelino is threshing at Passo di Cava to-day. If you have some other sin to confess, there's the arch-priest Bugno unoccupied—he's quite as good! a servant of God——"

However, seeing the canon-priest Lupi coming towards them, bowing at every altar, with his right hand dripping holy water and his three-cornered hat hanging in his left:

"Good-day to you, Sir Canon! How are you these days?"

The canon-priest, instead of replying, turned to Donna Bianca with a foolish smile on his sharp, swarthy, ferrety face.

"We are doing well, Donna Bianca! Recommending ourselves to the Saviour. I saw you entering the church as I was going to Don Gesualdo Motta's, close by, and I said: There's Donna Bianca making her visit to the forty hours of exposition, and she gives a good example to me, unworthy priest that I am——"

"Precisely!—here's the canon-priest!—If you have some other sin to tell him, Donna Bianca——"

"I can't, I'm sorry. Monsignor doesn't appoint me to hear confession, because he knows I haven't the time for it—" Then he added with a little smile, stroking his stiff-bearded chin: "Besides, your brothers wouldn't wish it——"

Donna Bianca, as red as if she had on her face all the reflection of the curtain which veiled the altar of the Crucifix, pretended not to understand. The canon-priest resumed, changing his key:

"I've got a lot of serious business on hand—my own and others'. I was going this minute to Don Gesualdo's on a commission from your aunt. You know the weighty affair they have together, with the baroness?——"

Donna Bianca shook her head.

"A weighty affair—There is talk of taking over the lease of all the communal lands in the county!—Don Gesualdo has a heart as big as this church!—and the cash as well! A good deal! a good deal, Donna Bianca! A good deal more than you think. A man who'll be as rich as Crœsus, with that clever head of his!"

Don Luca, as he was taking off his church vestments, his head inside his surplice, his arms in the air, his voice suffocated, suddenly let out:

"You should just see what he's harvested at Canziria, you should just see!"

"Ah, ah, have you been up there?"

"Yes, sir," said the sexton, drawing out his red, confused face. "Just, you know, for a bit of a walk—

I go every year for the church alms. Don Gesualdo
is a devotee of Saint Agatha."

"A heart of gold!—" interrupted the canon-priest;
"generous, charitable!—Pity that—"

And he put his hand over his mouth.

"Just what I was saying to Donna Bianca—" continued Don Luca, with renewed spirit, his little eyes
again rousing to interference.

"Enough! Enough! Everybody rules in his own
way in his own house. Now I'll leave you to your own
business.—My best wishes to Don Diego and Don
Ferdinando!"

Donna Bianca, embarrassed, wished to depart also:
but the sexton kept her.

"One moment! What must I say to Father Angelino, in case you wish to put yourself in God's Grace
before the feast of Saint John—"

The canon-priest also insisted:

"No, no, you stay, Donna Bianca, finish your business."

Then hardly had he let fall the door-curtain, going
out, than Don Luca winked:

"Is that it? what must I say to Don Gesualdo if
ever I see him—by chance?—"

She seemed to hesitate. She continued her way
towards the church-door, step by step, keeping her
eyes lowered, as if annoyed by the sexton's insistence.

"My brothers have already said no."

"And a silly thing they've said! I'd have liked to
lead them to Canziria to make them see if it isn't
worth all your smoky family portraits!—Excuse me,
Donna Bianca—I speak in your ladyship's own interest. Your brothers hang on to that nonsense because
they're old—they've got their feet in the grave as it

is!—But you who are young, what's to become of you? They've no business to ruin a sister like that!—Not even Saint Joseph, father of prosperity, will send you another such a husband!—Your brothers are mad to say no!—fit for the asylum!—All the lands of the County he'll be taking, will Don Gesualdo!—and then a finger in the pie everywhere. There isn't a stone built into a wall but he makes his profit on it. Lord upon earth! Bridges, mills, factories, high-roads! That demon puts the world upside-down. Before long we shall be able to go in a carriage as far as Militello, God first and then Don Gesualdo Motta!—His wife will go in a carriage from morn till night!—she'll walk on fine gold, as true as God's above. And Father Angelino will have given you the same advice as I'm giving you. I didn't hear anything, not to violate the seal of confession, but Father Angelino is a sensible man—he'll have advised you to take a good husband—to provide for yourself—"

Donna Bianca looked at him in consternation, her pointed Trao chin seeming convulsed. Then she raised her eyes wet with tears towards the crucifix, her pale lips pressed in a painful fold. At last she replied with those painful lips:

"My brothers are the masters—it is for them to decide—"

Don Luca, cut short in his arguments, remained for a moment almost stunned, planting himself in front of her so as not to let her escape, suffocated by the number of good reasons he'd got in his throat, stammering, waving his arms, scratching his head furiously, with his sparkling eyes seeming to probe her from head to foot to find the weak spot, shaking his clasped hands in front of her, threatening and imploring. At last he burst forth:

"But is it right, good God? is it right to make a gentleman who likes you so much suffer in this fashion? —Fairly kicking against fortune?—Excuse me, Donna Bianca, I speak for your own good. You must really think about it! You're not under age, when all's said and done!—If my blood gets hot for you—it's because I'm a good servant of your family—a great house!— pity it isn't what it has been!—Now you'll have a chance to restore the Trao name, though!—I call it being ungrateful to divine Providence—"

She continued her way to the door, irresolute, bending her head, Don Luca at her heels, getting more heated, harping on all the strings, changing his tune to every key.

"And one day, Donna Bianca!—there'll be one day that will dawn on your house!—But there, beg pardon, I only speak of it because I'm always running round to help you, along with my wife.—And then when your relations forget you're alive—! one winter's day, it may be!—But there!—And instead of that you can be queen of the place! you just think about it. Don Gesualdo would fetch the sun out of the sky and the moon as well, to please you!—He simply doesn't know what to do with himself!—He's like a proper mad-man, he is."

Donna Bianca had stopped arrested, her head high, on her cheeks a sudden flame that seemed as if it were cast by the lifting of the door-curtain at that moment, as someone entered the church. Appeared a skinny, thin woman with her ragged skirt lifted from her thin legs by her stomach that was big with child, dirty and unkempt, as if she had done nothing else all her life

but carry that belly in front of her;—the look of a
mother-hen stupefied by brooding her young, with two
round little eyes on her pointed parchment-yellow face,
and an invalid's torn handkerchief tied under her chin;
nothing else on her shoulders, being quite at home in
the house of the Good God. From the doorway she
began to moan as if her travail pains were upon her:

"Don Luca!—aren't you going to ring mid-day?—
the pot is nearly boiling—"

"What have you put it on so soon for? The sun is
on the threshold yet. The arch-priest raises the devil
because we ring mid-day before it's time.—But this
once—seeing the food's done—here's the tower-key."

Don Luca, still with his surplice under his arm, was
quarrelling with his wife, he as lank under his dirty
cassock-skirt as she, with her belly, was enormous.

"You, you've got the clock there, in your belly!—
You think of nothing but eating!—It takes some pro-
viding!—The neighbours are all in the fields yet—No,
there are Burgio's children—"

"They're waiting as well!" whined the wife, always
the same tune. "They're waiting for you to ring mid-
day—" And she went off with her belly in front of
her.

"Don Gesualdo's nephews!" resumed the sexton,
winking significantly at Donna Bianca as he turned
round. "They are there spying! Their mother, neighbour Speranza, sends them on purpose to find out what
we're doing. She's got her eye on the property, she
has!—as if it was her own!—She's got her designs on
it!—When she meets me she looks as if she'd devour
me."

He pretended to go in front of Donna Bianca to lift

the door-curtain for her, but really to keep her another moment.

"He makes me really sorry for him!—Looks absolutely ill!—He talked to me all the while about your ladyship. He says perhaps the canon-priest Lupi didn't manage the embassy well—that he'd like to speak to you—to see—to hear—"

Donna Bianca went red as fire.

"He's in love, and there you are. Madly in love. You'll have to speak to your brothers about him. Send him a kind word—a more christian answer. I'll come myself and take it, after midday, when Don Diego and Don Ferdinando are in bed—under the pretence of the flowers for the Madonna. Yes? What do you say?"

She bent her head rapidly, passing under the curtain, and went out. Don Luca, imagining he saw that she wanted to feel in her pocket, followed her, running after her:

"What are you doing? No! You offend me! Another time—later—when you can—I thought I'd better send my wife to take your ladyship's answer. I don't want your brothers to suspect that the canon-priest has sent me, if they see me hanging round the house—"

After vespers he finished off the church service as fast as possible and ran to Canziria; a five- or six-mile climb, bless your life, for love of Don Gesualdo, who was worth it, indeed.

"She's going to give in, Don Gesualdo! She hasn't said yes with her own mouth, not yet; but you can see she's wavering, like the pear when it's ripe. I understand these things because I see the women in church every day coming to the tribunal of repentance—before and after.—I've wet my shirt through with sweat!—

But I tell you now the pear is ripe! Another shake and it'll fall into your arms; I'm telling you! You ought to go quick to the village and strike while the iron's hot."

However, Don Gesualdo did not seem overjoyed by the arrival of the ambassador at that moment.

"Look you, Don Luca, I've got all the harvest on the threshing-floor. I've been at it since last night. I haven't got the wind in my pocket, to be able to thresh when I like—"

The threshing-yard was as big as a village-square. Ten mules trotted round continually, and after the mules ran Nanni l'Orbo and Brasi Camauro, sinking up to their knees in the chaff, panting, calling, singing, yelling. On one side a white cloud, a squad of peasants armed with wooden forks, their shirts flying open, seemed to be digging in the corn, tossing it to the wind, while Uncle Carmine, on the top of the stack, black with the sun, kept throwing more sheaves down. Sledges arrived every minute from the corn-fields around, loaded with more harvest; lads were putting the grain into sacks and carrying it into the barn, where the dirge of Pirtuso never ceased as he sang "e viva Maria" every twenty bushels. All around fluttered throngs of hens, a cloud of pigeons in the air; lean asses munching famished in the straw, their eyes spent; other beasts of burden were scattered here and there, and little barrels of wine passed from mouth to mouth, enough to put out a fire. Don Gesualdo was always on the go, with a bundle of tally-sticks in his hand, marking the sacks of wheat, making a cross for every little barrel of wine, counting the sledges that came up, shouting at Diodata, arguing with the agent, calling to the men in the distance, sweating, his voice almost gone, his face kindled, his shirt open, a cotton kerchief tied round his neck, and an old straw hat on his head.

"You can see whether I've got any time to lose just now, Don Luca!—Wine here! Give Don Luca something to drink!—Yes, yes, I'll come; when I can. At the present I couldn't stir, not if the world fell!— Diodata!—Mind the wind doesn't carry the flame to the threshing-floor, saints and blessings!—No, Don Luca! I'm not angry with her brothers because of their refusal—Come up here, closer, it's no good letting everybody hear our business!—Every man thinks in his own way. And after all it's for her to decide. If she says yes, I shan't draw back on my side. But I can't come to-day—nor yet to-morrow. Well!—the day after to-morrow! The day after to-morrow I've got to come for the affair of the communal lands, so we can talk then."

Don Luca suggested he should send two lines on paper.

"We've got my wife on the spot to take them quietly to Donna Bianca, without rousing any suspicions.—A nice little letter, with two or three words that do the trick with the girls! You know what I mean, your honour! Ciolla's a good hand at that. I'll speak myself to Ciolla in secret, without bothering you, your honour; and that'll make you cut a fine figure in her eyes. Then with a three-gallon jar of wine we'll quiet Ciolla."

Don Gesualdo wouldn't hear of any letter.

"Not to save the wine; but what tales are you telling me? If she wants to do the thing, where's the need of so much chatter?"

"All right! All right!" finished Don Luca. "I only

said it to drive the nail home. But you're the master."

Don Luca went back quite satisfied, with a lamb and a cheese. For prudence's sake he sent his wife to make the embassy, under a pretext.

"About that talk you had with my husband, your ladyship, he says that the confessor will come the day after to-morrow to take the answer!—The confessor will expect the answer on Sunday!"

Don Ferdinando, who had heard the street-door open, appeared at that moment like a spectre.

"The confessor!" Goodwife Grazia began to repeat without anybody having asked her anything—"Donna Bianca wanted to confess!—To-day the confessor can't hear her—nor to-morrow either. But he can on Sunday, if you'll let him know you are ready—"

The poor woman, under Don Ferdinando's staring eyes which seemed to search her through and through, suspicious, anxious, became confused, stammered, fumbled for her words. Then, seeing that he stood silent and did not move, emaciated, she was silent too, and began to look into the air, her mouth open, her hands on her stomach. Bianca, to make an end, took her to the store-pantry to give her an apronful of beans. Don Ferdinando, always after them, sewed to their heels, silent, looking in every corner, suspicious. He also bent over the heap of beans, protecting it with his person, measuring it with his eye, touching it with his hand. And after the sexton's wife had gone, like a duck rearing her full apron on her enormous stomach, he began to grumble:

"Too many!—You gave her too many!—They're nearly all gone!—Your aunt won't send any more before Christmas."

His sister wanted to go; but he kept on hunting, rummaging, reckoning up the stuff in the store-pantry; two lean little sausages hung on a big ring; a cheese gnawed by the rats; some rotten pears on a plank; a little pitcher of oil hung inside a receptacle that would have held twenty gallons; a sack of flour at the bottom of a bin as big as a corn-chamber; a big rush basket that was still waiting for the corn from Aunt Rubiera.

At length he added:

"We need God's help!—We are three mouths to feed in the house!—Does it seem to you little? We really want a drop of broth now and then for Diego— I've not been satisfied with him for some time now!— Have you seen how he looks? The same face as our dear departed, do you remember?—when he went to bed not to get up any more!—And the doctor doesn't come, because he's afraid he won't get paid—after all the money he swallowed during the last illness of our dear departed!—Aunt Rubiera has forgotten we're alive—Aunt Sganci as well—"

So grumbling he followed step by step behind his sister, bending down to pick up the beans that had fallen from Grazia's apron. Then, as if waking from a dream, he asked:

"Why don't you go to Aunt Rubiera's? She would have sent a pair of pigeons, knowing Diego is not well —to make him a drop of broth—"

Bianca became as red as fire, and dropped her eyes. Don Ferdinando waited for a moment with his mouth open for her reply, blinking his eyes. Then he went back to the store-pantry to put back the beans he had picked up. A little later she saw him appear before her once more, with that dismayed look.

"If the sexton's wife comes again don't give her

anything, next time. Leeches they are! The beans
are nearly gone, didn't you see!—And another thing—
You'll have to go to Aunt Sganci for a drop of oil—
to borrow it. Tell her plainly that you just want to
borrow it, because we aren't born to go begging for
charity;—since your aunt hasn't thought of us.—Before long we shall be in the dark—and Diego so ill—
all the night!—"

And he stretched wide his eyes, motioning again with
his hands and his head, a vague terror on his wondering face. In the distance they heard from time to
time the cough which was devouring Don Diego, coming through the closed doors and along the corridor,
grievous and implacable, all over the house.—Bianca
started every time, her heart going as if it would burst,
bending to listen, or else she fled as if terrified, stopping her ears.

"I can't bear it, no! I can't bear it—"

At last God gave her the strength to appear before
him again, the day that Don Ferdinando had told her
her brother was worse, and there she found him in his
dirty little bedroom, stretched out in a bed no better
than a kennel. Don Diego was neither better nor
worse. There he was, waiting for what God sent him,
like all the Traos, without complaining, without trying to escape his destiny, careful only not to trouble
others, to keep his pains and his miseries to himself.
He turned his head on seeing his sister enter, as if a
shadow had fallen on his parchment face. Then he
signed to her with his hand to come near the bed.

"I'm better—I'm better—poor Bianca!—You, how
are you?—Why do you keep out of sight?—why do
you?—"

He caressed her hand with his wasted, dirty hand

of a poor sick man. On his hollow cheeks scattered with grey hairs, lingered a flame-heat.

"Poor Bianca!—I'm always your brother, you know!—your brother who is so fond of you—poor Bianca!—"

"Don Ferdinando told me," she stammered timidly —"Would you like a little broth?"

The sick man at first shook his head, looking into the air, supine. Then he turned his head, fixing her with avid eyes from the depths of the sunken sockets, that seemed empty, sooty.

"Broth, did you say? Is there a bit of meat?"

"I'll send across to my aunt's—to Aunt Sganci's," hastily added Bianca, a flush coming unawares on her cheeks. Another similar flush had passed over her brother's face.

"No! No!—I don't want any."

Neither did he want the doctor.

"No, no! What good will the doctor do me?—all a fraud!—to fleece one of money. The true doctor is above!—Let it be as God wills. Besides, I feel better—"

He seemed really to improve, from then and for some days: good broth, a little old wine which Aunt Sganci sent, helped him to get up out of bed, still shattered, short of breath. Donna Marianna even came in person to see him, kind, with a reproving smile on her good-natured face:

"Why now! Are you in that state and I never knew? Are we among the Turks? Are we relations, or aren't we? Always secretive and savage, all you Traos!—lurking like bears in this den! One of these fine days you'll all be found unawares dead, and shame on all your relatives!—And neither have you said one word to me about that business of the marriage—!"

Then she began to recite this other rosary: They were mad, or else what were they, to refuse an offer like that?—A man on the way to being as amazingly rich as Don Gesualdo Motta!—"Don Gesualdo! yes, yes indeed! Leave mad people out of question!—You see plainly enough to what a state they've reduced you!—A brother-in-law who could help you in every possible way—who'd relieve you of so much strain!—Ah!—Ah!"

Donna Marianna looked round the squalid little room, shaking her head. The others didn't breathe; Bianca with her head dropped; Don Ferdinando waiting for his brother to speak, fixing his owl's eyes on him.

Don Diego was at first only astounded, grumbling: "Mastro-don Gesualdo!—Have we got as far as that?—Mastro-don Gesualdo wanting to marry a Trao!"

"Of course!—Whom do you expect to marry her? —without a dowry? And she's not a child neither!— It's a betrayal pure and simple!—What will she do, when you two close your eyes, you and your brother? —be a servant, eh? Aunt Rubiera's servant, or somebody else's?"

Don Diego got out of bed just as he was, in flannel undershirt, handkerchief on his head, his thin legs trembling like reeds in his worn-out drawers: an Ecce Homo! He went wandering about the room, making gestures and talking incoherently, coughing, breathing heavily, blowing his nose as if he was blowing a trumpet.

"—Mastro-don Gesualdo!—Have we come to this,

that a Trao should marry Mastro-don Gesualdo!—
And would you consent, Bianca?—would you?—You
would say yes?—"

Bianca, very pale, slowly nodded her head, saying
yes, without raising her eyes from the ground.

He threw his trembling arms in the air, and couldn't
utter another word. Don Ferdinando also did not
breathe, aghast that Don Diego couldn't succeed in
persuading Bianca.

"What do you want her to say?" exclaimed their
aunt. "Does it seem to you a nice future, to look forward to growing old like you two—in all this want?—
Excuse me, I speak because we are relations. I do all
I can myself to help you—but it's not very nice for you,
even that isn't.—And now that fortune offers itself,
you answer it with a kick.—If you'll excuse me, I call
it abominable!"

All at once Don Diego began laughing as if an inspiration had struck him, winking his eye, rubbing his
hands, and nodding his head with great portentousness.

"Right you are! Right you are!—This is all it
amounts to?—because now at the moment we're in
rather straitened circumstances?—It worries you, eh?
—it worries you, this straitened life, poor Bianca.
You're afraid for the future?"

He rubbed his scrubby chin with his skeleton hand,
winking all the time, trying to make his pale smile
look sly.

"Come here!—I say no more to you!—You as well,
Aunt!—Come and see!"

He climbed all trembling on to a chair to open a
little cupboard in the wall, over the window, and drew
out piles of old papers and parchments—the documents
of the law-suit—which would be the great revival re-

source of the family, when they'd got the money to prove their rights against the King of Spain; yellow tomes, worn out and dusty, which made him cough every time he turned a page. And on the bed was spread out a great genealogical tree, like a sheet; the family tree which bathed its roots in the blood of a libertine king, as their coat-of-arms proclaimed—red, with three golden lilies, on a bar of the same gold, and the motto which glorified the fall of their first foundress: *Virtutem a Sanguine Traho.*

He had put on his spectacles, leaning his elbow on the side of the meagre bed, face down, his eyes kindling in the depths of their livid sockets.

"Six hundred years of interest are owing to us!—A fine sum of money!—We shall be beyond every trouble, once and for all!"

Bianca had grown up among such talk, which had helped to pass the sad days. She had all her life seen those wretched books spread upon rickety tables and lame chairs. So she said nothing. Her brother turned his head at length to her, with a kindly, melancholy smile.

"I speak for you two others, for you and Ferdinando. At any rate you'll enjoy it. As for me—it is nearly over.—Here!—here's the key!—you keep it!"

At this Aunt Sganci went off like a spring gun:

"My dear nephew, you behave like a child—!"

But soon she calmed herself, with the indulgent smile which tries to make the child really see reason.

"All right!—Right, quite right!—First marry her to the husband that offers now, and then, if you become so many Crœsuses, all the better."

Don Diego was staggered seeing that his sister did not take the key, and started afresh:

"You too, Bianca?—Do you say Yes as well?—"

She, sitting overwhelmed on her chair, silently bent her head.

"Oh, very well!—Since you want it—since you haven't the courage to wait—"

Donna Marianna continued expounding the case for Don Gesualdo, saying that that marriage was a golden business, a fortune for them all; congratulating her niece, who was looking out of the window, her eyes bright with tears; turning even to Don Ferdinando, who was looking at all the lot of them in bewilderment; patting Don Diego on the back, though he seemed not to hear, his eyes glued on his sister, a tremor passing over all his body. At a certain point he interrupted his aunt, stammering:

"Leave me alone with Bianca—I must say two words to her. Leave us alone—"

Bianca raised her eyes, afraid, face to face with her corpse of a brother, after her aunt and Don Ferdinando had gone out.

The poor man still hesitated to add that which he still had to say, looking at his sister with a grief more piercing and profound. Then he seized her hands, shaking his head, moving his lips without being able to utter a word.

"Tell me the truth, Bianca!—Why do you want to go away from your home?—Why do you want to leave your brothers?—I know! I know!—Because of that other!—You are ashamed to stay with us after the calamity that happened to you—"

He kept on nodding his head, his voice and his face terribly broken, bitter tears running down between the grey, bristly hairs of his chin.

"God forgives.—Ferdinando knows nothing!—I—I

—Bianca!—Like a child I love you!—You are my daughter—Bianca!—"

He said no more, overcome by a burst of weeping.

She, more dead than alive, shook her head and mumbled:

"No—no—It is not for that reason—"

Don Diego slowly let fall the hands of his sister, slowly, as if an abyss opened between them.

"Well!—Do what you like—do what you like—"

And he turned away from her, bent, without saying more, dragging his feet.

VII

In the old house of the La Gurna family, which Don Gesualdo Motta had taken on lease, they were expecting the bride and bridegroom. Before the door was a swarm of youngsters, whom Burgio's boy, in his quality of relative, struggled to keep back, threatening them with a stick; the staircase sprinkled with orange leaves; a torch-lamp with four flames on the balustrade of the landing; and Brasi Camauro, in a hunting jacket of blue cloth, a starched shirt, new boots, giving the last sweep with the broom inside the newly white-washed courtyard door. Every moment arose a false alarm. The children shouted:

"Here they are! Here they are!" Camauro dropped the broom, people crowded at the illuminated balconies.

About an hour after dark arrived the Marchese Limòli, making himself a passage with his malacca cane. He saw the light, the orange leaves, and said: "Bravo!"—But going up the stairs he nearly broke his neck, and started swearing:

"The fools!—They've made a nice mess here!"

Brasi Camauro ran quickly with the broom:

"Shall I sweep it all away, my lord? Shall I throw everything away?"

"No, no—I'm through it now. Don't scratch too much with that broom, either—there's smell of the stable enough—"

Hearing voices, Santo Motta, who was waiting upstairs, presented himself on the landing dressed in new

clothes, riding breeches and a long waistcoat of flowered satin, just struggling into his tail-coat.

"Here I am! Here I am!—I'm here!—Ah, my
lord marchese!—Kiss your hand!"

He stood somewhat confused, seeing only Limòli.

"Your servant, your servant, my dear Santo!—
Don't go kissing anything—now that we're relations."

At the top of the stairs appeared also Donna Sara
Cirmena, the only one of all the bride's relations who
had deigned to come, with a bushel of artificial flowers
on her head, a silk dress that had creased like paper,
lying in the chest, the family earrings tearing down her
ears, herself annoyed at having waited so long in a
stew of preparation.

"And what are they doing? Is there something else
amiss?" she began to scream from above.

"Nothing! Nothing!" replied the marchese, coming
up very gradually. "I came out first so they shouldn't
see that I was the only one there, of all the relations—
I've just come to take a glance at things here—"

Don Gesualdo had indeed spent some money; new
furniture, brought specially from Catania, mirrors in
gilt frames, stuffed chairs, lamp with cut lamp-glasses;
a suite of illuminated rooms which, seen like that, with
all the doors wide open, seemed to lead into the distance like a cosmorama.

Don Santo went in front giving explanations, every
moment pulling up his sleeves which came right to his
finger-tips.

"What? Nobody come yet?" exclaimed the marchese when they had arrived in the nuptial chamber,
that was decked out like an altar. Neighbour Santo
drew his head inside his velvet collar, like a tortoise.

"It's not me that's missing. I've been here since the Ave Maria. Everything is ready—"

"But I thought at least the rest of your family would have come—Master Nunzio—and your sister—"

"No, sir—they're shy. There's been the devil of a row! I've come to look after the refreshments—"

And he opened the door to show him: a big table loaded with sweets and liqueurs, still in the fancy paper as they had arrived from town, scattered with carnations and Arabian jasmine, all there was in the village, because the Captain's lady had sent to say that if they wanted flowers—; as many candlesticks as they could borrow, from Saint Agatha and the other churches. Diodata for her part had arranged all the serviettes splendidly, rolled each one up to a cone, like so many skittles each with a flower at the top.

"Splendid! Splendid!" approved the marquis. "Never saw anything so fine!—And these two here, what are they doing?"

On either side of the table, like the Jews at the Holy Sepulchre, were Pelagatti and Giacalone, like papier-mâché figures, so washed and combed.

"To serve the refreshments, that's why!—Master Titta and the other barber, his assistant, wouldn't come, they sent an excuse! Those beggars will only go into the noble houses! They were frightened of dirtying their hands here, they who handle so much dirt—"

Giacalone, very eager, ran at once with a bottle in each hand. The marchese waved him back:

"Thank you, thank you, child!—You'll be ruining my clothes if you don't mind!"

"Over there are the tubs with ice-cream!" added Don Santo.

But as they opened the door into the kitchen they saw scuffling of women who had been looking through the keyhole.

"Yes, yes; I see, cousin. Leave them alone; don't frighten them."

At that moment they heard a hubbub in the street below, and ran on to the balcony in time to see the carriage arrive with the bride and bridegroom. Nanni l'Orbo, on the box, his hat down to his ears, cracked the whip like a coachman and shouted:

"Make room!—Oh, you!—Mind yourselves!—"

The mules, just taken from the herd, were rearing and snorting, so that the canon-priest Lupi proposed they should get down there where they were, and Burgio had already got up to open the door of the carriage. But the mules all at once put down their heads and dashed through the doorway top-speed into the courtyard.

"Sudden death!" exclaimed the canon-priest, grinning, with his nose on the knees of the bride.

They went up arm in arm. Don Gesualdo with a glittering pin plump in the middle of his satin cravat, shiny shoes, his coat with gold buttons, a wedding smile on his newly shaven face; only his velvet collar, too high, bothered him. She seeming younger and more graceful in that white spumey dress, with bare arms, a bit of bare breast, the angular profile of the Traos softened by the coiffure that was then in fashion, her hair curled at the temples and then gathered on the top of the head with a tortoise-shell comb; a circumstance which set the canon-priest's tongue clicking as the bride went bowing her head to right and left, pale as death, timid, almost frightened, all that nakedness of hers which blushed to show itself for the first time under so many eyes and so many lights.

"Long life to the bride and bridegroom! Three cheers for the bride and bridegroom!" the canon-priest began to shout, becoming lively, waving his handkerchief.

Bianca received the kiss of her Aunt Cirmena, the kiss of her uncle the marchese, and entered alone into the fine room, where there wasn't a soul.

"Hey? Hey? Mind you don't lose your husband!" cried the marchese behind her, amid general laughter.

"Is this all of us?" muttered Donna Sarina *sotto voce.*

The canon-priest hastened to reply:

"Yes, ma'am. Not much company and a happy time!"

Behind him Alessi came up the stairs, cap in hand, abashed by all those lights and preparations. From the doorway he began to stammer:

"Baroness Rubiera sends to say—she can't come because she's got a headache. She sends to greet her niece, and Don Gesualdo also—"

"Go into the kitchen, this way," replied the marchese.. "Tell them to give you something to drink."

Don Gesualdo profited by this moment to recommend his brother, *sotto voce:*

"You be careful before all these folks!—Sit down and don't stir again. And do what you see me do."

"All right. Leave it to me."

Aunt Cirmena had taken the bride in charge, and had assumed a matronly air which made her look as if she were angry. After everybody had taken their places in the fine drawing-room with the mirrors, silence fell; they all stared around, in order to do something, nodding their heads in admiration. At last the canon-priest felt he must break the ice:

"Don Santo, sit here. Come on; don't be afraid."

"Mean me?—" replied Santo, who heard himself even called Don.

"He is your brother-in-law," said the marchese to Bianca.

The lawyer remarked a moment later:

"Look! look! It might be the landing of Christopher Columbus!"

In the doorway of the antechamber was seen a bunch of heads which crowded, between curiosity and timidity, almost as if a mine was going to explode. Among the other youngsters the canon-priest discovered Nunzio, the nephew of Don Gesualdo, and made him signs to come in, winking at him. But the boy ran away like a savage; and the canon-priest, continuing to smile, said:

"A little rascal—just like his mother—"

The marchese, stretched out in an arm-chair near his niece, seemed like a president, chattering all alone:

"Bravo! Bravo! Your husband has done things well! There's no lack of anything in this house! You'll be set up like a princess!—You've only to say a word—express a desire—"

"Then tell him to buy different mules," put in the canon-priest, laughing.

"That's true; you're rather pale. You were frightened in the carriage, were you?"

"Those mules are too young—just taken from the herd—they aren't used to it. Nowadays they use horses for a carriage," said the canon-priest.

"Certainly! Certainly!" Gesualdo hastened to reply. "As soon as I'm able. Money is made to spend —when there is any."

The marchese and the canon-priest Lupi kept up a lively conversation, Don Gesualdo approving, nodding his head; the others listened; Aunt Cirmena with her hands on her stomach and an amiable smile that made the words simply fall from your mouth; a smile which said:

"One must really! Since one has come!—It was quite worth while dressing oneself up, indeed!—"

Bianca felt a stranger in the midst of all that luxury: and her husband also was embarrassed in front of so many people, his wife, friends, servants, and before all those mirrors in which one saw oneself from top to toe, in new clothes, forced to watch to see how the others did it if one only wanted to blow one's nose.

"The harvest has turned out well?" asked the marchese in a louder voice, so that the others should follow his lead. "I ask because I want to know. Eh? Eh? Farmer Fortunato?"

"Yessir, thanks to God!—It's the prices which don't amount to much."

"There must be a lot to be done in the country! There's nobody left in the village."

Aunt Cirmena couldn't restrain herself at that.

"I saw Cousin Sganci on the balcony—I thought she was coming as well—"

"Who knows? who knows? That shower of rain we had has made the road like glue!—I nearly broke my neck. However, they say it will do the vines good. Eh?—eh?—Farmer Fortunato?"

"Yessir, perhaps it will—"

"Everybody will be getting ready for the grape-harvest. Only not you and me, Donna Sarina! We

drink our wine without praying to God for the rain!
—You must take your bride to Giolio for the grape-
harvest, Don Gesualdo!—You'll see what vines,
Bianca!—"

"Of course—she's the mistress—of course!"

"One moment!" exclaimed the canon-priest dancing
to his feet. "I think I hear somebody—"

Santo, who kept on the alert, his eyes on his
brother, made him a sign to ask if it was time to begin
with the refreshments. But the canon-priest returned
from the balcony almost at once, shaking his head.

"No!—country labourers coming back into the village. To-day is Saturday, and they keep coming in till
late—"

"I knew it!" answered Dame Cirmena. "I'm sharp
on the ear!—Who are you expecting, then?"

"Donna Giuseppina Alòsi, by Jove!—She never
misses, she doesn't—"

"The cavaliere will have kept her," blurted the
marchese, losing patience.

Santo, who had already risen, came back very quiet
and diminished, to sit down again.

"Excuse me! Excuse me!" said the canon-priest.
"One moment! I'll be back in one moment."

Donna Sarina ran after him into the antechamber,
and they heard the canon-priest replying loudly:

"No! Near here—at the Captain's—"

The marchese, who was listening with all his ears,
pretended to be still admiring the furniture and the
rooms, and began to repeat again:

"Beautiful! Splendid!—A gentleman's house!
You were lucky to be able to set up in the nest of the
La Gurnas!—Eh! eh!—These rooms have seen some
fine feasts—this very room!—I remember—for the

baptism of the last La Gurna—Corradino. Now
they're gone to live at Syracuse, all the family, after
they sold up what was left!—*Mors tua vita mea!*—
Here you'll live like princes!—Eh! Eh!—I am old
and know what I say!—we should do well also, here,
we also, eh, Donna Sarina?—eh?—"

Donna Sarina waggled on her chair in her efforts to
hold her tongue.

"As for me," she said, "thank God!—My testimony
is that the La Gurna boy, Corradino, comes to me for
his summer holidays. He's not to blame, poor innocent—"

"No, no, it's better to be sitting in a nice soft chair
like this, than to go earning your bread here and there,
like the La Gurnas!—when they can manage to earn
it, moreover!—And to have a good table spread, and
a carriage to drive out a few steps after, and the vineyards for the summer holidays, and all the rest!—
Above all a good table!—I'm an old man, and sorry
I am that the marquisate can't dish itself up at table.—
Smoke is only good in the kitchen—smoke and vanity
—I'm wise now.—There's more smoke in the kitchen
than roast-meat on the table of many houses—those
that have the biggest coats-of-arms on the entrance
door—and curl their noses most! If I've got to be
born again I hope I'll be called plain Master Alfonso
Limòli, and be as rich as you, nephew.—To enjoy my
money all by myself, without inviting anybody—
no!—"

"Hush!—I hear the bell!" interrupted Donna
Sarina. "Somebody's been ringing for quite a time
while you've been preaching."

However, it was the humble tinkle of poor folks.
Santo ran to open, and found himself face to face with

the sexton, who was followed by his wife, who had under her arm a napkin that looked like a sack, as if she'd come for the house-removal. For a moment Don Luca was embarrassed, seeing the brother of Speranza, since that lady had sent him to say a thousand insults to her husband Burgio; but he didn't lose spirit, any the more, and soon found his cue.

"Is the canon-priest Lupi here?—My wife has told me he got into the carriage with the bride and bride-groom."

Gossip Grazia then entered unfolding bit by bit the serviette, and out she drew a flask of perfumed water, corked with a tuft of rags.

"The holy-water!—We thought of it for Donna Bianca."

And there they stood calmly waiting in the middle of the drawing-room, husband and wife.

At that moment returned the canon-priest Lupi, to prevent any questions he went straight to the master puffing, red in the face, wiping away his sweat. And of the house, smiling, with a free and easy air.

"Don Gesualdo—if you intend to taste all the good things!—It seems to me the right time now! I've got to say mass at dawn, before going into the country."

"Should I go?" Santo popped out at once. "Shall we set to?"

The bride rose; all the others rose after her and stood in their places waiting for somebody to lead the march. The canon-priest almost waved his arms off, signalling to Santo, then seeing the fellow didn't understand, he prompted, in the deep chest voice he used in church when something went wrong with the service:

"Now then there!—Give your arm to your sister-in-law!"

But the brother-in-law did not feel equal to this. At last they shoved him forward by force. Uncle Limòli meanwhile had gone on with the bride, and the canon-priest muttered in Don Gesualdo's ear:

"Would you believe it?—even the Captain's dame is playing the haughty! She who never fails to turn up where there's a plate to lick. Even she playing the high-and-mighty! As if we didn't know where that grand lady came from!—No! No! What are you doing?"—he cried suddenly darting after neighbour Santo.

That gentleman, having quite lost his patience, silently and deliberately rolled up the sleeves of his coat. By good luck his sister-in-law was talking to her uncle Limòli and didn't notice. The marchese, for his part, was divided in his attention, seeking to avoid Giacalone and Pelagatti, who were bent on serving him at any cost.

"Those two fellows will do some damage or other!" he muttered.

Even Bianca smiled faintly at the remark, and both of them kept away from the table to be out of danger.

"She doesn't want anything!" brother-in-law Don Santo went back saying, as if a great weight had been lifted from his stomach. "As for me, I've offered it her!"

"Not even a glass of Perfect Love?" put in the canon-priest gallantly.—Aunt Cirmena began to laugh, and Santo looked at his brother to see what he was to do.

"Eh! Eh!" added the marchese, with his little cough.—"Eh! Eh!"

"You'll take something, uncle?"

"Thank you, no thank you, Bianca dear.—I've neither teeth nor stomach any more—I'm invalided out. I can only look on—can't do anything else—"

The canon-priest let himself be pressed for a while, then he drew from his pocket a handkerchief as big as a sheet. Meanwhile Aunt Cirmena filled the satchel she carried on her arm, a satchel embroidered with a whole dog, and which held a rare quantity of stuff! The canon-priest, however, who had pockets that went down to his knees, under his cassock, proper saddle-bags, was able to slip out of sight everything he wanted, without attracting attention. Then Bianca with her own hands presented her brother-in-law Santo with a box of sweets.

"For your sister and the children—"

"Say that she sent them herself—her sister-in-law—" added Don Gesualdo, pleased, giving her a smile of gratitude.

They were a little apart, while all the others crowded round the table. So he said to her, with a certain tenderness:

"Well done! I'm glad you are wise, and try to have peace in the family. You don't know what it's been!—My sister especially!—They simply turned me to poison even on my wedding-day."

As she inspired him with confidence, with her gentle face, he was going to tell her all about it, unreservedly, when Aunt Cirmena came to interrupt him, saying:

"Remember the sexton; he's there waiting with his wife."

Don Luca, seeing so many good things coming his way, pretended to be surprised.

"No, sir! We didn't come for the sweets—Don't you trouble yourself, your honour!"

Meanwhile his wife was spreading out a tablecloth that looked as if it belonged to the altar. He, however, to show his gratitude, pretended to be staring into the air, arching his brows with surprise.

"Look, Grazia!—Such furniture!—There's been some money spent here!—" And then the moment Don Gesualdo turned his back he helped as hard as he could to pack up the stuff.

"As if they had the plague!" murmured Donna Sarina, re-entering with her full satchel, alone with the canon-priest Lupi. "Not even her brothers have come! —Did ever you see!—"

"Poor things!—Poor things!" replied the other, waving his hands in front of his forehead as if to say that they no longer had the sense for anything. Then looking round and lowering his voice: "They seemed as if they were weeping for the dead, when we went to fetch the bride! Two loonies, nothing more nor less!—They went looking from room to room, in the dark! Two loonies, nothing more nor less!—But Donna Bianca wanted to do things nicely—if only for human decency's sake!—Now that at last she's induced herself to take the step—"

He made another sign, with his forefinger and his thumb crossed on his mouth. And detecting out of a corner of his eye the re-entrance of Bianca and her husband into the drawing-room, he said loudly, as if following on from what he was previously saying, showing his full handkerchief:

"These are my dues!—fruits of the sacred office—"

The sexton's wife, who had not noticed the bride, put in:

"They are still there, both of them, standing at the window in the dark, looking into the square where there isn't a soul!—like two mummies, for all the world!"

Donna Bianca heard these words as she passed.

"Best of health to you!" interrupted the sexton, seeing the lady of the house. "It'll be a feast for those children when we get home! Five little ones, Donna Bianca!—"

Then turning to his wife who was going off staggering with that other burden on her stomach:

"Health and boy-children! Property you've got already! Now we'll pray to the Lord to give you children.—We want to see you like Grazia in nine months' time—"

The marchese, to cut short this farewell oration:

"Very well! Good evening, my dear Don Luca!"

In the other room, hardly had the guests left than there rose the deuce of a commotion. The neighbours, the house-folk, Brasi Camauro, Nanni l'Orbo, the family crowd, pounced upon the remains of the refreshments, falling out over the sweet-meats, tearing them from each other's hands, coming to blows with one another. And neighbour Santo, under the pretence of defending the stuff, laid hands on whatever he could seize and stuffed it wherever he was able, in his mouth, in his pockets, in his shirt. Nunzio, Burgio's boy, had come in like a cat and had clambered on to the table, and there he raged with kicks and blows, screaming like one possessed, the other children creeping underneath. Don Gesualdo, enraged, wanted to rush in and end this uproar with a stick: but the marchese his uncle held him by the arm:

"Leave them alone—so far!—"

Aunt Cirmena, who had at least enjoyed herself just a little, planted herself right in the middle of the room, staring people in the face as if to say it was time for them to go now. And at that juncture the sexton came running back, panting, with an air of great mystery:

"There's all the village!—down there in the street, watching! Baron Zacco, the Margarones, even the wife of Mendola—all the leading gentry of the place! Your wedding is making a stir, Don Gesualdo!—"

And he went off as he had come, in a scuffle, fatuous.

Aunt Cirmena murmured:

"How annoying!—If only there was another way out!—"

The canon-priest, however, curious, wanted to go and see. Right opposite, at the corner of San Sebastiano, there was a group of people; you could see white frocks showing in the dark of the street. Others were passing slowly on tiptoe, close to the wall, looking up. You could hear people talking in low tones, and stifled laughter, and furtive footsteps. Two people who were coming back from the direction of Santa Maria di Gesù stopped, seeing the balcony doors open. And everybody scuffled away hither and thither. Only Ciolla remained, pretending to be going about his own business and singing:

"Love, oh love, what hast thou made me do? . . ."

Donna Sarina and Marchese Limòli had also drawn near to the balcony. Then the latter said:

"You'll be able to go now, Donna Sarina. There's nobody left below there—"

Aunt Cirmena went off like a spring:

"I'm not afraid, Don Alfonso! I do what I choose

and please! I'm here to take the mother's place to
Bianca . . . since there's no nearer relation. We
can't leave the bride as if she was a waif and stray—
for the sake of the family decorum, if for nothing
else—"

"Ah? Ah?"—mocked the marchese.

Donna Sarina turned on him, restraining her voice
with difficulty:

"Don't pretend you don't know it as well as I do,
Don Alfonso!—You know it better!—It behoves
you to, since you're one of the family. We must do
it for the sake of other folks—if not for her own
sake!"—And continuing still to hold forth, she passed
through the door of the nuptial chamber.

"All right, all right! Don't get angry. It seems
we'd better be going!—Hey, hey! canon!—Methinks
it's time we went!—Practise a little prudence—!"

"Ah! Ah!—Ah! Ah!—" clucked the canon-
priest.

"Good-night, my children. I give you my blessing,
that costs nothing—"

Bianca had become pale as a washed-out rag. She
also rose, a slight tremor showing in the muscles of
her chin; her beautiful blue eyes seemed bewildered,
her new dress hampered her.

"Uncle!—listen, uncle!—" she stammered. And
she drew him aside to speak to him in an undertone,
vehemently.

"They are mad," interrupted the marchese loudly,
growing heated also. "Fit to be shut up! If I've got
to be born again, I'll say to them too, I want to be
called Master Alfonso Limòli—"

"Bravo!" mocked the canon-priest. "I like to hear
you say that."

"Good-night! Good-night! Don't think of it! I'll go to them to-morrow morning.—And in nine months' time, don't forget, I want to be invited again for the christening. Canon Lupi and I—only us two.—There won't even be any need of Cousin Cirmena."

"Not much company and a happy time," concluded the other.

Don Gesualdo accompanied them to the door, annoyed inside himself by the compliments of the canon-priest, who kept on telling him that he'd done things in style:

"Pity all the guests didn't come! They'd have seen that you spend like Cæsar. I'm surprised at Madame Sganci! And Baroness Rubiera would have been pleased to see how you respect her niece—that you're not one of the close-fisted sort—since in a little while you're to be partners—"

"Eh! Eh!" replied Don Gesualdo, who felt his ill-spent money boil up again in him at that moment. "There's time! there's time! A lot of water has got to flow first under the bridge that isn't in existence any more. Tell her so, my lady the baroness."

"What? What? It was an understood thing? You were to be partners?"

"My partners are these here," repeated Don Gesualdo, slapping his purse. "I shouldn't like to think the Baroness Rubiera was going to be ashamed of having me associate with her—and you can tell her so!"

"He is right!" said the marchese, stopping halfway down the stairs. "He's got the *amour propre* of his own money, deuce take it!—Cousin Rubiera might have condescended. She wouldn't have turned her blood by such a trifle, not she."

"Who knows!—Who knows why she didn't come!
—There must be some other reason. . . . And then,
business—that's another pair of shoes.—Just think it
over! You'll want some support! Else you'll have
them all enemies!"

"All enemies—that's nice! Why?"

"Because of your money, what else! Because you
can put your finger also in the pie! Then you're one
of their relations now!—that's a slap in the face, my
dear chap! You've given them a slap in the face, all
the lot!"

"Do you know what I've got to tell you?" shrilled
the marchese, lifting up his head—"That if I hadn't
my annuity as a Knight of Malta, to save me from
starving to death, I should have to give them a slap
in the face as well, all my noble relations—I should
have to go as a road-sweeper—"

And he went off grumbling to himself.

"Don Gesualdo—" said Nanni l'Orbo, peeping
out of the kitchen—"there's the servants here to
kiss the hand of the mistress, if everybody has
gone——"

"Hurry up with them," replied the latter, irritated.

At first they crowded on the threshold like a flock
of sheep; then, after Nanni l'Orbo, they filed one behind the other, a silly smile on their faces, cap in hand,
the women curtseying to the ground as in church, huddled in their mantles.

"This is Diodata," said Nanni l'Orbo. "A
poor orphan whom the master has kept out of
charity—"

"Yes, my lady!—Best of health to you!—" And
Diodata couldn't say another word.

"A real large heart, has Don Gesualdo!" added

Nanni l'Orbo, getting vehement. "He has given her a dowry! God bless him for it."

Don Gesualdo was putting out the lights. He turned to them, all in his new clothes, so that Diodata didn't dare even to lift her eyes to him, and he said:

"All right. Are you satisfied?"

"Yessir," replied Nanni l'Orbo, looking tenderly at Diodata—"Pleased as pie!—and she can say the same!"

"Neighbour Nanni has had his eye on those silver shillings for a long time, so they shouldn't escape him," added Brasi Camauro. "He was born with his cap on."

"He is marrying Diodata," Don Gesualdo told his wife. "I am marrying her to him."

The keeper added further information, laughing:

"They were running after one another! I had to keep watch over them as well!—The master will have to give me a bit of something for this extra job, which wasn't in the bargain!"

A general laugh broke out, because neighbour Carmine was usually being funny! The girl, red as fire, gave him a glance like a wild animal.

"It's not true; no, sir; no, Don Gesualdo!—"

"Yes! yes! and Brasi Camauro as well! and Giacalone, when he came for the cart!—All in love and all in agreement, all together!"

The laughter had no end; Nanni l'Orbo, the leader, holding his sides. Only Diodata, red as fire, protesting with all her might:

"No, sir!—it's not true!—how can you say it, neighbour Carmine?—have you no conscience?—"

Donna Sarina appeared once more in the doorway,

her arms crossed, not uttering a word; but the flowers shaking on her head spoke for her.

"Enough now!" said the master. "Go along, it's late."

They saluted once more, bowing gawkily, stammering confusedly in chorus, jostling one another as they went out, and finally departing with a stamping of feet like a drove of cattle. Hardly outside the door they began to laugh and make game among themselves; Brasi Camauro and Pelagatti charging into one another; Nanni l'Orbo and neighbour Carmine bandying bad language and atrocious insults back and forth, their arms round one another's necks, like two brothers grown merry with wine. A roystering that made even Don Gesualdo himself laugh.

"They're like animals!" he said, coming in again. "Don't take any notice, Bianca."

"One minute!" squealed Aunt Cirmena, pushing him back with her hands almost as if he had wanted to do her violence. "You can't come in now. Out with you! Out with you!"

And she shut the door in his face.

Diodata came running back in distress at that moment, tears in her eyes.

"Don Gesualdo!—They won't let me go my way!—Can you hear them, down there?—neighbour Nanni and all the others—"

"Well? What's it matter? Isn't he going to be your husband?—"

"Yessir!—He says that's why!—that he's the master. They won't let me go in peace!—all of them!"

"Wait! Wait while I get a stick!"

"No! no!" yelled Nanni from the street. "We're going home. Nobody will touch her."

"You hear? Nobody will touch you. Go on then—Now what are you doing?"

She, standing two stairs lower, had secretly taken his hand and was kissing it like a real faithful, affectionate dog.

"Good-bye! Good-bye!"

"Now the snivelling begins again!" he snorted. "I haven't a moment's peace, this evening."

"No, sir—without snivelling—All health to your honour!—and to your wife as well!—I only wanted to kiss your hand for the last time!—My legs are trembling a bit—You've been so good to me, your honour!—"

"Right! right!—You be gay as well!—It's supposed to be a joyful day, to-day!—You've found a good husband also. He won't let you starve—And when bad times come, remember there's always my barn open . . . Aren't you satisfied? What?"

She replied that she was satisfied, nodding repeatedly, since she had a knot in her throat and couldn't speak.

"All right!—now go and be content—without thinking of anything, you know—without thinking of anything!—"

As she looked at him in a certain fashion, with her hurt eyes which seemed to read also the secret hurt in his heart, he began to shout so as not to think of it, almost as if he were in a temper:

"And without looking for the skin in the egg!—without thinking of this, that and the other.—The Lord is for everybody—Even you who are a poor foundling, the Lord has helped you! And in case of accidents, there is me here! I'll do all I can—I haven't got a stone for a heart, no I haven't! And you know it! Go then, go; and go contented!"

But Diodata, who had turned away and stood leaning her breast against the balcony, felt she would die of heart-break, and could not suppress the sobs that shook her from head to foot. Then her master burst out swearing:

"Saints and blessings!—Saints and blessings!"

At that moment Aunt Cirmena appeared at the head of the stairs, her shawl over her head, the satchel on her arm, and her eyes wet with tears, as became her rôle of mother which she had to play for once.

"Here I am then, Don Gesualdo! here I am!—" And she stretched out her arms like a crucifix to fling them round his neck. "I've no need to preach to you! —You are a man of sense—Poor Bianca!—I'm so upset, just look!"

She looked for her cambric handkerchief in her satchel, among all the stuff it was crammed with, and she wiped her eyes. Then she kissed the bridegroom again, wiping her mouth after with that selfsame handkerchief, and called her servant who was waiting below with her lantern.

"Don Camillo! Light up, it's time to be going. Don Camillo? Hello! What are you doing? are you asleep?"

From the street Ciolla answered, passing and repassing with the guitar:

"Love, oh love, what hast thou made me do? . . ."

And other impudent wretches went behind him, making an accompaniment of grunts.

"No!" exclaimed Aunt Cirmena planting herself in

front of her nephew, as if to prevent him from doing something dangerous. "Don't take any notice . . . they are drunk—scum of the earth bursting with envy! Better go to your wife. I beg you to be careful with her—she's not to be handled the same as other girls. We are made of a different clay—all the family. I feel I'm leaving my own blood in your hands now! I never had a girl of my own—I've never been through anything like this before! I feel dreadfully upset!— No! no! Don't bother about me! I shall get quieter —You, Don Camillo, go forward with the light—"

He turned away.—"Such a lot of cackle! Are we husband and wife by now, or aren't we?"—Going into the nuptial chamber he heaved a heavy sigh.

"Ah, pray God, it's over! It's taken some doing— but it's finished, pray God!—I wouldn't do it again, I swear to heaven, if it had to be done afresh."

He wanted to make his bride laugh, to put her in a bit of a good humour, so that they might be easier together, have more confidence in one another, as should be between husband and wife. But she, seated before the mirror with her back to the door, started, hearing him enter, and her face flamed. Afterwards she seemed more livid than before, and her delicate features seemed to sharpen all at once.

Just as Aunt Cirmena had said. A girl who quivered at nothing, and made your hands and your tongue go confused. It exasperated him, completely! that wedding day that hadn't given him one single good moment.

"Hey?—Why don't you say something?—What's amiss?—"

He remained a moment embarrassed, not knowing

himself what to say, humiliated in his fine new clothes, among his furniture that had cost him an eye out of his head.

"Listen!—if that's how it is—if you're going to take it like that, you as well—Then good-night! I'll go and sleep on a chair, as God's above!"

She stammered some unintelligible words, a gurgle of timid and confused sounds, and bent her head obediently, to begin to take out her tortoise-shell comb, with delicate hands somewhat roughened at the tips, hands of a poor girl used to doing all the housework.

"Bravo! Bravo! That's the way for me!—If we get on together and you do as I tell you, our home will flourish—flourish rarely. Did you see this evening, how they wouldn't come to the wedding?—So much money thrown away!—Did you see how I swallowed my spleen, and laughed?—He laughs longest who laughs last!—Come now, come now, why do your hands tremble?—aren't I your husband now?—in spite of the envious ones!—What are you afraid of?— Hark!—that Ciolla!—he'll make me do something I shouldn't do!—"

She murmured again a few indistinct words, which died on her livid lips once more, and then for the first time she raised her eyes to him, those gentle blue eyes which gave him promise of the loving, obedient wife they had told him about. Then he was glad, and with a broad laugh which opened his face and his heart, he replied:

"Let him sing. I don't care now about Ciolla—him or any of them! They are bursting with envy because my affairs are going full sail, thanks to God. You won't repent, no, never, what you've done!—You are

good-hearted——You haven't got the stuck-up pride of
the rest of your people——"

An unusual tenderness swelled his heart, as he helped
her to comb her hair. Actually his big hands helping
a Trao, and feeling themselves become light as feathers
among her fine hair! His eyes kindled on the lace that
veiled her white, delicate shoulders, on the short,
puffed sleeves that almost gave her wings. The golden
down that bloomed on the last nodes of her spine
pleased him, as did the scars left by the inexpert vacci-
nation on her slim, white arms, and the little hands
that had worked like his own, and that trembled now
under his eyes, and her bent neck that flushed and
paled, all those humble signs of privation that
brought her near to him.

"I want you to fare better than a queen, if we get
on together and you do as I tell you! I want to put
all the place under your feet! All those swine who
laugh now and mock us behind our backs!——You'll
see! You'll see!——He's got a good stomach, has
Mastro-don Gesualdo!——able to store up for years
and years anything he wants to——and good legs as well
——to take him when he wants to go.——You are good
and beautiful! a delicate fine thing! a delicate fine
thing you are!——"

She shrank her head between her shoulders, like a
trembling dove that is just going to be taken.

"Now I like you really, I do!——I'm afraid to touch
you with my hands. I've got rough hands because I've
worked so much——I'm not ashamed to say it——I've
worked hard to get to where I am.——Who could have
told me?——I'm not ashamed, no!——You are beautiful
and good! . . . I want to make you like a queen——
Everybody under your feet!——these little feet!——You

wanted to come yourself—with these little feet—into my house. . . . The mistress!—my own beautiful lady!—Look, you make me talk nonsense!—"

But she was listening elsewhere. She seemed to be looking in the mirror, far off, far away.

"What are you thinking about? about Ciolla still? —I'll go and end in prison, the first night of my married life!"

"No—" she interrupted stammering, with a faint voice. "No—listen—I must tell you something—"

She seemed as if she hadn't a drop of blood left in her veins, she was so pale and broken. She moved her trembling lips two or three times.

"Tell me then," he replied—"everything you want. I want you to be content as well—"

As it was July, and very hot, he took off his coat, waiting. She drew back brusquely, as if she had received a blow full in the chest, and she went stiff, deathly white, with black rings round her eyes.

"Speak, speak up!—Tell it me in my ear—here so that nobody can hear—"

He laughed quite pleased, with his broad laugh, in the new rush that began to make his head turn, stammering and talking at random, in his shirt-sleeves, pressing her delicate body on his heart that beat right in his throat, her body that he felt shudder and almost rebel; and as he lifted her head gently he felt his arms fall. She wiped her feverish eyes, her face all painfully contracted.

"Ah!—it's a nice thing!—Aunt Cirmena was right! —A rare pleasure!—After all the struggles and all the bitterness in my mouth!—all the money spent!— We could be so happy here—two people who were fond of one another!—Not a bit! not even this do I

get! Not even on my wedding day, God love us!—
Anyhow tell me what's the matter!"

"Don't mind me—I am too much upset—"

"Ah! that Ciolla!—again!—As God's above I'll
throw a flower-pot down on him this time!—I want to
give him a treat as well, on my wedding night!"

SECOND PART

SECOND PART

I

"One guinea fifteen!—One!—two!—"

"Two guineas!—" answered Don Gesualdo impassively.

Baron Zacco got up, red as if he was having an apoplectic fit. He grasped around looking for his hat, and made as if to depart. But from the threshold he turned rushing back, foam at his mouth, almost beside himself, and yelling:

"Two five!—"

And he stood panting in front of the writing-table of the judges, annihilating his opponent with looks of thunder. Don Filippo Margarone, Peperito and the rest of the Town Council presiding at the auction of the communal lands, talked in each other's ears. Don Gesualdo took a pinch of snuff, quietly continuing to cast up his accounts in his pocketbook, that lay open on his knee. Then he raised his head, and retorted in a calm voice:

"Three guineas!"

The baron became suddenly as limp as a washed-out rag. He blew his nose; jammed his hat on his head, and bolted through the door exclaiming:

"Ah!—when it's like that!—since they make it!—a personal attack!—Good-day to the rest of you!"

The sworn-councillors fidgeted on their seats as if they had colic. The canon-priest Lupi got up suddenly and ran to say a word in Don Gesualdo's ear, passing his arm round his neck.

"No, sir!" replied the latter in a clear voice. "I've nothing to do with such rubbish. I attend to my own interests, and no more."

A murmur ran through the audience who were attending at the auction. All the other bidders had drawn back, dismayed, sticking their tongues out to the full length. Then the young Baron Rubiera rose to his feet, throwing his chest out importantly, stroking his scanty beard, not heeding the signs Don Filippo was making him from the distance, and let fall his own offer, with the sleepy air of one to whom money does not matter.

"Three guineas and three—!—I say it!"

"For God's love," whispered Lawyer Neri in his ear, pulling his coat-tails. "Baron, Baron, don't let us do anything mad."

"Three guineas and three!" repeated the young baron without heeding, giving a triumphant look around.

"Three five."

Don Nini went red, and opened his mouth to answer; but the lawyer put his hand over the open mouth. Margarone deemed that the moment had come to take on a presidential air.

"Don Gesualdo!—We are not here to play about! —You may have money—I won't deny it—but this is a considerable sum—for one who was carrying stones like a navvy yesterday—if I may say so without giving offence. To be sure: *Mind what I am, not what I was* says the proverb. But the parish must have its guarantee. Consider well what you're doing!—About five hundred square furlongs—That would make— that would make—" And he put on his spectacles, scribbling figures underneath figures in columns.

"I know how much it makes," replied Mastro-don Gesualdo, laughing. "I thought it out while I was carrying stones. Ah, Don Filippo, sir, you don't know what a satisfaction it is to have got as far as this, to be face to face here with your honour, and all these other patrons of mine, each of us speaking up for himself and doing his own business."

Don Filippo put his spectacles down on the papers; turned a stupefied look on his colleagues to right and to left, and remained ignominiously silent. In the crowd thronging the doorway arose a tumult. Master Nunzio Motta wanted to come in at any cost, to lay hands on his son who was throwing money away in this fashion. Burgio tried to stop him. Margarone rang the bell for silence.

"Very good!—yes, very good!—But, however, the law says—"

As he was trying to get on with his stammering, that yellow-faced Canali suggested him an answer, while pretending to blow his nose.

"Of course!—Who is your guarantee?—The law says—"

"I am my own guarantee," replied Don Gesualdo putting on the table a little sack of guineas which he fetched from under his hunting-jacket.

Then all the eyes opened. Don Filippo was dumfounded.

"Gentlemen all!" squealed Baron Zacco re-entering infuriated. "Gentlemen!—look at that!—look what we've come to!"

"Three five!" repeated Don Gesualdo, returning to the attack. "I offer three guineas five shillings a furlong for the tax on the public lands. Continue the auction, Don Filippo, sir."

The young Baron Rubiera went off like a spring, all his blood in his face. Chains wouldn't have held him now.

"Four guineas!" he stammered, beside himself. "I make a bid of four guineas a furlong."

"Take him out! Take him away!" squealed Don Filippo, half rising to his feet. Several people were clapping their hands. But Don Nini persisted, white as his shirt now.

"Yessir! four guineas a furlong! Write my offer down, secretary!"

"Halt!" cried the lawyer, raising both his hands in the air. "For the legality of the offer!—I make my reservations—"

And he threw himself on the young baron, as if they were having a fight. There, in the balcony-opening, face to face, with his eyes starting out of his head, breathing fiery breath into the other's face:

"Baron, my dear sir—when you want to throw money out of the window!—go and play cards!—play with the money out of your own pocket only!—"

Don Nini snorted worse than a mad bull. Peperito had signalled the canon-priest Lupi to come to him, and they were confabbing in an undertone, leaning over the writing-table, shaking their heads like two hens pecking in the same spot. The canon-priest was so upset that his hands trembled on the papers. The cavaliere took him by the arm and they went to join the lawyer and the young baron, who were disputing excitedly in a corner of the hall. Don Nini began to give in, his face lax and his legs weak. The canon-priest then made a sign to Don Gesualdo also to approach.

"No," winked the latter, without moving.

"But listen—it's that affair of the deposit-money.— The bridge has gone, joy go with it!—We might manage to arrange that affair of the deposit-money now—"

"No," repeated Don Gesualdo. He was like a stone wall. "The bridge business—a trifle in comparison."

"Boor! obstinate mule! cuckold!" the baron began to inveigh once more, *sotto voce*.

Don Filippo, after the first burst of agitation, had sat down again, wiping his perspiring face heavily. While the canon-priest was talking in a subdued voice to Don Gesualdo, the lawyer began making signs from the distance. Don Filippo leaned over to speak in Canali's ear. Stealthily, in a falsetto voice, the auctioneer reiterated:

"The last offer for the parish lands! At four guineas a furlong!—One!—two!—"

"One moment, gentlemen!" interrupted Don Gesualdo. "Who guarantees this last offer?"

At this remark they were all left open-mouthed. Don Filippo opened and shut his own mouth without being able to bring forth a word. At last he answered:

"Baron Rubiera's offer!—Eh? Eh?"

"Yessir. Who is guarantee for Baron Rubiera?"

The lawyer threw himself on Don Nini, who seemed to want to commit murder. Peperito twisted about as if somebody had given him a box on the ear. The very canon-priest was dumbfounded. Margarone stammered overwhelmed:

"Who is guarantee for Baron Rubiera?—who is guarantee?"

All at once he changed his tone, turning it into a joke: "Who is guarantee for Baron Rubiera?—Ah! ah!—Oh lovely! that's a good one!—" And many of the others following his example, held their sides with laughter.

"Yes, sir," repeated Don Gesualdo imperturbably. "Who is guarantee for him? The property belongs to his mother."

At these words the laughter ceased, and Don Filippo began to stutter again. People crowded the doorway like at the theatre. The canon-priest, who seemed paler under his four-days' beard, pulled his companion by the coat. The lawyer had succeeded in driving the young baron against the wall, while the latter, in the midst of all that turmoil, vomited forth:

"Fool!—booby!—woman-saver!"

"The baron's word,—" said Don Filippo at length. "Baron Rubiera's word is worth more than your guineas!—Don—Don—"

"Don Filippo," interrupted the other without losing his fine calm. "I have witnesses here to put everything down in the report."

"All right. Everything shall go into the report!— Write that the young Baron Rubiera has made the offer on his mother's account."

"Well and good!" added Don Gesualdo.—"Then at that rate write down that I offer four guineas five shillings a furlong."

"Madman! Assassin! Enemy of God!"—came the scream of Master Nunzio from the crowd in the other room.

And then there was an uproar. The lawyer and Peperito pushed the young baron out of the door, while that young man roared and threw his arms about. On the other hand, the canon-priest, convulsed, flung himself on Don Gesualdo, and clasped him close, almost sitting on his knees, his arms round his neck, conjuring him desperately in a low voice and with fiery words, pouring himself down his ear, shaking him by the lapels of his coat as if he wanted to tear him in two to make him hear reason.

"A madness!—What are we thinking of, dear Don Gesualdo?"

"Don't be afraid, Canon. I've made my reckonings. I don't lose my head, I don't."

Don Filippo Margarone had been ringing the bell five minutes, for a glass of water. His colleagues also wiped their brows, done up. Don Gesualdo alone remained seated at his post like a stone, near his little sack of guineas. At a certain moment, out of the tempest in the other room burst Master Nunzio Motta into the hall, glaring wildly, trembling with rage, his white hair bristling on his head, towing behind him his son-in-law Burgio who was trying to hold him by the sleeve of his coat, like a madman.

"Don Filippo, sir! am I his father, or aren't I?— do I rule, or don't I?—If my son Gesualdo is mad!— if he wants to ruin us all!—there is the public force, Don Filippo, sir!—Send for Don Liccio Papa!—"

Speranza, in the doorway, her baby at her breast, was tearing her hair and screaming as if she was being slaughtered.

"For the love of God! For the love of God!" pleaded the canon-priest, running from one to another.

"The money for the bridge!—He wants to ruin me! —Enemy of his own father, he is!" howled Master Nunzio.

"Was it your money, maybe?" the canon-priest then let out. "Wasn't it the blood of your son?—hadn't he earned it with his own toil?"

Everybody was standing up shouting. Canali was

heard squealing louder than the rest, to quiet Don Nini.
Baron Zacco, absolutely having lost heart, was leaning
with his shoulders against the wall and his hat on the
back of his head. The lawyer had come down in a
rush, taking the stairs four at a time, to run to the
Baroness Rubiera. On the stairs was a come-and-go
of inquisitive persons; people arriving every minute,
attracted by the uproar they heard in the Town Hall.
From the square Santo Motta was pointing at the
balcony and shouting that he didn't want to hear anything about his brother's extravagance. Even Donna
Marianna had appeared, with her little umbrella, shading her eyes with her hand.

"As God's above!—I made him, and I'll unmake
him!" howled the old man Motta, become ferocious.

"Make way!—make way!" cried somebody out of
the crowd.

Appeared Don Giuseppe Barabba, shaking a letter
aloft.

"Canon! Canon Lupi!"

The latter pushed forward with his elbows.

"All right," he said, after he had read the letter.
"Tell Madam Sganci all right, I'll be with her in a
minute."

Barabba ran on this errand into the other room.
The throng almost suffocated him. The canon-priest
got a rip in his cassock while the baron stretched
out his hand to read the note. Canali, Barabba and
Don Nini quarrelled among themselves. Then Canali
began to cry: "Make way! Make way!" and he
pushed smiling towards Don Gesualdo.

"The young Baron Rubiera is here and would like
to shake hands with you."

"At your service! At your service entirely! I'm not angry with anybody."

"That's what I say!—What the deuce!—Now that you're relations!—"

And pulling the young baron forward by his coat he brought them together in an embrace, almost making them kiss one another. Then Baron Zacco came running to throw himself also into their arms, sparks flying from his eyes.

"Let the devil be damned!—I'm not made of bronze!—what nonsense!—"

At that point the lawyer joined them. First he went to glance at the secretary's report, and then began to clap his hands.

"Hurrah for peace!—Hurrah for concord!—I've always told you!—"

"Look what your aunt Madam Marianna Sganci writes me!" said the canon-priest, quite moved, holding out the open letter to Don Gesualdo. And turning to the balcony he waved the sheet of paper in the air, like a white flag; while Madam Sganci replied with nods of her head from the balcony.

"Peace!—Peace!—You are all one family!"

Canali ran to lay hold of Master Nunzio, Burgio, even Santo Motta in his shirt sleeves, to thrust them into the arms of their new relations. The canon-priest went so far as to embrace Gossip Speranza and her infant. The very stones could have wept.

"For the wife's sake—you are cousins—"

"It's true," added Don Ninì, still rather red in the face. "We grew up together, Bianca and I—like brother and sister—"

"Dear Don Nunzio!—you remember the lime-kiln —near Fontanarossa?—"

The old fox shrugged his shoulders, to shake off the
heavy hand of Baron Zacco, and replied rudely:

"My name's Master Nunzio, Sir Baron! I've not
got my son's swelled head."

"And why?—For why you want to quarrel? Who
wouldn't enjoy so much money thrown away?" concluded Canali fervidly.

"Madness! Childishness!—Blood went to his head!
—The hot day!—A fool's obstinacy—a misunder-
standing.—Now it's done! Let us go! Don't let
us set the whole place laughing!—" And the lawyer
tried to lead them all away, all the lot.

"Just a moment!" interrupted Don Gesualdo. "The
candle is still alight. Let us see first if they have
written down my last offer."

"What, what do you mean? What are you talking
about?—What do you mean?—Are we going to start
all over again?"—the din rose up once more.—"Aren't
we friends any more? Aren't we relations?"

But Don Gesualdo insisted, worse than a mule.

"Yes, sir, we are relations. But we've come here
for the tax-auction of the communal lands. I have
made an offer of four guineas five shillings a furlong—"

"Boor! Cuckold—!"

In the midst of that bustle Don Filippo was forced
to sit down again on his seat, snorting. He emptied
the glass of water at one draught, and rang the bell.

"Gentleman!" shouted the secretary. "The last
offer—at four guineas five—"

Everybody had gone to discuss and shout about in
the other room, leaving Don Gesualdo alone before
the writing-table. In vain the canon-priest breathed
into his ear:

"Don't take it on, no!—They have come to an understanding among themselves—"

"At four guineas five shillings a furlong!—final offer!—"

"Don Gesualdo! Don Gesualdo!" shouted the lawyer as if he wanted to bring the hall down.

Then they all re-entered in procession: Baron Zacco fanning himself with his hat, the canon-priest and Canali talking together in a low voice; Don Ninì more restive, in the rear of the others. The lawyer made a circular gesture with his arms to group them all round him.

"Don Gesualdo!—Hark here!"

He threw a conspirator's glance round, and lowered his voice:

"A serious proposal!"—and he made another significant pause. "First of all, the deposit-money—a large sum!—The misfortune happened as it did—but through no fault of yours, Don Gesualdo—nor of yours, Master Nunzio.—It is only fair that you should not lose this money!—We'll arrange the matter!—You, Baron Zacco, sir, you regret relinquishing lands which have been in your family for forty years?—Very well!—Baroness Rubiera now wants her share also, does she?—she has more than three thousand head of cattle on her hands.—Once more, very well!—Don Gesualdo, here, has money to spend, for his part; he would like to speculate in the lease.—Then very well and good! Divide the lands among you three—without quarrels, without being exacting or obstinate, without falling out for other people's advantage.—to whose advantage is it, after all?—the commune's! That means nobody's!—Let us throw over the auction —I'll find a reason to give!—In a week's time we open

the sale afresh, at the original price; and we make one
single offer.—Not I—nor these gentlemen either!—
The canon-priest Lupi!—in your name, Don Gesualdo
—And we will trust one another—We are gentlemen!
One offer only at the original price; and the lands shall
be knocked down to you without a farthing's increase.
Only a little brokerage for me and the Canon.—And
the rest you divide among you three, fair and square—
in friendship and harmony. Do you like it? Are we
agreed?"

"No sir," replied Don Gesualdo. "I'll take all the
lands myself."

Just as the others were all pleased approval, nodding their heads to the triumphant glance which the
lawyer cast around him, came this answer like a bucket
of cold water. At first the lawyer was left dumbfounded; then he turned on his heel and went off humming a tune. Don Ninì bolted without saying a word.
The baron this time pretended to put his hat on for
good. The canon-priest himself jumped up viperishly:

"Then I've done with you too!—If you want to
crack your cranium, the balcony's there, wide and open!
—They offer you a good arrangement! They hold
out their hand to you!—I've done with you, I leave
you to yourself, as God's above!"

But Don Gesualdo persisted, with his foolish-seem-
ing little smile, the only one who didn't lose his head
in the turmoil.

"You're a fool," he replied, smiling continually.

The canon-priest opened his eyes and became docile
again, wanting to see what that devil of a Mastro-don
Gesualdo was at now.

The lawyer, wary, was able to control himself

sooner than the rest, and came back with a smile on his lips and his snuff-box in his hand.

"So then?—you want them all!"

"Eh! eh!—What else are we here for!" replied the other.

Neri offered him the open snuff-box, and replied in a low voice, in a tone of cordial confidence:

"What the devil will you do with them?—nearly five hundred square furlongs of land?—"

Don Gesualdo shrugged his shoulders.

"Dear lawyer, do I try to poke my nose into your old books, eh?"

"If it's like that, Don Gesualdo, then hark—we'll discuss it between us. We won't make a point of anything. We won't talk of friendship. We'll stick to business—"

At every phrase he bowed his head first to left and then to right, with a cadenced manner that was meant to be very persuasive.

"If you want all the land, we'll make you pay double, and there's half your gains gone in smoke at once—without counting the risks—bad seasons!—Leave us our skins, dear Don Gesualdo. Stop our mouths!—Because we've got teeth, and we can bite! We shall be running to break our necks, we others and you as well!—"

Don Gesualdo shook his head, grinning, as if to say: "No sir! Go and break your necks, you others by yourselves.—" He kept repeating:

"Do I try to poke my nose into your old books?"

Then seeing that the lawyer was going green with bile, he wanted to make a concession from his side.

"I will explain you the mystery in two words, since I see you speak to me with your heart in your hand.

I will take the lease of the communal lands—and of the County lands, even—all the lot, you understand, Master Notary?—Then I command prices and harvests, you understand?—I tell you because you're a friend, and because to do what I say wants a great deal of capital in hand, and a heart as big as the plains of Santa-margherita, dear notary. That is why I will push the auction to where you others can't come up. But mind! at a certain point, if it doesn't suit me, I shall draw back, and leave you with a weight on your shoulders that'll break your backs—"

"And this is the end?—"

"Eh? eh?—Do you like it?"

The lawyer turned this way and that, as if he was looking for something on the ground, thrust his hat on his head definitely, and turned away.

"Good-bye to the rest of you!—We're going!— We've nothing more to do."

The canon-priest, who had listened open-mouthed, pressed himself upon his partner with enthusiasm the moment they were left alone.

"What a stroke, eh? Don Gesualdo! What a deep one you are!—I shall have my share, shan't I?"

Don Gesualdo nodded reassuringly to the canon-priest, and said to Margarone:

"Don Filippo, sir, let us get on—"

"I'm not going an inch further," Margarone replied finally, in a rage.—"The law says—There's no competition any more!—I don't have any guarantee!—I must consult my colleagues." And he began to gather the papers together in frenzy and rage.

"Ah! That's the way, is it?—that's how you behave?—All right! Oh right you are! We'll talk about this later, Don Filippo.—A memorial to His

Majesty!—" So the canon-priest, with his cloak on his arm like a Roman orator, perorated the cause of his friend, threatening. Don Gesualdo on the other hand, calmer, took up his money again and the pocket-book full of figures.

"I shall be always here, Don Filippo, for when you open the auction again."

"But gentlemen!—but just look!—what we've come to!" grumbled Margarone.

On the steps of the Town Hall, and in all the village, was a row going on, when it was known what an attempt had been made to take out of Baron Zacco's hands the communal lands that had been in his family for forty years, and the price to which the lands had risen. People crowded to the door, to see Mastro-don Gesualdo pass by.

"Just think of it, my sirs,—what we've come to!"

Cool as a glass of water, that Mastro-don Gesualdo, going home with his hands in his pockets. He'd got more money in his pockets than hairs on his head!— and he was too much for the first gentlemen in the place!—

In his ante-chamber he found Don Giuseppe Barabba, waiting in livery.

"Don Gesualdo, sir, there's my mistress inside, paying you a visit—yessir—"

Donna Mariannina was seated in all her finery on the silk sofa, under the big mirror, in the fine yellow drawing-room.

"My dear nephew, you've been going it strong! You've raised old Harry in the whole family! Really! —The wife of Cousin Zacco came to show me her bruises!—The baron seems to have gone off his head! —He starts raving to everybody he meets. So does

Cousin Rubiera as well—she says it's a piece of treachery!—that the canon-priest Lupi had brought into agreement and sympathy, and then all at once—. It is true, my dear nephew? I came on purpose to have a chat with Bianca—Come, Bianca, you help me. Let us try and set it right. You, Don Gesualdo, you will do this kind act for your wife's sake. Eh? What do you say to it?"

Bianca looked timidly first at her then at her husband. She was curled in a corner of the sofa, her arms in her lap, and round her head the silk kerchief she had put on hastily to receive her aunt. She opened her mouth to say something, made bashful by Donna Mariannina, who kept on pressing her:

"Eh? What do you say? It's your business as well now."

Bianca turned to look at her husband, and was silent, embarrassed. But he relieved her of all doubt.

"I say no," he replied simply.

"Ah? Ah? Is that what you say?"

Donna Mariannina herself remained open-mouthed for an instant. Then she became as red as a cock.

"Ah, you say no?—Excuse me—It's not my affair. I came to talk to my niece, because I don't like quarrels and disagreements between relations.—With your brothers as well, Bianca—I don't know what I haven't done, to try and persuade them—specially Don Diego, who is so obstinate! A calamity, a real affliction!—"

"What can you expect!" replied Don Gesualdo. "All our bargains aren't good ones. Me as well, if you did but know. I don't speak of the wife I have taken, no! I don't repent it!—Good, careful, obedient —I tell you so, in front of her.—But as for the rest— we'll leave it alone!"

"You say well, we'll leave it alone. So I just came to have a talk with Bianca, because I know you are fond of her. Now you're husband and wife, as God has chosen. And she is mistress as well—"

"So she is, she's the mistress. But I am her husband—"

"Which is as much as to say that I've made a mistake," said Dame Sganci, touched on the quick.

"No, you haven't made a mistake, my lady. The point is that Bianca doesn't understand these things, poor child. Isn't it true, Bianca, that you don't understand?—Yes?"

Bianca said Yes, nodding her head obediently.

"Let it be as if we hadn't spoken. Enough said, we'll say no more. I've done my duty as a good aunt, trying to make peace between you—And the same to-day there in the Town Hall, did you see?—what I sent to say to you, by the canon-priest Lupi?"

"*Lupus in fabula!*" exclaimed that individual entering as if he was in his own house, his hat on his head, his mantle floating behind him, rubbing his hands. "You were speaking ill of me, eh? My ears were burning."

"You, is it, you woolly sheep! You look as if you'd just won first prize in the lottery."

"First prize in the lottery? You're taking a rise out of me also, are you? A poor devil who is kept running round from morning till night!—"

"We were talking about the auction of the communal lands," said Don Gesualdo calmly, taking a pinch of snuff. "Just for the sake of talking—"

"Ah! Ah!" replied the canon-priest, and he took to staring into the air. For her part Aunt Sganci examined the new furniture, turning her head from side to side.

"Lovely! Lovely they are! Cousin Cirmena told me—! Pity I wasn't feeling well on the wedding day—"

"Like all the others, Donna Mariannina, Ma'am!" replied the canon-priest with a laugh. "Quite an epidemic!"

"No! No! I can assure you! Upon my word!—Madam Rubiera, poor thing!—Her son as well—I hear him always complaining—*Aunt, how could I?—*" Donna Mariannina interrupted herself. "But we have said we wouldn't speak about it any more. But really he's sorry he can't come and pay his respects.—Dissension there always is, say I, even between brothers and sisters. But it will pass, with God's help.—Do you know, Bianca, your cousin is going to get married. We needn't make a mystery of it now, because it's all settled. Don Filippo gives the property of Salonia, thirty furlongs of land! A fine dowry!"

Bianca flushed with a wave of blood in her face, then she became white as a sheet, but she neither moved nor said anything.

The canon-priest replied in her stead, still chewing his bile—

"We know it! We know it! We guessed as much to-day, at the Town Hall!"—But in the end he couldn't contain himself, as if the wound burned in him.

"Baroness Rubiera tried to give me the kick, did she?—me who proposed the whole affair to her!—She went over and joined with the adversaries!—Everybody against us!—The relations of the wife joining forces against the husband!—Such a scandal as was never heard of!—They've invited new applications for the contract for the bridge—so as to make the unlucky man here lose his deposit! Every form of extortion!—

And for making the new roads they are bringing contractors even from Caltagirone and Lentini, to compete!—"

" 'Anyhow from over there they won't get another relation coming down on them'; said Baron Mendola with his own mouth, in the pharmacy."

Donna Mariannina turned all colours and bit her lips to keep herself from spitting out what was in her mind. Don Gesualdo, however, laughed quietly, sprawling on his fine soft sofa, and at a certain point he even put his hand over the mouth of the canon-priest, to silence him.

"Leave it alone!—This is the sort of chatter that brings no grist to the mill. Everybody minds for himself."

"I was only answering Donna Mariannina. Do you want to hear another, eh? the best of all? They have all joined together to sell the corn at any cost, to lower the prices. A camorra! The young baron said it didn't matter to him if he lost a hundred guineas, so long as he could make Don Gesualdo, who's got his barns full, lose a thousand. Does that to his cousin's husband! Shameful! I've got twenty quarters of corn myself, you know, your honour! A piece of rascality!"

The canon-priest was getting more and more excited, turning to Mastro-don Gesualdo.

"You've earned a fine wage by relating yourself to them. Who would have thought it—eh? You made a mistake!—Excuse me, Donna Bianca!—I don't speak of you, we know you are a treasure!—Well then, my dear Donna Mariannina!—well then, when it's like that, let Samson die along with all the Philistines."

"And we'll let them die," said Madame Sganci, rising. "The world won't end even for that."

As her niece rose also from the sofa, mortified by all this talk, her arms crossed in front of her, Donna Mariannina continued laughing and fixing her eyes on the young wife:

"Is it true, Bianca, that you're not going to let the world finish, anyhow?"

Bianca became red again.

"Well done! I congratulate you. Now you've got this fine house you ought to have a grand christening in it—with all the relations—in friendship and harmony. Else, why have you spent all this money?"

Don Gesualdo did not want to seem beaten before all his enemies, but he was gnawed inside himself, because really all that money he had spent had not brought him much return.

"Eh, eh," he replied, with that sort of good-humour which he wanted to make the most of just then. "Patience!—it'll be of use to those who will come after us, in God's will."

And he patted his wife's shoulder, affectionate and smiling, while thinking in reality that if his children were going to have the same fate as himself, it was really all money thrown away, so much weariness, the very profits even, always with that weary result. Then, when Aunt Sganci had gone he began to grumble at Bianca for not having put on a better dress to receive her aunt.

"What good is it your having things! They'll say I keep you like a servant. It's a nice thing to spend money and nobody to enjoy it, neither ourselves nor anybody else!"

"Let us drop that nonsense, and talk about serious

hings!" interrupted the canon-priest, whose face had louded again. "There's the devil of a row. They're rying to set all the place against you, saying you've ot a long arm, and that you want to lay hold of all he land you set your eyes on, to starve everybody. That swine Ciolla is going round preaching for them— They want to let loose even the labourers against you— gainst you and me, my friend! They say I hold the ack. I daren't stir out of my house—"

Don Gesualdo shrugged his shoulders.

"Ah, the labourers! We'll talk about them after-vards, when winter comes. What are you frightened of?"

"What am I frightened of?—for—my!—Don't you know that they've made a revolution in Palermo."

He went on tiptoe to shut the door, and came back pensive, his face dark.

"The Carbonari, you know!—And they've brought his nice novelty even here. I can speak about it, since I haven't had it under seal of confession. We've got the sect here as well."

And he explained what the new attempt was: to make new laws and overthrow all those who had com-manded up till then.

"A political faction, you know. We'll put Tavuso in place of Margarone; have all that lot bossing the show. Every labourer wanting his own portion of land! big fish and small fry, all together. They say that the son of the king is one of them: the Duke of Calabria, no other."

Don Gesualdo, who had been listening with his eyes wide enough open, blurted out:

"If it's like that—I'm for it! Suit me entirely!—

And you tell it me with a face like that? You gave me a rare fright, holy God!"

The other remained open-mouthed.

"What are you laughing at? Do you know what revolution means? What they did in France, you know? But you don't read history——"

"No, no——" said Don Gesualdo. "It's no matter to me."

"It matters to me though. Revolution means turning the basket upside-down, and those who were underneath coming cock o' the walk; the starving, the good-for-nothings!——"

"All right! What was I twenty years ago?"

"But now you're not! Now you've got something to lose, holy saints! Don't you know how it is? To-day they want the communal lands; and then to-morrow they want yours and mine as well! Thank you! Thank you very kindly! I haven't given my soul to the devil for so many years just so that——"

"Of course! You've got to look out for yourself that you don't go to the bottom of the basket, dear Canon! We've got to keep on top, cock of the walk, if we don't want the labourers to help themselves with their own hands. I know them—and I know what to do, never fear."

He explained his idea better; pull the chestnuts out of the fire with the paws of the cat; bring the water to his own mill; and if he could manage to get hold of the ladle for a quarter of an hour, and deal out the soup, and so give a kick to all those big-wigs whom he had not succeeded in conciliating even by marrying one of them without dowry or anything; why, so much the better.

His eyes wandered at that moment to Bianca who

was still huddled on the sofa, livid with fear, looking
from one to the other without daring to open her
mouth.

"I don't speak about you, lass, you know that. I'm
not sorry for what I've done. It's not been your fault.
All bargains don't pan out alike. Then if you happen
to do good, at the same time—"

The canon-priest began to get the hang of it, with his
mouth and his eyes twisted, very thoughtful, so he
supported his partner's speech with his own: One
didn't want to do anybody any damage—if one did
happen to get the ladle into one's hands for a little
while—such a lot of things one could do—

"You ought to do one thing!" interrupted Don
Gesualdo. "Talk with those that have got the handling of this business, and tell them we'd like to be one
with them."

"Eh? what are you saying?—a clergyman?"

"Leave that alone, Canon!—Besides if the King's
son is one of them, you can be one as well."

"Oh yes! They won't go cutting the King's son's
head off, whatever—"

"Don't be afraid. They won't cut your head off.
Nay, if it's as you say, they ought to be cutting the
head off all the village. Do you think I haven't reck-
oned up what I'm doing, these days!—When we're
there, we can see what's boiling in the pot.—We've got
to get near the ladle—with a bit of discretion—and a
bit of money.—I know what I'm talking about."

Then Bianca began to stammer:

"Oh Lord God!—What are you thinking to do?—
The father of a family!"

The canon-priest, undecided, looked at her uneasily,

as if he felt the noose already round his neck. T
reassure him Don Gesualdo added:

"No, no. My wife doesn't know what she's saying
She speaks out of too much affection, poor thing—
Then as he was accompanying his partner into th
antechamber: "You see! She begins to be fond of m
Children are a great bond. Let us hope at least tha
they may be happy and content; for I—. Shall I te
you, Canon, as if I was on my deathbed? I have kille
myself with work—I have killed myself getting th
property together—Now I risk even my neck, accord
ing to you!—And what have I had out of it all, eh?—
tell me then, just you tell me!—"

II

There was a great ferment in the village. They
were expecting the news from Palermo. Bomma
holding audience in the pharmacy and Ciolla spouting
all round the place. Agitators were rousing even the
peasant-labourers with speeches that made them open
their eyes: the communal lands which were leaving
the Zacco family for the first time for forty years;
—a price such as had never been seen the like of!—
That Mastro-don Gesualdo had too long an arm.—If
he'd made the lands go up to that price, it meant that
there was still something to be gained by it.—All out
of the blood of the poor!—Communal property—
Which meant that everyone had his right to it!—
Very well, why shouldn't everyone take his own bit!

It was a Sunday, the feast of the Assumption. The
evening before had arrived from Palermo a letter that
put a spark to the powder, as if everybody had read it.
From the break of day you saw the Great Square cram
full of peasant-labourers; a swarm of white stocking-
caps; a threatening buzz. Fra Girolamo of the Mer-
cenaries, sitting there in the shadow, along with other
persons of evil intention, on the steps in front of
Lawyer Neri's office, as he saw Baron Zacco going
by with his tail between his legs, showed him the pistol
which he carried in his wide sleeve.

"See that, Baron Zacco?—The times of arrogance
are over!—From now on we are all equal!"

A lot of talk was going round, about what Fra
Girolamo intended to do: leave his cassock in his cell,

take himself a property at Passaneto, and Margarone's daughter to wife, the youngest one.

The lawyer who had come to fetch some interesting papers out of his office, had to raise his hat to Fra Girolamo.

"Allow me!—gentlemen!"

Then he went to rejoin Don Filippo Margarone in the little square of Santa Teresa.

"Listen here; I want to tell you something!—"

And he took him by the arm, turning homewards, talking in low tones as they walked. Don Filippo went paler and shrank at every gesture that cut upon the air; but he kept on saying no, yellow with fear. The other pulled him hard by the arm, crossing the lane of the Masera to go up towards Sant'Antonio.

"See them? Hear them? Do you want them to lay hold of us, the peasants, and show us what for?"

The square at the end of the little street seemed a hive of wasps. Nanni l'Orbo, Pelagatti, other agitators, in a wild state of excitement went about from one group to another, shouting, gesticulating, spitting bile. Master Titta's clients appeared every moment. In Bomma's pharmacy they were wrangling with their fists in one another's faces. Opposite, on the pavement in front of the Café of the Gentry, Don Anselmo had set out the chairs in the open as usual; but there was nobody there, except Marchese Limòli with his stick between his legs, looking calmly at the threatening crowd.

"What do they want, Don Anselmo? What the devil's got them to-day? Do you know?"

"They want the communal lands, my lord marchese. They say that up to now you gentry have enjoyed them, and now it's our turn, because we are all equal."

"At their service! At their service entirely! I'm not going to contradict them! All equals!—Bring me a glass of water, Don Anselmo."

From time to time, out of the Rosary Street and the street of San Giovanni issued a flood of people—and a more threatening murmur that spread like thunder. Then Santo Motta came out of the tavern of Pecu-Pecu, and with his hand at his cheek began to shout:

"The communal lands!—Who wants the communal lands?—One!—two!—three!—"—and he finished with a shout of laughter.

"Make way!—Make way!—"

People ran towards the Masera. Above the crowd the young baron was seen, flourishing his whip over the head of his horse that snorted with fear. The estate keeper who ran at his side, armed to the teeth, shouted like one obsessed:

"Your Lordship—Sir!—This is no day for—! You need to be prudent to-day!"

From the Sant'Agata district the Captain also showed himself for a moment, to intimidate the muti-nous crowd by his presence. He took his stand at the top of the steps, leaning on his malacca cane, Don Liccio Papa behind him, glittering in the sun with such an expanse of white sword-belt across his stomach. But seeing that sea of heads they suddenly decamped, the pair of them. Anxious faces were peeping at the windows, behind the shut panes, as if it was raining. The Sganci mansion hermetically closed, and Don Giuseppe Barabba perched on the attic window-sill. Friend Bomma had got rid of his friends earlier than usual, for fear of his window-glass. From time to time, on the Margarone's terrace, above the roofs which piled up towards the castle, appeared the hood and the yellow face of Don Filippo. At mid-day, as soon as high mass rang, everybody went off about his own business; and in the deserted square only Santo Motta remained shouting:

"Do you see how it's turned out?—"

Even Ciolla ran off to his dinner. Don Liccio Papa, now there was nobody left, once more put in an appearance in the streets, his hand on his sabre, glaring proudly at the closed doors. At length he entered Pecu-Pecu's, and sat down at a table with neighbour Santo.

"You see how it's turned out?—"

Ciolla usually swallowed his dinner as fast as he could, his hat on his head and his stick between his knees, so as to get back into the square at once, to chew over his last mouthful there, carrying in his pocket a handful of boiled lupin seeds or of broiled chick-peas, in winter also a little warming-pot of hot ashes under his cloak, lounging, saying his say to everybody, spitting right and left and scattering the ground with husks.

"You see how it's turned out?—"

He made his first call at the cobbler's, then to the coffee-house as soon as it was open, without ever drinking anything there, following the shade in summer, and in winter following the sun. And things happened just as he foretold, according to Ciolla. Giacinto put out the little tables for the ice-cream, Don Anselmo arranged the chairs on the pavement in front of the Café of the Gentry. Only the last clouds of the storm remained: assemblies here and there, in front of Pecu-Pecu's shop and before the Town Hall; people who looked anxiously about, or inquisitive persons who came running and crowding at the least noise. But for

he rest everything had resumed its Sunday aspect.
The Archpriest Bugno licking up his ice-cream with his
little spoon, making it spin out for an hour; the marchese and the other gentry seated in a row in front of
the Café; Bomma preaching in the midst of his usual
set, in the pharmacy doorway; a swarm of peasants a
little way off, at the required distance; and every ten
minutes the ancient carriage of Baron Mendola, in
which drove the Baron's mother, deaf as a mole, back
and forth from the Rosary to Santa Marie di Jesu;
the hairy, weary ears of the mules wagging through the
crowd, the coachman perched on the seat with his whip
between his legs, beside the chasseur in fine uniform,
whose white stockings looked as if they were stuffed
with nuts, and the yellow plumes of the baroness' big
hat passing and re-passing above that sea of peasants'
white stocking-caps.

All at once there was a helter-skelter; some sort of
row in front of the tavern. Don Liccio Papa was try-
ng to arrest Santo Motta, because he had shouted
that morning, and the Captain was encouraging him
from the distance, brandishing his malacca cane:

"Halt! Halt!—the law—!"

But Santo freed himself with a shove, and began to
run towards Sant'Agata. The crowd whistled and
howled after the policeman who was trying to follow him.

"You see! You see!" said Bomma, who had climbed
on to a chair to look. "If they don't respect the authorities any longer!" Tavuso signed to him to be quiet, putting his forefinger across his mouth.

"Hark here, Don Bastiano!"

And they began to talk in low tones, drawing aside.
The lawyer came down from the Maddalena quarter

cautiously, step by step, his stick behind his back.
Bomma began to make signs to him from the distance;
but the attorney pretended not to see; he nodded to
the Captain who was making his way towards the
College, and, then passed into the church through
the little door. The Captain, as he passed before the
pharmacy, withered the free-thinkers with a look, and
muttered, turning to the ring-leader:

"Remember you have wives and children—"

"Blood of—! Body of—!" The chemist began to
rave. At that moment the bell rang for benediction,
and everybody in the square kneeled down. A little
while after, Ciolla, who was passing his time chewing
broiled beans, sitting in front of the ice-cream shop,
saw something that made him prick up his ears;
the lawyer Neri coming out of church again with the
canon-priest Lupi, and mounting again towards
the Maddalena parish, lingeringly, talking in low
tones. The lawyer shrugged his shoulders, looking
furtively here and there. Ciolla tried to join them,
but they repulsed him. Bomma stared after them
from the distance, wagging his head.

"Mind what you're up to!—You mind your skin!"
said the Captain to him as he passed again close by.

"Cuckold!" the chemist would have shouted after
him. "You mind yourself first—!"

But the doctor shoved him by force into the shop.
Ciolla had run up San Sebastiano Street after the
canon-priest and Lawyer Neri, and saw the pair of
them still standing under the arch of the Conduit, in
spite of the stench, almost in the dark, talking in low
tones, and gesticulating. The moment they saw Ciolla
they made off in haste, one this way, the other that.
The lawyer went on up the little stony street, and the

canon-priest came down again at breakneck speed towards San Sebastiano, stopping Ciolla as if by accident.

"That lawyer—he's let me in nicely!—He had an agreement with Farmer Sbrendola—a safe, straight contract—and now he says he remembers nothing of it!"

"No you don't, no you don't, you don't get me to swallow that!" murmured Ciolla to himself as soon as the canon-priest had turned away. And he ran at once to the pharmacy.

"There's big things happening! Cats and dogs are consorting together! There's big things happening!—"

Tavuso swelled his cheeks without answering. The apothecary, however, blurted out:

"I know it! I know it!"

Then he clapped his open hand over his mouth, withered by the severe look from the doctor.

About two hours after dark Don Gesualdo was just sitting down to supper when with great mystery arrived the canon-priest dressed up as a shepherd, looking for him. Bianca very nearly had a miscarriage, with fright.

"Don Gesualdo, we are ready, if you are coming; friends are expecting you."

But the poor devil's voice trembled. And Don Gesualdo as well, when it came to the point of throwing himself into that affair, had some unpleasant thoughts in his head; he turned pale, and his fork fell from his hand. Then Bianca rose convulsed, stumbling about the room, quarrelling with the canon-priest for dragging the father of a family into that mess.

"If it's like that!" stammered the canon-priest.—

"If you cast the evil eye on it beforehand—then good-
night!"

Don Gesualdo tried to laugh it off, with white lips.
"Bravo, Canon! Now we shall see if you are a
man!—I am glad, look you, Bianca! I am glad to go
up to the precipice brink, if it shows me that you're
beginning to get fond of me and of the home—"

Sweating, his hands trembling a little, he muffled
himself up inside a hood, for prudence's sake, and they
went down to the street. There wasn't a living soul
about. On the college terrace an unknown hand had
even extinguished the lamp in front of the statue of
the Immaculate Virgin: something to make your flesh
creep, that evening! And then he felt his heart contract with an unwonted tenderness, thinking of his
home and his relations.

"Poor Bianca! Did you see? She is good-hearted,
yes she is, at the bottom—I didn't believe it, really—!"

"Hush!" interrupted the canon-priest. "If you let
them recognise your voice, it's no good our muffling
ourselves up and sweating like animals!"

Every minute they kept turning round, afraid they
were being spied on. When they got into the Street
of San Giovanni they saw a shadow going up toward
the square, and the canon-priest said softly:

"See?—That's one of us!—He's going where we
are—"

It was in a store-barn of Grancore, down among the
little tortuous streets that seemed made on purpose
towards San Francisco. A low little house with one
window lighted as a signal. They knocked three times
in a special way at the little door which they reached
by descending three steps; they crossed a large, dark,
broken courtyard, and at the end they came to a large

room where, from the buzzing that was heard beyond
the closed door, they concluded many people were talking together. The canon-priest said:

"It is here!"—and he gave the proper signal.

Both their hearts jumped in their throats. By good
luck another accomplice arrived at that moment,
muffled up as they were, walking on the tips of his toes
among the stones of the yard, and he repeated the
signal the same.

"Don Gesualdo,"—said the lawyer Neri, putting his
nose out of a big scarf. "Is it you? I recognised you
by the canon-priest, who looks like a scarecrow, poor
chap!"

The lawyer took it livelily.—He told them that at
Palermo they had done it grand; they had killed the
Prince of Aci and had seized Castellammare.—"And
the one in command now is a priest, one called
Ascenso!"

"Ah?"—replied the canon-priest, feeling himself
concerned. "Ah?"

"Silence for the present!—We'll go slowly! Do
you know how it is?—it's a question of who will bell
the cat! And every gentleman would rather *not* put
his foot in the trap. But there's a fair number of us—
There is even Baron Zacco this evening."

"Why are we waiting to go in, gentlemen?" interrupted Don Gesualdo, brave as a lion when he heard
that news.

When they came out again, however, after a long
while, they were all more dead than alive. Bomma
forced himself to bluster; Tavuso did not say a word;
and the lawyer also was plunged in thought. Zacco
ran to take Don Gesualdo's arm, as if they had really
become brothers for good.

"Listen, Cousin, I want to tell you something—"

And they went on, arm in arm, in silence.

"Ssh!—a whistle!—towards the Capucin Monastery!—"

The baron put his hand on his pistol: all felt their hearts beating wildly. They heard a barking of dogs.

"Hold!" exclaimed the canon-priest *sotto voce*, clutching the arm which held the weapon, as the baron stared round in the dark. "It is Fra Girolamo, who had rather not be seen in these parts!" Hardly had they heard the door closing again upon the glimpse of white cassock they had seen in the doorway, than the apothecary murmured gasping:

"We've had a rare escape, upon my word!"

The baron for his part pressed the arm of Don Gesualdo tight, without saying anything. Then he let everyone go his own road, Bomma uphill, towards the Great Square, the canon-priest to the foot of the steps that led up to San Sebastino.

"This way, Don Gesualdo—come with me."

And he made him go all round by the Capucins, then mount towards Santa Maria di Jesu by certain dark little streets where you didn't know where to put your foot down. All at once he stopped, looking his new friend full in the face, with eyes that glittered in the dark.

"Don Gesualdo, did you hear all those fine things we talked about! Now we are all brothers. We're going to swim in milk and honey, from now on—You believe it, eh?"

The other neither said yes nor no, prudent, waiting for what was coming.

"Because I don't—I don't trust all these brothers of mine that my own mother never bore."

"Then why did you come, your honour!"

"So that you shouldn't have it all your own way, do you see? I don't deal in mysteries. We are playing at cutting the grass under one another's feet, we who have something to lose, and this is what it leads to. Cooking the meat for the cats, and risking our own property and heads!—I am looking after my own interests, as you are after yours.—I'm not full of fools' conceits like the rest of them.—Relations, ten times relations! I'm perfectly willing.—Then let us come to an understanding between ourselves—"

"All right? What do you want to do?"

"Ah! What do I want to do?—Is that your tune? You play the simpleton to me?—All right then, nothing said—Every man for himself! Brothers! Carbonari! We'll make a revolution! We'll put the world upside-down as well!—I'm not afraid!"

In the heat of his discourse the baron had leaned against the door of a courtyard. A dog began to bark furiously. Zacco, terrified, took to his heels with his pistol in his fist, and Don Gesualdo behind him, panting. Before they got into the Square of Santa Maria di Jesu a man who came running towards them stopped him, putting his hand on his breast.

"Don Gesualdo, Sir! where are you going?—the police are in your house!"

Just as the canon-priest had feared! Just as Bianca had feared! He ran on in the dark, without knowing where, with a great confusion in his head, and his heart almost bursting out of his chest. Then, hearing the fellow limping behind, with a peculiar noise as if he was knocking with a stick:

"And you, who are you?"

"Nardo, the labourer, the one who lost his leg on the

bridge. Don't you know me, your honour? Donna Bianca set me to keep night-watch."

And he told how the Armed Force had come unexpectedly, at four hours after dark. The Captain and others of the Armed Force were in Don Gesualdo's house. Above, towards the Castle, lights were seen gleaming; there was, moreover, a lantern hung in front of the stable doors, at the Poggio, and soldiers dressing down the horses. Further off, near the Great Square, from time to time voices were heard: a confused murmuring, foot-steps resounding in the night, dogs barking all over the village.

Don Gesualdo stopped to reflect.

"Where are we going, your honour?" asked Nardo.

"I've thought it out. Don't make a sound. Ah! Holy Madonna of Peril! Go and call Nanni l'Orbo. You know him? The husband of Diodata?"

It was beginning to dawn. But in the insignificant back alleys they had taken they did not meet a soul. The miserable little house of Diodata was hidden among a heap of blackish hovels and thickets of cactus, where the mud did not dry up even in summer. There was a vine-trellis over the terrace, and a light which leaked out through the dilapidated door-frame.

"You knock, in case——" said Don Gesualdo.

Diodata, seeing her previous master appear before her panting and worn out, began to tremble like a leaf.

"What do you want of me at this hour?—For the love of God leave me in peace, Don Gesualdo!—If my husband comes in!—He's gone out this minute to gather one or two prickly pears—just near here."

"Fool!" he said. "I've got something else on my mind! I've got the police at my heels."

"What's happened?" asked Diodata, terrified.

He made her a sign with his hand, to keep quiet. At that moment Nardo came running back; you could hear the wooden leg some distance off, on the cobble-stones.

"Here he is!—here he comes!—"

Entered Nanni l'Orbo, surly, the pointed cane for gathering prickly pears on his shoulder, and his squinting eyes glaring this way and that. Diodata, her arms crossed over her breast, vowed and swore.

"But master!" exclaimed Nanni. "What game are we playing at? This isn't the way to—!"

"Fool!" cried Don Gesualdo at length, losing patience, "I've got the gibbet before my eyes, and you talk to me of jealousy!"

At the row the neighbours were running up.

"You see?" repeated Nanni infuriated. "What sort of a figure do I cut before them all, master? In all conscience, the bit you gave her to get her married is a misery, seeing the fool you make of me!"

"Be quiet! You'll bring up the police with that row! What do you want? I'll give you what you want."

"I want my own honour, Don Gesualdo! My own honour which can't be bought with money!"

All the dogs in the neighbourhood began to bark.

"Do you want the Carmine field?—a bit of land to make your mouth water."

At last neighbour Nardo succeeded in bringing them to an agreement about the Carmine field.

"Body of Judas! Property comes in handy for these things: prison, illness, and persecution. . . . You got it together, and now it comes in handy to save your skin——"

Don Gesualdo, with a face like a funeral, grumbled:

"You can talk? You can hold forth! You're righ
of it! Now you're right of it, you are!"

"But take into consideration your fellow-man, you.
honour! A wife to keep—The children that will b
born . . . And if those others come home to me
those that arrived beforehand, I shall have to keep
them as if they were my own—because I am the hus
band of Diodata. Folks will say in any case it wa
me who put them in the world—"

"Shut up! Shut up! Haven't I said Yes about the
field!"

"Word of a gentleman? Before these witnesses
If it's like that then—even though you say you hav
come only to save your skin, you can stop as long a
you like. I'm a good-natured devil, I am, you
know!—"

It had become late. Neighbour Nanni, completely
restored to good humour, proposed also to go and see
what was happening out there:

"You make as free here as if you were in your own
home, Don Gesualdo.—Neighbour Nardo will come
with me. When I come back, for a signal I'll knock
three knocks on the door. But don't you open for
anything else, not even to the devil."

There was a reign of terror in the village: door
and windows still shut, men of the Armed Force in the
street, noise of sabres and of spurs. The Margaron
young ladies, wearing their trinkets and with thei
heads bristling with ribbon-ends, like a fireworks, ran
on to the balcony every moment. Don Filippo
triumphant and with his chest thrown out proudly, wa
now seated along with the Civic Captain and the Fisca
Attorney in the Café of the Gentry, making anybody
who passed tremble with a mere look. In Don Gesu

ıldo's stable the police runners were grooming the
ıorses, while their commander, in his slippers, was
ımoking on the balcony as if he was in his own house.

Nanni l'Orbo came back laughing fit to split. Before
entering, however, he knocked three times as he had
ıaid, coughed, blew his nose, then remained talking for
ı while in a loud voice with a neighbour who was
combing her hair on her terrace. Don Gesualdo was
eating a salad of onions, to keep him from having an
ıllness brought on by fright.

"Eat well! eat well, Don Gesualdo! I found
ıtrangers in your house, just the very same as you
ıere in mine. Baron Zacco is still running!—He was
ıeen before dawn beyond Passaneto, would you believe
ıt! Very devil's business!—behind a hedge, more dead
than alive!—His wife is going on like a madwoman.—
I went to find Lawyer Neri as well, thought he might
write a word or two about this Carmine field which
you're giving to my wife for services rendered.—Not
that I don't trust you—you know that as well as I
do—life or death. But nobody knows where he is, the
ıawyer! They say he's hidden in the monastery of
San Sebastian—dressed as a woman—yessir!—The
police are hunting everywhere! But you've nothing
to be frightened of here, your honour.—Hark! Hark!"

He seemed to take a delight in making the blood
freeze in the veins of his fellow-man, did that rascal.
There came as a matter of fact a sound of gossips'
voices, a running of heavy-shod feet, squealing of
children. Diodata clambered right up to the granary
attic-top to look.. Then Nanni came to say:

"It is the viaticum, God preserve us!—It is going
up to Sant'Agata. I saw the Canon-priest Lupi carry-

ing the Host—looking down at the ground—and a face
like a saint, as God's above!"

"This evening, as soon as it is dark, I'll get somebody to find me a mount down at the Masera, and
something to disguise myself a bit," said Don Gesualdo, who looked more livid than ever in the light of
the attic window.

"Why? Don't you like stopping in my house? Has
Diodata done something to put you out?"

"No, no—It seems a thousand years to me till I can
get away—"

"But you've got nothing to be frightened of here—
The police runners won't come to look for you here!
In your own house of course. Look you!—"

As a matter of fact Bianca had had the Captain of
the Armed Force appearing at three hours after
dark, the evening before: a fine man with a fringe
beard and military moustaches, bringing the notice that
he was billeted in the house. Bianca, already anxious
about her husband, not knowing what to do, had sent
for her uncle Limòli, who arrived yawning and in a
bad temper. In vain did the Captain of the Force
caress his moustaches, which he had only lately let
grow, and say to her in a deep voice:

"Don't be afraid!—Calm yourself, dear lady!—We
soldiers are gallant men where the fair sex is concerned!—"

"But then," added the marchese, "these fellows are
just so-to-speak soldiers; like me who have taken the
vow of chastity by way of being a Knight of Malta."

The Captain frowned, but the other, without heeding, continued, patting him familiarly on the shoulder:

"I know, Don Bastiano!—You were only so high,
with your little open breeches, in the days when I was

having escapades with your father.—And my vow
bothered me then as your rapier that you wear at your
side bothers you now.—Happy days!—A fine man
your father! Heart and purse always open!—Don
Marcantonio Stangafame, of the Stangafames of
Ragusa!—one of the first families in the County!
Pity there are so many of you. You must have found
it so before you had yourself appointed Captain of the
Force! Two hundred guineas a year to be responsible
for all the thefts out in the country. It's a nice sum of
money—And it goes every penny into your pocket—
because the district is quiet!—Just a trifle of a dozen
soldiers whose keep you have to provide—eightpence
a day apiece, eh!—"

"Drop it, body of—Bacchus!" shouted the Captain,
hitting his sabre on the ground. "Do you want to
make game of me, body of Bacchus!"

"Hey, hey! gently, Mr. Captain! I am Marchese
Limòli, and I've still got friends at Naples, to uncap-
tain you and to shave off your new moustaches, you
know!"

At that moment arrived the sexton's boy, who came
on an errand of great importance, muddling himself
up, always going over the same thing again, red with
shyness. The marchese, who was beginning to be a bit
deaf, snapped at him and frightened him still more,
squealing:

"Eh? What the deuce do you want?"

But Bianca uttered a lacerating cry, a cry which left
her uncle open-mouthed, and ran round the house looking for her mantle, looking for something to throw
over her head, to go out in, to run at once.

III

Every day for years, at the same hour, Donna Giuseppina Alòsi on her balcony knitting as she waited for Peperito to pass, Don Filippo Margarone as he turned the tomato paste which was drying on the terrace, the arch-priest Bugno as he hung out his canary in its cage, even those who were yawning in Bomma's pharmacy, were accustomed to turn their eyes upwards towards the castle, above the roofs, and to see Don Diego and Don Ferdinando Trao, one after the other, peeping at a window, cautiously, each of them looking to the right and then to the left, then up into the air, and then withdrawing his head like a snail. After a few minutes the doors of the big balcony gradually opened, screeching on their hinges, shakily, shoved apart bit by bit, and Don Diego appeared, bent, cadaverous, with his cotton bonnet pulled right down to his ears, coughing, spitting, clinging to the iron balustrade with one hand; and behind him Don Ferdinando, yellow, gaunt, a real spectre, bringing the watering-can. Don Diego watered, trimmed, attended to Bianca's flowers; he bent down to pick off the dry twigs and the withered leaves; he stirred up the earth with a bit of broken pot; counted over the new buds, and treasured them as he looked at them. Don Ferdinando followed his every movement, most attentive; he bent down his white-washed face also to every plant, making his nose more pointed, knotting his brows. Then they leaned their elbows on the rail, and remained like two fowls perched on the same perch, turning their heads first this way and then that, according as there appeared one of Farmer Burgio's mules loaded with grain, or as the girl who sold eggs came up the Rosary Street, or the sexton's wife crossed the square to ring the Ave Maria. Don Ferdinando was intent on counting the number of persons he saw cross that bit of street which he could see beyond, between the roofs of the houses that descended in a huddle down the slope of the hill; Don Diego for his part following the last rays of the sun as they rose slowly towards the elevation of the Paradiso and of Mount Lauro, and rejoicing at seeing the sudden sparkle of the windows of the little houses which were already disappearing among the fields, like whitish blotches. Then he smiled and pointed his trembling, skeleton finger, nudging his brother with his elbow, while the latter nodded Yes and smiled as well, like a child. Then he told what he had seen himself:

"Twenty-seven to-day!—twenty-seven people gone past. The arch-priest Bugno was with cousin Limòli!—"

For a few days, towards the beginning of August, Don Ferdinando had come alone to water the flowers, trailing himself along with effort, his grey hairs flying loose, slopping himself all over at every step. When again appeared Don Diego, he seemed like Lazarus risen from the dead: all nose, his ears purple, buried alive in an old great-coat, coughing his soul away at every stride; a weak cough that one could hardly hear any more, but which shook from head to foot both him and his brother on whose arm he leaned as he went making his bow before every pot of flowers. And this was the last time. From that time forward the two grey heads of the brothers were seen at rare intervals behind the window-panes that were patched with paper, as they looked for the sun. Don Diego spitting and staring at the ground every moment. The day when there was that uproar in the Town Hall, so that the voices were heard right up in the little Square of Sant' Agata, the top of a white, trembling bonnet appeared for a moment at the window. But when the day came for the procession of San Giuseppe to stop before the great door of the Traos, paying the traditional homage to the family, the windows remained shut, in spite of the shouting of the crowd. Don Ferdinando went down to buy the picture of the Saint, swollen with asthma, his eyes burnt with lack of sleep, his body bent double, his blackened hands trembling so much that he could hardly find the two farthings in his purse to pay for the card. The procurator of San Giuseppe, who was conducting the procession, said to him :

"You'll see how miraculous that image is! How much health and abundance to all in your house!"

And he trusted him with the saint's silver staff, to put at the bed-head of the sick man : one touch is health. But however that didn't help either.

Neighbour Cosimo and Pelagatti, leaving for the open fields at two hours before dawn, or returning after dark, saw the light always in Don Diego's window. And the Motta's black dog howled through the square, like a lament. Then, towards nine, Don Luca's boy came knocking at the big door, bringing a glass of milk. Occasionally Don Giuseppe Barabba came with a plate covered with a napkin; or the servant of the Fiscal Attorney brought a flask of wine. Gradually, however, even these visits became fewer. Doctor Tavusa had gone away the last time shrugging his shoulders. The children of the neighbourhood played the whole day long against that great door which never opened any more. One evening, late, the neighbours who were eating their supper, heard the hoarse voice of Don Ferdinando calling for the sexton, there across the way; a voice to make the bread drop from your mouth. And immediately after a loud bang at the battered door, and steps hurrying away into the distance.

That was the same night that the Armed Force came. A tumult all over the village. At the unusual noise even Don Diego opened his eyes for a moment. Burgio, on his own terrace, stretching his ears towards the big square, whence he heard all that uproar, seeing people on the Trao's balcony, asked uneasily:

"What is it?—What's amiss?"

"Don Diego," replied the sexton; and he made the sign of the cross, as if Don Diego could see him in the dark; "alone like a dog!—they leave him on my hands! I've sent Grazia for the doctor—at this time of night!—"

"Hark, down there, towards the square!—do you hear?—What sort of day will to-morrow bring, God save us!—"

"Sufficient that you've got a clear conscience, Farmer Fortunato. I've always been a poor devil! I kiss the hand that gives me bread—"

"The doctor!—him, yes!—I bet he's got the trembles at this moment!—And the canon-priest Lupi too, they say!—Good-night!—Walls have ears in the dark!"

In fact, Doctor Tavuso, who was leader of all the jacobins in the village, at present hiding in the wood-shed, trembling like a leaf, now felt that his last hour had come, hearing someone banging at the door with such fury.

"The police!—The Armed Force!—"

When they told him it was the wife of the sexton, however, come to fetch him to Don Diego, who was dying, he got into a bestial rage.

"Still alive, is he?—Send him to the devil!—They come and frighten me out of my life!—at this hour!—in times like these!—The father of a family!—Go and fetch his own relations instead—or the viaticum, if you want something better!—"

Neither did Aunt Sganci want to open. Barabba replied from behind the closed door, that was bolted to such a degree:

"My good woman, these are not the times when you can go running about the streets at night. To-morrow morning, by God's will, those that are alive will see each other again."

Luckily Grazia had nothing to fear; her husband would have sent her without misgiving among a company of soldiers. Going round so late at night, and on such a night, was really terrifying. Even Baron Rubina, who had left the Margarone's house early, had a man with a lantern to go with him.

"Nini! Nini!" squealed Donna Fifi with her thin voice, as if her fiancé was running to throw himself over a precipice.

"Don't be afraid—no!" replied the young man, with a deep voice.

Hearing people in the little square, at the big door of the Traos, which resounded like a cannonade, Don Luca came running out.

"Oh, Baron—sir!—Your cousin Don Diego is

dying!—alone like a dog!—There's not a soul in the house!"

Facing the black, wretched mansion of the Traos shone the lit-up balcony of the Margarones, and in the light the shadow of Donna Fifì, reminding the young baron of that other shadow that used to wait for him once on a time at the window of the dilapidated mansion. Don Ninì went off in haste, his head dropped, carrying with him in his eyes the memory of that closed, dark window.

"Lot of swine!—They leave him on my hands!—me all alone!"—grumbled Don Luca, returning to the chamber of the dying man.

Don Ferdinando was seated at the foot of the bed, without saying a word, like a mummy. From time to time he went to look into his brother's face; then he looked at Don Luca, bewildered, and went back to sit with his head hanging over his breast. At the outburst of the sexton, however, he got up suddenly as if someone had given him a shove, and asked softly, in the somnolent voice of one who speaks in his sleep:

"Is he asleep?"

"Yes, he is asleep! You go and get to sleep yourself, won't you?"

But the other did not stir. At first the sick man asked every minute what time it was; then, towards midnight, he didn't ask anything any more. He lay still, with his nose to the wall, and the bedclothes up to his ears. Grazia, on her return, had set the door ajar, put the light near, on the little table, and had gone to see to her own house. Her husband settled himself as best he could on two chairs. Don Ferdinando from time to time got up again and went on

tiptoe to lean over the bed, like a bird of ill-omen, and
returned to whisper in Don Luca's ear:

"What is he doing? Is he asleep?"

"Yes! Yes!—You go to sleep yourself, won't
you!—go on!"

And he went with him to his chamber, to get rid of
the bother of him. Don Ferdinando dreamed that the
black dog of the neighbour Motta was crouched on
his chest and wouldn't go away, no matter how he tried
to shake him off, and to shout out. The tail of the
dog, so long that there was no end to it, was twisted
round his neck and arms and was squeezing him, suffocating him, strangling his voice in his throat, when he
heard another voice that made him jump out of bed,
with his heart beating wildly.

"Get up, Don Ferdinando! This is no time to be
sleeping."

Don Diego seemed to be snoring loudly, you could
hear him from the other room; stretched out, his eyes
open wide and spent, his nostrils going black; a face
that you couldn't recognise. As Don Ferdinando
called him softly, softly, and began again calling him
and shaking him, all to no purpose, the few hairs that
poor Don Ferdinando had on his head fairly stood on
end, and he turned to the sexton, dazed, pleading:

"What is he doing now?—What is he doing?"

"What is he doing?—You can see what he's doing!
Grazia! Grazia!"

"No!—Don't do that!—Don't open now!—"

It was clear day. Donna Bellonia in her petticoat
stood on the terrace to spy towards the Great Square,
at her husband's request, terrified by the great hubbub
that had been heard all through the night in all the
village; and Burgio was grooming the mule tied to

the big door of the Traos. At the shouting of Don
Luca he lifted his head towards the balcony and asked
with a toss of his head what was the matter. The
sexton also replied with a wave of the hand, making
a sign of one who is going away.

"Who?" asked Madam Margarone, who also perceived it. "Who? Don Diego or Don Ferdinando?"

"Yes my lady, Don Diego! They leave him all on
my hands!—I'm going for the doctor—at least for the
receipt of the viaticum, deuce take it!—my sirs, is it
right for a Christian to go like this, without doctor or
apothecary?"

Speranza began by screaming at her husband who
had tied the mule to the house of a dying man:—

"It's bad luck! And we need that, I must say!—"

Then she went on to conjure the numbers of the
lottery along with Donna Bellonia, who had run to get
the book of Rutilio Benincasa. Donna Giovannina
appeared, wiping her face; but she didn't see anything
except the sexton running to fetch Doctor Tavuso, a
few yards further on, at the little green door there with
the bell-cord tied up high so that folk shouldn't come
bothering him in the night. He knocks and knocks
again, and then the servant of Tavuso at last calls to
him through the key-hole:

"Oh stop the noise, the doctor isn't going out not
if the world falls. He's more ill than anybody, himself."

Bomma, yellow as saffron, was pounding cream of
tartar at the back of the pharmacy, as lonely as if he
had the plague. Don Luca entered in a rush, gasping:

"Don Arcangelo, Sir!—Don Diego Trao is dying
this minute. The doctor won't come—What am I
to do?"

"What are you to do?—Make the dead man his coffin, plague on you! You frightened me to death! That's not the way—to-day when every gentleman has his heart in his mouth!—Go and fetch the priest then—there, at the college, there's the canon-priest Lupi in a frenzy saying mass and matins all the time till dawn, to show himself in church!—He always falls on his feet, he does! He laughs at the police!—I am the apothecary! I am pounding cream of tartar since I can't pound anything else.—I can't come!"

But seeing Ciolla going by handcuffed like a robber, he bit his tongue and bent his head over the mortar.

"Sirs, my sirs!" vociferated Ciolla—"just look here!—a gentleman who is only standing in the square minding his own business!"

The Armed Force, without heeding him drove him forward with shoves; Don Liccio Papa as escort carrying an unsheathed sabre, shouting:

"Make way! Make way for the Law!"

The Civic Captain, from the top of the steps of the Café of the Gentry, moralised:

"We've got to make an example of one of them! They'll kick us, we all know where, if we give them time!—a set of scoundrels!—A village like ours that was a convent of friars till now!—To the castle!—to the castle! Don Liccio, here are the keys!—"

Thank the Lord they could breathe once more. The well-disposed began to show themselves on the streets again towards evening, so late in the day; the arch-priest in front of the Café; Peperito up and down the Rosary Street; Canali going arm in arm with Don Filippo towards the wax-chandling cousin; Don Giuseppe Barabba taking Donna Marianna Sganci's little dog for a walk once more; then the Captain's lady all

dressed up as if it was her birthday, now there were
so many soldiers about, her embroidered satchel on her
arm, her little hat loaded with plumes, wagging her
tail, laughing, flirting, towing behind her Don Bastiano Stangafame, or the lieutenant, or any other col-
league of her husband, which latter gentleman stood
looking on like a real booby, with his malacca cane
behind his back, while his own colleagues strolled
with his wife, splitting themselves in their stride like
pairs of compasses, laughing at the top of their voices,
staring proudly at the women who dared to show
themselves at the windows, making the whole place
ring with a noise of sabres and the clinking of spurs, as
if they had bells at their heels. The Margarone girls,
cooped on the terrace, were dying of jealousy. Especially of the lieutenant, who had moustaches like the
tail of a horse, and two rows of buttons along the front
of him that shone in the distance.

So that in this holiday air the little bell of the viaticum rang more sadly. Also sinister rumours were
afoot.—A battle had taken place!—men condemned
to death!—One of the men who carried the tall lantern behind the canopy said that the Host was going
to the Trao house.—"Another great family dying out!"
gravely observed the Fiscal Attorney, baring his head.
The Captain's lady, skipping on her toes to show her
silk stockings, was launching back at Don Bastiano a
smile calculated to damn him:

"I know! I know! Sailor's vows!—"

The Captain of the Force winked at Donna Bianca
who was passing just then, as if to say: "Her as well!
—but is it my fault?"—taking off his hat with servile
obsequiousness. But the poor thing did not answer.
She was almost running, spent, with her mantle slip-

ping down her shoulders, her face pale and anxious.
Donna Fifì Margarone drew back from the balcony
with a grimace as she saw her come into the square
from the Sant' Agata steps.

"Ah!—at last!—the good sister!—how condescending of her!"

"Bianca! Bianca!" cried Uncle Limòli, who could
not keep up with her.

In front of the big doorway whose two doors were
wide open, the children of Burgio and Don Luca were
crowding. The sexton's wife came out at that moment,
dishevelled, yellow, and without any stomach. She
began dealing smacks to right and left.

"Be off! Be off from here!—What do you want?—
is there a treat?"

Then she darted into the church. Gossips stood at
their windows, inquisitive. At the top of the stairs
Don Giuseppe Barabba was shaking out some black
banners, gnawed and holed by the rats, that bore the
coat-of-arms of the Traos: a red splotch all moth-
eaten. Aunt Macrì had come running at once with
her daughter, and Baron Mèndola stood near her; a
come-and-go throughout the house, a smell of incense
and of candle-wicks, a confusion. In the background,
through a half-open door, the foot of a low bed could
be seen, and a flickering of lighted candles, funereal in
the light of day. Bianca saw nothing else, in the midst
of all those relations crowding in there, blocking her
way.

"No!—let me go in!"

The dazed face of Don Ferdinando appeared for
a moment, like a phantom; then the door closed.
Friendly arms supported her, affectionately, and Aunt
Macrì repeated:

"Wait! Wait!"

The wife of the sexton came back panting, carrying candlesticks under her apron. Her husband, who showed himself again at the door, said:

"The viaticum is coming—the extreme unction— But he knows nothing—"

"I want to see him!—Let me in!"

"Bianca!—At this moment!—Bianca!"

"Do you want to kill him?—upsetting him?—If he recognised you!—Don't go on like that, don't, Bianca! —A glass of water!—quick!"

Donna Aggrippina ran to the kitchen. They opened the door again before the gleaming of a procession. The priest, the canopy, the tall lanterns of the viaticum passed like a vision. The marquis, bowing to earth, murmured:

"Domine salva me—"

"Amen!" replied the sexton. "I've done what I could—alone like a dog!—twice to the doctor!—in the middle of the night!—And to the apothecary as well!—he says the account is already a long one— and he hasn't got the herb of Lazarus Risen, he says!—"

"Why?—Why don't you let me in?—What have I done?"

She was trembling so much that her teeth tinkled on the glass, almost beside herself, facing people with her terrified eyes.

"Let me go in! Let me go in!"

Her uncle the marchese hastily got out his handkerchief to wipe away the water she had spilled down her. Baron Mendola and Aunt Macrì were talking in the big window-bay.

"A long illness!—The Traos are all like that!—there's nothing to be done—"

"Look!" said the Baron, who had been watching for some time. "They've opened a little window on to my roof!—down there!—that thief of a Canali!—good thing I noticed it!—I'll have him up for it!—he's guilty, as black as pitch!"

"Don Luca! Don Luca!" somebody was calling. The door flew open all at once and Don Ferdinando appeared waving his arms in the air. Don Luca came running as fast as he could: screams, agitated voices, a mad running here and there, Donna Agrippina looking for the *Vinegar of the Seven Thieves,* the others struggling to restrain Bianca, who was behaving like a mad-woman, foam at her mouth, her eyes flashing lightning, so that you could hardly recognise her.

"Why not?—Why won't you?—Let me! Let me! —let me go in!"

"Yes! Yes!" said the marchese. "It is nothing but right that she should see him!—Let her go in!"

She saw a long, stiff body on the low bed, a sharp chin bristling with a greyish beard, sticking up into the air, and two wide-open, glaucous eyes.

"Diego!—Diego!—Oh my brother!"

"Don't go on like that, Donna Bianca!" said Don Luca quietly. "If he is still conscious, think what a fright for him!"

She stood still shuddering, terrified, her hands in her hair, looking around dazed. Then she fixed her dry, burning eyes on Don Ferdinando, who was gesticulating frantically as if he wanted to drive her from the bed.

"Not a thing!—not a thing did you let me know!—I

don't count any more—a stranger!—Shut out of heart and home!—shut out!—from everywhere!"

"Be quiet!" stammered Don Ferdinando, putting a trembling finger on her mouth. "Besides!—besides! —Be quiet just now!—So many people, you know—"

"Bianca! Bianca!" pleaded the others, taking her in their arms, pushing her, pulling her by her dress.

"Take her away!" cried Aunt Macrì from the door. "In her condition, poor thing—there'll be another tragedy if we don't mind—"

In the meanwhile arrived Donna Sarina Cirmena, exhausted, bathed in perspiration.

"I've only just heard!" she stammered, letting herself sink on the leather arm-chair in the midst of the relations gathered in the great drawing-room.—"What can you expect! with all that hubbub there's been in the village! If it hadn't been for the viaticum which I saw coming this way—"

The marchese nodded towards the door of the other room. Aunt Cirmena, huddled in the arm-chair, with her handkerchief to her eyes, whimpered:

"I can't bear these scenes!—I'm simply prostrate—!"

And as she continued interrogating with her eyes first one and then the other, Donna Agrippina replied *sotto voce,* afflicted, making the sign of the cross:

"Just now!—five minutes ago!"

Don Giuseppe came bringing the bundle of mourning flags.

"Here you are!—I've told the joiner."

Baron Mendola rose to go and hear what he wanted.

"All right! all right!" said Mendola. "We shall attend to everything just now. Don Luca? Hey, here, Don Luca! Don Luca!" Just as the sexton's head appeared in the doorway, came screams to tear your heart.

"Poor Bianca!—do you hear her?"

"She's like a mad-woman!" Don Luca confirmed. "Tearing her hair!"

Baron Mendola asked him before everybody:

"You've thought of everything, have you, Don Luca?"

"Yessir. The catafalque, the banners, as many masses as there are priests. But who's going to bear the expense?"

"Go away! Go!" interrupted Aunt Cirmena sharply, pushing the sexton by the shoulders towards the death-chamber, where the confusion was increasing.

"I'm sorry," said Aunt Macrì, rising to see how far the sun had got. "I'm sorry it's so late, and there's nobody at home to see to a mouthful of food."

Don Luca came out of the death-chamber, troubled in countenance.

"It's a risky thing!—She'll have to be taken away by love or force!—It's a risky thing, I tell you!"

"Is it allowed? May we?"

It was the big voice of the game-keeper who accompanied Baroness Mendola, with the plumed hat and the stockings stuffed with nuts. The old woman, without needing to hear more, stiff and straight as a distaff, went to take her place among the relations who had all gone quiet when she appeared, seated around on the old arm-chairs, with long faces and their hands in their laps. The Baroness looked around, crying in a high voice:

"And Madam Rubiera?—and Cousin Sganci?— What are we doing nowadays?—The relations must be told, for the funeral."

"There she goes!" said Donna Sarina in Dame Macrì's ear. "If the world fell—she'd be there! Did you see the commotion in the streets?"

Her cousin replied with a pale smile, implying that the old woman feared nothing because she was deaf.

"As a matter of fact—" began the baron.

But at that moment they came out carrying Bianca in a dead faint, her arms hanging, while Donna Agrippina and the sexton, red in the face, panted and gasped under the burden.

"As if she was dead," puffed the sexton, "her bones weigh."

"There, there in her own room," advised Aunt Macrì.

"As a matter of fact," resumed Baron Mendola, drawing his cousin Limòli and Sarina Cirmena aside— "as a matter of fact we shall have to club together for the funeral. And now you'll see brother-in-law Motta's relations coming forward.—We shall make a fine show—side by side with Burgio and Master Nunzio Motta!—But we can't leave her husband out.—It's a calamity, I don't say it isn't—but we've got to reckon with Mastro-don Gesualdo, eh?"

"Of course! of course!" replied Aunt Cirmena.

She wanted to raise some other objection, but Marchese Limòli put in his word.

"Leave it alone, my dear cousin!—In any case—the dead are dead, and won't speak again—"

"For all that," persisted Dame Cirmena, growing red, "it's simply disgraceful that Mastro-don Gesualdo hasn't even showed himself here."

Mendola went on to the landing to tell Barabba to run to the Sgancis.

"It'll cost some money! Did you hear the sexton? 'Who's going to bear the expense?'"

Aunt Macrì pretended not to hear, talking in a low voice with Dame Cirmena.

"Poor Bianca!—in her condition! How many months is it? Do you know?"

"Seven! it must be seven!—Really it's a risky thing—"

Marchese Limòli who was discussing with Mendola and Barabba the preparations for the funeral, concluded:

"I would invite the White Fraternity, seeing it's a question of a man of some distinction—"

"Of course!—We must do things properly—spare no expense—"

But everybody sheered off into generalities when it came to the point of laying down a farthing. Meanwhile in the death-chamber continued the conflict between the sexton's wife, who wanted to make Don Ferdinando leave the room, and Don Ferdinando who insisted on staying; like the whining of a little dog, and the shrill voice of Auntie Grazia squealing:

"Holy Madonna! Don't you understand a thing, don't you?—You are an out-and-out child! My boy would have more sense, believe me!"

And all at once, in the midst of the group of relations who were talking in low tones, appeared Don Ferdinando, dragging his legs, with his hair all ruffled, his shirt open, a face like a corpse on him too, bringing an old paper which he went round showing everybody.

"There's the privilege!—The diploma of King Martin—You must put it in the death notice—you must let them know that we've the right to be buried in the royal tombs—*una cum regibus!* Have you thought of

the banners with the coat-of-arms? Have you thought
of the funeral?"

"Yes, yes, don't be afraid—"

As everybody avoided taking direct responsibility,
turning away from him, Don Ferdinando went from
one to the other mumbling, with tears in his eyes:

"*Una cum regibus!*—My poor brother!—*Una cum
regibus!*"

"All right, all right," answered Marchese Limòli.
"Don't think about it any more now."

Baron Mendola, who had been confabbing with folks
outside on the landing, came back gesticulating.

"Gentlemen!—if you did but know!—I've fallen
out of the clouds!"—

"Quiet, quiet!" the marchese motioned to him.
"What is it now?"

In Bianca's room a great bustle was heard; anxious
and pleading voices; a fluttering as of people in a
quarrel; delirious cries of pain and anger; then a
scream which made everybody start. The door was
banged open violently, and the marchese suddenly came
out, in distress. A moment after appeared Aunt
Macrì crying:

"A doctor! Quick! Quick!"

Other relations now arrived one after the other,
afflicted, in black gloves. And above all the noise of
chairs shifted rose the cry of Aunt Macrì again:

"Quick!—a doctor! quick!"

IV

"Though an agglomeration of ceremonious phrases forms not the theme of these lines, homage remains undiminished. Out-pourings less false and more enduring are the only prayers I esteem. The favour of one look from you is what I sigh for, and this the reward I covet for these awkward lines of mine.

"At 7 o'clock on the 17th.

"Baron Antonino Rubiera."

"Of course!" added Master Titta who was standing on the threshold of the box while Donna Fifi perused this note. "He gave it me himself, did the young baron, to hand it over secretly to the leading lady. But for mercy's sake! I'm father of a family—Don't make me lose my daily bread."

Donna Fifi, yellow with bile, answered never a word. In private, behind the parapet, she unfolded the letter with feverish hand. Then she passed it to her mamma, who stammered:

"But let us hear—What does he say?"

"I'll be going," continued the barber humbly. "I'm going round to the back of the stage, because she murders her first love just now, and I've got to comb her with her hair down over her shoulders.—My respects, Donna Fifi—Don't you betray me!—"

"Whatever does he say?" repeated the mamma.

Nicolino stuck his head between them, and got a kick for his pains. At his cries Don Filippo came running in. He had been walking in the corridor, because the box was chock full.

"What's the matter!—As usual!—We shall have all theatre turning on us—nobody but us!—"

Canali also poked his head into the box.

"You must attend now! This is the scene where they kill one another!—"

"Let them!" muttered Fifì between her teeth.

"Eh? What?"

"Nothing. Fifì has got a headache," replied Don Filippo. Then softly to his wife: "May we ask what's amiss?"

"It's really stifling!" added Canali. "Can you make me a bit of room?—Just look up there—what a lot of people! I'd take my coat off as leave as not."

There was a hedge of heads. Peasants standing on the benches of the gallery, holding on to the beams of the ceiling in order to look down into the pit; boys almost hanging outside the balustrade, as if they were pruning olives and hanging on the boughs; such a crowd, that the Captain's lady in the box opposite threatened every minute to faint away, her bottle of smelling-water under her nose.

"Why doesn't she let the Force Captain unlace her?" said Canali, who was addicted to such little jokes.

Baron Mendola, who was paying a visit to Donna Giuseppina Alòsi in the next box, turned round with his foolish laugh that was heard all over the hall. Donna Giovannina went red. Mita stretched her eyes wide, and the mamma pushed Canali out of the door. Then she said to Fifì:

"Look out! The Captain's wife is watching you through her glasses."

"No! She's not watching me," replied the other, shrugging her shoulders.

"Do you want to hear the latest?" said the baron,

persisting in poking his head through the doorway.
"There's the deuce to pay, at the Captain's lady's.
She's having the lodging-house where the leading lady
is stopping put under surveillance!—Her husband himself, poor fellow!—Apparently they've found out some
pretty doings!—The Force Captain, really annoyed,
had to get a bit of his own back: Why don't you attend
to what's happening in your own house, my dear col-
league?"

"Hem! hem!" coughed Don Filippo gravely.
From the pit, however, they called for silence, the curtain having risen. Then Donna Bellonia fetched out
her spectacles to read the note, sheltering behind Fifi's
back.

"But what does he say? I don't understand a thing!"

"Ah, you don't understand?—He's never once written me one single nice word!—the villain! the traitor!"

The fact is that Ciolla, who prided himself on being
literary, had distilled the quintessence of his brain into
the epistle as he sat with the young baron shut up in
absolute privacy in the back of Giacinto's shop.

"But what's it about?—Can one get an idea?"

"Sssst!" they hissed from the pit.

You could have heard a fly buzz. The leading lady,
all white except her hair, which hung loose down her
back, as Master Titta had combed it out for her, made
the flesh creep on the bones of all those who were
listening to her. Some, for sheer anxiety, had risen
to their feet, in spite of the protests of those who
were sitting behind and couldn't see a thing. Canali
himself, profoundly moved, blew his nose like a
trumpet.

"Look!—Look!—Now!"

' "I!—I myself!—with this right hand which thou didst clasp, swearing me eternal faith!—" '

The lover, a mingy little fellow whom she could have put in her pocket, recoiled step by step backwards, with one hand on his velvet vest and the other, in the act of horror, among his curls.

"I can't stand it, I can't!" muttered Canali. And he fled away, just at the moment when the applause resounded.

"What an actress, eh? What talent!" exclaimed Don Filippo, also getting out of hand.—"Peste!—you clown!"

Nicolino, scared, kicked and floundered towards the door, head downwards, squealing that he wanted to go home. An earthquake down below in the pit. Everybody standing up, shouting and banging. The leading lady bowed her thanks to one side and to the other, wagging her hips, stretching her neck to right and left like a tortoise, sending kisses and smiles on her finger-tips to all the crowd, her lips gathered into a rosette, her breasts escaping quivering out of her bodice every time she bent forward.

"Blood of—! body of—!" exclaimed Canali who had come back to applaud. "I am a married man. I am father of a family—! But I shall be doing something I shouldn't!—"

"Oh papa, papa," broke forth Donna Fifì, bursting into tears. "If you love me, Oh papa! have that trollops whipped as she deserved."

"Eh?" stammered Don Filippo, arrested with his mouth open and his hands uplifted. "What's got you now?"

Donna Bellonia, Mita, Giovannina all rose together to calm down Donna Fifì, surrounding her, pushing

her into the background, towards the door, to hide her.
In the boxes opposite, and down in the pit, there was
a wave of uplifted faces, bursts of laughter, and a set
of inquisitive individuals pointing their glasses at the
Margarone box. Don Filippo, to put an end to the
scandal, posed himself in the front row along with
Nicolino, leaning on the parapet, saluting the ladies
with a superficial smile on his lips, while he muttered
in an undertone :

"Stupid donkey! Your brother, little as he is, has
more sense than you !"

Also in the next box there was a scuffle. Madam
Alòsi in a great bustle, her bottle of smelling-waters
in her hand, and Baron Mendola turning his back on
the theatre, shaking by the arms a boy as white as his
shirt, who lay fainting in a chair.

"The young La Gurna is taken bad—" said Baron
Mendola from Donna Giuseppina's box. "He under-
stands like a grown-up !—A nuisance !"

"Like my Fifì—just now !—Blessed children ! They
take everything so seriously."

The boy, pale, with big, timid, intelligent eyes, was
still looking at the stage whose curtain was fallen.
Donna Giuseppina, after her young nephew had somewhat come round, out of courtesy offered her smelling
bottle to the Margarones. Don Filippo kept grumbling under his breath :

"Just exactly like the La Gurna boy, who is no more
than seven years old !—Shameful !—You don't play
that dodge on me again, my word you don't !"

But he held his peace seeing Mendola enter on a
visit, dressed up in a bottle-green cut-away coat, apple-
blossom knee-breeches, only his cravat black in mourning for his Cousin Trao. He went making visits from

box to box in this fashion so as not to have to pay for a seat.

"Don't disturb yourselves—an inch of room—in a corner—you, Canali, can go to Donna Giuseppina next door here, there's nobody there!—No, no, really nobody! Sarino, her little lad—the boy as tall as her fan—you know the song—and Corradino La Gurna, the child of her aunt Trao. Donna Giuseppina takes him with her wherever she goes to serve as a screen— when she is expecting certain particular visits—you know what I mean! They sent him on purpose from Syracuse to bleed our pockets!—" "And then, as soon as Canali had gone:—"Peperito will be coming as well just now!—I don't like playing gooseberry!"

He closed one eye in a wink. Nobody answered him. Then, seeing all their long faces, he resumed, changing his tone:

"What a performance, eh! The woman especially! —She made me cry like a child!"

"Same here! Same here!" replied Don Filippo, pretending to turn it into a joke.

"Ah, Donna Fifi?—cheer up, they make friends again here in the third act. He is only wounded. A girl who loves him secretly saves him, and then vice-versa they discover that she is his foster-sister.—A play that was produced twice on two successive evenings at Caltagirone.—Oh-ho! Oh-ho!—What is it now?"

The Captain of the Force, in the box opposite, thinking he wasn't seen behind the back of the Captain's lady, made a sign towards them with his white handkerchief, pretending to blow his nose. Mendola, on turning round, surprised Miss Giovannina with her handkerchief at her face. She dropped her eyes suddenly and became as red as a pepper-pod.

"Ah! Ah! A splendid company! Lucky to get them in these parts. Specially the leading lady!—She is lodging there facing my house in Nanni Ninnaro's lodging-house. You should just see, every evening after the performance!" And he finished his sentence in the ear of Don Filippo, who went: "Hem! Hem!"

"I'll slap your face," threatened the mamma meanwhile *sotto voce,* as she glared at Giovannina. "I'll cool you down—"

"Of course!" continued the baron in a louder voice, so that the girls should not understand what had happened. "Master of the bunch is that noble father, the one that wears the long white beard. They pretend to quarrel every evening on the stage—But then, at home, you should see!—It's the truth I'm telling you! I made a hole on purpose in the granary window-cover, looking right into her room. There are the casuals, however, the three-farthing worshippers, you know! those who come to bring their offering—Lawyer Neri's son ransacked the pantry, that time when his father had fled away—sausages, the remains of the dried figs, whole cheeses—every day he brought something in his pocket! Ha-ha!"

The Captain's lady was of a mind to leave before the end. Standing in the front of the box, she had rudely taken the scarf from the Force Captain's uniform, and had given it to the lieutenant, who was putting it on her bare shoulders, adjusting it there under the nose of his superior, leisurely, calmly taking his own time, without caring a bit about all the eyes that were staring at him. Don Bastiano on the other side of the box, holding the fan in his hand, and the lady's own pacific husband, both looked on in silence. Mendola nudged Margarone, and these two then began to stare into space, scratching their chins. Canali remarked from the next box:

"A bit for everybody, and no harm to anybody——"

"You mind yourself though!—You mind yourself!"

"Yes, yes, I saw him come.—Now I'm off, before he's here, the cavaliere."

He ran into Peperito right in the doorway on to the corridor.

"Oh Cavaliere!—What a blessing to see you! Somebody hereabouts was anxious about you—honest truth!"

"Why?" stammered Peperito, going red.

"Why!—A performance that brings the whole place crowding like this—They were all saying—but how is the cavaliere?"

Peperito hesitated a while, trying to find an answer, not knowing what to do with himself, he was so angry. Then he banged the door in the other's face.

"Now they'll just do for the picture of the four innocents," added Canali laughing. "I'm going into the pit to look at him from down below."

"Cheer up, Donna Fifi!" then said Baron Mendola. "You're neither dead nor dying!—If we can't make you laugh whatever we do, it will mean——"

Just then a rustle of silk was heard in the corridor, and a noise of sabre and spurs. Donna Giovannina went red as fire, feeling her mamma's eyes on her. The Captain's lady pushed open the door of the box, and put her curly, smiling little head inside.

"No, no, don't move. I just came for a moment to say how do you do. This performance is really indecent—I'm going, so as not to hear any more—And the woman's dress!—did ever you see, when she bends forward——"

I

"Eh! Eh!" went Don Filippo, with a motion indicating his girls there.

"Exactly! A mother can't bring her girls to the theatre—"

"That's a fact," observed Don Filippo then. "The authorities ought to take action."

The lieutenant, who was very chirpy owing to the courtesy of the Captain's lady, added:

"I am the authority. I'm just going on to the stage to see if it is as I say—I want to touch with my own hand, like Saint Thomas."

But nobody laughed. Only the Captain's lady gave him a tap on the arm, and bent smiling to confide in Donna Bellonia's ear what it was that the lieutenant affirmed:—"But I say it's not so.—Look at Donna Giovannina—She is almost as fat as the leading lady, and yet one doesn't see any signs—Just a bit, maybe—from near to—perhaps from her stays being too tight——"

"Very graceful!" stammered the Force Captain from the corridor. "Very elegant!"

Zacco, who arrived just then, was for going back when he saw the uniforms, he had such a fear on him since that affair of the Carbonari. But then he took courage, so as not to arouse suspicion, and went round shaking everybody's hand, smiling, and yellow as death.

"I have just left Cousin Bianca Trao. She is still at her brother's house, poor thing! She can't move!— She had to have her baby right there in her own old home!—I didn't know a thing, having been in the country looking after my business."

"But what are they waiting for, that they don't baptise that child?" asked Margarone. "Archpriest

Bugno is raising the deuce for the soul of that innocent girl-baby, which is in every danger of going to hell—"

Then the Civic Captain spoke up:

"They are waiting for the mandate from His Majesty, God love us.—Marchese Limòli's idea, to carry on the Trao name in the collateral branch, now that the male line dies out.—I had the papers in my hands."

"Yes, a great family—a great house," added the Captain's lady. "I went to see Donna Bianca. I saw the baby too—a nice little face—"

"Well and good!" concluded Zacco. "Then Mastro-don Gesualdo finds that even his own child isn't his own."

The joke raised a laugh. Canali, returning with his pockets full of roast chestnuts, wanted them to tell it him again.

"Good-night! Good-night! I won't hear any more!" exclaimed the Captain's lady smiling all over her face, stopping her ears with her little gloved hands. "No—I am off—really!"

They were all in the corridor, Donna Fifì chewing a smile between her yellow teeth; Nicolino behind Canali, who was distributing chestnuts; also Donna Giuseppina had opened her box door, so as not to give occasion for talk. Only Donna Giovannina remained in her seat, nailed there by the black looks of her mamma. Don Ninì, who came on the quiet so as not to arouse suspicion in his fiancée, a little bunch of roses in his hand, was rather taken aback seeing everybody in the corridor. Donna Fifì darted a look at him, and rudely dragged away her brother who was climbing all over the young man to search in his pockets. The Force Captain caressed the boy, and said, looking into the Margarone box with those burning eyes of his:

"What a fine lad!—so attractive!—A fine family!"

Donna Fifì replied with a fetching smile, right under the very eyes of her fiancé. The Captain's lady also gave a wry smile; she looked at Donna Giovannina, whose eyes were shining; and as Peperito was just caressing Corradino La Gurna so as to pay court to Donna Giuseppina, saying the boy had a distinguished look, just like the Traos, she added, with her honied little voice:

"It is surprising what a family likeness there is between them all. Have you noticed how like Don Ninì Bianca's little baby is?"

"What the deuce!" muttered Canali in her ear. "What tales are those you are trumping up?"

Then followed some moments of embarrassing silence. Zacco went off humming. Canali announced that they were going to start the last act. There was an exchange of kisses and pungent smiles between the ladies; and Donna Fifì let herself go as far as to clasp with soft abandon the hand which the Captain held out to her in the foreign fashion.

"Here, come in for a moment," said Donna Bellonia to the young baron. "You will sit in the back of the box with Fifì, since you are quarrelling out with one another. Nobody will see you. Get up from there, Giovannina."

"Always the same!" muttered the latter who was furious with her sister. "I've always got to give way to her, I have!"

"Mamma—let him go—if he wants to quarrel!— He can see the play from behind the scenes!" sneered Fifì.

"I?"

But she turned her back on him. Mendola had stuck himself in front of everybody else in the box, to see the act which he had described, and at every verse-end he explained: "Hark now!—Here they find out that the foster-sister is the daughter of the other one—"

"Such things do happen," observed Canali from the doorway.

"Be quiet! Be quiet! Spiteful!"

All eyes turned on the young baron, even those of the girls. He pretended not to hear.

"If you are in a temper—," muttered Donna Fifì—"since you stand there like an owl—why don't you go?"

"I?"

"There you are!" interrupted Mendola in triumph. "There now—you see!"

"I'm a married man," Canali began once more.—"I'm father of a family.—But that leading lady would easily make me do something I shouldn't do!—She's even got a lovely name!—Aglae!"

"Aggly—Ugly!—What a name!" jeered Baron Mendola. "I shouldn't know what to do—face to face with her!—"

Don Filippo cut in.

"She's a famous actress—a leading lady on the placards—So you can guess——"

"Why yes," ejaculated Don Nini rashly, so as to say something.

"Ah!—You like her as well, do you?"

"Certainly—that is—I mean—"

"Say it, say it then!—We know all about it!" Mendola smelt a storm and rose to clear out. "I know the rest that's coming. Good-night. If you'll allow me, Don Filippo—Listen, Canali—"

As ill luck would have it, the leading lady, who ought to have kept her eyes turned to heaven whilst declaiming: 'It is written above—by Fate—' let her looks wander into the Margarone box. And then Donna Fifì could not restrain herself.

"Yes, we know all about it! The agglomeration of ceremonious phrases!—these awkward lines of mine!—"

"I?—these awkward—?"

But she flew at him as if she wanted to set her teeth in his face:

"You may well make a brazen face!—Yessir, the letter with the awkward lines!—here it is!—" and she waved it under his nose, bursting into tears of rage. Don Ninì remained at first overwhelmed. Then he went off like a fury, looking for his hat. In the doorway he ran into Don Filippo, who was rushing up at the noise.

"You are a fool!—an imbecile!—You've brought up your daughter in a nice fashion!—Thank God I shan't set foot in your house again!"

And he went off in a rage, banging the door. Don Filippo, who had stood open-mouthed, bolted into the box the moment the young baron had gone, and in his turn flew at his wife:

"You are a fool!—A fine way you've brought up your daughters!—You see what I've had to listen to! You ought never to have brought that knave to my house—"

The rupture created a stir. Five minutes later nobody was talking of anything else in the theatre. It was a wonder the performance didn't end in whistling. The leading actor rounded on the leading lady, who was ruining him in the eyes of the first families in the place. But she vowed and swore that she didn't even know him by sight, that baron, and that he didn't matter a straw to her. Master Cosima, the carpenter, and everybody behind the scenes heard them. Don Nini, furious, went immediately next day to find Ciolla, who was going his own ways after those twenty-four hours under lock and key in the Castle.

"You've made a nice fool of me with your awkward phrases!—The whole place knows your letter off by heart—"

"All right! What does it signify? It's a sign that they all like it, if they know it off by heart."

"Like be damned! She says she doesn't care a straw about me—"

"Oh! Oh!—that's impossible!—That letter would have fetched a wall down! As a matter of fact it's your fault, Don Nini.—I don't speak of your physical appearance. But you ought to have made some sort of present to her along with it, dear baron! Powder makes the ball fly! Did you think you were going to do the trick with your handsome face?—with two farthings' worth of satin note paper?—Because you haven't given *me* anything, you know."

In vain did friends and relations try to intervene to patch up the quarrel. The mamma repeated:

"What can one do?— Men—! Even your father!—"

Don Filippo tried another tune:

"Follies!—Youthful pranks!—It was just circumstances—the novelty.—Leading ladies don't come every year, not by any means.—You are a Margarone, when all's said and done! He certainly won't change a Margarone for a comedian!—And then, if I forgive him, because it's I who have most to forgive—"

But Donna Fifì was not to be placated. She said she wanted to have nothing more to do with him, a simpleton, a stingy creature. Baron Awkward Lines!— Anyhow, she would never lack for a swain twenty times better than he—She went about vilifying him among friends and relations. There was nothing Don Ninì couldn't have done, for rage. He swore that he wanted to throw her over at any cost, and have the leading lady, if only out of spite.

"Ah! I'll show her, that witch! Powder makes the ball fly!"

And he sent presents of sausages, fine cheese, and a four-gallon jar of wine. They filled the table of the lodging-house. People talked of nothing else in all the village. Baron Mendola told how he saw the Marriage Feast of Cana every night through his hole. Presents upon presents, till the baroness had to hide the key of the store-pantry. Master Titta came at length to tell Don Ninì:

"She resists no longer, your honour! The leading lady has lost her head. . Every night while I'm combing her hair she talks of nothing else to me."

"You must get me the satisfaction I told you of!— Right under Donna Fifì's own eyes I want that satisfaction! I want to make her die of consumption!"

But the first meeting was a fraud. Signora Aglae pretended to be a poor unsuspecting creature, and had her face painted like a mask. Nevertheless she received him like a queen, in the hole at the back of the scenes, that stank of candle-wicks, and she presented him to a bit of a man who was rummaging in the chest, in his shirt-sleeves, and who didn't even turn round.

"Baron Rubiera, the distinguished agriculturalist—Signor Pallante, the celebrated artiste—"

Then she threw a look at the back of the celebrated artiste, who went on rummaging and grumbling, another longer look at Don Nini, and added in a half-tone:

"I have known him for some time!—I see him every evening in the pit!—"

Then he began excusing himself that he hadn't been to the theatre because the family was in mourning; but at that, Signor Pallante turned round with his hands dirty with dust, his face also plastered up, and on his head a bladder-skin from which hung greasy hair.

"It isn't there," he said in a deep voice that seemed to come from under the ground. "I told you so!—be damned to it!" and he took himself off growling.

She looked round with a mysterious air, her eyes bewildered in the midst of the black circles around them; she stole on tiptoe to close the door, and then turned to the young man, one hand on her bosom, and a pallid smile at the corner of her mouth.

"Strange how my heart beats!—No—it is nothing. Be seated!"

Don Nini looked round for a chair, his brain on fire and his heart beating indeed. At last he perched on the trunk, trying to find some appropriate phrases that might take effect, whilst she was burning a bit of cork in the smoky flame of the oil-lamp.

Another visitor arrived, Mommino Neri, who when he found Rubiera there, became suddenly ill-tempered and didn't say a word, leaning on the door-frame, sucking the knob of his walking-stick. Signora Aglae alone kept up the conversation: a fine town—a cultured, intelligent public—handsome young people there too—"

"Good-night!" said Mommino.

"You are going already?"

"Yes—you can't stir inside here—Too many of us—"

Don Ninì looked after him with a grin, and kept up a drumming of the big drum with his heels upon the chest. She caught his grin and raised her shoulders with a fascinating smile, sighing as if a weight was lifted from her stomach.

The young baron, transported, began:

"If I am in the way too—" and he looked round for the hat he was holding in his hand.

"Oh no—you no!" she said earnestly, bowing her head.

"May we come in?" asked the cracked little voice of the scene-shifter behind the door.

"No! No!" cried Signora Aglae with as much agitation as if she had been caught in the act.

"We are going on!" came the deep voice of Signor Pallante. "Hurry up." Then she, lifting towards Don Ninì her resigned face, said with a sad smile:

"You see!—I haven't a moment's liberty!—I am a slave of the arts!"

Don Ninì took up the refrain: The arts—a splendid thing—It was her own kingdom—her own altar!—Everyone filled with admiration of her!—all the hearts she made beat!

"Ah yes!—I have given myself entirely to my art—I have given myself entirely."

And she opened her arms, turning herself towards him, with such abandon, as if offering herself to her art, there in front of him, that Don Ninì sprang down from the chest.

"Take care!" exclaimed she in a low voice, rapidly. "Take care!"

Her hands trembled as she stretched them instinctively towards him, as if to keep him off. Then she rubbed her eyes, suppressing a sigh, and stammered as if just waking up:

"Oh forgive me.—One moment—I must dress—"

And a malicious smile flashed in her eyes.

That nuisance of a Mommino Neri was still there, leaning against a side-scene, and talking with Signor Pallante, who was already dressed as a king, with a furred gown and a paper crown. This time it was Don Nini's turn to look black. She, as if she knew, half opened the door again, leaning out her naked arm and shoulder:

"Baron, if you wait till the end of the act,—I have got those verses that you want to read there at the bottom of the trunk."

No! no woman had ever given him such joy, such a hot flame at his heart and in his head; neither that first time when Bianca abandoned herself in his arms, quivering; nor when a Margarone had inclined her superb head, showing herself together with him in the midst of the murmur which they excited in the crowd. It was a real access of madness. It put him in such a state that he would have borrowed money wherever he could, in order to make her presents. The baroness in desperation warned the tenants not to lend a farthing to her son, unless they wanted to reckon with her.

"Ah! Ah!—they shall see! My son has got nothing of his own. And for certain I shan't pay!—"

There had been violent scenes between mother and son. He more obstinate than a mule, worse than ever since Signora Aglae had not even let him come up the stairs at the lodging-house. At last she had told him why, one evening, in the dark there on the threshold, while Pallante had gone up to light the lamp.

"He is jealous!—I am his!—I have been his!—"

And she had confessed all, with her head drooped, and her beautiful sonorous voice suffocated with emotion. He, a great gentleman disinherited by his father on account of that unlucky passion, had loved her for years, madly, desperately; such a love as one reads of in books; he had devoted himself to Art, to follow her; had suffered in silence; had implored, had wept— At last one evening—when—still all trembling and palpitating with the emotions which art aroused—pity —sacrifice—she did not herself know how—while her heart was soaring to other skies—flying far away to another ideal—But afterwards, never again!—never again!—She had recovered herself!—ashamed—repenting—implacable—He, who loved her always, the same as before—more than before—loved her to madness—he was jealous; jealous of everything and of everybody, of the air, of sleep, of thought—and of him also, Don Nini!—

"Hey!" they heard the deep voice on the stairs. "Do you want them fried or with tomato sauce?"

Over her face, sweetly veiled in the semi-darkness, strayed an angelic smile.

"You see?—Always the same!—Always the same devotion!"

Ciolla, who was Don Nini's confidant, said to him later:

"What a silly you are! That fellow's nothing but

a—an old pimp. They swallow together the stuff you and Neri's son send."

Indeed he had often met Mommino on the stage, and even outside the door of the lodging-house, up and down like a sentinel. Mommino was now all smiles and sweetness for him. When it seemed to him that he was really made a fool of, he got in a rage.

"Ah!—You want that?" she said to him in fevered tones. "Well!—well—if there's no other way of proving to you how I love you—If I must be lost at any cost—this evening—after midnight!—"

There was a smell of stables on those dark stairs whose steps were dirty and broken by the iron-shod boots of all the clientele. At the top, a thread of light, and a white figure which offered itself entirely, brusquely, with hair all loose.

"You want me—your Indian slave—your oda-lisk?—"

There were dirty plates on the table, upon the bed a damask mantle worked with arabesques, carnations and a lighted night-light on the cupboard-top under the little picture of the Virgin, and a scent of incense rising from a pomade pot which was smoking on the floor. Over the doorway which led into the other room was nailed a beautiful turkish shawl, spotted with oil; and behind the turkish shawl could be heard Signor Pallante snoring upon his jealousy.

"To tell the truth she has bewitched him," wrote the canon-priest Lupi to Mastro-don Gesualdo, pro-posing that they should do a good one on the young Baron Rubiera. "Don Ninì is up to his ears in debt, and doesn't know which way to turn. The baroness swears that while she lives she won't pay a farthing.

But she's got no other heirs, and one day or another she'll have to leave him everything. As you see, it's a good opportunity, if you have the courage—"

"How much?" replied Mastro-Don Gesualdo. "How much does he want, young Baron Rubiera? If I can manage it, I am ready—"

Later, when it was known in the village what a large sum Don Gesualdo had advanced to Baron Rubiera, everybody said he was mad, and that he'd lost his money. He replied with his own peculiar smile:

"Don't you trouble. I don't lose money. The baron is a gentleman—and time is a better gentleman than he."

So the proverb says truly that woman is the root of all evil. And when it comes to an actress—

Don Ninì had hoped to keep the negotiation a secret. But for some time his mother had been refusing to leave him alone, seeing him so changed, disrespectful, with his face shining and his chin shaved every morning. At night she couldn't close her eyes for worrying where her son managed to find the money for all those silk kerchiefs and bottles of scent. She had set Rosaria and Alessi on his track. She asked the farm-bailiff and the country people. She kept the key of the pantry and of the store-barn under her pillow. How her heart talked to her, poor thing! Her cousin Limòli had been so kind as to point Aglae out to her, as the actress was waggling her hips and tinkling with trinkets.

"See her? that's the one. How do you like the looks of her, eh, for a daughter-in-law? Like her, do you?"

For all the world as if Don Diego Trao, dying, had cast the evil eye on her.

In little towns there are people who would walk miles to bring you a piece of bad news. One morning the baroness was seated in the shade under the awning on the balcony, basting together one or two sacks of rough canvas which she handed on to Rosaria to sew properly, as the girl squatted there on the outer stairway, pursing her mouth and screwing up her eyes so that the needle shouldn't escape from her coarse, roughened hands, turning round from time to time to look down into the narrow, deserted street.

"And three!"—Rosaria blurted as she saw Ciolla

passing back and forth with that police-bailiff's look on his face, examining the baroness' house from top to bottom, stopping every two strides, turning round as if he expected her to call to him. Dame Rubiera, who had been following that come-and-go for some time, from under her spectacles, finally leaned forward to fix Ciolla with a look that said plainly enough: "What are you up to and what do you want?"

"How do you do?" He started the conversation himself. And he stood there with his feet apart, leaning against the wall opposite, his hat over his eye and in his hand his stick that looked like the land-surveyor's measuring cane, waiting. In answer to his greeting the baroness asked with a bitter-sweet smile:

"What are you after? Valuing the house? Do you want to buy it?"

"I—no! I don't, dear Madam."

"No, I don't," he said again more emphatically, seeing that she had begun her sewing again. Then Madam Rubiera leaned again towards the narrow street, her spectacles shining, and she and Ciolla remained eyeing one another for a moment, like two basilisks.

"If you've got something to tell me, then come up—"

"No, nothing," said Ciolla; and yet he made for the big door. Rosaria pulled the cord, and began to mutter: "What does he want now, that fellow? In a minute it'll be time for lighting the fire."

However, the clamour of the live-stock was heard from the court-yard, and the steps of Ciolla coming up very leisurely. He entered with his hat on his head, very polite, repeating: *"Deo gratias! Deo gratias!"* and praising the order which reigned everywhere in that house.

"Managers like you aren't born to-day, Baroness. There you are, there you are, always on the go, ruining your eyes with work. They've got some property together, those hands have!—And they have squandered nothing, that I *can* say."

The baroness, who was listening with all her ears, began to be uneasy. Meanwhile Rosaria had cleared a chair of the sacking which had been piled over it, and stood there listening, scratching her head.

"Go and see if the hen has laid an egg," said her mistress. And then she turned to talk to Ciolla, more affable than before, so as to get out of him what he had to say. But Ciolla wouldn't let it out yet. He spoke of the weather, of the crops, of the ferment which the Force Company had left in the village, and of the troubles that had come upon himself.

"Poor folks get pitched on, dear Madam, and the folks who've made the mischief go scot free. Blessing for you that you stop at home and mind your own business. You're right of it! You do well! Everything you've got here is of your own making. I don't say it to praise you. Bless your hands that can work! Your husband, rest his soul!—but there, we won't speak of the dead!—everything slipped through his fingers, as it does with all the Rubieras'—The property all mortgages up to the hilt—and the house— What was the Rubiera house, when all's said and done? —Those five rooms there—"

The baroness pretended to sup up the praise, giving him the information he wanted, following him from room to room, explaining to him where the doorways had been opened to put the old into communication with the new.

Ciolla kept looking round with his bailiff's eyes, nodding his head, pointing with the cane:

"Precisely! Those five rooms there! All the rest belongs to you. Nobody can set their claws in your belongings while you live—God send you may live to a hundred! A house like this—a real palace! big as a monastery! It would be a mortal pity if your enemies went and broke it up again for you—for enemies has every man!"—

She felt herself going pale, but pretended to smile; a smile that simply got his pecker up.

"Well, what? Have I said something funny? Enemies has every man. Mastro-don Gesualdo, for example, if you like!—He's one that I wouldn't like to have mixed up in my affairs—"

Then he too pretended to look around suspiciously, as if he saw the long hands of Mastro-don Gesualdo everywhere.

"That man—if he's made up his mind to get inside your house—bit by bit—if it takes a hundred years— like the hedge-hog—"

The baroness had returned to the balcony to take the air, without answering him, so as to get the remainder out of him. He hung back a little still, pretending to be going, taking off his hat to give it a rub, looking for his cane which he had in his hand, asking her to excuse him for all the chatter he had been filling her ears with till then.

"You've got so much to do, eh? You ought to be getting dressed to go to the baptism of Don Gesualdo's baby? It will be a choice christening—in the Trao house!—See how the devil puts his spoke into everything, that the baby of Mastro-don Gesualdo goes and is born in the Trao house!—All the relations will be there—a general peace—you are relation as well."

The baroness kept on laughing, and Ciolla kept up with her, each looking the other in the face with eyes alone remaining serious.

"No? You're not going? You are right. You beware of that man. I say no more.—Your son is a fool!—I say no more!"

"My son has his belongings and I have mine—If he's made a fool of himself he will pay—if he can pay—Because I shan't! He can pay out of his own belongings, those five rooms there that you saw. He's got nothing else, worse luck.—But I shall keep what I've got for myself.—I don't mind if my son enjoys himself. He's young—young folks must enjoy themselves. But I'm not going to pay for it, that I'm not."

"That's what everybody says. Mastro-don Gesualdo thinks himself very smart. But this time, for once, he's found somebody smarter than himself. He'll look lovely, if he's got Don Ninì's mistress to keep!—He'll be able to fancy he is sowing his own wild oats, for his young self!—"

The baroness laughed so much that she had to hold on to the furniture lest she should fall.

"Ha—ha! that's a good one!—You are right there, Don Roberto!—"

Ciolla kept pace with her, pretending to laugh also, spying her out of the corner of his eye, irritated that she took it so cheerfully. But Rosaria, when she came to take the sacking, found her mistress so pale that she was going to shout for help.

"Fool! What are you doing? What are you standing stuck there for? Can't you see Don Roberto to the door!—"

So Ciolla finally made up his mind to go, grumbling as hard as he could to the servant:

"How jolly your mistress is! I'm pleased to see it! Laughter is good for the blood and makes you live long. Splendid! Splendid!"

When Rosaria got upstairs again she saw her mistress in a fearful state, rummaging in drawers and cupboards, with eyes that saw nothing, foam at her mouth, dressing herself in haste to go to the christening at cousin Motta's.

"Yes, I'm going——We'll find out what it really is.—— Better know the truth."

People seeing her going down the street haggard and with her bonnet on one side, didn't know what to think. In the small square of Sant'Agata there was great curiosity, as the guests arrived to the christening in the Trao house, and Don Luca the sexton was running back and forth with the candlesticks and other sacred implements under his arm. Speranza came out on to her terrace every other minute, shaking her skirts and planting her fists on her hips, and she began to rail at that baby which was robbing her brother's inheritance from her:

"It'll be a famous christening! The house is full of them—all the swells—Only not any of us! We're not going—so the grand relations needn't blush. We've nothing to do with it, we haven't. Nobody has invited us to my niece's christening——You can see that it's no blood of ours——"

Old man Motta had also refused, that morning, when Gesualdo had gone to ask him to put the holy water on his grandchild. Seated at table—he was just eating a mouthful—he told him No, holding up the wine-flask which he had had at his mouth. Then, wiping his lips with the back of his hand, he gave him a black look.

"Go yourself to your daughter's christening. It's your own business! I was never born to mix up with your grand gentry. You can come for me only when you need me—to stop folks' talking—No, no—when there's something to be earned you don't come to fetch me, no indeed!—Don't you know?—The contract for the road—the communal lands—"

Master Nunzio wanted to recite the whole litany of his grievances, now he'd started. But Gesualdo, who already had his house full of people, and who knew he'd never make him come round if once he had said no, went away with heavy heart and drooping shoulders. He wasn't feeling very cheerful either, poor fellow, although he had to make a smiling face for all the congratulations and the deep bows he would get. Then at last he burst out at Nanni l'Orbo, who was at the bottom of the stairs more impudent than ever, asking him for sweets and money:

"Yes!—It goes without saying!—It goes without saying a man must be skinned even to the roof-beams, now that a child is born in this house."

Barabba and the chasseur of Baroness Mendola had swept a bit, and dusted, and set the rickety altar on its feet, after it had been shut up for so many years in the wall-cupboard of the big drawing-room that served as a chapel. The room itself was still draped in the mourning remaining from the death of Don Diego, the portraits covered and the chandeliers wound round and round with black cloth for the relations to come to the funeral, as was the custom in old families. Don Ferdinando, newly shaved, in one of Cousin Zacco's black coats that hutched up on his back, went poking his long-faced nose in everywhere, his arms dangling out of his short coat-sleeves, smeary, suspicious, asking everybody:

"What is it?—What's happening?"

"Here is your brother-in-law," his aunt Sganci said to him as she entered the room along with Don Gesualdo Motta. "Now you must embrace one another and be really nice with one another, now that that little creature has come to bring you together."

"How do you do! How do you do!" muttered Don Ferdinando; and turned his back.

But the other relations had more sense, and were nice with Don Gesualdo; Mendola, the Zacco cousins, all the lot. Already times had changed: the whole village had been upside-down for twenty-four hours, and you never knew what might happen from day to day. Anyhow, by love or force Mastro-don Gesualdo had established himself among all the relations, and now they had to reckon with him. All of them therefore wanted to see the baby—a flower, a rose of Mary!—Aunt Rubiera kissed Bianca like a mother who has found her lost child again, wiping her eyes with her handkerchief wet as a sponge.

"No! I've not got the feelings of a horse!—I couldn't believe it was true, I couldn't, after I'd reared you like a daughter!—Oh dear, I'm a fool—I am as I always was, a simple country woman—just like my own mother, rest her soul—with my heart in my hand."

Bianca, who was all decked out under the canopy of the bed, so pale that she looked like wax, dazed with all that crowd, didn't know what to say, looked at the people, bewildered, trying to rake up a smile, stammering. Her husband, however, played his part among all those friends and relations and congratulations, with his face open and jovial, his shoulders broad and genial, his ear on the alert to catch the things that were being said around him and behind him. Aunt Cirmena, infatuated, said in answer to those who wished the parents a fine boy-child later on, that girls are absolutely like twitch-grass, and that in the end they clear everything worth having out of the house, when they've got to be married——

"Eh—children!—you've got to take them as God sends them, boys or girls. If we could go and pick them in the market—Don Gesualdo wouldn't want for money to buy himself a boy."

"Don't talk to me!" said Aunt Rubiera at length. "You don't know what boys cost you!—The amount of trouble!—I know——"

And she continued to unburden herself into Bianca's ear, watching Don Gesualdo out of the corner of her eye to see what he would say. Don Gesualdo said nothing. Bianca for her part kept her eyes dropped and changed colour continually.

"I don't know him, I don't!—and I'm his mother who bore him!—Do you remember, what a good child he was, good as gold!—quiet, loving, obedient!—And now he'd even turn on his mother, for the sake of that beastly stranger-woman—a strolling actress, do you know her? They say she's got false hair and teeth. She must have cast some evil spell on him! Strolling actress and a stranger, just imagine!—he can't think of anything else.—Spends the very blood out of his veins;—and bad people—scoundrels they are, they help him. But I'm not going to pay, no I'm not.—No, that I shan't do!"

"Aunt!" stammered Bianca, all her blood in her face.

"What do you think of it! He is my cross! If only I knew how much, though——"

Don Gesualdo kept on chatting with Cousin Zacco, each of them with his heart in his hand, oh so friendly! Then the baroness spat out the question that was boiling inside her:

"Is it true that your husband lends him money—on the quiet?—Have you seen him come here to him?—Tell me, what do you know?——"

"Certainly, certainly," replied Don Gesualdo at that moment. "You must take children as they come."

To confirm this Zacco, pointed to his own girls, ranged in a row like so many organ-pipes, modest and pleasing.

"Look you! I have five girls, and I'm fond of them all alike."

"Why, of course!" replied Limòli. "That's why you don't want to marry any of them off."

Donna Lavinia, the eldest, threw an ugly look behind her.

"Ah, are you there?" said the baron. "You are always ready, like the devil in the litany, you are!"

The marchese, who was to be godfather, had put on his Cross of Malta. Don Luca came to say that the canon-priest was ready, and the ladies passed into the drawing-room, with a great rustling of silk, behind Donna Marianna who was carrying the baby. Through the open doorway was seen a twinkling of little flames. Don Ferdinando was peeping at the bottom of the corridor, curious. Bianca wept softly for tenderness. Her husband, who had remained on his knees, as Dame Macrì had told him, with his nose to the wall, got up to calm her.

"Be still—Don't let them see you!—Before them all you've got to keep a smiling face—"

All at once down in the square below there exploded the deuce of a noise of crackers. Don Ferdinando fled in terror. The others who were attending to the christening ran to the balcony with their tapers in their hands. Even the canon-priest in gown and stole. It was Santo, Don Gesualdo's brother, celebrating the baptism of his niece in that fashion, in his shirt sleeves, on all fours down below there, with a lighted fuse. Don Gesualdo opened the window to pour out a sackful of abuse.

"Fool!—You'd have to be doing something!—Fool!—"

The friends calmed him.

"Poor chap!—let him alone! It's one way of showing his pleasure—"

Aunt Sganci triumphantly put his daughter into his arms.

"Here you have Isabella Trao!"

"Motta and Trao! Isabella Motta and Trao!" corrected the marchese.

Zacco said it was a successful grafting: the two families becoming one. Don Gesualdo, however, was still somewhat gloomy as he held the child in his arms. Meanwhile Don Luca, aided by Barabba and the chasseur, served the ice-slush and the sweets. Aunt Cirmena, who had brought the La Gurna nephew along with her on purpose, filled his pockets and his handkerchief. The Zacco girls, because the eldest had disdained to take anything, all said no, one after the other, devouring the tray all the while with their eyes. Don Luca encouraged them to take something, saying:

"They're all quite fresh. I went myself to order

them at Santa Maria and the college. No expense spared."

"The deuce!" said Zacco, who was seeking an opportunity to appear amiable. "The deuce! I am pleased to see this day."

The others chimed in in chorus:

"Now the house of Trao is resuscitated. God's will it is. The child herself chose to be born in the maternal home."

The canon-priest Lupi also arrived to present his congratulations, along with Marquis Limòli who had thought out this means of not letting the Trao house become extinct with the death of Don Ferdinando.

"Of course, of course—" grumbled Don Gesualdo. "It was an understood thing—I agreed to it before— and when I have given my word—"

He went to put the baby in the arms of its mother, who was robbed of it again by all the aunts in turn. Baroness Mendola wanted to know what everybody was saying. Zacco, very considerate, came to ask for sweets for Don Ferdinando, whom nobody had thought of.

"Of course, of course. He is the master of the house."

"You see," observed Dame Rubiera. "There's soon plenty of folks in the world ready to carry off your child and your property."

There was a burst of laughter. Donna Agrippina twisted her mouth and bent to earth her great eyes which said so many things, as if she had heard something indecent. Don Gesualdo was also laughing, carrying everything off pleasantly. In the end even he risked his joke:

"And when she marries she'll leave her Trao name

behind her again—But she won't leave her dowry behind—"

Dame Rubiera, deeming the moment propitious and not wanting to lose the opportunity, drew him privately to the side of the bed, whilst Mendola and Don Ferdinando were heard quarrelling at the end of the corridor in loud voices, and everybody was running to see.

"Listen, Don Gesualdo. I'm not one of your mealy-mouthed sort. I wanted to speak to you about my scamp of a son. You help me, Bianca."

"I, aunt?"

"You must excuse me, I speak with my heart in my hand,—just like my mother who made me. Now that you're a father yourself, Don Gesualdo, you'll understand what I feel—what a thorn I've got in my heart —what a torment—!"

She looked now at her niece and now at her niece's husband, with that simple, good smile, which her parents had taught her to put on when making a thorny bargain. Don Gesualdo listened quietly. Bianca, embarrassed by this exordium, seemed like a wax statue with her child in her lap.

"You know all the talk that's going round, about Nini and that actress, don't you? All right. As for her, I don't care a thing. She's not the first and she won't be the last. His father, rest his soul, was just the same. But I've kept him from making any great mess so far. And now he's got into bad company, a set of scoundrels and—bad companions! Hark here, Bianca, I wouldn't have given my daughter to that canon-priest to baptise—"

Bianca, dismayed, moved her lived lips without uttering a word. Don Gesualdo, however, had twisted his mouth to a smile as the baroness let out that remark.

She, hearing everybody coming back, at last asked openly:

"Tell me the truth. He has asked you to lend him money, hasn't he!—Have you given him any?"

Don Gesualdo grinned wider. Then seeing the baroness going red as a pepper-pod, he replied:

"Excuse me—excuse me—You see—why not ask him himself?—This won't do—I'm not your son's confessor, you know—"

Mendola burst into the room telling amid noise of laughter the scene he had just had with that bear of a Don Ferdinando, who didn't want to come and make peace with his brother-in-law. Dame Rubiera, without saying any more, wiped her lips with her handkerchief that was still sticky with the sweet-stuffs, while the relations were taking their leave. As they departed they all had a word of praise for the way in which everything had gone off. Donna Marianna said to Dame Rubiera that she, the baroness, had done well to come, so as not to let anything appear exceptional or to give occasion for spiteful talk.—The other replied with a glance which Donna Agrippina caught as it passed:

"A lot of help it's been to me! Serpents they are! I'll say no more. But we've taken the viper into our bosom—! You'll see before long—"

Don Gesualdo, left alone with his wife, quaffed in one draught a large glass of water, without saying anything. Bianca, her face haggard, as if she felt ill, followed every movement of his with frightened-seeming eyes, pressing the baby to her bosom.

"Here, do you want a drink?" said he. "You must be thirsty as well—"

She nodded assent. But the glass trembled so much in her hand that she spilt all the water down her.

"Never mind, never mind," said her husband. "There's nobody to see you now."

And he began to wipe the sheet with his handkerchief. Then he took the baby in his arms, because it had begun to cry, dancing it to soothe it, carrying it round the room.

"Did you see the folks, eh?—the loving relations? But they don't take your husband in, not they."

Outside in the square all the neighbours had gathered to see the guests leave. At the Margarone window away in the background, above the roofs, there were other sort of people peeping every moment. Dame Rubiera began saluting from the distance with her fan, with her handkerchief, whilst she talked so vehemently with Marchese Limòli that the pair of them seemed as if they were coming to blows.

"Race of serpents! Rogues of all rogues! They'll swallow him in one bite, that reprobate of a son of mine!—But first they'll have to reckon with me! Look, come with me to the Margarones' for a minute—We've not seen anything of one another for some time—But there's really no reason why we should have done with our old friends—for a mere childishness. You are a man of the world—and sometimes—a word in season—"

Donna Giovannina came with a glowering face to open the door. In the background you could see the parlour door open, and through the door the furniture with the covers taken off. A ceremonial air, in short.

"What is it?" asked the marchese entering. "What's happening?"

"I don't know at all," exclaimed Donna Giovannina, who seemed on the point of tears. "There's somebody come to see us, I believe. But I know nothing."

"Poor lass! poor lass!" The marchese lingered in the ante-chamber, caressing the girl. He had taken her plump chin between two fingers, winking wickedly at her, looking round as he said in a low voice:

"What do you expect, though? Patience! First come first served. Donna Fifi and your mamma, eh, receiving visits? Don Bastiano, eh? the Force Captain?——"

Don Bastiano was actually there, in the parlour, dressed in civilian clothes, a fine new suit that shone on his back, newly shaven, seated on the sofa next to Mamma Margarone, like a suitor, letting slide a languid, sentimental look from time to time towards the young woman, stroking his new moustaches that refused to be caressed into form. Donna Fifi, seeing Dame Rubiera appear, bridled superbly, triumphant, cooing apart with the stranger in order to insult her.

"Oh, oh——" said the marchese, saluting Don Bastiano who was looking rather sheepish. "Are you here then? Good! Good!"

And he began to talk with the Captain, while the ladies chattered all together, asking him why the Force Company had departed without him; if he intended to stay for some time, if he liked the village and if he wanted to quit his epaulettes. But Don Bastiano kept to generalities, praising the locality, the climate, the inhabitants, underlining his words with expressive looks at Donna Fifi, who was pretending to gaze out of the balcony windows, with eyes full of poetry, and was bowing her head and blushing, at every compliment, as if it had been paid to her herself. The marchese asked all at once whether Don Filippo was not at home, and they answered that he had gone to take Nicolino for a walk.

"Ah good! good!"

Dame Rubiera bit her lips waiting for the marchese to turn the conversation to the things she wanted. Meanwhile she watched on the sly the languid airs of Fifì, who seemed to be melting under the fiery looks of Don Bastiano Stangafame, and couldn't keep still on her chair, with her flat bosom heaving like a pair of bellows, and her restless little feet speaking so many things as they showed themselves every minute from under the hem of her dress. The conversation languished. They talked of the christening and of the people who had been there. But everybody was thinking of his own affairs, chattering more or less, trying to say something, with an absent smile on the lips. Only the marchese seemed to take a great interest in the Captain's talk, as if the game wasn't his business. Then, catching sight of the red face of Donna Giovannina who was hanging round to spy through the half-open door, he called her in a clear voice:

"Come in, come in, my pretty dear. We want to see your lovely face. We're alone here, *en famille*—"

The mamma and the elder sister darted two black looks at the girl who remained in the doorway, hiding her servant's hands under her apron, ashamed of being caught like that, in her house-dress. Limòli, without noticing anything, asked in a low tone of Donna Bellonia:

"When shall we marry this handsome child? The eldest comes first, naturally. But then remember that I'm here to play the intermediary,—*gratus et amore,* of course—We are old friends!—"

Donna Bellonia kept giving him looks, though the marchese pretended not to see. Then she said to him, *sotto voce:*

"What are you saying?—What ideas are you putting into her head! She's too young yet—She's hardly out of short frocks—"

"I see, I see!—" replied the marchese eyeing the white stockings of Donna Giovannina. Donna Fifì had taken the Captain to look at her flowers on the balcony. She plucked a carnation, breathed its scent in a long breath, half closing her eyes, and gave him the flower.

"I see, I see," repeated the little old man.

Then Dame Rubiera wanted to go, chewing a smile, the yellow flowers on her bonnet trembling. While the ladies were exchanging kisses and embraces, the marchese turned to the Captain.

"I'm very pleased!—I'm very pleased indeed—really—Don Bastiano!"

"Why?—What about?"

The Captain, surprised and embarrassed, tried to find a response to retaliate with. But the other had turned away, and was saluting the ladies with a kind word for each; he caressed Giovannina in a paternal manner, while that young lady was still scowling.

"What's amiss? What's amiss? What do you mean by it? Girls ought to be pleased and lively. Did you hear what your mother said? She says you've plenty of time to grow up. Now then, now, cheer up!"

Dame Rubiera felt herself bursting under her mantle; after she had turned round in the street to wave her hand to all the Margarones arrayed there on the small terrace, she began to mutter:

"Did you realise, eh?"

"*Diamine!* It didn't need many wits. But we've got to put Giovannina's heart to rest also—"

"Why yes, yes! I'd put her heart to rest with all

he pleasure in the world.—A flirt!—Did you see the
game with that carnation? We should have been in
for something, my son and I—He almost deserved it,
really! The reprobate; the enemy of his own
mother!—"

A few yards further on they met Canali who was
going to the Margarones', and had seen all the hand-
kissing exchanged between the street and the terrace.
Canali made an important face, and stopped the baroness to greet her, leading the conversation round
about, ferreting in her face with two inquisitive eyes.

"You've been to see Donna Bellonia, have you?
Well done. An old friendship like yours!—Pity that
Don Nini—"

The baroness also wanted to draw him out, assum-
ing a nonchalant air, fanning herself and enticing the
dog through the barn-yard.

"Ah well—follies—the follies of youth—"

"No no, pardon me!" returned Canali. "I'd just
like to see how *you* would feel—! A father must keep
his eyes open and mind whom he gives his child to.—I
don't speak of your son—A good young fellow—a
heart of gold. The trouble is, he's let himself be taken
in—surrounded by false friends. There are always
plenty of rascals.—They've got him to sign something
or other—"

The baroness marched off, leaving him standing
there.

"You hear?—You see?" she mumbled to her cousin
Limòli. And then she left him also, since he couldn't
keep up with her.

"Good day! Good day!"

And she ran to Lawyer Neri, pale and overcome, to

K

see—to hear. The lawyer knew nothing—nothing positive, at least—

"You know, Don Gesualdo is a sharp fox.—There are things that are done on the quiet, you know. They'll have had the contract drawn up by some strange lawyer. Lawyer Sghembri from Militello, they say— But there! There's no need for you to get into such a state for a thing like that—I don't like the looks of you."

Rosaria, who was busy cleaning out the fowl place when her mistress came home, all at once heard a fearful scream from the courtyard, as if they were cutting the throat of some large beast upstairs, a scream that made her lose her slippers as she ran. The baroness was still there, where she had begun taking off her things, leaning against the chest of drawers, bent double as if she had colic, moaning and lamenting, while the saliva ran from her mouth and her eyes started from her head:

"Assassin! unnatural son!—I won't let him devour my property!—I'd rather leave it to the poor—to the nuns—I want to make my will!—I want to make donations! Fetch me the lawyer—quick!—"

Don Ninì was fooling with his Aglae, in that wretched lodging-house room which had become an inferno for him ever since he had saddled himself with that debt to Mastro-don Gesualdo. The bed in disorder, the dirty clothing, the uncombed hair, even her caresses, and the meat stews which friend Pallante cooked for them, had all turned to poison for him since they cost him so dear. Seeing Alessi appear, coming to fetch him, and talking of lawyers and donations, he went suddenly pale. In vain did the leading lady clasp him round the neck, her dress all ungirdled, heedless of

Pallante who ran from the kitchen and of Alessi who
stood there open-eyed, rubbing his hands.

"Ninì! My Ninì!—Do not abandon me in this
state!—"

"Damn it all! Let me go—the lot that you are!—
Do you think it's a joke?—That woman is capable of
everything!"

Don Ninì, once more entirely under the spell of the
love of property, was moved neither by the scene nor
by the fainting. He left the poor Aglae there lying
stretched out on the floor where she was, like the last
act of a tragedy, and Pallante pulling her dress down
over her stockings, whilst Ninì himself ran home without his hat. There at home ensued a terrible scene between mother and son. At first he wanted to deny it;
then working himself up to a frenzy, he complained
that he was kept like a slave, worse than a child, without a shilling to spend; and the baroness threatened to
go herself to the lawyer, to dispose of her property,
so just as she was, in her petticoat, that very moment,
if they wouldn't send and fetch him. Then Don Ninì
went down to double-lock the street door, and put the
key in his pocket, threatening to break every bone of
the lad's body if he so much as breathed.

"Ah, this is my reward!" mumbled Alessi. "Next
time I shall really go to the lawyer's."

At last, by love or force, they succeeded in getting
the baroness to bed, while she struggled and screamed
that they wanted to kill her outright so as to squander
her property.

"Mastro-don Gesualdo!—Yes—It's he who is devouring all I've got!"

Her son tried to calm her with fair words and foul.

"Don't you see you're poorly? Do you want to g
really ill, to drive me to perdition?"

And then all night he never closed his eyes, risin
every minute to run and hark if his mother was sti
crying out, terrified that the neighbours would hear he
and would come into the house with the lawyer and th
police, cursing the leading lady in his heart, that he'
ever come across her, troubled, if he dozed off for
moment, by a host of bad dreams; Mastro-do
Gesualdo, the debt, people crowding in and filling th
house, a great crowd.

Rosaria came to knock at his door early in th
morning.

"Don Ninì, oh Baron, sir, come and see—The bar
oness can't speak!—I am frightened—if you saw—

The baroness was stretched out in her bed like a
ox felled by the butcher, with all her blood in her fac
and with her tongue hanging out. Bile, and bitterness
all those ill humours which must have accumulated upo
her stomach, were seething inside her, and came out a
her mouth and nostrils, running out on to the pillow
And how she tried to help herself, still, in that state
how she tried to grasp with her heavy, swollen hands
how she tried to call, in those inarticulate tones tha
were swamped in the viscous slime.

"Mamma! Oh mamma!"

Don Ninì overcome, still puffed with sleep, was cry
ing from room to room, striking his head with his fists
running to the balcony in despair, whilst the neighbour
knocked and stormed at the locked door below. Afte
a while, doctor, barber, relations, inquisitive folk
filled the house. The very dream of the night before
Don Ninì told everybody the same thing, wiping hi
eyes and blowing his nose as if he was blowing

rumpet. As soon as he saw Lawyer Neri there, he
wouldn't move from his mother's bedside, asking the
doctor every moment:

"What do you think, doctor? Will she recover her
speech?"

"In time, in time," replied the doctor at last, annoyed. "Damnation, do you think it's as easy as
sneezing?"

You would hardly have known Don Ninì any more,
from one day to another; with a long beard, dishevelled
hair, fixed at his mother's bed-head, or else immersed
in the business of the establishment. Not a bean went
out of the store-pantry unless it passed through his
hands. So true it is that trouble teaches a man sense.
His mother would have told him so herself, if she
could have spoken. You could see it in the way she
looked at his hands, her eyes all bloodshot, every time
he came to take the keys that were hung on the door-
post. And even he understood, now that the stuff was
passing through his own hands, how much misery he
must have given to the poor woman; he repented, and
tried to win forgiveness, with patience and loving care,
keeping always near her, watching over the sick woman
and the visitors who came to see her, growing pale
every time his mother tried to loosen the bonds of her
tongue in the presence of strangers. He felt a great
tenderness when he thought that the poor paralytic
could neither move nor speak to take the property
away from him, as she had threatened.

"No, no, she won't do it! Those are things one says
in a moment of anger—I would like to see her—!
When all's said and done, I'm her own flesh and
blood—She'd be the first to die of a stroke if she had
to leave away all she's got to one body and another—"

trumpet. As soon as he saw Lawyer Neri there he
couldn't move from his mother's bedside, asking the
[...] moment.

"What will you think, doctor? Will [...]
[...]?"

"[...] time," replied the doctor at last, un-
moved. "Damnation, do you think it's as easy [...]
[...]ing?"

You would hardly have known Don Nini any more,
from one day to another, with a long beard, dishevelled
[...] fixed at his mother's bed-head, or else unmindful
of the business of the establishment. Not a bushel went
out of the store-pantry unless it passed through his
hands. So true it is that trouble teaches a man sense.
His mother would have told him so herself, if she
could have spoken. You could see it in the way she
looked at his hands, her eyes that were all blood-shot, every time
he came to take the keys that were hung on the door-
post. And even he understood now that the stuff was
passing through his own hands; how much misery he
must have given to the poor woman; he repented, and
was now in forgiveness, with patience and loving care,
keeping always near her, watching over the sick woman
[...] the visitors who came to see her, growing pale
every time his mother tried to loosen the bonds of her
tongue in the presence of strangers. He felt a great
darkness when he thought that the poor paralytic
could neither move nor speak to take the property
away from him, as she had threatened.

"No, no, she wouldn't do it! Those are things one says
in a moment of anger—I would like to see her—"
When, she said and done, I'm her own flesh and
blood—he'd be the first to draw a stroke, if she had
[...] we'll all be got to one body and another—"

THIRD PART

THIRD PART

I

Little Isabella, even before she was five years old, was put in the Maria College. Don Gesualdo, now that he had his own property under the sun, and was on a level with the best people in the place, wanted his daughter to be on the same level: to learn fine manners, and reading and writing and embroidery, and the Church Latin as well, everything like a baron's daughter; the more that, thanks to God, she wouldn't be lacking in dowry, as Bianca did not seem as if she would give him any other heirs. She had never been well after her baby was born, and seemed to decline from day to day, gnawed by the same worm that devoured all the Traos, so that it was certain she would have no more children. A real chastisement from God. A failure, the marriage, although the gentleman himself was careful not to complain even to the canon-priest. When you've made a mess of something, better keep still and say nothing of it, so as not to show yourself beaten before your enemies.

Nothing, nothing had that marriage brought him, neither dowry, nor male child, nor the help of the relations, nor even that which Diodata gave him formerly, a moment of happiness, an hour of pleasantness, such as a glass of wine brings to a poor man who has worked all day! Not even that!—A wife who wasted away between your hands, who made your caresses go cold, with that face and those eyes and that being frightened, as if you were going to make her fall into mortal sin, every time; as if the priest hadn't made the sign of the cross over you both, in the beginning, when she had said yes. It wasn't Bianca's fault. It was the blood of her race which refused. You can't graft peaches on an olive tree. She, poor thing, inclined her head, and even went so far as to offer herself, all blushing, so as to obey the commandment of God; as if she was paid to do it—

But he wasn't taken in, no. He was a peasant, but he had the subtle shrewdness of a peasant too! And he had his own pride, even he. The pride of a man who has managed to earn with his own hands, and his own work, the fine linen sheets in which they both slept turning their backs on one another, and those good meals which he had to eat on the end of his fork, finicking, under the eye of the Trao wife—

At least he wanted to order the feast in his own house. And if the Lord God had punished him precisely in that matter of the children he wanted to put into the world according to His law, giving him a girl instead of the legitimate heir he wanted, Isabella at least should possess everything he lacked himself, she should be a lady in name and in reality. Bianca, as if she felt she had not long to live, didn't want to be separated from her daughter. But the master was he, Don Gesualdo. He was good, loving in his own way; he let her lack for nothing: doctors, drugs, exactly as if she had brought him a big dowry.—Bianca hadn't words good enough to thank God, when she compared the house in which the Lord had set her with that in which she was born. There her brother himself lacked bread by day and covering by night.—He would have died of want if his relations had not helped him well, without letting him know it. Only from her, Don Ferdinando wouldn't accept anything whatsoever, while

Don Gesualdo would not have let him go short of any-thing, with a heart as large as the sea, that man! Her own relations said of him:

"You haven't words good enough to thank God and your husband. Let him do as he will, for he is the master, and you do your best for your child."

Then she considered that it was the Lord who pun-ished her, that He did not want that poor innocent to be in her husband's house, and at night she soaked her pillow with tears. She prayed God to give her strength, and consoled herself as best she could, thinking that she suffered in expiation of her sins. Don Gesualdo, who had so many other things on his mind, such weighty affairs on his shoulders, and who was used to seeing her like that, with that face, didn't even notice. Some-times, seeing her rise more deathly pale than ever, more haggard than usual, he said to her to encourage her:

"You will see that when you've sent your child to college, you'll be more contented yourself. It's like pulling a tooth out. You can't look after your child, when you are so poorly in health. And when she's big she's got to know all the things that plenty of other folks know, who aren't so rich as she is. Children must get used to the yoke while they're young, each one according to his own estate.—I know it, I do.—And I've had nobody to help me myself! That child is born ready clad."

Nevertheless at the last minute there were tears and laments, when they took Isabella to the parlour of the convent. Bianca had been to confession and to com-munion. She heard mass kneeling, feeling herself fail, feeling her child torn once more from her bowels, as the little creature hung round her neck and didn't want to leave her.

Don Gesualdo did not mind any expense to keep Isabella content in her college; sweets, books with pictures, images of the saints, walnuts with the wax Infant Jesus inside, a manger of Good Saint John which took up a whole table; everything that the children of the leading gentry had, his little girl had the same; and the nicest things to eat, the first-fruits of the whole country, cherries and apricots brought specially from a distance. The other girls stared with all their eyes, and stifled such great sighs. The youngest of the Zacco children, and the Mendolas of the second marriage, who had to be satisfied with the onion and black olives which passed at the convent for lunch, saved their faces by talking of the riches which they had at home and on their lands. Those that had neither riches nor lands made the most of their noble relations, the Civic Captain who was mamma's brother, the baroness aunt who had the chasseur with the feathers, Daddy's cousin who had five estates touching one another, in the district of Caltagirone. Every holiday, every New Year, when the little Isabella received still more costly presents, a silver crucifix, a rosary with the glory-be-to-the-father beads made of gold, a mass book with a tortoise-shell back for her to learn to read from; new little wars arose, new little slights, alliances made and unmade according as a sweet or a saint's picture was given or not given. There were young eyes glittering with haughtiness and jealousy, little faces flushed red, tears, and afterwards everything poured into the ears of the mammas, in the convent parlours. Between all the little girls of all the families arose the same devilment which Don Gesualdo had aroused

among the grown-ups in the village. You didn't know
any more who could spend money and who couldn't.
A competition between all the parents as to who could
throw away most money in ridiculous trifles, a general
confusion among those who had always formed the
front rank and those who ought to come second. Those
who really couldn't, and those who couldn't find in
their hearts to spend their precious money to suit
Mastro-don Gesualdo, let fall certain allusions and
remarks about him which fermented in the heads of
the little scholars. The nuns also took part in this
internecine warfare, according to their relationship or
their sympathies, and the party which triumphed even
wanted to overthrow the Mother-Superior. They took
sides even down to the portress, even to the lay sisters
who felt themselves humiliated at having to serve
without any extra pay the daughter of Mastro-don
Gesualdo, a creature who had sprung from nothing,
like themselves, and who had only got rich yesterday.
The outside enmities, discords, strife of interests or of
vanity passed right into the cloister, and occupied the
hours of recreation, and broke forth inside the sacred
precincts in small spite and small reprisals, and in ugly
words.

"Do you know what they call your father?—*Mastro-don Gesualdo.*"

"Do you know what you have to do at your house?—
You've had to sell a pair of oxen to be able to get the
ground sowed."

"Your aunt Speranza spins thread for anybody who
will pay her for it, and her children go barefoot."

"The bailiffs have been to your house to make a
mortgage inventory."

Little Alimena even hid herself on the tower stairs

on Sunday to see if it was true that Isabella's father
wore the peasant's stocking-cap.

He found his daughter still flushed, her breast heav
ing with sobs, looking timorously behind her lest sh
should see the malicious eyes of the other little girl
glittering behind every grating, staring at his hand
to see if they were really dirty with lime, drawing bach
instinctively when his rough skin pricked her as h
kissed her. Just like her mother.

"You can't graft peaches on an olive tree—"

So many pin-pricks; the same evil fate which hac
always poisoned everything for him every day; th
same implacable warfare which he was forced to wag
all the time against everybody, and everything; and i
wounded him even there, in the quick of his love for hi
child. He held his peace, he did not complain, for h
wasn't a baby and he didn't want to set his enemie
laughing; but meanwhile his own father's words cam
back into his mind, the same rancours, the same jeal
ousies. It had to be so. He stilled his own heart, bu
in that heart the thorn remained always. All that h
had done and did for his daughter only removed her
further from him: the money he had spent to educat
her like a lady, the company among which he had her
brought up, the extravagance and luxury which sowec
pride in the heart of the little girl, the very name he
had given her by marrying a Trao—a fine prize he had
won! The child always said:

"I am a daughter of the Traos. My name is Isabella Trao."

The war burst out more fiercely, between the girls,
when Don Niní Rubiera got married:

"If it's true that you are relations, why didn't your

uncle send you any sweets? That's because they don't want you for relation."

Isabella, who already replied like a grown up, returned:

"My father will buy me sweets. We've fallen out with the Rubieras because they owe us so much money."

The daughter of the wax-chandler, who was on her side, added many other stories:

The young baron had been thrown over. Fifì Margarone wouldn't have any more to do with him. He had married Donna Giuseppina Alòsi, who was older than himself, because he couldn't find anybody else and must have money:—all the gossip that went on in her mother's shop, in every café, in every druggist's, and from door to door.

In the village they talked of nothing but the marriage of Don Ninì Rubiera.

"A marriage of convenience," said the Captain's lady, who always talked in such a mincing fashion. As years went on the Captain's lady had also fallen into the vices of the place; she busied herself with other people's affairs now she had none of her own to hide. When she met Cavaliere Peperito she made a malicious little face at him that made her look twenty years younger, smiles which wanted to find out so many things, shaking her head, offering so graciously to listen to his confidences and his jealous outpourings, threatening the cavaliere with her fan, as if to tell him he'd been a terrible rake, and that if he'd let another man carry off his mistress now, it showed that he must have had his own good reasons for so doing.—Sooner or later——"

"No!" retorted Peperito, who was beyond all grace.

"Neither sooner nor later! You can go and tell Donna Giuseppina so! If I couldn't have her and be her master, I'm not going to be there for her when it suits her, you understand!—play the stud-cock—You understand? Donna Giuseppina can rest quite assured about that."

And now he was spreading all the dirty stories about Dame Alòsi in the square: if for a miracle she sent you a basket of grapes, she asked you to send the basket back; and she sold on the sly the stockings she knitted, servants' stockings as thick as your finger—yes, and she had showed him these stockings when she'd got them on also, just in order to rouse him—to get out of him just what suited her.—But no, he wasn't having any!—

In fact, he went round saying things hot and cold. There were some nice talks at the Café of the Gentry. Ciolla followed him round to pick up all the bits of spite and carry them further on his own account. One day there was a real treat for him when Signora Aglae was seen to arrive in the village, along with Signor Pallante, to make a scandal against Baron Rubiera, and to take what belonged to her if her seducer was not ready to go to the altar with her. She came on purpose from Modica, spitting bile, waxed, painted, loaded with cock-feathers and bits of glass, trailing along with her the innocent proof of Don Ninì's villainy, a real love of a little girl. And so folks said that Don Ninì had always been one for the fair sex, and that if he'd married Madam Alòsi, who was old enough to be his mother, it meant that there must have been some serious money interest. The matter was threshed out in one way and another. The young baron stopped the mouths of those who came to congratulate him in order to get the truth out of him, with a few words. Madame Sganci, who had arranged the marriage, held her tongue when her friends went to visit her. Don Gesualdo perhaps knew more than most, but he shrugged his shoulders. All they could get out of him was answers like this:

"Well, what would you? Everybody minds his own business. Baron Rubiera will have found that it suits his own advantage to marry Madam Alòsi, that's all."

The truth was that Don Ninì had had to take the Alosi woman so as to save that bit of a house which Don Gesualdo wanted to turn him out of. It is true that he'd become wise now, given over altogether to money; but his mother, buried alive in her arm-chair, didn't leave him master of a farthing; she made him give account of everything; everything had to pass under her eyes; without being able to speak, without being able to move, she succeeded in making her own people obey her even better than before. And she struck like an oyster to her belongings, forcing herself to live so as not to have to hand over what she'd got. Meanwhile the debt increased from year to year; so that poor Don Ninì spent whole nights without being able to close his eyes, sometimes; and when the money fell due, with capital and interest it amounted to a considerable sum. The canon-priest Lupi, who went in the young baron's name to ask for an extension of time for payment, found Don Gesualdo worse than a wall.

"What are we playing at, my dear Canon? I've neither seen interest nor capital for more than nine years. My money is useful to me just now, and I want to be paid."

Out of sheer necessity Don Ninì was reduced to going to plead with his Cousin Bianca, after so many

years. He started with her from a distance:—Such
a long time since they had seen one another! He hadn't
had the face to call on her, to tell the truth. He didn't
want to excuse himself. He had been a young scamp.
Now he had opened his eyes, too late, when there was
no help for it, when he found on his back all the burden
of his own mistakes. But absolutely he couldn't pay
just then. "I am a gentleman. And in the end I've got
the wherewithal to pay. But at this moment I absolutely can't! You know what your aunt is! What a
stubborn head! You and I have had to suffer for her
stubborn head. But anyhow she can't last forever,
in the state she's in—"

Bianca had scarcely been able to breathe at first
when she saw him, going white and red in turns. She
didn't know what to say, she stammered, broke into a
cold sweat, had a convulsion of her hands, and so tried
to hide them, smoothing the two corners of her apron
mechanically. All at once there was blood in her
mouth.

"What's the matter? What's the matter? Something the matter with your gums? Have you bit your
tongue?"

"No," she replied. "I have it sometimes. Don
Diego had it as well, you remember. It's nothing."

"Good, good. Then do me a kindness; speak a word
for me to your husband. At this moment I absolutely
can't.—But I am a gentleman, I believe!—My mother
hasn't got anybody else to leave everything to, between
now and a hundred years hence—"

Bianca tried to excuse herself:—Her husband was
the master. He did everything according to his own
mind, he did. He didn't like anybody poking their
nose in his affairs—

"Then what are you his wife for?" retorted her cousin. "It's a nice thing! A fellow who wasn't fit to look you in the face!—He ought to thank God and my mother's obstinacy that he's been so lucky!—You'll do all you can to persuade him to grant me this extension, won't you then?"

"And you, what did you say to him?" asked Don Gesualdo, finding his wife still upset, after that visit.

"Nothing—I don't know—I felt ill—"

"Good! You did well. Don't you bother, I'll look after things. Serpents in your sleeve, are relations.— What, did you see! Coming round *you*, now that they want to make use of you; the rest of the time he doesn't care whether you're alive or dead. Leave him to me, I'll send him his answer by the police bailiffs, that cousin of yours—"

So that marriage had come to pass, after the baron had turned heaven and earth to find the money to pay Don Gesualdo; and at last Donna Giuseppina Alòsi, who had fine property in land, had given him a mortgage. Don Gesualdo, having got hold of that fine inscription on her land, said no more about needing money.

"Give them time," he confided to his wife. "Leave them alone. They pay neither interest nor capital, and in time that land will come in for Isabella's dowry. What do you think of it? Couldn't you laugh! Uncle Rubiera scheming to get together the dowry for your daughter—!"

He has these outbursts of humour at times, when he was alone with his wife, and pleased with his day, before going to bed, while he was putting his night-cap on, in his shirt-sleeves. In private with her he showed himself as he really was, rough and not ill-natured, with his wide laugh showing his big white teeth, and afterwards passing his tongue over his lips as if he already tasted the taste of something good, like the man greedy of possessions, which he was.

When Isabella had grown up a bit she was sent from the Maria College to the first convent-school in Palermo. Another blow for the poor mother, who feared she would never see her again. Her husband, in order to comfort her, in the state that she was in, said:

"Look you, we're killing ourselves to do our best for her, each of us as we can, and the day will come when she'll never even think of us. That's how the world is. And so you'd better get it into your head that you can't have your daughter for ever with you. When she marries she'll go somewhere else, away from here. Here there's nobody to marry her, with the dowry she'll have. If I've done so much for her, I want at least to know who I'm giving my own flesh and blood to. At this minute the man is already born, somewhere or other, who will enjoy the fruits of all my labours, without even saying thank you to me—"

He had his heart full also, poor devil, and if he let himself go sometimes, all alone with his wife, just by way of talk, still he did not shrink from doing his duty. He went to see his girl in Palermo, when he could, when he was able to leave his business, that is once a year. Isabella had grown into a beautiful maiden, a little frail still, rather pale, but with a natural grace in all her subtle person; the delicate skin and the aquiline profile of the Traos; a flower from a rare plant, in short; fine, well-bred stuff she was, so that even her father himself when he went to see her felt shy in front of the girl, who had now the same bearing as her companions among whom she was educated, all girls of the first families, each one bringing into the school all the baronial haughtiness of every corner of Sicily. In the parlour they called him Signor Trao. When he wanted to know why, Isabella blushed red. The same tale here as at the Maria College. And his daughter would have had to suffer the same humiliation here again, on account of her parentage. By good luck Signorina di Leyra, whose affection Isabella had won with presents, had taken up the sword vigorously on her behalf. She knew the Trao name, one of the first families of the South, down there where her brother the duke had his estates. The little duchess had a high name and a high-handed manner of speech, even though she was there in the college without paying, so that the companions let the Trao pass. But Don Gesualdo also had to let it pass, and have himself called by that name, out of love of his daughter, when he went to see her.

"You'll see how lovely she's grown, your daughter," he came back to say to his wife, who was always ailing.

The mother saw her at last when she left her college in 1837, when the first rumours of cholera began to spread already in Palermo, and her father hurried to fetch her away. It was like a blow in the breast for the poor mother when, after so long a time, she heard the mule-litter stop before the big door.

"My child! my child!"—with her arms stretched out and her legs shaky, rushing down the stairs. Isabella coming up also at a run, with her arms also open.

"Mamma! Mamma!"

And then they clung round each other's necks, the mother rocking her child from side to side again, as she had done when Isabella was tiny.

Then came the visits to the relations. Bianca had got her strength back, to carry her child round in triumph, to the Sganci house, to the Marchese Limòli, to all the houses where she had gone as a child, before she had been sent to college; and now she was already a big girl, with a straw hat and beautiful blond tresses —a flower. Everybody came out to see her go by. Aunt Sganci, who had grown deaf and blind, touched her face so as to know her again.

"A Trao! You can't say anything else!"

Her uncle the marchese praised her eyes, eyes blue and bright as two stars.

"Eyes which could see sin coming," said the marchese, who had always got his little jest ready.

Then when they took her to see Uncle Don Ferdinando, Isabella, who had always been recalling to her school companions her mother's home, in her outbursts of ingenuous ambition, felt a sense of surprise and depression, disillusion, seeing it again. Anybody who liked could now enter the collapsed great door. The courtyard was mean, cumbered with stones and rubbish. You came by a path through the nettles to the dilapidated flight of steps, shaky, also stifled in weeds. At the top the falling door was hardly held shut by a rusty latch; and the moment you entered, a heavy, humid atmosphere took hold of you, a smell of mould and of cellars rose from the floors of glazed tiles blazoned with coats-of-arms and historic scenes, and littered with stubble and broken bits fallen from the vaulted ceiling whose plaster was all dropping off, a thick air came from the corridor that was dark as a tunnel, and from the dark rooms which you could just make out stretching in a long row, empty and abandoned, revealed by strips of light which wavered in through the dilapidated windows. At the end was her uncle's little room, sordid, smoky, with the ceiling coming undone and ready to fall, and the shade of Don Ferdinando coming and going like a spectre.

"Who is it?—Grazia—come in—"

Don Ferdinando appeared on the threshold, yellow and lean, looking at his sister and his niece in stupefaction through his spectacles. On the unmade bed still lay Don Diego's old great-coat, which he was just patching. He rolled it up hastily, along with a bundle of other old rags, and thrust it in a drawer.

"Ah—is it you, Bianca?—What do you want?"

Then realising that he still had the needle in his hand, he put it in his pocket, ashamed, always moving with the same mechanical movement.

"Here is your niece come to see you," stammered his sister with a tremor in her voice. "Isabella—you remember her?—She has been away at school in Palermo."

He turned on the girl those blue, bewildered eyes of his, which shifted all the time from side to side, and murmured:

"Ah!—Isabella!—My niece!"

He looked uneasily round the room, and from time to time, as he caught sight of some forgotten object lying on the table or on the lame chair, a knot of dirty thread, or a cotton handkerchief put in the sun to dry, he ran quickly to hide it. Then he sat down on the edge of the little bed, staring at the door. While Bianca was speaking, her heart wrung inside her, he kept looking round with suspicious eyes, thinking of something else. All at once he went to lock the writing-desk.

"Ah!—My niece, do you say?"

He looked at the girl once more with the same hesitating look, then turned his eyes to earth.

"She is like you—the very image—when you lived here—" He seemed to be trying to find something to say, his eyes wandering round, avoiding the looks of his sister and his niece, his hands trembling slightly, his face colourless and blank. For a moment, while Bianca was whispering in his ear, begging something of him, as if she was going to break into tears, he suddenly straightened his bent back so that he seemed very tall, a shadow in his light-coloured eyes, a wave of the Trao blood colouring his pallid cheek.

"No—no—I don't want anything. I have no need of anything.—Go away now, go away—you see—I've got such a lot to do—"

It fairly wrung your heart. A ruin and a state of want that humiliated her ambitious memories and her fantastic romances born during imaginative confidences made to her school-friends, the illusions that the maiden's little head was full of, now she had come back to her home village intending to play the leading rôle there. The paltry luxury at Aunt Sganci's, her own cold and melancholy home, the tumble-down mansion of the Traos, which she had so often recalled with childish pride, while she was away, all had now dwindled, gone black, poor, sad. There opposite was the Margarone's terrace, which she had so often remembered as vast and full of sun and flowers and happy girls who dazzled her with the display of their elegant clothes, then, when she was a child. And how little and squalid it was in fact, with the leprous wall that gloomed above it!—and how old Donna Giovannina had become, always seated smiling in the midst of the dusty flower-pots, knitting, in a black dress, enormous! At the bottom of the little road squatted the little house of Grandfather Motta. When her father took her there they found Aunt Speranza spinning, grey-haired, with disagreeable wrinkles in her face. There were loose tiles to stumble over, a lad in his shirt-sleeves who lifted his head from a pack-saddle he was mending, without greeting her, Master Nunzio moaning with rheumatism in bed under a dirty coverlet:

"Oh, you've come to see me! Did you think I was dead? No, no, I'm not dead. Is this your girl? Have you brought her to show her off to me?—She's a young lady, you can't say anything else! You've given her a fine name! Your own mother was called Rosaria! Wasn't she? Excuse me, my dear niece, if I receive you in this hovel—I was born here, so what's the odds! I hope I shall die here—I wouldn't change it with the fine house where your father wanted to shut me up. I'm used to going into the street the minute I get up. No, no, better think about it in time. Everybody as he is born."

Speranza grunted out something which one couldn't hear. The lad followed them with his eyes as far as the door, when they left.

Meanwhile rumours of cholera began to go around. At Catania there had already been an upheaval. Arrived Don Bastiano Stangafame, from Lentina, along with Donna Fifì, who looked as if she had the sickness already on her, green, lean, telling tales that would turn your hair grey in a day. At Syracuse, a young woman as lovely as the Madonna, who did dances on the backs of trained horses in the theatre and went spreading the cholera in that way, had been killed by the enraged people. Uneasy people waited to see, making all preparations for decamping from the village at the first sound of alarm, and spying at every new face that passed.

Just then there appeared two pedlars selling ribbons and silk handkerchiefs. They went from house to house selling their things, and looking in at the doors and courtyards. Dame Margarone, who was always ready to spend money to deck herself out, as if she was still a young chicken, made many purchases; however, as she hadn't got any change, those gentlemen said they would call for it next day.

Instead the Judgment Day dawned. Ciolla ran to the justice of peace to complain that his hens had been poisoned; he took them with him in his hands as a proof, still warm. Don Nicolino went back home beside himself, ordering his sisters to bar the doors and not to open to any living soul. Doctor Tavuso even had the door of the village draw-well closed. The gentry, remembering what a doubtful subject that Ciolla was, since he had been handcuffed and put in the castle sixteen years before, armed themselves to the teeth and prepared to scout the country, ready for if he took it into his fancy to go fishing in troubled waters again. The order was, fire without mercy at the first alarm. The two pedlars were seen no more. Before evening loaded carriages began to pass, fleeing into the open country. After vespers not a living soul went into the streets. Quite late arrived a litter bringing Don Corrado La Gurna, dressed in black, his handkerchief at his eyes. The dogs barked all night long.

The panic knew no bounds when they saw Baroness Rubiera, paralysed, escaping carried in an arm-chair, because she couldn't get into the sedan-chair, she was so enormous: four men struggling to carry her, with her head hanging on one side, her great face livid, her purple tongue coming half out of her slavered lips, her eyes alone alive and anxious, her dead hands troubled by a continual trembling. And following after, the young baron looking twenty years older, bent, grey, burdened with children, with his wife beside him again in the family way, and the children of the first marriage going along with them. They filled the road wherever they passed: something terrifying. The poor people who were forced to remain in the village stood watching overwhelmed. In the churches they had exposed the Holy Sacrament. Old rancours were now forgotten, and labourers were seen restoring to their masters the things they had stolen. Don Gesualdo opened his arms and his barns to the poor and to his relations; all his houses in the country, at Canziria and at Salonia. At Mangalavite, however, where he had vast establishments, he talked of gathering the whole family together.

"Now I'll run to my father to try and get him to come with us. And you go to your brother," he said to Bianca. "Make him understand that these are times when you must bury the past, even with somebody who has betrayed you.—We've got the cholera on top of us.—Blood isn't water, when all's said and done! We can't leave that poor old fellow alone in the middle of the cholera. People would have some right to talk against us then, I'm thinking—"

"You've got a good heart," stammered his wife, feeling her heart go tender. "You've got a good heart."

But Don Ferdinando was not to be persuaded. He was terribly busy sticking strips of paper on all the cracks in the window-frames, with a little pot hung round his neck, perched at the top of a ladder.

"I can't leave the house," he replied. "I've so much to do!—See how many holes?—If the cholera comes—I must stop them all up—"

In vain his sister prayed and implored him again.

"Don't leave me with this remorse, Don Ferdinando!—How am I going to close my eyes at night, knowing you're alone in the house?"

"Ah! Ah!" he replied with a silly smile. "They won't give me the cholera in the night!—I shall stop up all the cracks—look!"

And he began reiterating again:

"I can't leave the house by itself—I've got to look after the family documents—"

The sexton's wife, seeing Bianca leave the door in distress, ran after her, weeping:

"We shan't see one another any more!—Everybody is going.—There'll be nobody to ring the mass for and the matins—"

Master Nunzio also had refused to go with his son.

"I eat with my fingers, my son! You'd blush for your father at table—I'm a boor, I am—I'm not fit to mix up with your gentry! No, no, better think in time! Better be finished off with cholera than with spleen!—And then you know I'm used to being master in my own house—I'm a country fellow—I'm not used to lying down and letting my wife walk over me, I'm not!"

Speranza pointed to Burgio, who was also in bed with malaria.

"It's not like us to fly from danger!—My husband can't move, and so we shan't move!—That's how we're made, we are!—And you know what it takes to keep

a whole family, with your husband fastened to his
bed—!"

"But I've always told you you shall be mistress!—
Everything you want!—" exclaimed Don Gesualdo
at last.

"No—I've not come begging from you!—We shan't
take a thing from you, unless we're forced to—thank
God!—And then you're giving us charity. We shall
go to Canziria. Don't be frightened, people won't
be able to say you left your father in the middle of
the cholera!—You can think of sending us some pro-
visions—We can't live on grass, like cattle!—But here
—If you happen to have a frock that your daughter
has left off, that she absolutely can't wear any more—
She's a lady, I know, but it would come in useful for
poor folks like us—"

The Margarones left at once for Pietraperzia; all
still in mourning for Don Filippo, who had died of
heart-troubles brought on by his son-in-law Don Bastiano Stangafame every time he beat Fifì when her
father didn't send money. They darkened a whole
street. Baron Mendola, who was paying court to Aunt
Sganci, took her to Passaneto, where she caught malarial fever, poor old woman. Zacco and lawyer Neri
left for Donferrante. All the village was in squalor.
At eleven o'clock there was nobody to be seen down
the Street of San Sebastiano except Marchese Limòli,
taking his usual little walk after dinner. And they let
him know that even he aroused suspicion by his move-
ments, and they were going to let him see something
the first case of cholera that occurred.

"Eh?" said he. "See something? You'd better
think about it first, you lot, because you'll have to pay

for the show. I shall do what I've always done, even if I die for it."

And to his niece who begged him to go with them to Mangalavite:

"Are you frightened I shan't be here when you come back?—No, no, don't be frightened; the cholera won't bother itself about me."

While Bianca and her daughter were just getting into the litter, arrived Aunt Cirmena, desperate.

"Do you see? Everybody's going. The relations have turned their back on me!—And I've even got that poor orphan of a Corrado La Gurna saddled on me. A tragedy in his home—Father and mother in one night—struck down by cholera.—Nobody else has the heart I have!—A poor woman without help and with nowhere to go! Won't you give me the keys of the two rooms you've got out there at Mangalavite, near to your villa!—the rooms of the mill. You are the only relation I can turn to, you are, Don Gesualdo!"

"Yes, yes," he answered. "But don't tell the others."

"I shall tell them, indeed!—I want to throw it in every one of their faces, if I live!"

nices. Aunt Cirmena swore she had seen single luminous rockets away towards Donfernite. And at

II

What they called the villa, at Mangalavite, was
a great building nestling at the bottom of the small
valley. From her window Isabella could see the broad
alpine avenue bordered with olive trees, the dense
green thicket which indicated the cave where the
water rose, the steep rocks among which wound the
footpaths, and higher up the rustling slopes of the
sumach trees. Budarturo bare and rocky in the sky,
looking like enamel. The only gay touch was a hedge
of dog-roses always in flower at the entrance to the
avenue, forgotten and neglected.

Amongst the precipices every cave, all the cabins
hidden in the thickets of cactus, were inhabited by poor
people who had run away from the village in fear of
cholera. All around you could hear the crowing of
cocks and the crying of children; old rags spread out in
the sun, and fragile columns of smoke rising here and
there, above the trees. Towards vespers the cattle-
herds came home from the olive groves round the
homestead, whole droves of colts and oxen gathered
in the immense courtyards. Then all the night was
a restless stamping of feet, sudden outbursts of moo-
ings and of bleatings, a shaking of cattle-bells, such
a wild encampment that Isabella couldn't sleep a
wink. From time to time a mad volley of firing
passed through the distant shadows; and sometimes
wild cries of alarm reached even down there; peasants
appeared the day afterwards telling how they had
come upon shadows lurking furtively among the preci-

pices; Aunt Cirmena swore she had seen single luminous rockets away towards Donferrante. And at once they sent people to enquire if there had been cases of cholera. Baron Zacco, on the contrary, who was staying in those parts, said that the lights were seen towards Mangalavite.

Don Gesualdo, apart from the fears of the lights which were seen at nights, and the suspicion aroused by every new face that passed along the footpaths clambering above among the crags, lived there like a patriarch, among his herds, his lands, his own peasants, his own activities, always on the go from morn till night, always shouting and showing his masterful face everywhere. Then at evening he rested, sitting among his own people, on the flight of steps which went up to the avenue, there before the great gateway, in his shirt-sleeves, enjoying the cool of evening and the freedom of the country, listening to the interminable laments and rambling talk of his own peasants. He would say to his wife, who felt worse in health in the country air, wanting to console her:

"Any way you're not afraid of catching cholera here. So long as there's no cholera, the rest doesn't matter."

There he was as safe from cholera as a king in his own kingdom, guarded night and day. He had given every peasant a fine gun for himself, old flint-locks hidden underground since '12 or '21, and he kept mastiffs that could have devoured a man. He was good to everybody; there wasn't a man but would have been killed to save him from hurt, those days. Grain, beans, a barrel of wine that was a little spoilt. Everybody who was in need ran to him to ask him for the loan of whatever was lacking. He with his hands open like Providence. He had given shelter to half the village, in the hay-barns, in the stables, in the shepherds' cabins, in the caves above on Budarturo. One day arrived even Nanna l'Orbo with all his troop, winking his eye and drawing him aside for his own ends:

"Don Gesualdo—there's your own belongings here as well. Look at Nunzio and Gesualdo how like you they are! Four measures of bread a month they eat, good luck to them! You can't shut the door in their face—You have been so charitable to everybody. Be it for us then, in God's name."

"I'm sure the devil has been and put this in your mind!—I've got my wife and daughter here now!—At least go up to the mill, and don't show yourself in these parts."

But all his kindness was turned into poison for him by the obstinate refusal of his own relations to put themselves under his wing. He often raved to Bianca, at night, when doors and windows were shut and they were safely alone.

"We are saving so many people from the cholera—So many people under our wings, and only our own blood scattered all about. They do it on purpose—to keep us in anxiety—to let us have a thorn inside us! I won't mention your brother, poor fellow—he doesn't realise. But my father!—He'd no business to give me this thorn in my flesh, he hadn't."

He didn't know the other trouble that his daughter was preparing for him, poor man! Isabella, who had come home from school with so many fine things in her head and had imagined that at Mangalavite she would find so many fine things, like at Favorita near Palermo, marble seats, statues, flowers everywhere,

big trees, avenues kept like so many ball-rooms, now
got hold of a new illusion. She had found steep rocky
paths, stones which turned her shoes on one side, dusty
vines, burnt-up stubble-fields that blinded her with
their long white straw, rocky peaks scattered with
sumach trees that looked like rust at that height, and
where the sunset rapidly saddened the evening. Then
days following one another all alike, in that Thebaid;
continual suspicion of everything, doubt concerning
the water that one drank, of people who passed by,
of the dogs that barked, of the letters which arrived,—
a heap of damp straw permanently in front of the
gateway to fumigate everything that came from outside—the rare letter received on the end of a cane,
across the smoke—and for sole entertainment the gossip of Aunt Cirmena, who arrived every evening with
a lantern in her hand and her knitting-basket on her
arm. Her nephew came with her occasionally; he pre-
ferred to remain at home, brooding and thinking of his
troubles and of his own dead, who knows.—Aunt Cirmena said in his excuse what a great talent that boy
had, all the livelong day shut up in his own room, his
head in his hand, filling up sheets of paper bigger
than a packsaddle, with poetry that would make the
stones weep. Don Gesualdo went to sleep with their
talk. The girl's mother also talked little, always short
of breath, always between bed and lying-chair. The only
one to pay any attention to the aunt was Isabella herself, stifling her yawns after those empty days. To her
school-friends, who were also scattered here and there
about the country, she could find nothing to write.
Marina di Leyra sent her every week little crested
sheets of note-paper full of adventures and interesting
confidences. She roused her curiosity, questioned her

and asked for her confidences in return. It seemed to Isabella in every letter that she had her friend there before her, with her haughty eyes and beautiful red mouth, leaning to whisper in her ear things that brought the blood to her face, made her heart beat, as if she had a hidden secret of her own which she must confide to her friend. Each had given the other a little diary-book, and had promised to write in it her most intimate thoughts, everything, everything, without hiding anything. The beautiful blue eyes of Isabella, the eyes of which Uncle Limòli had spoken, without wishing it, almost without looking, seemed to be seeking for those thoughts. In that little head, whose hair still hung down her back, there started a buzzing as if a swarm of bees had brought in all the voices and all the perfumes of the country, from beyond the rocky heights, from beyond Budarturo, from far away. It seemed as if the open air, the rustling of leaves, the hot sun had set her blood on fire, penetrated into her blue fine veins, come to bloom in the coloring of her face, and filled with sighs her bosom that was just gently swelling under the bib of her apron.

"See how the country suits you!" said her father. "See how pretty it makes you!"

But she was not happy. She felt an unrest, an ennui which made her sit with her hands idle upon her embroidery, made her hunt out particular places in which to read her few books, those little volumes which she had kept hidden under her linen, in school. In the shadow of the walnut trees, near the water-source, at the end of the avenue which sloped upwards in front of the villa there was a great silence in which you heard the dripping of water in the cave, the leaves rustling like the sea, the sudden cry of some kite which hung like a dot in the immense blue. Such a lot of insignificant things which drew her little by little, so that she sat for hours at a time watching a line of ants following one another, a fire-fly which showed itself timidly at a crevice-opening, a dog-rose dangling above the low wall, the light and the shadows changing and mingling upon the lands. A sort of drowsiness overcame her, a serenity passed into her from everything, and took possession of her, and kept her there, with her book on her knees, her eyes wide open and fixed, her mind wandering far away. A melancholy sweet as a soft caress descended on her, and her heart contracted at times with a vague desire for unknown things. From day to day a new sensibility rose in her, from the poetry she read, from the sunsets which made her sigh, a vague exaltation, a subtle intoxication, a mysterious and timid disturbance which she felt she must hide from everybody. Often in the night she quietly, softly rose from her bed, so that her mother should not hear, and without lighting the candle went to lean at the window, dreaming, looking at the sky that swarmed with stars. Her soul vaguely followed the noises out in the country, the lament of the owl, the far-off yelping of dogs, the confused forms which travel in the night, all those things that cause a delicious fear. She almost felt as if the moon were sending down rain on to her face, on to her hands, a great sweetness, a great prostration, a great wish to weep. She seemed to see moving in the great white glow, dimly, beyond Budarturo away in the distance, well-known forms, dear memories, fantasies which had luminous intermittency like the light of certain stars: her friends, Marina di Leyra, another unknown face which Marina was always showing her in her letters, a face which wavered and changed its form, now blond, now dark, sometimes with tired rings round the eyes and the melancholy fold of the lips like Cousin La Gurna. She was gradually penetrated with the spirit of things about her, the sadness of the water-source, as it distilled drop by drop through the maiden-hair leaves, the lostness of the solitudes stretching away across the country, the desolateness of the deep little valley where the moonlight never came, the splendour of the rocks that were rimmed with silver, away above at Budarturo, outlined distinctly in the great gleam of night like magic castles. Up, up, in the silver light, she seemed to rise on her thoughts as if she had wings, and tender words came on to her lips, harmonious voices, verses which made you weep, like those that flowered in the heart of Cousin La Gurna. Then she thought again of the youth whom she hardly ever saw, who remained shut up in his own little room, imagining, dreaming as she dreamed. Down there, beyond that hill, the moon would be glittering on his window-panes, the same sweetness would be entering in to him. What was he doing? What was he thinking about? A shiver of cold passed over her from time to time as the trees rustled and brought to her so many voices from the distance.

"White moon, lovely moon!—What are you doing, moon? Where are you going? What are you thinking about, you also?—"

She looked at her delicate thin hands, white also as the moon, with a great tenderness, a vague sense of gratitude and almost of pride.

Then she fell down from her heights, tired, her mind inert, irritated by her father's snoring, which

filled the house. Her mother next to him hardly dared
to let her breathing be heard; just as she hardly dared
to show all her tenderness for her daughter, before
her husband, with those sad eyes and that pale smile
which said so many things in the most humble words.

"Daughter! My daughter!"

Only the clasp of her thin arms and the expression
of the eyes which turned anxiously towards the door,
told the rest. As if she had to hide the caresses she
gave to her own child, as her trembling hands sought
the girl's face, her troubled eyes watched her closely.

"What's amiss with you? You look pale!—Don't
you feel well?"

Aunt Cirmena, seeing the girl so frail, wan-looking,
with those puffs under her eyes, tried to amuse her,
teaching her new bits of work, little frames woven of
straw, oranges and canaries made of wool. And she
told her tales, and brought her in secret the poetry
which her nephew Corrado had written, hidden under
her knitting in her basket.

"They are piping fresh, written yesterday. I took
them off his table just now when he'd gone out for a
walk. He's a difficult creature, is that blessed child.
So shy! Needs somebody to help him, with all the
talent he's got, more's the pity!"

She suggested remedies also for Isabella's delicate
health, Mars syrup, and nail-heads in a bottle of
water. She worked herself into a great sweat, helping in the kitchen, with her skirt tucked up round
her waist, making a good bone broth for her niece
Bianca, or some tasty stew for Isabella, who was eating nothing.

"Let me see to it. I know what she needs. All you
Traos are as whimsical as new-hatched chickens."

A real arm of the sea that woman! She was such
a one, that if you were good to her, you didn't lose by
it entirely. Often she made Corrado come along with
her in the evening, to liven up the company.

"You who can do so many things, with your books
and your talk, you'll make a bit of entertainment:
goodness me! if you're always going to sit penned up
with your books, how is anybody ever going to know
what you're worth."

Then when he wasn't there she sang even a plainer
song:

"At his age!—He's not a child any more—You've
got to help yourself in this world—He can't always
live on his relations—"

He was proud as Lucifer if you please, rearing on
his hind legs and growing restive if anybody tried to
help him, or to make him show to advantage, or if
his aunt did her best to open people's eyes to her
nephew's worth, and stole his old papers, taking them
off to show to everybody at Cousin Motta's in the
evening, cracking him up, getting as hot as an auctioneer who is trying to enhance the value of his goods,
while Don Gesualdo was gradually dropping to sleep,
nodding yes, yes, yawning, and Bianca was looking
at Isabella who sat there with her eyes wide open in
the shadow, the expression of her delicate face changing every minute, as waves of blood illuminated it
again and again. Donna Sarina all intent on her reading noticed nothing, only stopped to settle her spectacles now and then, leaned towards the light, or else
grumbled against her nephew for his small fine writing.

"But what a talent, eh! As a director—what shall
I say—to superintend work in the country—to direct
a farm, that boy would be worth his weight in gold.

My heart tells me, Don Gesualdo, that if you were to commission him to carry out any of your affairs, you'd make money by it! And—now that he's not present to hear—for very little salary either! The lad has his eyes shut, so to speak—without guile still—and would be content with little! You would do a work of charity as well, you would!"

Don Gesualdo said neither yes nor no, cautious, the sort of man to move his tongue seven times in his mouth before he let out any nonsense. He thought about it, calculated the consequences, watched his daughter even while he snored, one eye open. He didn't want the girl to get ideas into her head from all this nonsense, while she was still so young, so inexperienced, with no notion what it meant to be rich or to be poor. He was ignorant, one who knew nothing, but he knew that these nice tales were traps to catch gabies. Just the same dodges as the folks who could read and write would use to catch you and tie your hands or make you say something you didn't want to say, when you were driving a bargain. He had wanted his daughter to learn everything that was to be learnt at school, because she was rich, and one day or other she would make an advantageous marriage. But just because she was rich, so many people would have their designs on her. In the end Aunt Cirmena's continual talking became objectionable to him, as did the behaviour of her nephew who held the sack with that aloof manner of his, like one whom you have to press to come to table, or who wants to sell his goods dear. And then the long looks of his little cousin, the obstinate silences, her chin nailed down on her breast, her rage for hiding herself away with her books in certain lonely places, she being literary as well, a girl who ought rather to have been thinking about laughing and amusing herself—

However, it was only child's play so far; nonsense to be made fun of, or else knock their two young heads together, the young madam who was leaning in the window to watch the flies flying, and the youth who stood astrologising in the distance, his straw hat showing above the low wall or above the hedge, hanging round the villa, hiding himself among the plants.—Don Gesualdo had good eyes. He couldn't guess all the nonsense that was fermenting in those two mad young heads—the kisses blown into the air, and the sun and the clouds taking part in the duet—a mile apart; but he knew the meaning of fresh foot-prints, and of dog-roses found picked to pieces on the path, and of the ingenuous air of Isabella when she came downstairs to look for her scissors or her thimble when by chance her cousin happened to be in the room; and of the youth's slyness as he pretended not to look at her, like one at a fair who passes and re-passes in front of the heifer he wants to buy, without so much as glancing at her. He saw also in Nanni l'Orbo's thievish face, when the latter pretended to be suspicious of him, and in the silly manner the fellow put on, when he stretched on tiptoe among the sumach trees, shading his eyes with his hand to look away below into the avenue, or hid himself on all fours among the cactus plants, or came to bring him bits of paper he had found near the spring, or bits of plaster chipped off from the seat, putting on a silly air:

"Don Gesualdo, was it your honour who was up there?—Now and then—taking a bit of a walk.—The grass on the lawn is all trampled down as if a donkey had been rolling on it. It won't be thieves, eh?—I'm more frightened of cholera people."

"No—in the daytime?—what the deuce!—fool that you are! Don't you be afraid, we are keeping our eyes open."

And he was waiting, as a matter of fact, cautiously, and so as to avoid scandal, waiting for the cholera to end so that he could sweep the house and finish clean with Donna Sarina and all that belonged to her, without giving occasion for evil talk; giving Aunt Cirmena a set-back now that she had become knowing and had started talking rather hoity-toity, cutting her short in her rambling speeches that made you yawn from the heels upwards. One day, in front of everybody, he spat out what he had to say:

"Ha!—poetry! That stuff won't fill anybody's belly. You know!"

Aunt Cirmena took umbrage at length.

"You take everything by weight and measure, Don Gesualdo! You don't know what poetry means—I'd just like to see you try!"

Then, in the joking way he had, he raked together into a heap the books and newspapers that lay on the table, and threw them into Donna Sarina's lap, laughing loudly, pushing her by the shoulders as if he wanted to turn her out, like the agent does at the end of a bargain, shouting so fiercely between his laughter that it sounded like anger:

"There then—take them if you like them—You can live on 'em!—"

They all looked one another in the eyes. Isabella rose without saying a word, and went out of the room.

"Ah!" muttered Don Gesualdo. "Ah!—"

But seeing that it wasn't just the right moment, he swallowed his bile and turned the thing into a joke.

"She's the same—she likes bits of poetry. As a pastime—with the guitar—now that we're in the country—I don't deny. But hard work has been done for her, hard work in sun and in wind, you know!—And if she's got the obstinate head of the Traos, neither are the Mottas fools, when it comes to—"

"Quite," interrupted the aunt. "But that is another story."

"Ah, you think that's another story?"

"Look here!" broke out Donna Sarina, suddenly turning on her nephew. "Your uncle is speaking for your good. You won't find another relation who's as good to you as he is, mind."

"Why yes, why yes—you're a sensible woman, Donna Sarina, and you're quick at taking a hint."

Dame Cirmena then began to show that a young fellow with talent could get on in anything he set his mind to, whether it was secretarial work, or farm-managing, or as steward of a large estate. He didn't lack for protection, to start with—

"Certainly, certainly," Don Gesualdo kept on repeating. But he didn't commit himself further. He busied himself putting the chairs back in their place and shutting the windows, as if to say: "Now go away!" But as the youth turned his back without replying, showing all the haughtiness of all impoverished relations, Donna Sarina could contain herself no longer. Scraping together in a fury her knitting needles and her spectacles, and slinging her little basket on her arm without a word to anybody.

"I should like to know if this is what you call right! Is this all the thanks that relations get for all their

worry and trouble? I'll wash my hands of it—like
Pilate!—Charity begins at home—"

"That's a fact, Donna Sarina. Charity begins at
home. Wait a moment and I'll see you home.—Eh?
Eh? What is it?"

For some time, while talking, he had been listening
acutely to the barking of the dogs, and to all the devil
of a row which the geese and turkeys were making in
the courtyard, and to somebody's hasty running. Then
a strange voice was heard amongst the chatter of his
own people. In the gateway appeared the estate-
keeper, rolling his eyes, making signs to him.

"I'm coming, I'm coming, wait a moment."

He came back after a few moment, another person,
upset, his straw hat pushed back from his forehead,
wiping away the sweat. Donna Sarina wanted to know
at all cost what had happened, pretending to be afraid:

"Nothing—The stubble on the hill will have taken
fire.—I'll see you home. It's nothing at all."

In the barnyard a hubbub. Master Nardo, in the
open shed, was saddling Don Gesualdo's bay mule as
fast as he could. At the garden fence Nanni l'Orbo
and several others were listening open-mouthed to an
outside peasant who was telling great tales, excited,
gesticulating, showing his clothes reduced to rags.

"Nothing, nothing," repeated Don Gesualdo. "I'll
see you home. There's nothing to bother about."

It was obvious, however, that he was upset, he stammered, great drops of sweat ran down his forehead.
Donna Sarina insisted on being afraid, standing stock
in front of him, searching around with inquisitive
eyes, scrutinising him to see what there was underneath him.

"A case of cholera, eh? They've brought it even

here? Some scoundrel? They've caught him in the act?"

At last Don Gesualdo put his hands on her shoulders, looking her fixedly in the whites of the eyes.

"Donna Sarina, what are we playing at. Let me look after my own business! Saints and blessings!"

And he turned her out, marched her plainly down the little road, over the little bridge. Returning again he began to abuse all the workpeople, who seemed almost in a state of mutiny, Gossip Lia who had left off mixing the bread, and her daughter who had come running with her hands also covered with flour.

"What's amiss? What's amiss? You, Master Nardo, go ahead with the mule. I'll join you on the way. There, that way, by the footpath. There's no need to let all the place know whether I'm going or staying. And the rest of you, look after your own jobs. And stitch your mouths up, see!—and don't go blowing the trumpet and talking about what happens to me, all over the place!—"

Then he went upstairs, feeling his legs broken. The moment Bianca saw his face, she got frightened. But he said nothing. He was afraid the mice would play while the cat was away. While his wife was helping him on with his boots, he kept telling her what to do:

"Look after the house. Look after our girl. I'm going, but I shall be back directly. Just as far as Salonia to see my father, who is not well. Keep your eyes open while I'm not here, mind!"

Bianca, kneeling as she was, lifted her face stunned.

"Rouse up! What the deuce has taken you? Just like your brother Don Ferdinando, you are. Your daughter is letting her fancies run away with her. We've made a mistake, putting so many bees in her bonnet. Who knows what she's got in her mind now? And those others as well—Donna Sarina and that lot! Serpents in your sleeves!—Mind then, no more visits till I get back—and keep your eyes open about your daughter. You know what girls are when they get something in their heads! You've been young yourself.—But I'm not going to be led by the nose like your brothers, mind—! No, no, be still!—I'm not finding fault with you. You did it for my sake, moreover. You've been a good wife, submissive and obedient, and all for your home. I'm not sorry I did it. I'm only telling you so that you'll know what to do, now. Girls never think of anything, once they want to get married. But anyhow you didn't do anything crazy.—And you've never repented it either, have you? But this affair now is another pair of shoes. Now we've got to mind that we're not robbed as if we were in a wood—"

Bianca, standing motionless near the door, white-faced, opened wide her eyes with a vague terror in their depths, and a pathetic dismay, and the painful intermittency of a clouded reason such as showed in the eyes of Don Ferdinando.

"Ha! Now do you understand at last? You've noticed it as well? And you never told me about it!—All alike, you women—you all hold the sack for one another!—in a conspiracy against anybody who is striving for your own good!"

"No!—I swear to you!—I know nothing!—It's not my fault. What do you want me to do?—You see what a state I'm in."

"You didn't know! Then what are you doing, not to know! Is that how you keep a watch over your child?—And this is the mother of a daughter!—Everything falls on my shoulders! I've got a broad back. I've got a bellyful of troubles—and I'm well and strong, I am! I've got a thick skin."

And he went off with his back bent, under the strong sun, ruminating on his troubles. The messenger who had come to fetch him to Salonia was waiting at the top of the path, with Master Nardo who limped along leading the mule. As the man saw him in the distance he began to shout:

"Hurry up, your honour. If we get there too late, by bad luck, it'll be all my fault!"

As they travelled he told things to make your hair stand on end. At Marineo they had killed a passer-by who had come hanging round the water-cistern in the heat of the day, ragged, barefoot, covered with dust, his face inflamed, with one blind eye, trying it on in the very teeth of the Christians who were watching from a distance, suspecting him. At Callari they had found a corpse behind a hedge, swollen like a water-skin: they'd found it out by the stench. At evening there were lights like fireworks everywhere, a rain of rockets, just like San Lorenzo's Eve, God preserve us. A woman with child, who had let some unknown person help her to carry a load of wood to Trimmilito, had suddenly died the same night, without as much as saying "Christ help me!" with her belly full of prickly pears.

"Your father fairly wanted to get the cholera, he did, your honour. Everybody said to him: Don't open door or window before the sun is up!—But you know what a stubborn head he's got. A straying fellow brought us the cholera to Salonia, one who went round with a saddle-bag over his shoulder. In these times, just imagine it! Somebody saw him sit down, dead tired, on the low wall near the farm-place. Then all

the night noises on the roof and behind the doors—
And spots of grease that we found here and there, when
it was day!—Like slime which a snail leaves, yes your
honour!—That fool of an apothecary kept on preaching about sweeping the houses and driving away the
pigs and the fowls, to keep off the cholera! The
Lord's creatures bring the poison now, which haven't
any badness in them!—did ever you hear, your
honour!—Enough to make you murder the lot of
them, doctors, priests, apothecaries, all the lot, because,
you know, for every Christian they send into the next
world, they get a couple of florins each from the king—
And Archpriest Bugno actually had the courage to
preach from the altar:—'My children, I know you are
angry with me because of the cholera. But I am innocent. I swear to you upon this consecrated Host!'—I
don't know whether he was innocent or not. I only
know he's caught the cholera himself, because he kept
in his house those bottles that they sent from Naples to
be the death of Christian folks. I don't know. I only
know the dead are dropping like flies: Donna Marianna Sganci, Peperito—"

III

When they got to Salonia they found all the other inmates of the farmstead loading mules and donkeys to flee away. In vain did Bomma, who had come from the vineyard close by, burst his throat shouting:

"Fools! it'll be some sort of pernicious fever!—some sort of horse-fever! You don't die of cholera if you've got fever!"

"It doesn't matter to me whether it's pernicious fever or not!" grumbled Giacalone at last.—"This is what doctors are paid for."

Master Nunzio was really very bad: death had pinched his nostrils and put a finger-mark under his eyes, a sooty shadow which tinged his nipped nostrils, sunk his eyes and his toothless mouth to the bottom of black holes, and veiled his earthy face that was dirty with grey hairs. He opened those eyes of his heavily, hearing his son Gesualdo beside his bed, and said in a hollow voice:

"Ah! So you've come to see the fun, at last!"

Santo, like an owl, was seated on the door-step, not saying a word, with tears in his eyes. Burgio and his wife were struggling to get a bit of corn into a sack, so that they shouldn't starve in the place they were going to as soon as the old man had closed his eyes. In the courtyard were mules laden with stuff. Don Gesualdo seized Bomma by the coat as he also was preparing to be off.

"What can we do, Don Arcangelo? Tell us! Anything we can possibly do for my father—everything we've got!—Don't spare any expense—"

"Eh, you'll not have to spend much—There's nothing to do—I came too late. Quinine doesn't work any more!—a first-class pernicious fever, my dear man! But anyhow he's not dying of cholera, and there's no reason to frighten all the neighbourhood as they are doing."

The old man was listening, with anxious, suspicious eyes in the depths of his eyesockets. He watched Gesualdo pressing round the apothecary, Speranza crying and sobbing as she helped her husband in the preparations for departure, Santo stupefied and motionless, the grandchildren scattered about the house and the yard, and Bomma turning his back on him, shaking his head and making signs of impatience. Speranza at length came to hand over the keys to her brother, grumbling all the time.

"Here! I'm glad you've come—Now you won't be able to say that we laid hands on your belongings, I and my husband, the moment our father's eyes were closed—"

"I'm not dead yet, no I'm not," lamented the old man from his corner. Then the other son, Santo, rose up like a fury, his face all sticky with tears, shouting and raving at everybody:

"Aren't you going to give him the viaticum, race of swine?—Are you going to let him die worse than a dog?"

"I'm not dead yet," whined the dying man again. "Let me die in peace, first."

"It's not for the property, no, no," son-in-law Burgio replied, drawing near the bed and bending over and speaking as one speaks to a child. "No, it's for your

own sake we want you to confess and to take the com-
munion before you close your eyes."

"Ah!—Ah!—You can't wait, can't you!—Leave me
alone—leave me!—"

Evening came and the night passed in this way.
Master Nunzio in the shadow lay still and motionless,
like a log of wood, only every time they forced him to
swallow his medicine, he moaned and spat and complained that it was bitter as poison, and that he was
dead, and that they were waiting to get rid of him.
At last, so that they shouldn't bother him, he turned
his nose to the wall and moved no more.

It might have been midnight, though nobody dared
risk opening the window to look at the stars. Speranza
went on tiptoe to the bedside of the sick man every now
and then, and touched him, and spoke to him very
softly; but he kept still. Then she went back to talk
in an undertone with her husband who was quietly
waiting, squatted on the stairs, dozing. Gesualdo sat
elsewhere with his chin between his hands. From the
far end of the big room came Santo's snores. The
grandchildren had already gone off with the goods,
together with other tenants, and a cat that was left
behind went miauing round the farmhouse, like a soul
in Purgatory; a thing that made them all lift their
heads, startled, and they crossed themselves as they
saw those eyes gleaming in the dark, through the beams
of the roof and the holes in the walls; and on the dirty
wall all the time they could see the shadow of the old
man's nightcap, gigantic, giving no sign of life. Then,
three times, they heard the screech-owl cry.

At last, by God's will, when day had come, after the
daylight had for some time been leaking through
the window-frames, making the light on the barrel look

pale, Burgio decided to open the door. It was a heavy day, a grey low sky and a great silence over the livid, rocky plain. Blackish little houses here and there, and the tail of the village seen on a hill in the background, seemed to rise slowly out of the dimness, lost and silent. Not a bird, not a murmur, not a breath of wind. Only a rustle ran frightened through the stubble at Burgio's appearance in the doorway, yawning and stretching his arms.

"Farmer Fortunato!——come here, come!" called his wife at that moment, in a changed voice.

Gesualdo leaned over his parent's bed, called him, and shook him. His sister, dishevelled and all her clothes undone, looking more yellow than ever in that pallid light, got ready to scream. Finally, after a moment or two, Burgio hazarded the opinion:

"Gentlemen, he seems to me as if he'd been dead for a hundred years."

And then the tragedy exploded. Speranza began howling and scratching her face. Santo, wakened with a start, began hitting his own head with his fists, rubbing his eyes, crying like a child. The most upset of all, however, was Don Gesualdo, although he said nothing, looking at the dead man who himself looked back out of the corner of his dull dead eye. Then he kissed his hand and covered his face with the sheet. Speranza, inconsolable, threatened to run to the village to drown herself in the great cistern, and to let herself starve to death.

"Now what am I doing in the world any more? I've lost my support! the pillar of the house!"

This wailing lasted the whole day long. It was no good her husband's telling her in order to console her that Don Gesualdo would not abandon them. They were all his children now, needy orphans. Santo with his dirty face looked first at this one and then at that as they opened their mouths to speak.

"No!" persisted Speranza. "He's dead, he's dead now, my father! There's nobody now to look after us!"

Gesualdo, who had let her hold forth for some time, shaking his head, his eyes swollen, said to her at last:

"You're right!—I've never done anything for any of you! You're right to carry on at that rate!—"

"No," put in Burgio. "No! It's only words one says at the moment, brother-in-law."

Nevertheless the old man had to be buried, with not as much as a dog to help you, if you paid all the gold in the world. A joiner down at Camemi knocked together four boards to look like some sort of a coffin, and Master Nardo scraped out a hole at the back of the house. Then Santo and Gesualdo had to do the rest with their own hands. Burgio, however, stood looking on from the distance, frightened of infection, and his wife wailed that she hadn't it in her to touch the corpse. It hurt her heart, it did! Afterwards when she'd wiped her eyes and made the bed again and tidied the house while Master Nardo was getting the horses ready, and while they were all sitting waiting in a group, she began to talk seriously.

"And now, how are we going to settle?"

They all stared at one another at this exhortation. Farmer Fortunato twisted the tassel of his cap, and Santo made wide eyes. Don Gesualdo, however, did not catch the allusion, he stared into the air as if looking for what he should say.

"How are we going to settle? Why? Settle what?"

"We must speak about business, mustn't we? We've got to divide up the inheritance that that good soul has left us, may he rest in paradise! There's three of us—Every one his own part—according as your conscience bids you.—You are the eldest, you divide it up—and we will take our share.—If there'd only been a will—I won't say—But say what you think, and we'll see."

Don Gesualdo, being Don Gesualdo, was left openmouthed by this speech. Stupefied, he stammered for something to say.

"The inheritance?—The will?—Our share of what?—"

Then Speranza flew into a fury.—What? Why, this is what she was talking about. Weren't they all children of the same father? And the head of the house, who had that been? Up to now Don Gesualdo had had the making and meddling of everything, selling, buying.—But now everybody ought to have his fair share. All that good property, all that fine land, Canziria, and Salonia itself where they were at that moment: perhaps this had all fallen out of the skies like rain?—

Burgio, calmer, tried to put in a quiet word; he said that wasn't the moment to talk of it, with the dead man still warm. He shut his wife's mouth; he drove back his brother-in-law Santo, who had opened all his ears and was shouting:

"No, no, let her speak!"

Finally he wanted them to embrace, there, in the room where they had been left poor orphans. Don Gesualdo was a gentleman, a good-hearted fellow. He would never do them any dirty trick. "Don't go away! Hark here! Isn't it true? Aren't you a gentleman?"

"No! no! Let me hear what they've got to say. It's better to speak out plain."

But his sister wouldn't heed him any more. She sat on a stone outside the door, muttering to herself. Farmer Fortunato, however, tried another tune: the affliction that had come upon them, the hour that was really growing late. Meanwhile Master Nardo led by his feverish hands, during the long hours of wait- the mule out of the stable. They stayed out there a little longer to sulk with one another. Then Don Gesualdo proposed to take them all to Mangalavite. Brother-in-law Burgio locked the door and put on the pack-saddle the few clothes they had gathered into a bundle. Speranza did not reply at once to her brother's invitation, shaking out the shawl to wrap herself up for the departure, looking around with sullen eyes. At last she came out with everything she had on her chest.

"To Mangalavite?—No, thank you! What should I be doing there—Since you say it belongs to you? It would be a nuisance for your wife and your daughter— two ladies who are used to having all they want. We poor creatures must manage as best we can—We'll go to Canziria. Or we'd better go to the lime-kiln my father has left us, rest his soul—That's where we'll go! There at least we shall be in our own house. You won't pretend you bought the lime-kiln with your savings!—No, no, I'm not saying anything, Farmer Fortunato! We'll talk later, if we live. If you live the year round you'll see all the holidays. Good day to you, Don Gesualdo. It'll be as God wills. Blessings on that poor creature who is at rest now, under the ground!—"

She was still carrying on as she rode away, jogging to the ambling of the mule, her back bent, and the wind ballooning out her shawl behind her. Don Gesualdo also mounted, and rode away in the other direction, with his heart swelling at the ingratitude which he always received, turning back, from time to time, to look at the farmstead left shut up and deserted, beside the still fresh hole, and the cavalcade of his own folks passing away into the distance, in a file one behind the other, already no more than black dots in the naked countryside that was now going dark. After a while Master Nardo, having given it sufficient thought, pronounced the dead man's funeral oration:

"Poor creature! He has worked so much—to bring up his children—to leave them rich—Now he is under the ground! You remember, your honour, when the bridge broke down, at Fiumegrande, and he wanted to drown himself!—That's how the world is! To-day it's your turn, to-morrow it's mine."

His master gave him a sour look, and cut him short:

"Be quiet, fool!—You, now!—"

It might have been two hours after dark when they arrived at the Fountain of Cosimo, on a lovely starry evening, the sky all seeming to throb around Budarturo, above the expanse of the plains and the mountains that showed themselves dimly. The mule, smelling her stable near, began to bray. Then dogs barked; away below at the bottom, lights appeared in the darker shadow of the trees that surrounded the villa, and voices were heard, a hurried threshing of feet as of people running; along the path that rose from the valley was heard a rustling of leaves, stones bounding precipitously, as if someone were cautiously climbing upwards. Then silence. All at once, out of the dark, from the edge of the copse, came a voice:

"Hey, Don Gesualdo?"

"Hey, Nanni, what is it?"

Neighbour Nanni did not answer, pushing in and walking close beside the mule. After a minute he mumbled, as if unwillingly:

"What it is, is that I'm here to look after you."

Don Gesualdo asked no more. They went down the narrow road in single file. Only Nanni l'Orbo added after a while:

"You had a rosy time, eh?"

And as his master continued to keep silent, he went on:

"I could tell by the face you've got on you, your honour. World of troubles—! One on top of another!"

When they had arrived at last at the fountain, he said:

"We'll dismount here, eh? Master Nardo can go down the avenue with the mounts, and we'll go down here, to be quicker."

Don Gesualdo understood at once, and didn't let himself be told twice. They went in silence along the wall, as if they could see in the dark. At a certain point l'Orbo nodded with his head towards some stones scattered around, and a sort of breach between the dry thorns that crowned the wall, and he said softly:

"Look at that, your honour."

The other nodded, and climbed into the paddock. Nanni l'Orbo lit a sulphur-match with his flint and steel, and they went inch by inch following the foot-prints to the house. Under Isabella's window l'Orbo pointed in silence to the grass, that was all trampled down as if donkeys had really been rolling on it.

"And the dogs like as if they'd been drugged," observed neighbour Nanni, with that mysterious manner of his. "If it wasn't for me, who am sharp on the ear—I said to Diodata: While the master isn't here, we've got to keep our ears open, to look after his things.—So I sent Nunzio on to the log-bridge while I came down with Gesualdo from the mill—Yessir, where Donna Sarina is lodging with her nephew—Said I to myself, if the dogs keep quiet—"

"All right. Now be still. They might hear you upstairs."

The next day he was receiving the visits of condolence, standing dressed in a black suit, and unshaven. Hardly had Donna Sarina pronounced her eulogy of the dead man, wiping her eyes and rolling her sleeves up to run into the kitchen to help in the disorder, than Don Gesualdo stopped her in the passage and said without more ado:

"Do you know, Donna Sarina—the best help you could give me would be if you went away. Plain speech and good friendship, isn't that so? I really need those two rooms—for reasons of my own. I've said nothing up to now. You will have wondered at my prudence, eh?"

Dame Cirmena turned green. She smoothed her dress, smiling, taking it coolly:

"Very well, very well. I know what you mean. If you stand in need of those two rooms—If you've got reasons of your own—At once if you like, just as I stand—cholera or no cholera!—People can say what they like about your sending me away in the thick of the cholera! You're the master. Everybody knows the business of his own home. Only, by your leave, I'll go and say good-bye to my niece first. I don't know what she'd think if I went off with never a word!—The way folks talk, don't you know!"

Bianca couldn't take it in.

"What? going away? In the thick of the cholera? Why? What has happened?"

Aunt Cirmena put forward various queer reasons; force of circumstances; everybody has his own reasons; serious business at home; Corrado had received a most urgent letter.

"He's as sorry as I am, poor thing. It has fairly bowled him over. He's got so fond of this place— Why just now he said to me: Aunt, to-day is the last time I shall go to the spring for a walk—"

Don Gesualdo, who was all off his hinges, cut this rubbish short:

"Excuse me, Donna Sarina. My wife doesn't understand anything really. They all go like that in her family.—It's me you've got to deal with!—"

Isabella, however, had gone white as death. But she did not stir, and she said nothing, a real Trao, her face shut and impenetrable. She also returned the embraces and affectionate kisses of her aunt, with a thin fold between her brows. Then, when she was alone, all at once, with a desperate gesture she tore off the collar that was suffocating her, with a wave of blood to her face, a sudden dazzle in front of her eyes, a pain in her side, a sharp spasm that made her sway, uttering incoherent words, beside herself.

She wanted to see him, for the last time, at any cost, while everybody would be lying down after mid-day,

and not a soul would be stirring in the villa. The
Madonna should help her.

"Madonna!—Madonna!"

She repeated that and nothing else, a painful confusion among her ideas, her head in flame, the sun
beating down on her, her eyes burning, a fire devouring
her heart, and mounting to her brain, blinding her,
making her delirious.

"I will see him—whatever happens!—To-morrow
I shan't see him any more—never, never, never!—"

She did not feel the thorns, nor the stones of the
little sidetrack she had taken in order to come to him
secretly.—Panting, pressing her bosom with her hands,
stumbling at every step, spying out the way with
anxious eye. A little bird flew away frightened, giving
a sharp cry. The level fields were deserted, in a heavy
shadow. There was a low wall covered with gloomy
ivy, a little abandoned cistern in which aquatic plants
were rotting, and over the wall squares of vegetable
garden, divided by little abandoned avenues stifled between the box-hedges that bristled with yellow dead
leaves. Everywhere that feeling of abandonment, of
desolation, in the pile of wood that was going dry-
rotten in a corner, in the decayed leaves heaped under
the walnut trees, in the water of the spring that seemed
to be in tears as it distilled from the tufts of maiden-
hair fern that tapestried the cave. Only among the
weeds of the path along which he must come were
humble thistle-flowers glinting in the sun, and green
berries bending and swaying softly, saying: "Come!
Come! Come!" She cautiously crossed the avenue
that sloped down to the villa, with her heart leaping in
her throat, beating in her temples, and taking away her
breath. There among the dry leaves near the low wall

where he had sat so often, were scraps of half-burnt
paper, damp, still fluttering like live things; burnt
matches, torn ivy-leaves, shoots broken into tiny
bits by his feverish hands, during the long hours of
waiting, in the automatic activity of his fantastic
imagination. The chopping of an axe was heard in
the distance; then a melancholy song which lost itself
above, in the little road. What a long agony! The
sun slowly left the path; it died palely upon the naked
rock which made the deep valleys seem more gloomy
than ever, and she waited still, waited ever.

"Don Gesualdo, Sir—Come here, if I may ask you—
I've something to tell you."

Nanni l'Orbo, keeping on calling him from the
farmyard, affected not to be able to set foot in
the courtyard, looking mysterious, until his master
went to find out what the devil he wanted, giving him
a good hit to begin with:

"I've told you plenty of times not to show yourself
around here! What the devil!—As if you did it on
purpose—"

"No, sir! On purpose, I call you out here. We
must have a word or two together, about something
I've got to tell you.—Here in the garden. We are
expected."

As a matter of fact there stood Nunzio and
Gesualdo, Diodata's children, dressed in their best
clothes, with their hands in their pockets and a black
kerchief round their necks. Neighbour Nanni pointed
it out to his master.

"Blood is blood. You don't find fault with us?
Both of them—they wanted to put on mourning for
your father, rest his soul—out of respect, without
thinking anything—Only, your worship might help

them without putting your hand in your pocket. You know, they would like to work that bit of land under the fountain, at half profit. They're two good, hard-working lads. They're like you, Don Gesualdo—and if you show them a kindness, you can be sure anyhow that you're not doing it for strangers—"

Don Gesualdo hesitated, on the one hand suspicious at being taken so by surprise, and at the same time yielding in spite of himself to a certain inward voice which kept on repeating inside him all the arguments which neighbour Nanni put forth to persuade him.— Well, then, what did they want?—work—He who had so much in his power—a matter of conscience!— It wouldn't be a bad bargain either—

At a certain point l'Orbo proposed to send for Diodata so that they might hear what she had to say. Then Don Gesualdo blurted out, to get rid of the annoyance, to ease his conscience, as the other fellow said, looking pointedly at the two lads who followed behind them step by step, with their hands in their pockets, without opening their mouths:

"Well—well—if it's only a matter of that piece of land below the fountain—If you're not going to be like the hedgehog, putting all your thorns out afterwards—"

"Yessir! What does it amount to!" Nanni pounced on him at once. "Only that bit! No more than ten acres of land. We can go and look at it. It's just near. I'll put in the land-marks under your eyes, since you're here, and then you won't be frightened of being robbed—Just so!—and we've got witnesses as well, see—The young lady up there, under the big walnut tree—"

Don Gesualdo looked where l'Orbo was saying, and

suddenly went white in the face. All at once he changed complexion and manner, and sent off his companions roughly.

"All right, we'll talk about it—There's time. You don't take people by the scruff of the neck like that, saints and blessing! I've said Yes: now go away."

The two young ones made off mutely under that onslaught, while Nanni hid himself among the thickets to enjoy the scene from the distance. Don Gesualdo was already hastening up the avenue, as quick as if he was but twenty years old, all upset. Isabella saw him suddenly appear before her with a face which almost sent her into a faint, with fear. He said nothing to her. He took her by the hand, like a child, and led her back to the house. She let herself be led, like a dead woman, her heart dead in her breast, her eyes sightless, stumbling among the stones. Only from time to time she thrust her hand in her hair, as if she felt a great bewilderment, a great pain.

Bianca, seeing her arrive like that, began to tremble like a leaf. Her husband handed the daughter over to her, with a terrible look, wagging his head. But he said nothing. He began to walk about the room, from time to time wiping away the bile he had in his mouth. Then he opened the door with a slam and took himself off.

He roamed round like a mad bull, slamming the doors and attacking everybody he came across. All over the house you could hear his voice, making the place shake. "Nardo, where have you been all this time? Didn't I tell you to bring me those pruning-scissors to the vineyard?—Aren't the colts in yet? That brute of a Brasi will be laming some of them for me! I'll let him have it, when he does come in!—Hey,

Santoro! have you finished cutting the sumach trees up there?—What the devil have you been doing then all day?—As soon as the master is away for a moment!—Assassins, paid thieves!—Martino! light the lamp, Martino, to milk the ewes. You'll have all the milk on the floor, in the dark like this, fool!—They haven't lighted the lamp upstairs yet! What are they doing? Are they telling their beads?—Concetta! Concetta! We're in the dark still! What the deuce are you doing? What a house, the moment my back is turned!—What will become of it if I should close my eyes for ever?—"

After a time he came back knocking at the women's door, and as they didn't open at once he burst it open with a kick. Then Bianca turned fierce, like a hen defending her chickens, with such a face as had never been seen on her; the staring face of the Traos, in which the eyes now gleamed like a mad-woman's out of the pallor and the frightful thinness, covering with her own body the body of her daughter, who lay stretched face down on the bed, her face in her pillow, shaken by nervous shudders.

"Ah, you want to kill her for me, do you? You've not done enough? You've not done enough? You want to kill her for me?" You couldn't recognise the same woman. So much so that Don Gesualdo was disconcerted. Now he tried to be nice to her, overcome by an immense discouragement, the bitterness of so much ingratitude rising in his throat, as he felt his bones broken, his heart black as pitch. "You're right!—I'm the tyrant! I've got a hard heart and a tough skin! I'm the working ox—If I kill myself working it's for you two, and you know it. I should be satisfied with a piece of bread and cheese.—And you're going to tell me that I've worked as I have, to throw everything into the wolf's mouth—my blood and my belongings?—You are right!—"

Bianca tried to stammer some word or two. Then he turned on her in a fury, his hands in the air, his mouth open. But he did not say anything. He looked at his daughter who was leaning against the bedside trembling all over, with her face swollen and her hair slipped loose; then he dropped his arms and began to pace back and forth in the room, beating his hands one upon the other, puffing and blowing, his eyes staring on the ground, as if he was trying to find something to say, trying to find the way in which to make those obstinate heads understand reason.

"Come come, Isabella!—It's a lot of nonsense, you know. It's nonsense to upset yourself.—I don't want to upset myself—I've plenty of other troubles! My heart is heavy enough, as it is!—I'd like you to see for a minute the number of troubles I've got on my mind!—You'd begin to laugh, as God's above you would! You'd see what nonsense it is, all this other business!—You're young yet—There are some things you don't understand—The world, believe me, is a swarm of thieves. All they ever do is so to say: Get up from there and give me what you've got.—Everybody after his own ends—Don't you see, don't you see—what I tell you?—If you'd got nothing, nobody would bother you. It's first a business proposition, you know! One way of being set up for life. If anybody's poor, whether it's man or woman, I don't say it to offend anybody, but he makes a try where he can—He looks around; he sees what'll suit him—and then he tries every means he can to get it, every man in his own way.—One, let us say, will try his noble name;

M

and another will try something he is better at,—pretty talk and tender looks.—But if you've got any sense, on your own side, you keep your eye on your affairs. You see how silly it is to cry and make yourself desperate—"

But his words died in his mouth before the pale face and staring eyes with which his daughter looked at him. His wife as well could find nothing to say except:

"Leave her alone!—Don't you see how she is?"—

"How idiotic she is!" cried Mastro-don Gesualdo. And then, losing control of himself: "How she doesn't know and doesn't intend to know—! But I'm not going to be made a fool of, no I'm not!—I know what it all amounts to!—"

And he went away enraged.

IV

The fear of cholera had ceased, and they had hardly returned into the village, when Don Gesualdo was served with the summons from his sister, authorized by her husband Burgio, demanding her part of the paternal inheritance—that is, of everything he possessed—a real roguery; stating that his possessions had been acquired with the profits of the society of which Master Nunzio was the head; and that now he, Gesualdo, wanted to appropriate everything;—he who had been saddled with the lot of them, right up to that very day; who had had to submit to the bad speculations of the father; who had had to be the support of his brother-in-law Burgio in bad seasons; who paid the debts of his brother Santo at Pecu-Pecu's tavern!—Even Santo summoned him for his own portion, since he had been one of the famous society also, that idle good-for-nothing!

Now they insulted him by sending the police-bailiff; they called him robber; they wanted to put seals on everything, to sequestrate all his property. They dragged him through law-suits before lawyers and public prosecutors—a world of expense, and so many bitter morsels, such a waste of time, so much of his business going to pieces, and his enemies getting fat on it. In the café and at the druggist's they talked of nothing else—all against him because he was rich, and on his sister's side because she was poor! Lawyer Neri took up the case against him, *gratis et amore,* because of old quarrels, and new quarrels, that were between them. Speranza waited for him on the steps of the Magistrate's Court to vomit insults against him, trying in vain to incite against him her big, heavy children, inciting Santo against him, though Santo hadn't really the face to say anything against him, and tried to avoid him.

"You're all a chicken-hearted lot, just like my husband!—I'm the only one that ought to wear breeches among you! I shan't be able to bear myself if I don't send him to the galleys, that thief! I'd sell the clothes off my back. I want my own rights, blood of my own father."

It was still worse the first time the judge pronounced against her, and she lost her case.

"My sirs, look at that!—Everything is bought with money these days!—But I'll take it to Palermo, I'll take it up to the king, if there's any justice left in the world!"

Baron Zacco, having in mind certain negotiations with Don Gesualdo, that he wanted to bring off, intervened to please him. One Sunday he gathered all the Mottas together in his house, including Gossip Speranza's husband, who was a fool, and hadn't a word to say for himself. Santo, forced to meet Don Gesualdo his brother face to face, began to excuse himself.

"What was I to do?—It's not my fault. They took me to the lawyer—What could I do?—Why did we go to the lawyer for advice?—What the lawyer tells me to do I do."

Don Gesualdo showed himself amenable. Not that he was obliged, no!—the law recognized his right.—But out of good-heartedness. He had always done all the good he could to his relations, and he wanted to go on doing it. Whereupon began an altercation that there was no end to. Speranza, who saw her share of the inheritance going up in smoke once they began talking about good-heartedness, started to abuse her husband and children for not knowing how to defend themselves. Even Santo kept quiet, like a child who has done something he shouldn't. Lucky she was there to say her say:

"What do you want to give us, charity? A bushel of corn or two, as it pleases you, from time to time?— or a barrel of wine that's not good enough to sell?"

"What do you expect me to give you, the Alia farm, or the Donninga? Do you expect me to strip myself to fill your gizzards, you who have done nothing for it? I've got children. I can't meddle with my property—"

"Your property?—hark at that! You'd like to say then that our father, bless his soul, left nothing at all? And what about the lime business you were partners in? And what about the contract for the bridge which you took between you? There's nothing left of that poor departed soul, isn't there? All the profits have been yours, have they? to buy nice property in land? that you want to stick to because you've got children!— But there's a God above, let me tell you.—And what you want to take out of the mouths of my poor innocents, there's others that are ready to snatch it from betwixt your own teeth! Go and see for yourself, at night, what a promenading there is under your windows!—"

It ended in an uproar. The baron had to begin shouting and raising the deuce to prevent them from coming to blows there and then, instead of coming to terms. Speranza went off raving on the one side, and Don Gesualdo on the other, his mouth bitter, tormented also by another flea that his sister had put in

his ear. Now, in the midst of all the other vexations
and worries, he would have to keep his eye on his
daughter and that assassin of a Corrado La Gurna, as
well, whom Aunt Cirmena kept in the village at her
own expense, just out of spite, to hamper him. He had
to keep a sharp look-out upon every creature that came
and went, on the servants, on the sheets of note-paper
that were missing, and on his daughter, who went
about pale and haggard, looking as if she was hatching
some rare mischief.—She was eating her soul away, the
miserable creature. And he had to gnaw his own liver
and swallow his bile, not to make matters worse. At
last one evening he caught her at the window, in dog's
weather.

"Ah!—So the band's still playing!—What are you
doing here?—at this time of night?—Taking the air
in readiness for summer?—I'll teach you to count the
stars! You've not seen me yet when I really turn. I'll
teach 'em to go walking under my windows at night,
certain young gentlemen. I'll dust their jackets if I
come across them! You've seen me sweet up till now;
and now I'll show you the sour! I'll make you plough
straight, as I plough myself!"

From that day on there was the devil to pay, morning and evening. Don Gesualdo attacked Isabella with
fair words and foul, to drive that nonsense out of her
head; but she had it always there, in the slight fold
that was fixed between her brows, in the pallor of her
face, in her tight lips that said never a word, and in
her grey, obstinate Trao eyes which said plainly
enough:—

"Yes, yes, if I die for it."

She did not dare openly to rebel. She did not complain. But she lost her youth and health. She ate

nothing; but she never yielded an inch, block-headed, a real Trao, with the defiant nature of the Mottas into the bargain.

The poor man was reduced to examining his own conscience.—From her parents, that girl had inherited nothing but the defects. But love for her possessions, no, that she hadn't inherited! The sense to know who was for her and who was against her, the sense to look after her own interests, no! She wasn't even docile and obedient like her mother. She had even spoilt Bianca for him! Even his wife, seeing her daughter turning to skin and bone, had become for all the world like a cat when you want to take her kittens away, with her hair on end;—her back bent with illness and her eyes shining with fever. She unsheathed claws and tongue against him.

"Do you want to kill my child of a slow decline, do you? Don't you see what a state she's in? Don't you see how she's wasting from day to day?"

She would have helped her, by stealth, even to do something wrong, even to break her neck. She would have betrayed her husband for her child. She said to him:

"I'm going home to my brother's. I'm going with my child! How will you like that?"—This with her eyes like coals. He had never seen her in such a state. Once, in the wake of the doctor who came on account of Isabella, he saw a face that didn't please him at all: an old woman of the neighbourhood who carried the medicine for the apothecary, as Don Luca the sexton and his wife Grazia had carried his own love-intrigues into the Trao home. He was reduced even to examining the doctor's prescriptions and the pill-papers which Bomma sent. In a month he changed the maid-servant

five times. He might be a lunatic, but he wasn't a
ninny like the Trao brothers. He kept everything
under lock and key; he didn't let go a farthing that
might help in his betrayal. He was a chained dog
himself, poor man. At last to get out of that hell he
decided to put Isabella into the Convent, there in the
Mary College, just as when she was a child, in prison!
His wife had a rare weeping and despairing. But he
was master.

"Hear me!" said Bianca with clasped hands. "I
haven't long to suffer. Leave me my daughter till
I close my eyes."

"No," replied her husband. "The ungrateful creature hasn't even compassion on you. We've all slaved
ourselves to death to bring up an ungrateful creature.
She lost her love for her parents—while she was away
from home."

The betrayal took place there at the College: more
people whom he had been good to, that Sister Gerbido
the porteress, and Giacalone who came to bring Aunt
Cirmena's presents and to pass on the love-letters,
Bomma who kept open conversation in the pharmacy,
to suit Don Corrado La Gurna, who started telegraph-
ing to her the moment the maiden appeared on the
belfry tower. They did it for a few half-pence, or for
pleasure, or for nothing, for spite. All the lot con-
spired against him to rob him of his child and his
possessions, as if he had robbed them from other
people. One fine day at last, while the nuns had gone
up into the choir, during the forty hours of exposition,
the girl got her accomplices to open the door, and took
flight.

It was the second of February, day of the Virgin
Mary. There was a great concourse of devotees that

year at the festival, because it hadn't rained since Octo-
ber. Don Gesualdo had also gone to church, to pray
God to remove this cross from him. But the Lord
must have turned his eyes elsewhere that morning.
When he came home from mass, that memorable day,
he found the house upside-down; his wife with her
hands in her hair, the servants running hither and
thither. At last they told him what had happened.
It was like an apoplectic stroke to him. They had to
send rushing to fetch the barber to bleed him. Goodwife Lia got a bang at the side of the head that made
her teeth rattle. Bianca, more dead than alive, went
sluthering down the stairs as if to run away as well,
she was so frightened. He, purple with rage, with
foam at his mouth, was blinded by fury. He couldn't
see what a state the poor woman was in. He wanted
to rush to the magistrate, to the mayor, to turn the
whole village upside down; to fetch the Armed Force
from Caltagirone; to have them both arrested, his
daughter and her accomplice; to have him hung in
the public square, that rascal! to have him drawn and
quartered by the hangman; to make him rot in a
prison! "That assassin! that scoundrel! I want to
make him die in the galleys!—the pair of them—"

In the midst of this fury appeared Aunt Cirmena,
with her mass-book in her hand, and her quiet smile,
dressed up in her silk dress.

"Calm yourself, Don Gesualdo. Your daughter is
in a safe place. Pure as the Immaculate Mary! Calm
yourself! Don't make matters worse by making a
scandal! Look at your wife, who looks as if she was
going to give up the ghost, poor thing. She is a
mother! We can't imagine what she has in her heart
at this moment! I've come on purpose to settle the

hash. I haven't got the stomach of a horse, like some other people. I can't bear malice. You know I've always slaved for my relations. You turned me out, put me on the street—in your anger—with an orphan on my hands—But no matter. Here I am to settle the business. I've got a good heart, worse luck for me! for it's my loss! But I don't know what's to be done! We've got to begin and think how to mend matters. We shall have to marry those two children, now the mischief's done. There's no help for it. Besides there's nothing to be said against the lad—of good family."

This time Don Gesualdo lost all respect for her, opening his mouth as if he wanted to eat her:

"With that beggar?—Give him my daughter?—I'd rather let her die of consumption like her mother!— In the country! in a convent! A nice thing you let me in for!—and just like you!—It takes a rare brazen face!—You make me laugh with all this fine nobility!—I know how much it's worth!—and all the lot of you!—"

Then there was an uproar. Donna Sarina also unsheathed her sharp tongue, red as a cock in the face.

"You speak like what you are! At least you could hold your tongue about your wife, you peasant! Mastro-don Gesualdo! You're the shame of all the family!—"

"Ah! Ah! the shame. My word, you've some right to talk about shame, you have!—you procuress! You've lent a hand yourself! You're the accomplice of that thief!—A nice occupation at your age! I'll have you arrested along with him, Donna Sarina lick-my-boots! Donna, —— thing, for that's what you ought to be called!"

Arrived Uncle Limòli, in spite of his infirmities, for the sake of family decorum, to try himself to make peace, with nice words and nasty.

"Don't make scandals! Don't shout so, which is worse! Wash your dirty linen at home. Let us rather try and see how we can get out of this mess. The mess is made, my dear fellow, so now we've got to unmake it as quickly as possible. Bianca! Bianca, don't go on like that, you'll ruin your health—That won't help."

Don Gesualdo suddenly set off full speed for Caltagirone. He wanted the warrant of arrest, he wanted to bring the Armed Force. The marchese uncle for his part took steps to achieve the best result, with prudence and sagacity. First of all he went to fetch his niece immediately and took her to the Convent of Santa Teresa, recommending her to one of his relations. The house-servants, partly by bribes and partly by threats, were pledged to keep quiet. A little later came like a thunder-clap from Caltagirone the order for the arrest of Corrado La Gurna. Donna Sarina Cirmena, frightened, kept her tongue at home also.

Meanwhile the marchese worked quietly to find a husband for Isabella. She was an only child; Don Gesualdo, by love or force, would have to give her a fine dowry; and with his own numerous relations he was sure of finding her a good party. He wrote about it to his friends; he talked of it to persons who could be of use in such matters, the canon-priest Lupi, Lawyer Neri. The latter at last revealed to him what was to be done in the case: a great nobleman whose property was in charge of the lawyer, and who, though his affairs were in some disorder, between law-suits and debts, was of a great family and would give a fine name to the descendants of Mastro-don Gesualdo. But when, however, they came to speak to the latter about a dowry, it was another pair of shoes. He didn't want to let himself be eaten alive. Not a farthing! His money had been earned in the sweat of his brow, during his whole life. It didn't please him to let his veins be opened for the sake of somebody who would come from Palermo to drink his blood.

"Where do you expect him to come from then, from the moon? My dear fellow, these are words on the wind. You know how things stand. I'll tell you a parable, in your own fashion, to make you hear reason: Hail falls in your vineyard—A disaster happens to your herds—you've got to send to market the heifer with a broken horn, and shut your eyes as to price. You've got to bow your head, out of love or necessity. Besides, you have no other children—At least you can make a fine lady of her!"

At the same time the marchese went to pay a visit to his grandniece. He talked to her kindly, with all the discretion necessary for touching upon certain subjects.

"You are right! Weep away, you are right of it!—Tell me all about it, because I understand these things—A pain for you, something you feel you must die of! Your father doesn't understand anything, poor man. He's always been buried in his business, among his tenants and labourers;—a bit rough, if you like—But he has worked for you, to make you rich. You, with your mother's name and his money, you could take the leading part even in a big city, whenever you wanted to. Not here, in this hole. Here even I feel stifled. I have been young; and I've enjoyed my best years.—That's why I tell you. I can understand what you must be feeling now, in your little heart. When you're young you think there's no one in the world but just the one. Your father took the wrong way.—But if he declares that he'll give you nothing, that young fellow has got nothing either.—And then—if you have to start house-cleaning—and if he's got to seize the devil by the tail—It won't be a pleasant matter, you know! There'll come quarrels, and repentance, and long faces. And long faces won't suit either you or him, my dear. Then why insist? What's the good. If your father has said No it means no, that you won't marry him. You'll die here, in this sort of prison; here you'll waste your best years away. Corrado will remain in exile, at the mercy of the police, as long as your father likes; for he's got long arms now, your father.—Even to those you're most fond of, it won't be any good your holding out. Your cousin needs to keep his brain quiet, to work in peace, in order to earn an honest living.—Then on the other hand you may marry a great nobleman, and if it's true that that youth is so fond of you, he ought to be the first to be pleased about it. That's what one calls love.— A great nobleman, you understand! For the present you won't say anything to your companions—here in the monastery, you know, they'd die of jealousy.—But I know it's in the air that you should marry a great nobleman. You'd be a princess or a duchess! Something different from Donna So-and-So! Carriages, horses, a box at the theatre every evening, jewels and dresses as many as you like—With that pretty face I know how many heads you'd turn in a big city. When you come into the ballroom, in a low-cut dress, covered with diamonds, everybody asking:—"Who is that

beautiful woman?—and you hear the answer: Duchess
So-and-so, or Princess So-and-So!—There then, come
and see your mother who is still ill, poor thing! This
blow has finished her! You know what poor health she
has!—And your father as well is waiting open-armed
for you. He's a good sort, poor fellow! A heart of
gold, a man who has slaved himself to death working
to make you rich!—Now come back home—And then
we'll see—"

When at last the marchese uncle took the lost sheep
back to her parents' home, there was a scene to make
the stones weep. Isabella fell on her knees before her
mother's bed, finding her so changed, sobbing and asking for forgiveness; while her mother, poor thing, went
from one faint into another, her consolation was so
great. Then arrived Don Gesualdo, and they were
all of them silent. At last he began to speak, for he
too was moved, his eyes were swollen, for blood is not
water after all, and his heart was not a stone either.

"Well, you played me a nice trick. I never dreamed
of this. We have taken the bread from our mouths,
your mother and I, in order to make you rich!—See
how low she is brought, poor woman!—If she closes
her eyes she looks a corpse pure and simple!—But you
are our own blood, our own child, and we have forgiven
you. Now we won't talk about it any more."

However, Isabella was always talking about it, with
her uncle the marchese, with her aunt Mendola, with
Aunt Macrì, with all the relations; she asked them all
for help, even her confessor, like a mad-woman, desolate, washing the stones of the confessional with her
tears. Everybody said:

"What can we do, if your father isn't willing? He's
the master. He's got to lay down the money for the

dowry. He does it for your good; he is doing his best for you. Everybody gets married as their parents wish!"

The confessor himself brought forward the will of God. Even Aunt Cirmena, when she saw that even flight would not squeeze the money out of Don Gesualdo's hands, had turned to shrugging her shoulders.

"What can you expect, my dear? I've done all I could. But without money there's no Mass sung. Corrado has nothing: and you've got nothing either, if your father keeps on saying No.—You'd make a fine marriage! You see how it's turned out! That poor lad has even committed his liberty to your father's caprice! Leave him in peace now anyhow, because what with the letters he keeps writing to the relations every day, in all of them weeping about his troubles and begging for money, it's become a serious business—"

Marchese Limòli, however, took another line.

"My child, when a man isn't rich, he can't give himself the luxury of falling in love as he pleases. You two are both of you young yet, and your eyes aren't opened. You see only one thing! But you've got to see what would come later on, the pot to put on the fire and the shirt to patch.—You'd find it a rare amusement! You are well born on your mother's side, that I know. But look at your mother, what she's had to go through, and your uncle Ferdinando, and I myself—We are all of us born from Adam's rib, my child!—Corrado as well came from Adam's rib, But your father has got the pennies! And if he won't give you any, why you can both go road-sweeping, and in a month you'll be fighting with one another. On the

other hand you can make a splendid marriage, live like
a great lady, in a great city!——And then, when you've
got your chef in the kitchen, your carriage waiting for
you at the door, and your own good income secured
in the marriage settlement, then you can afford yourself the luxury of thinking about other things——"

About Easter-time the Duca di Leyra arrived in the
village, under pretence of putting in order his affairs
in those parts, not before they needed it. He was a
handsome man, thin, elegant, a little bald, and most
polite. He took off his hat even in answer to the
peasants' salutes. He had the same smile and the same
courteous manners for all the tedious persons by whom
he was constantly beset, from the very first day. In
the village they talked of nothing but him: What he
had said; what he had come for; how long he would
be staying; how old he was. The ladies declared he
didn't look more than forty. On the day of the Resur-
rection procession the Café of the Gentry was cram-
full of ladies. The Zacco females in hats that took
your eyesight; the Captain's lady withered in her
eternal struggle to be young, which made her still be
called the lovely little widow—as she had been for ten
years, ever since her husband had died. The Margarone women in great get-ups; green, red, yellow,
fluttering with feathers, and ribbons, and little curls
that had grown black with years, fat enough to burst,
and brick-red in the face. They all twittered away,
and made a great to-do trying to impress the strange
gentleman. The duke had got behind his uncle the
Baillie, so as to look younger—so said the spiteful
tongues: a fat little ruddy old man who was supposed
to be leaving him his property, and who meanwhile was

paying court to all the ladies—as men don't know how to nowadays!—observed the Captain's lady.

At the crucial moment, while the statue of the Evangelist came lurching from the Church of Jesu a Maria, and the people were all shouting: "Hail the Risen God!"—there appeared Don Gesualdo Motta's new carriage. He in his tail-coat with golden buttons, and a solitaire diamond in his shirt-bosom, his wife dressed up as well, poor thing, so that her new dress seemed fairly to weep upon her, she was so wasted, wasted to a skeleton, and her daughter also in a new gown that had been sent specially from Palermo. The crowd opened to let them pass, without need of force. Onlookers stared open-mouthed. The very duke asked who they were.

"Ah, a Trao! You can see it at once, though she looks as if she knew suffering, poor lady."

Marchese Limòli thanked him with an inclination of the head, and presented him to his niece. The Duke and the Baillie di Leyra made a separate group, on the pavement of the Café of the Gentry, with the family of Don Gesualdo and the Marchese Limòli. All around was a circle of impudent starers.

Baron Zacco tackled the coachman, to find out what there was underneath it all. Mendola pretended to be patting the horses. Canali winked from one to another:

"Look at that, gentlemen, what a wheel the world is!"

Nobody took any more notice of the procession. There was a great whispering all over the Café. Don Ninì Rubiera, from the distance, with the pole of the church-banner leaning against his shoulder, bit his lips with mortification, thinking how differently things had

turned out for him, Donna Giuseppina Alòsi for a
wife, a swarm of children, the law-suit for the house
which Mastro-don Gesualdo wanted to lay hands on,
after such a length of time—His wife, seeing him
staring so abstracted, his eyes fixed on his cousin, gave
him a sharp nudge in the ribs.

"When are you going to have done? It's scandal-
ous! Your own children are watching you! Dis-
grace!"

"But you're mad," he replied. "The devil! I've
got something else to think about these days. Don't
you see she's got white hair already? That she's nothing but a mummy!—You're mad!"

He himself had got old, as well, loose, bald, fat-
paunched, red-faced, with his cheeks and nose embroidered with sanguinous threads which threatened him
with the same illness as his mother. Now they looked
at one another like two strangers, he and Bianca, indifferent to one another, each having his own troubles
and interests. Even the spiteful talkers had forgotten
the gossip about the two cousins, after such a long time.
However, they envied Mastro-don Gesualdo who had
climbed so high, and Donna Bianca who had made that
famous marriage. Her daughter would go who knows
how far? Donna Agrippina Macrì and the Zacco
cousins launched fiery glances at Isabella's elegant
little hat, and at the attentions which the Duca di
Leyra was paying her, as he stood there gloved, with
a fine large satin cravat holding up his handsome nobleman's head, toying all the time with a thin gold-headed
cane. The Captain's lady turned to remark to Mommino Neri, who had been regarded as a dangerous rake
after the leading-lady affair:

"It's no good. You've only to glance at him once,

and you know whom you've got to deal with. And
he'll be talking rubbish just now—But it's the way he
says it!—Every word as if he offered it you on a
tray—"

His Grace the Duke went later to pay his respects
to the Motta household. Don Gesualdo was waiting
in the best drawing-room. They'd been busy all day
cleaning and airing, the servants, himself, Master
Nardo, all helping. His Grace, with his facile conversation, talked a little about everything, of agriculture with the master of the house, of fashion with the
ladies, of the old families with Marchese Limòli. He
had the whole list of all the noble families in the island
ready at his finger-ends. He went so far as to confess
that his own family had come originally from this
village. He wanted to pay his respects to Don Ferdinando Trao, and visit the mansion, which must be most
interesting. With the young lady, in the course of the
conversation, he turned the subject to the operas then
in vogue; he told anecdotes of the days when the court
was in residence in Palermo, about Queen Caroline,
and the English; he talked a little society small talk;
in fact a world of chatter, in which passed, as in a
magic lantern, great ladies, luxury, and feasts. In
leaving he kissed Donna Bianca's hand. On the stairways, from the fowl-house, on the threshold of the
woodshed all the domestics crowded to see him pass.
And all the evening after, they did nothing but talk
about him, in the kitchen, even the servant girls and
Master Nardo, who made wide eyes.

The Baillie di Leyra and Marchese Limòli, however,
had got another sort of conversation under way, talking from the edge of lips and keeping to generalities.
The next day the duke intervened, however, confessing

first of all that he was in love with the girl, a real flower
of the fields, a hidden violet; and he declared smiling,
that as to the rest—business, that is to say—he never
troubled about it, unfortunately for himself!—it
wasn't his *forte,* so he had asked Lawyer Neri to look
after it——

A real usurer, that lawyer, cunning, greedy, insatia-
be. Don Gesualdo would a thousand times rather have
done the business with his son-in-law, face to face like
gentlemen.

"No, no, dear father-in-law. It's not in my scope.
I don't understand such things. Whatever you others
arrange will suit me. As for myself, the treasure I
ask of you is your daughter."

However, the treaty took a long time. Mastro-don
Gesualdo tried to defend his own possessions, wanting
to weigh with his own hand to make sure that that
which my lord son-in-law was putting into the other
pan of the scales was refined gold. The duke had
great possessions, it is true: half a county. But they
said that everything was in a great mess, law-suits,
mortgages. He could put no trust in Lawyer Neri.
The other negotiator, Marchese Limòli, had never had
the sense even to look after his own interests. The
canon-priest Lupi wanted to intrude himself, protesting an old friendship. But Don Gesualdo replied:

"Thank you very much! Many thanks, Canon. But
once was enough for me! I wouldn't like to abuse—"

Everybody had an eye on his possessions. There
were advances and withdrawals, difficulties that rose
at every step, old papers in which they lost themselves.
Meanwhile his daughter, on the other side, had still
got the other fellow in her mind— She implored her

father and mother not to sacrifice her. She went weeping to the relations, begging them to help her.

"I can't! I can't!—"

At the feet of her confessor she opened all her
heart;—the mortal sin that she was in. That servant
of God didn't understand anything. All he did was to
tell her to sin no more, and he put her heart at peace
by giving her absolution. The poor child went so far
as to run into the Trao house, to throw herself into
the arms of her uncle.

"Uncle, keep me here with you! Save me! I've
nobody else in the world. I belong to your own blood.
Don't send me away."

Don Ferdinando was ill with asthma. He couldn't
speak, and besides he didn't understand a thing. He
made vague motions with his wasted hands, and called
for Grazia to help him, like a child, dismayed by every
new face that he saw.

"Yes, keep me here in place of Grazia. I'll serve
you with my own hands. Don't send me away. They
want to marry me by force!—in mortal sin!"

The old man then had the semblance of a gleam of
remembrance in his faded eyes, in his livid, wrinkled
face. All the grey hairs of his beard seemed to
tremble.

"Your mother as well got married by force.—Diego
didn't want it.—Go away now—if you don't go your
father will come to fetch you away! Go along, go
along—"

The marchese uncle, who knew more of the unpleasant gossip that was going on than anybody else, tackled
Don Gesualdo straight out:

"Will you realise, then? You've got to get your
daughter married quick. Give her to whom you please:

but there's no time to lose. Now have you understood?"

"Eh?—What do you mean?—" stammered the poor father, turning white in the face.

"That's what I mean!—You've found a gentleman who will take her—in good faith.—But you mustn't expect too much of him, you know!—"

So that Don Gesualdo, pressed on all sides, dragged along by the hair, let his veins be opened, and put his name in printed letters on the marriage-contract; Gesualdo Motta—under the signature of his son-in-law, which filled two lines: Alvaro Filippo Maria Ferdinando Gargantas di Leyra.

Magnificent presents arrived from Palermo, jewels and dresses which dried the bride's tears little by little, a pomp of grandeur which made her dizzy, and brought a pale smile even on her mother's lips, and which the marchese uncle went bragging about all round the place. Only Don Gesualdo muttered in secret. They expected great things from this wedding. The Captain's lady sent an express to Catania to the first tailor there. The Zacco women kept the house for eight days, stitching for the event. And then nobody was invited to the wedding: the bride and bridegroom in travelling dress, the parents, the witnesses, four candles and nothing else, in the paltry little church of Sant'Agata where Bianca was married.

How many memories for the poor mother, as she prayed there on her knees before that altar, with her elbows on the chair and her face between her hands! Outside was waiting the litter that would carry away the married couple. There was a general disappointment and anger among all the relations and in all the village. Spiteful comments and criticisms without end

were made about that marriage, that had been carried
out almost in secret. People had gone to visit the
Margarones or Donna Giuseppina Alòsi, to see if the
bride had turned white or red. The Captain's lady
was in a great fix, she made a rare effort not to give
in, saying that that was the fashionable way of getting
married nowadays. Donna Agrippina replied that
that sort of way didn't even seem like a sacrament to
her,—poor Isabella!—Dame Cirmena was chewing
other things between her teeth.

"Like her mother!—You'll see she'll be lucky, being
her mother's daughter!—"

Ciolla, seeing the litter pass through the square,
began to shout:

"The bride and bridegroom! Here's the bride and
bridegroom setting off!—"

Then he went round from door to door, to the Café,
to Bomma's pharmacy, to confide the news:

"And a letter has gone off to Don Corradino La
Gurna—It's a fact! A letter to foreign parts. I
don't know what was in it; but it didn't look to me like
Dame Cirmena's writing. I'd have given something
to know what was in it—"

The letter as a matter of fact said a lot of pretty
things, to send down the pill;—she and her little cousin
who was suffering and despairing far away.

"Addio! Addio! If you remember me, if you think
of me still, wherever you are, here is the last word of
Isabella who loved you so much! I have resisted, I
have struggled as long as I could, I have suffered—I
have cried so much! I have cried so much!—Good-
bye! I shall go away, I shall go far from these scenes
which still speak to me of you!—I shall go far away—

At the festivities, in the midst of all the pomp of the capital, wherever I shall be—no one will see the pallor under my duchess' coronet—No one will know what is in my heart—always, always!—Remember! Remember!—"

FOURTH PART

FOURTH PART

I

Six months had hardly gone by when new troubles
came for Don Gesualdo. Isabella threatened to commit suicide; the son-in-law had taken her travelling
outside the Kingdom of Naples, and talked of appeal-
ing for a legal separation, on grounds of incompati-
bility of temper. Other gossip reached the poor
father, in secret, and he set off hot-foot to the Villa di
Carina, where the duchess was kept for reasons of
health. He came back looking ten years older, and
quarrelled with his wife, who never understood a thing,
and cursed Aunt Cirmena and all the relations with all
his heart, because they had brought him nothing but
bitter vexations, and was forced to rush to the lawyer
to settle the business with his genteel son-in-law by dint
of money and more money. It was a great blow for
the poor fellow. He hid the real trouble from his wife,
so as not to distress her uselessly;—he kept everything
to himself; but he had no peace; it seemed to him that
people were pointing the finger at him; he felt the blood
come to his face as he went alone, thinking, or if he met
that infamous creature Cirmena. He was a peasant;
he wasn't used to such shame! And his daughter the
duchess cost him the eyes out of his head, moreover.
The Canziria estate to start with, and Alia and Donninga which he had assigned to her as her dowry, and
which made his heart bleed every time he saw them
now, let out to anybody and everybody, divided again
into bits and scraps after he had struggled so hard to
put them together, badly kept, badly worked, far from

the master's eye, as if they belonged to nobody. From time to time also other bad news reached his ear, giving him no peace, tormenting him like horse-flies or like stinging wasps; they said in the village that my Lord Duke was sowing debts with both hands, thick as hail, the same wild oats that devoured his own property and spread over his wife's possessions worse than locusts. That poor Canziria which had cost Don Gesualdo so many labours, so many privations, and where he had felt his blood stir as he set his foot for the first time upon his own soil! Donninga for the sake of which he had brought down on himself the hatred of all the village! the good lands of Alia, which he had brooded over, coveting them with his eye for ten years, morning and evening, good sunny land without a stone, loose and soft so that you could push your hands in and it felt warm and fat like living flesh—all, all was going in this gangrene! How could Isabella have held the pen in her hand and put her signature to so many debts? Cursed the day in which he had let her be taught to write! He seemed to see the shadow of mortgages stretching over the lands which had cost him so much sweat and blood, like a hoar-frost in March, worse than a heavy spring mist that blackens the young corn like fire. Once or twice, in serious circumstances, he was forced to let himself be bled in other ways. ' All his savings bled away from this open vein, all his toil, his sleep at nights, everything. And yet Isabella was not happy. What a state he had found her in, in the sumptuous Villa di Carina! He guessed what there must be underneath it all, when she wrote letters to him which set him in a fever, and which poisoned him with the delicate scent of those crested sheets, him who had thickened his own skin labouring even under malaria. The lord duke, however, conducted all this sort of business through the Lawyer Neri—*because they weren't his forte*—And when at last Mastro-don Gesualdo really turned, refusing to go any further, rearing and shying, he was told that his son-in-law said:

"It is obvious my father-in-law, poor man, doesn't understand what is needed for my wife to keep up the name she bears in decency."

"Decency?—I black my boots with decency! I eat bread and onions to keep the duchy going. Tell my noble son-in-law that! In a few years he has wasted a whole patrimony."

There was the devil of a row. Donna Bianca, who was already ill enough, spitting blood morning and evening, had a relapse which brought her to the grave's brink in a fortnight. In the village they all knew she had consumption; like all the Traos! a family which was dying out *of exhaustion,* said the doctor. Only her husband who was always out, busy with his own business, so many thoughts and troubles in his head, deluded himself thinking she'd be better as soon as he could take her out to Mangalavita, into that balsamic air, that would really bring the dead back to life. She smiled sadly and said nothing.

She was reduced to a skeleton, gentle and resigned to her fate, expecting nothing and desiring nothing. Only she would have liked to see her daughter again. Her husband had promised it her. But since they were at outs with their son-in-law he had said no more about it. Isabella was always promising to come, from one autumn to another, but she could never finally make up her mind to it, as if she had sworn to herself never to set foot in that accursed village again, as if she had

plucked it from her heart entirely. And Bianca, as
her strength ebbed, felt this hope also fade, as her life
was fading from her, and wasted herself in ruminating
on future projects, day-dreaming, her face flushing up
with the last flames of her life, her eyes veiled with
tears which might have been tears of tenderness and
were really tears of discouragement.

"I'll do this! I'll do that!"

She was like those caged birds who try over their
song for the spring they will never see. The bed in
which she lay seemed to eat away her flesh; the fever
consumed her with a slow fire. Now, when she was
seized with a fit of coughing, she was left gasping,
spent, with her mouth open, her eyes delirious in the
depths of the sockets which seemed so deep, so deep,
clutching with her poor wasted arms as if she wanted
to hold on to life with all her might.

"All right!" sighed Don Gesualdo at last, seeing his
wife in this state. "I'll do this as well, then!—I'll pay
the noble duke to let you see your daughter again!—
I'm made to carry the load, as I always was."

The doctor came and went, and tried all the remedies and all the nonsense he read in his books; there
was a frightful bill at the druggist's.

"Anyhow it'll help some way or other," grumbled
Don Gesualdo. "I don't mind what is spent for my
wife; but I want to spend my money so that she can
get some good by it and I can see it in her face—not
so that they can try all the new medicines on her like
at the hospital!—Now they've got it into their heads
that I'm rich, they all want to make what they can out
of it!—"

But the first time he ventured to make a veiled com-
plaint to the doctor himself, Saleni, another of these

medical fellows, this one worse even than Tavuso, rest
his soul, the man looked straight at him with his impudent eyes and said rudely:

"Then why do you send for me?"

And he had to beg and pray him to continue to do
as he liked, although it wasn't the slightest good actually. On the eve of the Immaculate Virgin it looked
as if poor Bianca was really going to yield up her soul
to God. Her husband, who had gone to wait for the
doctor on the stairs, said to him immediately:

"I don't like her, doctor! I don't like the looks of
my wife to-night."

"Eh! have you only just found it out? I haven't
liked the looks of her for some time. I thought you'd
have realised it."

"But isn't there anything we can do, your honour?
Do all you can. Don't mind the expense—Money is
meant to be spent for these things—"

"Ah, you tell me so now? Now you realise? Well
I'm glad to hear it, I must say!"

Saleni began the comedy all over again; the pulse,
the tongue, a bit of a chat seated at the bed-foot, with
his hat on his head and his stick between his legs.
Then he wrote the usual prescription, the usual rubbish
which was no good to anybody, and departed leaving
husband and wife to their miseries. The house had
become a forsaken cavern. Everybody gave it a wide
berth. Even the servants were afraid of the infection.
Zacco was the only relation who remembered them in
their trouble, since he and Don Gesualdo had formed
a company together for the contract for the high-road,
and so were friends again. The baron came every day
with all his family, the baroness lean and obedient, her

daughters filling the room, so over-ripe, fat and bursting, that they made you expect a cannonade.—

He wasn't afraid of infection! Lot of rubbish!—And then, when it's one's own relations—! He'd heard that evening in the town that his cousin Bianca was worse, so he had come sooner than usual. To take Don Gesualdo's mind off his troubles a bit, he drew him into the balcony opening and began to discuss their business with him.

"What do you say to this? Cousin Rubiera is going to bid at the auction for the other two sections of road—Yessir!—that fool!—Eh? Eh? What do you think of it?—Him who's not been able to pay you back that money for the leading lady yet!—There's hell to pay with his wife, about you, because she won't settle it with her money!—She brought him her children, for a dowry!—but she wants to keep her money for herself! He's fated, is that poor Don Ninì!—And do you know who else is coming in at the auction? Do you want to know?—Canali, just think of it!—Canali playing at being a joint contractor along with Baron Rubiera!—They've all got hungry for making profit nowadays!—Eh?—Wasn't I right to tell you?—Doesn't it make you laugh?"

But his friend was not really heeding him; he was uneasy, keeping his ear listening in another direction. Then he got up and went to see if Bianca was wanting anything. She didn't want anything, as she lay staring in front of her with those eyes of an innocent creature, putting her handkerchief to her mouth sometimes, and then hiding it again, along with her wasted hand, under the pillow. The Zacco girls were sitting round the bed, with their hands in their fat laps. Their mamma stammered timidly, in order to break the silence:

"She seems a little calmer—since we came—"

At those words the daughters all looked at one another and nodded approval.

Then the baron went up to the bedside, showing a great deal of interest in the sick woman.

"Yes, yes, there's no comparison!—her eye is more alive, and her countenance is more animated.—Naturally!—hearing some talk going on round her. She needs to be livened up, to have a bit of conversation. For a blessing you're in good hands. The doctor knows what he's doing. And then when you've got the means!—when you lack for nothing! I know plenty of others where it's different—well born too—of good family—and they want bread by day and covering by night!—old and ill, without doctor or druggist—"

He leaned to Don Gesualdo and twaddled out the rest in his ear. Bianca either heard or guessed, with her shining eyes which fixed people in the face, and she drew her white, wasted hand that was like a child's from under the pillow to make a sign to her husband to come near. Don Gesualdo had bent over her and was nodding Yes. The baron, seeing there was no longer need for mystery, spoke up.

"He won't come! Don Ferdinando has become a regular child. He doesn't understand a thing, poor fellow!—We must be sorry for him. We can say it here, among us relations—He needn't lack for anything—A brother-in-law with such a good heart as this one here!—"

The sick woman waved once more that hand that spoke by itself.

"Eh? What does she say? What does she want?" asked the baron.

Donna Lavinia, the eldest of the daughters, had risen, anxious to do for her anything she might require. Donna Marietta, the other daughter, for her part pulled her father's coat-tails. But Bianca had closed herself in a silence which sharpened her worn face like a knife, so that even the baron noticed it and changed the subject.

"The Lord God sometimes lengthens our days to try us with fresh troubles—I speak of the Baroness Rubiera, poor thing! Eh?—To live to see the property she'd got together go to pieces under her own eyes!—and not to be able to say a word or to move a finger—eh? eh? Her son is a fool. Her daughter-in-law grudges her the mouthful of food she eats!— As true as God's above!—She can't wait to be rid of her!—But she doesn't want to go! She wants to live just to see how her son will get out of that debt to Don Gesualdo—Eh?—I've been telling your husband just now of the great schemes Don Nini has got in his head—"

Don Gesualdo was silent, plunged in thought. Then, seeing that the baron was expecting his cousin Bianca to answer, waiting with that fixed little smile on his mouth, he growled:

"No, there's not so much to laugh at—I'll wager the canon-priest Lupi is at the back of it."

Zacco was staggered.

"That rascal? that trickster?—How do you know?—Who told you?"

"Nobody. It's my idea. But he won't take me in, you'll see.—Besides, I don't care. I've got something else to think about now!"

But the baron would give him no peace.

"What? You don't care! Thank you for that!

You know what they're saying, don't you? That they
want to take the communal lands away from us!—
They say they've found the way and means this time—
and that neither you nor me can help ourselves, do you
know!"

Don Gesualdo shrugged his shoulders. It seemed
as if really he didn't care a single straw about it now.
The baron gradually calmed himself down, in the midst
of the chorus of his women who were murmuring abuse
against the canon-priest.

"A trickster!—a swindler!—You can't stir in the
village but what he has to poke *his* nose in—"

Donna Marietta, more prudent, pulled her father's
coat-tails once more.

"Excuse me! Excuse me!" added he. "One chat-
ters to say a bit of something—to liven up the sick
woman. One doesn't know what to talk about.—Do
you know though what the malcontents like Ciolla are
going round saying?—that they'll be making the revolution in eight days' time—to frighten the gentle-
folks.—You remember, in twenty-one, eh, Don Gesualdo?"

"Ah!—What's the good of talking!—I've got a
revolution in the house now!"

"I know, I know—But then, it doesn't seem to
me—"

The baroness, who could speak when necessary,
turned to Don Gesualdo with that ill-omened face of
hers to ask if they had written to the duchess to tell
her what a state her mother was in.—Bianca had the
sharp ear of the very ill.

"No, no, there's no danger!" interrupted Zacco.
Meanwhile Donna Lavinia had risen to fetch a

glass of water. As the door-bell was heard to ring she
wanted also to run and see who it was.

"A two-handed sword!" exclaimed the baron *sotto
voce,* as if he was saying something in confidence, smiling complacently. "A real treasure of a girl to have in
the house—So sensible!—And she'd throw herself in
the fire for her cousin Bianca!—"

The mamma also smiled discreetly. At that moment
appeared the servant girl announcing Baron Rubiera
and his wife.

"Him? Well, it takes a cheek like his!" burst out
the baron, jumping up and looking for his hat which
he'd got on his head all the while.—"You'll see he's
come to talk about what I was telling you! Isn't there
another way out?—not to meet him face to face, the
fool!—"

His family was taking leave as fast as ever they
could, rushing round like him, looking for shawls, upsetting chairs, bumping into one another, as if Don
Ninì was going to burst into the room with a drawn
dagger. The poor ill woman, overcome by all that turmoil, let herself sink into unconsciousness, saying with
a thread of a voice:

"For the love of God!—I can stand no more!"

"No—But there's no help for it, cousin!—They're
relations, as well!—You'll see they've come for their
own purpose, to seize the opportunity—Pretending to
be coming to see you—We'd better be going, we had—
That's the way—First come first served—"

But the Rubieras did not put in an appearance as yet.
Don Gesualdo went into the anteroom, where he learnt
that they were waiting in the parlour, as they had heard
that the Zaccos were there—

"All the better!" observed the Baron. "That means

he wants a private talk with you, does Don Ninì!—So we won't stir. We'll stop and keep our cousin company, while you talk business.—And then we shall hear what that ninny has come to ask you!"

The servant had taken a little light into the parlour, and in the semi-obscurity Don Ninì looked really enormous, muffled in his great-coat, with a woollen scarf right up to his ears, in his neck a mane of hair that hadn't been cut since May. Don Giuseppina on the other hand, had gone round-shouldered, her face was flabby and wrinkled in her round hood, her hair, of a dirty grey, was ill combed, rolled up in a hurry with one hand and then held in place by the silk handkerchief that she had tied under her chin. Her hands were cracked and black, the hands of a good housewife, as she now gesticulated to defend her husband's interests; agitating herself inside her mud-splashed cape that covered her all over; showing in all her person the slovenliness and neglect of a rich lady who had no need to dress herself up, a wife who has left off bearing children and hasn't to trouble any more about pleasing her husband. And on her toothless mouth she kept all the time the smile of a poor person, the humble smile of one who comes to beg a favour. While Don Ninì fumbled for his words, turning his old hat in his hands, with that scarf up to his nose giving him a threatening look. His wife encouraged him with a look and began herself:

"We heard that cousin was worse—We came at once with Ninì—We're relations when all's said and done— the same blood—There are differences—and different interests—there must be, in all families—But everything goes under when certain things happen.—Ninì as well—poor fellow, he couldn't rest—always saying—I'd really like to know why—"

Don Ninì agreed with gestures and with all his person, which he had let sink on to the sofa, making it creak loudly. And quickly he broached the matter he had come for—his wife insisting absolutely that their cousin should sit down between the two fires—

"We've got that business of the new contract to consider, dear Don Gesualdo. Why should we fight amongst ourselves, say I?—for some outsider's benefit? —since we really are relations!—" "Of course!" interrupted the wife. "That's what we came about— How is our poor cousin?"

"As God wills she should be!—So that I've got the punishment of God on my shoulders!—I haven't got the head for business now—"

"No, no, I don't want you to bother.—I was just saying—you ought to trust yourself to a reliable person.—Not that it's anything to do with me, of course—"

All at once Don Ninì' face went dark, as he seemed to withdraw, watching the other man with suspicious eyes.

"Tell me though, do you trust Zacco, really? Eh? Do you trust him?"

Don Gesualdo, in spite of all he was feeling, twisted his mouth to a smile, as if to say he trusted nobody.

"Good! If you knew the sort of fellow he really is!—All the things he used to say about you once!— before he was hand and glove with you!—The talk he used to let out!—"

Donna Giuseppina had her cheeks pursed out and her lips nipped together as if to keep in all she might say.

"Anyhow, we won't bother! Talk won't grind us any corn. He's a relation as well! So let's come back to ourselves.—What have we to keep on falling out about? Why should we keep a lot of lawyers and judges at our expense? What is the trouble between us relations? Is it all for that trifle which I owe you?—For you it's no more than a pinch of snuff."

"Oh well, excuse me, so it is for you—"

Then chimed in Donna Giuseppina, telling over her troubles, her large family, her mother-in-law the baroness, who while she lived—

"Excuse me!—She doesn't come in.—It's the money that matters, you know. And I lent my money to your husband."

Don Ninì began to excuse himself, there in front of his wife.—Yes, he had borrowed the money—at a moment when he had lost his head—When you're young—you'd better cut your head off, sometimes—He would pay—in time—the last farthing—without law-suits or any more expense—as soon as his mother had closed her eyes.—But was it right to make him feel bitter against the baroness, good God? To make her do something foolish?—"

"Ah?" said Don Gesualdo. "Ah?"—And he looked at Donna Giuseppina as if to ask why *she* didn't pay.

Don Ninì, embarrassed, looked from one to the other. She at last put in, cutting her husband short with a wave of the pocket-handkerchief she had taken from her satchel:

"It's not only that.—The affair of the lands—You haven't mentioned that yet to Cousin Don Gesualdo, have you?"

"Yes—the affair of the communal lands—"

"I know—" replied Don Gesualdo—"The lease ex-

pires in August.   Whoever wants to come in at the
auction, can then—"

"No! no!—Neither you nor I will get them this
time."

"A new law," interrupted Donna Giuseppina with a
sour smile.   "The lands aren't going to be leased out
any more!   The parish is going to rent them—to the
poorest people—a little bit for everybody.—Everybody in the village will be a landowner in a little
while!—Didn't you know?"

Don Gesualdo pricked up his ears, putting aside his
own troubles for a moment.   Then he gave a weary
smile.

"It's as true as God's above!" added Baron Rubiera.
"I have seen the project at the Town Hall!   They say
the parish will be the gainer, and everybody will have
his own piece of land."

Then Don Gesualdo took out his snuff-box, smelling
a trap.

"That is to say?   That is to say?"

"Don Gesualdo!" called the servant from the doorway.   "Just a minute, your honour!"

"Do go, never mind us," said Donna Giuseppina.
"Don't you bother.   We'll wait."

"It's the mistress.   She wants to speak to your
honour!"

"Eh?   What do they want?   What do they say?"
The Zaccos fell upon Don Gesualdo the moment he
entered the sick room.

"It was I who sent for you," said the Baron with
a sly smile.

But the other didn't answer, bending over his wife.
Making her eyes and her poor, wasted white hand
speak for her, she said:

"No!—Don't have anything to do with him—if you want just for once to listen to me.—Don't join with my cousin Rubiera, don't do it!—Mind, I speak to you on my deathbed—"

She had a toneless voice, and eyes which penetrated into him, so fixed and shining. Zacco, who had also bent over the bed to hear, exclaimed triumphantly:

"Bless her! She speaks as if she could see beyond. You'll never do any good with that man! A fool! A weathercock! What your wife says to you at this moment is gospel, Don Gesualdo! Don't forget it. I'd be very careful before I disobeyed what she says, on my word I would—!"

"And Donna Giuseppina! Deceitful, spiteful!" put in Madame. "She has shortened her mother-in-law's days! She can't wait to be rid of her!"

"Go then, go and face the music. We are here. Go along, else they'll be there till to-morrow."

Don Ninì was still seated on the sofa, puffing with the heat of his woolen scarf, his hat on his head; and Donna Giuseppina had got up to look in the obscurity at the ornaments and things arranged carefully on the tables and stands: the coffee-service, the paper flowers under the glass dome, the clock which always pointed to the same hour. Seeing Don Gesualdo return she said immediately:

"Baron Zacco sent for you, didn't he? There was no need—We don't make any mystery—"

"We don't make any mystery—" repeated her husband. "It's only a question of coming to an agreement—all those that are well-disposed to one another —If he's well-disposed himself—that gentleman!—"

"But," observed Don Gesualdo, "if the thing is as

you say, I don't know what's to be done.—What do you want of me?"

Donna Giuseppina had also changed her face, darting her eyes like needles first to this one, then to that, chewing a smile with her black mouth. She put her husband altogether in the background, and took up the cudgels herself with her Cousin Motta.

"Yes, there is help for it!—there is!—" And she kept still for a moment, staring fixedly at him, to impress him more. Then, holding her purse tight between her hands, she came up to him with a peculiar motion of her hips, in confidence.

"We've got to get our own people to take the lands—on the quiet—" said the baron.

"No! no!—let me explain.—The communal lands are to be rented out in lots, aren't they? in bits and scraps so that every land-labourer can have his share. All right. Let them do it. And then, we'll put forward other applicants, on the quiet—shop-keepers, people who don't know what to do with land and haven't even the money for the rent. Everybody has the same right to apply, haven't they? Well then, with a bit of foresight, advancing a small sum to this one and the other—They will be in debt to us at the New Year, and we'll take the land in payment. Do you see what I mean? We've got to prevent as much as ever we can the real land-labourers from getting hold of it. Because once they do they'll never let go of their bits again. They'd die rather."

Don Gesauldo got up suddenly, his nostrils dilated and his face all at once reanimated, and began to walk up and down the room. Then, turning round to face the other two, who had also risen startled:

"*You* didn't think of this!" he exclaimed. "This is a good one. I know where this comes from!"

"Ah! Ah! You know? You see?" replied the baron triumphantly. "First of all you've got to stop Nanni l'Orbo's mouth.—With caution—and a little money— without doing anybody any hurt, of course!—The authorities—"

"You who've got a hand in the affair—The fellow is a ringleader, an agitator—capable of rousing the whole place against you. You who've got a hand in the affair, you must stop his mouth."

Don Gesualdo went to sit down again, repenting of having let himself be carried away by the first emotion, scratching his head.

But Baron Zacco, who was on the other side of the door listening with all his ears, could not contain himself any longer.

"Excuse me. Excuse me, gentlemen," he said, entering. "If I disturb you—if you have something to talk about in secret—I'll go—" And he straightway took a seat, with his hat on his head.

They were all silent, each one glancing furtively at his neighbour, Don Ninì with his nose in his scarf, his wife with her lips compressed. At length she said she was so sorry about Bianca's illness.

"Really! mourning in the whole village. Ninì has been preaching at me for a while now—Giuseppina dear, we must go and see how my cousin is—Money is one thing, and relationship is another—"

"Well now," resumed Don Gesualdo. "This fine idea of taking the communal lands on the quiet—who is responsible for it?"

It was no use pretending after that. Donna Giuseppina began to talk again about the ferment there was in the village, and of the revolution that was threatening. Baron Zacco fidgeted, making signs with his head to Don Gesualdo.

"Eh? Eh? What was I telling you just now?"

"When all's said and done," concluded Donna Giuseppina—"it's better to speak out plainly and shake hands with one another, all of us who have something to lose."

And she returned to the subject of that scoundrelly chopping up of the communal lands for the benefit of the poorest people, into so many morsels, a crumb for everybody, so as not to wrong anybody. She laughed till her stomach shook, with venom.

"Ah? ? ?" exclaimed the Baron, purple in the face, his eyes starting out of his head. "Ah? ? ?" And he said no more.

Don Gesauldo was also laughing.

"Ah? It makes you laugh? ah?"

"What do you want me to do? It matters nothing to me, I tell you."

Donna Giuseppina was staggered.

"How?—You!—"

Then she drew him aside, near to the corner where was the stopped clock, and was talking to him softly, with her hands over her eyes. Don Gesualdo said nothing, but stroked his chin, with that calm little smile that made people wild. From the distance the two barons kept their eyes fixed on him, like two mastiffs. At last he shook his head.

"No! no! Tell the canon-priest Lupi that I'm going to find no money for these dodges. They can have the lands who like—I've got my own—"

The others turned on him one and all in one accord, shouting, exciting one another. Zacco, now that he understood what was going on, raved worse than any of them.

"A genuine good idea! Coming from a man who knows what's what! The best way of getting out of that rascalry of dividing the communal property among a lot of good-for-nothings—Don't you understand?— What they mean is that what's mine isn't mine, and everybody wants his share of it!—"

Don Gesualdo, obdurate, only shook his head and kept repeating:

"No! No!—They don't catch me!"

All at once Baron Zacco seized Don Ninì by the scarf and pushed him towards the sofa as if he wanted to devour him, whispering in his ear:

"Do you want to hear? Should I tell you? What it amounts to is that he's got his own idea for making a fool of us all!—I know him!—"

At the commotion the Zacco cousins had appeared in the doorway of the anteroom. There was a moment of embarrassment among the relations. Zacco and Don Ninì calmed themselves suddenly, becoming ceremonious again:

"Excuse me! Excuse me! I don't know what cousin Bianca will think, hearing all this shouting—and all for nothing!—"

Zacco smiled good-naturedly, his face still kindled. Don Ninì wrapped his scarf up to his nose again. His wife, also with an amiable smile, took her leave.

"My best wishes to Donna Bianca.—We won't disturb her.—Let us hope the Madonna will perform a miracle—"

Don Ninì also growled out some inaudible word from under his muffler.

"Just a moment. I'll come with you," exclaimed

Zacco. And pretending to look for his hat and cane he came near to Don Gesualdo in the antechamber.

"Listen—You're wrong, upon my word you are! It's a serious proposition!—You're wrong not to join in with Baron Rubiera!—"

"No, I don't want the bother!—I've got so many other things on my mind!—Then my wife said no. You heard her yourself."

The baron was really getting into a rage at this.

"Ah!—your wife?—You attend to her when it suits you!" But he suddenly changed his tone:

"Well then—do as you will!—Do as you will, my dear friend!—Wait a minute, Don Ninì. We're coming now."

His wife couldn't get away. She seemed as if she couldn't tear herself from the bedside of the sick woman, straightening the bedclothes, smoothing the pillow, putting the glass of water and the medicine within reach, making a long face, sighing, and mumbling Ave Marias. Then she wanted her daughter to stay and sit up for the night, at least. Donna Lavinia consented heartily, also busying herself doing things, anxious to help, already taking possession of the keys, watching over everything, like a mistress.

"No!" murmured Bianca with her hoarse voice. "No!—I don't want anybody!—I don't need anybody!"

She followed them round the room with an anxious eye, suspicious, diffident, with a peculiar note of rancour in her hollow voice. She forced herself to appear stronger than she was, struggling to rear herself up on her trembling elbows, with her shoulders so sharp that they seemed as if they would pierce through her night-dress. Then as soon as the Zaccos had gone she dropped exhausted, making a sign to her husband to come near.

"Listen!—Listen to me!—I don't want them any more!—Don't let those women come here any more— They want you to marry one of them—as if I was dead already."

And she kept on nodding her head, saying yes, yes, that she was not mistaken, her sharp chin sinking in the shadow of her hollow neck, whilst he, bent over her, talked to her as if she was a child, smiling, but with his eyes swollen.

"They want to set Lavinia in the house for you— They can't wait for me to close my eyes—"

He protested that it wasn't so, that Lavinia wasn't of the least concern to him, that he would not marry again, that he had seen trouble enough. And the poor thing listened to him quite pleased, with her shining eyes that penetrated right into him, to see if he was speaking the truth.

"Listen—again—something else—"

She always motioned with her hand, because her voice failed her, her voice that seemed to come from afar off, her eyes that gradually were growing darker, becoming veiled. She had even made the effort to raise herself so as to clasp an arm round his neck, as if there was nothing left but him to cling to for life, to hold her to life, shaking her face, that had gone still sharper, as if she wanted to hide it in his breast, as if she wanted to confess herself to him. After a moment she relaxed her arms again, with her face rigid and closed, and her voice changed.

"Later on—I will tell you—But I can't now—"

II

Now everything was going to rack and ruin for Don
Gesualdo; the house all in disorder; the country labourers, far from the master's eye, doing what they
liked; the very servants left one by one, afraid of
catching consumption; even Mena, the last one remaining for the absolute needs, when they spoke to her
about washing the sick woman's clothes, that the wash-
erwoman refused to take to the river, for fear of losing
her other custom, said straight out:

"Don Gesualdo, you'll excuse me, but my life's worth
as much as yours, though you're rich.—Don't you see
how far gone your wife is?—It's a wasting decline,
God help us! I'm frightened of it, and so excuse me."

And that after she had grown fat in his house!
Now everybody abandoned him as if he was ruined,
and there was nobody even to light the lamp. It was
like that night at Salonia, when he had had to put his
father in the coffin with his own hands. Neither money
nor anything was any good any more. Then Don Gesualdo really lost heart. Not knowing what to do, he
thought of his old friends, those whom one remembers
in time of need, and he sent to fetch Diodata to lend
a hand. Instead of her appeared her husband, suspicious, looking around, careful where he put his feet,
spitting right and left.

"As for me—I'll risk my skin for you, if you want it,
Don Gesualdo! But Diodata is mother of a family,
you know—If anything was to happen to her, God preserve you and me—If she caught your wife's illness—

374

We are poor folks—And you're rich enough; but I shouldn't even have the money to pay the doctor and the druggist—"

In short the same old song, the same chanting to get more money out of him, to bleed him again. At last, after a bit of pulling and holding back, they agreed as to the recompense. He had to shut his eyes and bow his head. Nanni l'Orbo, quite content with the bargain he had made, wound up:

"As for us, you're the master even of our lives, Don Gesualdo. You've only to give your orders, night and day. I'm going to fetch my wife, and I'll bring her along."

But now Bianca had got another cause for suffering. She didn't want to see Diodata about the house. She wouldn't take anything from her hands.

"No!—You, no!—Go away with you!—What have you come for, you?—"

And she fretted against those greedy creatures who came to feed at her expense. How she clung to her possessions, now!—and how the old rancour awoke again in her now, a jealousy of her husband whom they wanted to rob away from her, those wicked people who had come on purpose to hurry her into her grave, to make themselves masters of everything that was hers. She had become absolutely like a child, suspicious, irascible, capricious. She complained that they *put something* in her broth, and that they changed her medicines. Every time she heard the door-bell there was a scene. She said they sent people away because they didn't want to let them see her.

"I heard my brother Don Ferdinando's voice!— There was a letter came from my daughter, and they wouldn't give it me!—"

The thought of her daughter was another torment. Isabella also was in poor health, so far away, that a journey would have prostrated her for ever, wrote the husband. For the rest they had known for some time how Bianca dragged herself from her bed to her lying-chair, and they would never have believed that the catastrophe was so near. But the poor mother would give herself no peace, she turned upon Don Gesualdo and everybody who was near her. It needed the patience of a saint. In vain her husband said to her:

"Look now!—What the deuce are you getting into your mind now?—Even you take it into your head to be jealous!"

She looked at him with such black looks as he had never seen. And with a certain tone he had never heard before in her hoarse voice, she said to him:

"You've taken my daughter away from me—even now when I'm in the state I am in!—I leave you to your own conscience!—"

Or else she threw it in his face that he had brought these other people around her. Or else she wouldn't answer at all, with her face turned to the wall, implacable.

Nanni l'Orbo had installed himself like a father in Don Gesualdo's house. He ate and drank, he came every day to fill his belly. Diodata looked after what there was to do, whilst he ran round in the market-place amusing himself, confabulating with his friends, holding forth about what was needed and what must be done, upholding the cause of the poor people in the matter of dividing up the communal lands, every man his own bit, as God had intended it, and every gentleman to have as many portions as he had children to bring up. He also knew by thread and sign all the manœuvres of the big-wigs who were trying to get the lands for themselves. On one occasion he started a grand discussion on this point with Canali, and they came to blows over it, now that the days of arrogance were over and every man might say his say.

The day after, Master Titta had gone to Canali's to shave him, when the door-bell rang and Canali went to see who it was, with all the soap on his chin. While he was sharpening the razor, Master Titta stretched his neck from simple curiosity, and saw Canali talking in the anteroom with Gerbido, and the pair of them with faces to make anybody open his ears full width. Canali said to Gerbido:

"So you rely on it, then?"

And Gerbido replied:

"Oh! ! !"

Nothing else.

Canali came back to be shaved, as quiet as if it was all nothing, and Master Titta thought no more about it. Only that evening, he himself didn't know why— but he had a presentiment, seeing Gerbido leaning against the corner of the Masera, with his gun behind him!—The words he had heard a while before came back to him.

"Who knows whom that pill is destined for," he thought to himself.

Things were already looking doubtful, and people had hurried home before Ave Maria was rung. Further on, meeting Nanni l'Orbo hanging around down there, his heart told him that this was the very person for whom Gerbido was waiting.

"What are you doing out at this hour, neighbour Nanni?" said Master Titta to him. "Better come along home. We'll be going the same way."

"No, Master Titta, I've got to go to the tobacconist's here, and then I'm going for a moment to see Diodata who is waiting on Don Gesualdo's wife—"

"Do me this favour, neighbour Nanni! Come along home now! I'll give you tobacco, and you can go to see your wife to-morrow. These are no fit times for roving round the street at this hour!—You believe me!—"

The other passed it off in joke; saying he wasn't frightened of their robbing him of money he hadn't got.—His wife was expecting him with a plate of macaroni—and plenty else.—For a plate of macaroni, God save us, you'd risk your skin!—

As soon as Master Titta heard the noise of the gun two minutes later, he said to himself:

"There's neighbour Nanni getting it."

Don Gesualdo had had other trials that morning. Speranza sent the sergeant-bailiff just when she knew it would make him most mad. They gave him no peace from year's end to year's end, and they'd made his hair go grey with those law-suits. And Speranza herself was become like nothing but a witch; she had eaten up the fields and the vineyard, egged on by everybody who had a grudge against her brother. She went round everywhere villifying him. She waited for him in the street in order to vomit insults upon him. She incited her children against him, since her husband didn't want to inflame himself—he was good for nothing but for taking his belly for a walk round the village, he was; and Santo himself, now that he wanted money, turned his coat and went over to Don Gesualdo's side, to spit back at his sister the same ugly things he had said before against his brother; a weathercock who spun round with the wind.

"It's a real villainy, that it is, Don Camillo! They come down on me with this, just when I'm up to my neck in trouble already. I've sown good and reaped evil from everybody, I have."

Don Camillo shrugged his shoulders.

"Excuse me, Don Gesualdo. I do my duty. Why did you fall out with the canon-priest Lupi?—About the contract for the high-road!—for a mere nothing— You need to keep friends with that servant of God. Now he blows the fire up against you with your relations. I don't want to speak ill of anybody; but he'll make it hot for you, my dear Don Gesualdo."

And Don Gesualdo was silent; he bent his back now that everybody could say his say against him, and anybody could throw stones at him.

As it was known that his wife was worse, Marchese Limòli came to visit his niece and had even brought Don Ferdinando as well, arm in arm the two of them, holding each other up. "Death and the dunce," said those who met them in the street at that hour, with the ferment there was in the village; and they crossed themselves, seeing Don Ferdinando still in the world of the living, with that old great-coat which hardly hung together any more. The two old men had sat down by the bed, their chins on their sticks, while Don Gesualdo told the story of the illness, and his brother-in-law turned his back on him without saying anything, looking towards his sister, who looked back first at one, then at the other, poor thing, with those eyes of hers which seemed to want to make everybody happy, when suddenly they heard a shouting in the street below, people running crying loudly, as if the expected revolution had really broken out. All at once, they heard a knocking at the street door, and a voice calling:

"Neighbour Diodata, open! Come quick. Come and see your husband, he's been shot—he's there in the pharmacy—"

Diodata ran just as she was, with her head uncovered, screaming down the streets. In a moment Don Gesualdo's house was all upside-down. Baron Zacco also came, suspicious, anxious, mumbling his words, looking in front and behind him before he opened his mouth.

"Did you see? They've done it! They've killed Diodata's husband."

Then Don Gesualdo lost patience.

"Well, what's it to do with me? I needed this, that I did! What the devil do you want with me?"

"Ah—what's it to do with you?—Excuse me! I thought you'd thank me—if I came at once to let you know—out of good feeling for you—as a friend—and as a relation—"

Meanwhile other people arrived. Zacco went to see who it was, half closing the door of the anteroom. Every minute there was a banging at the street door, so many shocks for the poor sick woman. Then Zacco came to say, quite overwhelmed:

"There's been the devil of a row at Palermo.—The revolution—They want to make it here as well.—That rascal of a Nanni l'Orbo did well to get himself killed just now!—"

Don Gesualdo still only shrugged his shoulders, like one to whom nothing mattered now, nothing except the poor dying woman. After a while the wife and daughters of Baron Zacco also arrived, dressed in their house dresses, with their yellow shawls down their backs, and long faces, never saluting anybody. You could see that all was over. Every minute the baroness went over to speak to her husband, in a low voice. Donna Lavinia had appropriated the keys. Seeing this Don Gesualdo went white. He hadn't even the courage to ask if the hour had come. Only his bright eyes interrogated first one and then the other.

But they answered him with half words. The baron pulled a long face, and his wife turned her eyes up to heaven and put her hands together. The girls, already sleepy, kept silent, sitting together in the next room. Towards midnight, as the sick woman had gradually become quieter, Don Gesualdo wanted to send them away to rest.

"No," said the baron. "We shall not leave you alone to-night."

Then Don Gesualdo breathed no more, since there was no more hope. He began to walk up and down, with bent head, and his hands behind his back. From time to time he leaned over his wife's bed. Then he went to continue his walking in the next room, muttering to himself, shaking his head, shrugging his shoulders. At last he turned to Zacco, his voice full of tears:

"I say we ought to send for her relations—eh?— Don Ferdinando—What do you think?"

Zacco made a grimace.

"Her relations?—Ah, all right—as you will—To-morrow—as soon as it's day—"

But the poor man couldn't contain himself, the words were burning inside him and on his lips.

"Don't you see?—Not even letting her see her daughter for the last time!—He's a swine, that noble duke! For three months he's been writing—we'll come to-day and we'll come to-morrow! As if the poor thing had got a hundred years to live! It's a true proverb: Out of sight, out of mind. He's stolen both child and dowry, that assassin!"

And he went on raving like this for some time with Zacco's wife, for she was a mother herself, and she nodded yes! yes! forcing her eyes to keep open, while they shut by themselves. He felt neither sleepy nor anything, and began grumbling again:

"What a night! What an endless night! How long this night lasts, Lord God!"

Day had hardly dawned when he opened the balcony doors to call Nardo the labourer, and sent him round to all the relations to say that Bianca was very bad, poor thing, and if they wanted to see her. Along the street there was an extraordinary come and go, and down in the square you could hear a great buzzing. On his return Master Nardo brought the news:

"They have made the revolution. There's the flag on the church-tower."

Don Gesualdo sent him to the devil. Little he cared about the revolution now. He'd got revolution enough at home now! But Zacco tried to calm him down.

"Careful! Careful! In these days we have to be careful, my dear friend."

A short time after, they heard a knocking at the street door. Don Gesualdo ran to open it himself, thinking it was the doctor or one or other of all those whom he had sent for. Instead he found himself face to face with the canon-priest Lupi, who was dressed in short clothes and with a ragged hat on his head, and the young Baron Rubiera, who stood aside.

"Excuse me, Don Gesualdo. We don't want to bother you—But it's a serious business—Hark here—"

He drew him aside into the stable to tell him in a

low voice what he had come for. Don Nini, in the distance, still scowling, nodded approbation.

"We've got to make a demonstration, you understand?—Shout that we want Pio Nono and liberty as well.—If we don't the peasants will turn on us. And you must join in. We mustn't give a bad example, good God!"

"Ah! The old song about the Carboneria?" burst out Don Gesualdo, infuriated. "Many thanks to you, Canon! I'm not making any more revolutions! We made a fine show of it at the start! They've got to like it now, and every little while they'll be making another, to get the money out of your pocket. I know what it all amounts to now:—*You get out, and give me what you've got!*"

"You mean to say you stick up for the Bourbon? Speak out."

"I stick up for my own possessions, bless you!—I have worked hard—with my sweat—And so—all right —But now I'm not going any more to do just what suits those who don't own anything or possess anything."

"Then they'll do it to you, you understand! They'll sack your house and everything!"

The canon-priest added that he came on behalf of those who had something to lose and who ought to unite together, in the present peril, for the common good.—Otherwise he wouldn't have set foot in his house—after the trick he had played him about the contract for the high-road—

"Excuse me—Since you want to play at being deaf— You know how many enemies you've got! Jealous persons—who would like to lay hold of—They don't look on you very kindly—They say you're worse than

the others, now you've got money. This is the time
to spend your money, if you want to save your skin!"

At this point Don Ninì chimed in also:

"You know they accuse us of having had Nanni
l'Orbo killed—to stop his mouth—you for the first!—
I'm sorry they saw me coming here the other evening
with my wife."

"Ay," observed the canon-priest—"we are honest
men. Whose concern could it be, after all, to stop
Neighbour Nanni from talking so much?—The devil's
own tongue he had, my sirs! The whole village knows
the history of Diodata. Now they're letting loose even
the children against you—You'll see, Don Gesualdo!"

"All right—" replied Don Gesualdo. "Good day.
I can't leave my wife in the state she's in, to listen to
your gossip." And he turned his back on them.

"Ah—" returned the canon-priest, following him up
the stairs. "Excuse me, I knew nothing about it. I
didn't think it had already got so far—"

Since they were there they could do no less than go
up and see Donna Bianca for a moment, he and the
young baron. Don Ninì stopped in the doorway, hat
in hand, without saying a word, and the canon-priest,
who understood these things, after a while nodded his
head to Don Gesualdo as if to say Yes, the hour had
come.

"I will go," said Don Ninì putting his hat on again.
"Do excuse me, but I can't bear it."

Don Ferdinando Trao was already there at the bed-
head, like a mummy, and Aunt Macrì, who was wiping
her niece's face with a handkerchief of fine linen. The
Zaccos were pale with having lost a night's sleep, and
Donna Lavinia could hardly stand. The Marchese
Limòli arrived with the confessor. Donna Agrip-

pina then turned them all out, all the lot. Don Gesualdo, behind that closed door, felt a knot in his
throat, as if they were taking his poor wife from him
before her time.

"Ah!" muttered the marchese. "What a comedy,
poor Bianca! We remain here to keep up the comedy
every day, eh, Don Ferdinando!—Even death has forgotten that we're in the world—"

Don Ferdinando listened blankly. Now and again
he looked timidly, furtively, at his brother-in-law,
whose eyes were swollen, whose face was yellow and
bristly, and he made as if to go away, frightened—

"No," said the marchese. "You can't leave your
sister at this point. You are like a child, bless my
life!"

At that moment Baron Mendola entered, out of
breath, beginning at once to make excuses in a loud
voice.

"I'm sorry—I knew nothing about it—I didn't
think—"

Then seeing around him such faces and such silence,
he dropped his voice and went to finish his discourse
in a corner, in the ear of Baron Zacco. The latter
began to talk about the night's sleep he had lost; his
daughters who had never closed their eyes, Lavinia
who could hardly stand. Don Gesualdo, it is true,
stared blankly around, but it was obvious he didn't
take it in. Just then the priest came out again, dragging his feet, and so moved that his hanging lips were
trembling, poor old man.

"A saint!" he said to the husband. "A real saint!"

Don Gesualdo nodded his head, his heart also swollen. Bianca now lay prostrate, her eyes unseeing, her
face as if veiled by a shadow. Donna Agrippina was

preparing the altar on the *commode,* with a damask tablecloth and silver candlesticks. What good would silver candlesticks do anybody now? Don Ferdinando went round touching everything, really like an inquisitive child. Then he stood right in front of the bed, watching his sister who was making her account with the Lord God at that moment, and he began to weep and sob. They were all crying. At that instant Donna Sarina Cirmena peeped in at the door, flustered, her mantle inside out, hesitating, looking round to see how she would be received, beginning already to rub her eyes with her embroidered handkerchief.

"Excuse me! Pardon me! I haven't got the heart of a stone—I heard that my niece—My heart is in the right place, and it's tender!—I've loved her like a daughter!—Bianca!—Bianca!—"

"No, aunt!—She is waiting for the sacrament. Don't disturb her now with wordly thoughts—" said Donna Agrippina.

"You are right," said Donna Sarina. "Excuse me, Don Gesualdo."

After she had taken the communion, Bianca seemed a little calmer. The choking passed off, and she managed to stammer a few words. But in a voice that was hardly audible.

"You see?" said Donna Agrippina. "You see, now she has made her peace with God!—Sometimes the Lord performs the miracle."

They put on her breast the relic of the Madonna. Donna Agrippina got the girdle of the tunic to push it under her pillow. Aunt Cirmena gave examples of miraculous healings: everything depends on having faith in the saints and in the blessed relics: The Lord can do as much and more. Don Gesualdo himself began to cry like a baby.

"Even he!" murmured Donna Sarina, pretending to speak in Dame Macrì's ear. "Even he hasn't got a bad heart, at the bottom. But I can't understand why Isabella hasn't come—duchess or not!—We've only got one mother!—Was it necessary to tell so many stories just to get this fine result here—"

"He's a swine!—a villain!—an assassin!" Don Gesualdo kept growling, glaring round, his lips compressed and his eyes glowing like a madman's.

"Eh? What did you say?—" asked Dame Cirmena.

"Ssh! Ssh!" interrupted Donna Agrippina.

Baron Mendola leaned over to say something in Zacco's ear. The other shook his dishevelled, swollen head once or twice. The baroness took advantage of this good opportunity to press Don Gesualdo to take a little refreshment from Lavinia's own hands.

"Yes, a drop of broth, for it's two days since the poor man opened his mouth!—"

As they went into the next room, which opened on to the street, they heard a noise like the sea in storm. Mendola then told what he had seen, coming along.

"Yessir! They've put the flag on the church tower. They say it's a sign that all food-taxes and land-taxes are abolished. So they'll be making the demonstration just now. The letter-carrier has brought news that at Palermo they have already done it—and in all the villages along the road as well. So that it would be vile if they didn't do the same here. However, what will it amount to? The band, four ells of muslin— Look! Look!"

From the Rosary Street dawned a tricolor banner

on a long cane, and behind it a flood of people shouting and waving arms and caps in the air. From time
to time also there was a gun-shot. The marchese, who
was deaf as a mole, asked:

"Eh? What is it?"

The end of the world it was! Don Gesualdo stood
arrested, basin in hand. A loud ringing was heard at
the street door, and Zacco ran to see. After a moment he poked his head through the door of the anteroom, and called loudly:

"Marchese! Marchese Limòli!"

They were discussing for some time, in low voices,
in the other room. It sounded as if the baron were
putting in a good word for a third party who had just
arrived, and the marchese was getting fiery.

"No! no! it's a swinish trick!—"

Whereupon Zacco re-entered, alone, his face in-
flamed.

"Listen, Don Gesualdo!—A moment—just a
word—"

The crowd had gathered right under the house; you
could see the banner there at the balcony height, as
if it wanted to come in. Shouts were heard: Hurrah
for—Down with—!

"One moment!" exclaimed Zacco then, putting every
consideration aside. "Come out here a moment, Don
Gesualdo. Show yourself to them, or else there'll be
I don't know what devil to pay!—"

There was the canon-priest Lupi carrying the por-
trait of Pope Pius IX, the young baron Rubiera, yellow
as a corpse, waving his handkerchief, and a lot more
people all shouting:

"Hurrah for—!—down with—!—death to—!"

Don Gesualdo, huddled in a chair with his basin in

his hand, kept shaking his head and lifting his shoulders, white as his shirt, looking a perfect wreck. The
marchese absolutely insisted on knowing what all those
people wanted down there:

"Eh: What is it?"

"They want all you've got!" burst out Baron Zacco
at last, quite beside himself.

The marchese began to laugh, saying:

"Welcome! Welcome every time!"

At that moment Donna Agrippina Macrì passed in
a frenzy, her puce-coloured tunic flapping behind her,
and in the dying woman's room was heard a great
commotion, chairs upset, women crying. Don Gesualdo jumped up, swaying, his hair on end; he put
the basin on the little table, and began to walk up and
down, beside himself, hitting his hands against one
another and repeating:

"The game's up!—it's over!"

III

A letter arrived from Isabella a little later; she knew nothing of the catastrophe as yet, and her letter would have made the stones weep. The duke also wrote—a small sheet of notepaper with a black border as thick as your finger, and the crested seal, that black as well, enough to break your heart—inconsolable for the loss of his mother-in-law. He said that the truth had to be hidden from the duchess, by the doctors' advice, for it would have come like a thunderbolt to her, ailing as she was, and just on the eve of starting off to see her mother!—He wound up by asking for some memento of the dead woman, for his wife; some trifle, a lock of hair, her mass-book, the wedding-ring she wore on her finger—

He wrote also to the lawyer to enquire whether the defunct, rest her soul, had left any property outside her dowry—Then it came out through Don Emanuel Florio, the post-master, who nosed out the business of everybody in the village, that the lawyer never even answered the letter, and that he only went round grumbling among his intimate friends, like the peevish old man he had become with age:

"It strikes me that the noble duke is driven to fishing for the moon in a pond, that's what it strikes me!"

The poor dead woman had gone to the grave in haste, between four candles, amid the hubbub of the mutinous populace who wanted this, that, and the other, stuck in the market-place from morning till night, bawling, with their hands in their pockets and their mouths open, waiting for the manna to fall down from the flag on the church-tower. Ciolla had become somebody at last, with a black feather in his cap and a velvet blouse, so that he looked a perfect child, at his age, and he walked up and down the square, looking here and there as if to say to folks: "Hey! You mind yourselves!"—Don Luca, carrying the cross in front of the coffin, winked amicably, so that the people would make way for him through the crowd, and he smiled to his acquaintances as he heard all the chants of praise which they vented along the street after Mastro-don Gesualdo.

A thief! an assassin! A fellow who had got rich, while so many others were left poor and more needy than ever! a fellow who had his store-barns full of stuff, and sent round the sergeant-bailiff to collect the debts from other people.

Those who shouted loudest were such debtors as had eaten their corn in the blade, before it came to ear. They reproached him, moreover, with having been the most obstinate against letting them have the communal lands, each his own bit. They didn't know whence the accusation had arisen, but it was a fact. Everybody said so: the canon-priest Lupi armed to the teeth, Baron Rubiera in his fustian hunting-jacket, like any poor devil. They were always in the midst of the land-labourers, handy and jolly, with their heart on their lips:

That Mastro-don Gesualdo was always alike! he had let his wife die without so much as sending to Palermo for a doctor! A Trao! One who had raised him up to honour in the world! What good had it done her, being so rich?—

The canon-priest let out more things against the

other man, in confidence:—He had begrudged the very
masses for the soul of the poor woman!—"I know it
for certain. I was in the sacristy. If he has no feeling even for his own flesh and blood!—Don't make
me talk, I've got to say mass to-morrow morning!—"

Gentry and plebeians, after the first shock, had become all one family. Now the gentry were fervent
protectors of liberty: priests and friars with the crucifix on their breast, or the cockade of Pius IX, and with
muskets on their shoulders. Don Nicolino Margarone
was nominated captain, with spurs and a striped cap.
The Captain's lady went round collecting to buy firearms, dressed in the tricolour, a short red overdress,
a white skirt, and a Calabrian hat with green feathers
that was a perfect love. The other ladies carried
stones every day to the barricades, outside the gates,
with their little baskets ornamented with ribbons and
the band playing in front. It was like a festival, morning and evening, with all those flags and that crowd
down the street, the shouting of Hurrah for! and of
Down with! every moment, the bells chiming and the
band playing, and later on the illumination. The only
windows that remained shut were those of Don Gesualdo Motta. He alone had retired into his lair like
a wolf, the enemy of his village, now that he'd got
rich, doing nothing but complain because they came to
him every day to ask for something, the commission
for the poor, the forced loan, the requisition of firearms!—They put him at the head of the list, and made
him pay twice as much as anybody else. He had to
defend himself and contend with them. The gentlemen of the Committee returned from his house worn
out and telling fine tales. They said he didn't understand anything any more, absolutely stupid, nothing

but a shadow of Mastro-don Gesualdo, a real corpse, who kept on his feet still to defend his own property, but the hand of God would fall on him sooner or later.

Meanwhile the peasantry and the starving people who stood about the square from morn till night, open-mouthed expecting the manna that never came, inflaming one another as fast as they could, talked of the fraudulent way they'd been treated, the hardships they suffered in winter, while there were folks who had store-barns full of stuff, and fields, and vineyards!—They could do with the real gentry, who were born to it—But they couldn't rest for thinking that Don Gesualdo Motta had been born poor and naked as themselves—They all remembered him a poor navvy— Speranza, his own sister, preached there in front of the flag hoisted on the Town Hall, that now at last the moment had come to make restoration of ill-gotten gains, to take justice into one's own hands. She incited her own children against their uncle, and now that her boys had grown big and strong they would have been able to make themselves felt, if they hadn't been two ninnies, like their father, who had quieted down the moment his brother-in-law had sent a handful of money, when Bianca was so ill, saying he wanted to make peace with everybody, and he had only too many troubles already. Giacalone, whom Don Gesualdo had made to pawn his mule to pay for the harvest-debt; and Pirtuso's heir who was still fighting him in a law-suit about certain moneys which the agent had carried with him into the other world; all those who were against him for one reason or another, now blew up the fire, saying he was a shady one, telling all the dirty tricks of Mastro-don Gesualdo, crying him down in every little drinking-tavern and in every club, even rousing up those who had nothing against him, with the story of the communal lands which were going to be divided amongst everybody, so that everybody was expecting his bit from day to day, and yet nothing was really decided about it, and anybody who talked about it they had him killed to stop his mouth.—They knew well enough where the shot had come from! Master Titta had recognised Gerbido, the former servant-boy of Don Gesualdo, as he ran away hiding his face in his handkerchief. And so came up again the story of Nanni l'Orbo who had taken on Don Gesualdo's woman and the children she had had by him, poor foundlings who went hoeing in their father's fields to earn their bread, and kissed his hands into the bargain, like that fool of a Diodata who if you gave her a kick said Thank you for it.

So on and so on, they managed to let loose even these two upon him, one evening when they had drawn them into the tavern with their talk, and the two lads hadn't even the money to pay for a drink for their friends. Then, at that hour, Don Gesualdo saw appear before him Nunzio, the more fiery of the two.— His grandfather's name, yes, that he had given him; but the property, no!—As near as nothing they were to coming to blows, father and son. There was a great shouting, a row that lasted for half an hour. Nunzio, rolling drunk, stuck up for himself there to his father's face, and told him everything he could lay his tongue to, him and her as well. Uncle Santo, who had made it up with his brother after the death of his sister-in-law, helping him to live through his grief, eating and drinking at his expense, seized the wooden bar to make peace between them. Poor Don Gesualdo went to lie down, more dead than alive.

In the midst of so many worries he had really got ill. It poisoned his blood to hear all the talk that went on. Don Luca the sexton, who had come and established himself in the house, as if it was already time to bring him the extreme unction, made out that Don Gesualdo ought to open his store-barns to the poor, if he wished to save body and soul. He himself had five children to keep, five mouths to fill, six with his wife. Master Titta, when he came to bleed him, sang the rest of the song, lancet in air:

"You see! If they don't use a bit more sense, some of them, it'll come to a bad end this time! People can't stand any more. I've been cutting hair and letting blood for forty years, and I'm not changed, I'm not!"

Don Gesualdo, ill, yellow, with his mouth always bitter, had lost appetite and sleep; he had cramps in his stomach like mad dogs inside him. Baron Zacco was the only friend he had left. And people said that even he had something to gain by being friends with him, some scheme up his sleeve. He came to see him morning and evening, and brought his wife and daughters, all dressed in black, so that they darkened the street. He left him his daughter to look after him.

"Lavinia is a splendid hand at making decoctions— Lavinia is a demon for keeping her eye on things about the house—Let Lavinia do it, she knows how to manage things—"

On the other hand, the baron looked black if Diodata dared so much as to show her face there, at Don Gesualdo's, with a black kerchief on her head, loaded with children, already grey and bent like an old woman.

"No, no, good woman. We don't want you! Better

look after your own affairs, we don't keep lavish open house here any more——"

Afterwards he babbled his paternal advice to his friend.

"What the devil do you want with that old woman? —You've no business to have her hanging round, now she's a widow!—Especially seeing that you used to have her in the house when she was a lass—You know what the world is, and how it talks!—Then that other business of her husband's death—Though it's true he deserved it!—But anyhow it's as well not to let people talk!—Besides, you don't need anybody, now we have my daughter here——"

He himself took upon himself to order and dispose of everything in the house of his cousin Don Gesualdo, poking his nose into all his business, running up and down with the keys of the store-houses and the cellar. He advised him, moreover, to put out his ready money to interest, supposing he had any by him, for fear things should get worse.

"Give it out on loan, with a good lawyer's security —a bit for everybody, for those who shout loudest, because they've nothing to lose, and are threatening now to break in to your store-houses and burn your house. Then they'll be quiet for the time being. Then, if they do manage to get hold of the communal lands, you can jump on them with a fine mortgage. Things can't go on always like they are now. Things will change round again, and you'll have got your claws in in time——"

But he wouldn't hear of money. He said he hadn't any, that his son-in-law had ruined him, that he'd rather meet them with guns, the folks who came to burn his house or to break in to his store-barns. He had become like a wild beast, green with bile, the illness itself making him frantic. He shouted, threatening:

"Ah! My own property! I'd like to see them! After I've been forty years getting it together—penny by penny!—Better cut out my liver and all the rest at once, for I'm rotten inside with miseries.—With guns, I say! I'd like to murder a dozen or so of them first! If a man wants to take from you what you've got, you take his life from him!"

So he had armed Santo and Master Nardo, the old labourer, with sabres and carbines. He kept the door barred, and two fierce mastiffs in the courtyard. People said that his house was like an arsenal; that at night he received Canali, Marchese Limòli and others, to conspire with them, and that one fine morning you'd find the gallows set up in the market-place and all those who had made the revolution hanging on it. So his few friends had abandoned him so as not to be looked upon with dislike. And Zacco really ran an ugly risk by keeping on going to see him, with all his family.

"Pity that soap and water don't wash with you!" the baron said to him more than once. The baroness at last, seeing that there was no coming to a conclusion with that man, decided to explode the bomb one day when Don Gesualdo was just nodding on the sofa, yellow as death, and her daughter was playing sicknurse, sitting on guard by the window.

"Excuse me, cousin! I'm a mother and I can't keep quiet any longer, I can't—you, Lavinia, go out a minute while I speak to Cousin Don Gesualdo.—Now that my daughter's gone, tell me what's in your heart, Cousin —tell me plainly what is your intention.—As for me,

I shall be very pleased—so will the baron, my husband.
—But we must speak out plainly—"

The poor wretch opened his sleepy eyes wide, still
a wreck after the colic—

"Eh? What do you say? What do you mean? I
don't understand you."

"Oh! You don't understand me? Not when my
daughter Lavinia is here doing everything for you?
An unmarried girl! And you're a widower at last,
and you ought to have reached years of discretion, so
that you can make up your mind and know what you
want to do."

"Nothing. I don't want to do anything. I want
to be left in peace, if you'll leave me alone—"

"Ah? So that's it? Then stay as it suits you—
But anyhow it's not right—you know it!—I am a
mother—"

And now, resolute, she ordered her daughter to
take her mantle and come away home. Lavinia
obeyed, also in a fury. The two of them, as they left
that house for the last time, drew a cross savagely on
the threshold.—

A veritable galley, that hole! Poor Cousin Bianca
had left her bones there with a slow decline!—Zacco
went that very evening to visit Baron Rubiera, instead
of boring himself to death with that farm-labourer of
a Mastro-don Gesualdo who spent the whole time
whining, holding his stomach, in the dark in order to
save the light.

"You don't mind my coming, eh? Cousin Rubiera
—Donna Giuseppina—"

Don Ninì had gone out to some secret meeting or
other, to decide some weighty matter. While waiting
for him, Baron Zacco wanted to pay his respects to the

dowager baroness, since he had not seen her for some time. He found her in her room, nailed in her chair facing the matrimonial bed, near which still hung her husband's gun, rest his soul, and the crucifix which they had laid on his breast when he was dying. She was bunched up in an old shawl, her helpless hands in her lap. The moment she saw her cousin Zacco come in, she began to cry with emotion, childish:—big silent tears which welled little by little in her dull eyes, and fell slowly down her loose cheeks.

"Good, good, that's right, Cousin Rubiera! Your head is all right! You know people when you see them!"

She also wanted to tell him of her own troubles, mumbling, puffing, and confusing herself, with her thick tongue and her violent lips frothing with saliva. The baron bent over her, listening closely and affectionately.

"Eh? What! Yes, yes, I understand! You are right, poor thing!"

Whereupon arrived the infuriated daughter-in-law.

"She doesn't understand a damn thing," said the baron. "It must be a purgatory for you who are closely related to her."

The paralytic looked daggers at them, lifting more than she was really able, her head which was bent over her shoulder, while Donna Giuseppina scolded her like a child, wiping her chin with a dirty handkerchief.

"What's the matter?—What do you want?— Stupid!—You'll ruin your health!—She's a real infant, God bless us! You don't have to believe what she says! It takes the patience of a saint to put up with her, it does."

The mother-in-law now made big eyes, looking round in dismay, drawing her head in between her shoulders, as if she was afraid of being beaten.

"You see! Blessed patience!"

"As I told you," concluded the baron. "You've got your purgatory here on earth, you can go straight to heaven after this."

Don Ninì came in to take the keys of the cellar. Finding his cousin there, he put on a silly sort of look.

"Ah—Cousin!—What's the latest? Is your wife well?—Here you can see what it is—trouble by the shovelful. What's amiss, mamma?—the same old worries? Excuse me, cousin Zacco, I must go downstairs a moment—"

The keys always hung there on the door-post. The paralysed woman followed them with her eyes, without being able to say a word, forcing herself to turn her head more than she could, following every stride her soon took, while splotches of sick blood burnt again all at once in her cadaverous face. Then Zacco began to recite the rosary against Mastro-don Gesualdo.

"Lord God, I blame myself, and I repent! I've kept on only too long with that fellow! It seemed to me a miserable thing to abandon him in his need—in the midst of all his enemies—if it was only out of Christian charity.—But no more! it's too much—Not even his own relations can put up with that man! Think of it! not even a simpleton like Don Ferdinando! He'd rather stop at home than be forced to put on the new suit his brother-in-law sent him.—As long as he lives, you understand? He's a man of character! And really I am tired, you know. I don't want to ruin myself for love of Mastro-don Gesualdo. I've got a wife and children. Must I carry him hung round my neck like a stone to drown myself with?"

"Ah!—I told you so! Why look, in all conscience! What was Mastro-don Gesualdo twenty years ago?— And now he puts his foot on all our necks. Just look, my sirs, a Baron Zacco blacking his boots and quarrelling with all his relations on account of him!—"

The other bowed his head in contrition. He confessed that he'd been wrong, but in a good cause, to prevent the man from doing any more harm and to try and get out of him the little good that was in him. Once in a lifetime one may make a mistake.

"But you know now? Now you know which of us two was right?"

His wife stopped the words in his mouth with a nudge of her elbow.

"Let him speak. It's his business now to tell us what he wants of us—what he's come for—"

"All right," returned Zacco with a good-humoured smile. "I've come to play the Prodigal Son, my word! Does it please you?"

Donna Giuseppina was pleased with a sour mouth. Her husband looked first at her, then at his cousin Zacco, and didn't know what to say.

"All right," resumed Zacco once more. "I know that those lads want to make a bit of a row in the streets to-night. You've just got the keys of the cellar in your hand, to keep them good-tempered. And you remember that I'm not one of your mealy-mouthed sort, if some of them take it into their heads to come and annoy me under my windows. I've got my own stomach full of stuff, and I don't want to have a lot of enemies to my credit, like Mastro-don Gesualdo—"

Husband and wife looked at one another meaningly.

"I'm father of a family!" the baron went on. "I've got to defend my own interests.—Excuse me—But if we play at kick who can amongst ourselves—!"

Donna Giuseppina took up the reply, scandalised.

"Why whatever are you talking about?—Excuse me, really, if I speak about your business. But, after all, we're relations."

"That's what I say. We are relations! And it's better to hang together, among ourselves—in these days!—"

Don Ninì held out his hand.

"What the devil!—what nonsense!"

Then he unbuttoned altogether, looking frequently at his wife.

"Come to the theatre this evening, for the singing of the hymn. Show yourself along with us. The canon-priest will be there as well. He says it won't be a sin, because it's the Pope's hymn.—We'll talk about it.—But you'll have to put your hand in your pocket, my friend. You've got to spend and treat. See me?" And he shook the cellar keys before him. The old woman, who had not lost a word of this conversation, although nobody was paying any heed to her, began to growl in the obstinate anger of a child, on purpose making the veins of her neck swell till she was purple in the face. Then the racket began again: son and daughter-in-law scolded her together; and she tried to howl more loudly, shaking her head infuriated. Rosaria appeared, with a huge belly, and with her dirty hands in her greyish, towsled hair, and she too began threatening the paralytic:

"Just you look! She's become as wicked as a sandy-

coloured ass! What does she want, eh? She eats like
a wolf!"

Rosaria never knew when to finish this tune. Baron
Zacco thought well to take his leave out of that upset.
"Well, good evening till the cantata."

coloured ass! What does she want, eh? She eats like a wolf!"

Rosaria never knew when to finish this time. Baron Zacco thought well to take his leave out of that upset.

"Well, good evening till the capital—"

IV

There was a full theatre because entrance was free. Lights, singing, applause rising to the stars. Signora Aglae had come on purpose from Modica, at the village expense, to declaim the Hymn of Pius IX and other suitable poems. Seeing her dressed in Greek robes, with all that flesh on her, good luck to her, Don Ninì Rubiera amid the general emotion felt tears come to his eyes, and clapped louder than anybody, murmuring to himself:

"Body of—! She is still a fine-looking woman!—Blessing my wife isn't here!"

But those who were shut out, who pushed without being able to get in, went off at last to shout Death! and Hurrah! on their own account; and all those who were in the theatre, hearing the uproar, went out into the square, leaving the leading lady and Signor Pallante to embrace alone, with the flag in their hands. In a moment a great crowd gathered, and kept on increasing like a river. There was an immense shouting, and yells which in the darkness and the confusion sounded threatening. Don Nicolino Margarone, Zacco, Mommino Neri, all the well-disposed, burst their throats shouting "Out with the lights!" so that they could see better, so that trouble should not arise.

The crowd kept on shouting this way and that for a time. Then it burst in a torrent down the street of San Giovanni. In front of Pecu-Pecu's tavern there was a bench with dishes of fried vegetables and things, and this went flying—pumpkin and tomato all underfoot. Santo Motta, who was as if shopkeeper and at home there, seeing all this stuff go to waste, screamed like one possessed:

"Fools! animals!—Don't you eat good food, don't you?"

They were very near to pounding him too, in the fury. Giacalone and the most fervent proposed to bash in the church-doors and carry round the saint in procession, to make more impression.—Yes and No.— Curses and knocks on the jaw, there in the dark, in the sacred place. Master Cosimo meanwhile climbed the belfry and rang unceasingly. The cries and the clash of bells were heard even at the Alia, even as far as Monte Lauro, like the ravings of a hurricane. Lights were seen running in the upper village—an end of the world. All at once, as if some word of order had been given, the crowd poured tumultuously towards the Fosso, apparently following some precious leaders.

Mendola, Don Nicolino, and canon-priest Lupi himself, who had buried himself in the thick of the tumult to do what good he could, in vain yelled:

"Stop! Stop!"

Baron Zacco, not having young legs any more, landed out right and left with his stick, biff! bang! to make the bereft hear reason.

"Hey? What are we up to?—Gently, gently, my masters! We're not going to begin doing dirty fools' tricks! In these things you know where you begin but you don't know—"

Just as many of them had lent their ears to the talk about smashing in doors and taking out all the saints for a dance, so now the mob thronged before the store-houses of Mastro-don Gesualdo. They said they were full to the roof.—A man who was born poor as Job, and now who had got stuck-up, and was sworn enemy of the poor and of the liberals—! With stones, with cudgels!—Some of them had armed themselves with a big stone and were smiting the street-door with blows that sounded like cannon-shot. The shrill voice of Brasi Camauro was heard whining:

"My sirs! There's no religion left! They won't have any more to do with Christs and saints! They want to let us starve to death every one of us!"

All at once out of the commotion came yells to make your flesh creep. Santo Motta, torn and bleeding, by rolling himself on the floor succeeded in making a bit of space in front of the store-house door. And then the gentry, also yelling, shoving, fighting, drove back the most riotous. The canon-priest Lupi, clinging on to the iron grating of the window, tried to make himself heard:

". . . like this? . . . religion! . . . other people's possessions!—The Holy Father! . . . if we begin—"

Other shouts responded from the multitude:

". . . equal . . . poor people . . . dragged by his feet! . . . fat ox!—"

Giacalone, in order to excite the mob, pushed forward Diodata's two bastards who were there in the crowd, yelling:

". . . Don Gesualdo! . . . if there is justice anywhere! . . . abandoned on the streets . . . the Lord God Himself weeps at such a sight! . . . go and reckon with him! . . ."

From the Square of Santa Maria di Jesu, from the first houses of San Sebastiano, the neighbours, terrified, saw a flood of people passing, a great commotion, weapons glinting, men's arms waving in the air, flushed, fiery faces, showing convulsed in the light of the torches. Doors and windows slammed to. From the distance came screams and weeping of women, voices crying:

"Holy Mother of God! Oh, holy Saints!"

Don Gesualdo was sick in bed, when he heard somebody knocking at the little side-door opening on to the alley, knocking as if they would break it down. Then the rumble of the tempest supervened. That very evening a kind soul had run to warn him:

"Beware, Don Gesualdo! They're threatening you because you are for the Bourbons. Lock yourself in the house!"

He, having got so much other trouble on him, shrugged his shoulders. But now, seeing it was really turning out seriously, he jumped out of bed just as he was, with handkerchief round his head and a cataplasm on his stomach, pulling on his trousers anyhow, putting his pains aside at the sound of that voice crying:

"Don Gesualdo!—quick!—escape!"

A voice he'd not forget if he lived to be a thousand. Dishevelled, half-dressed, with his eyes glittering like a wild-cat's and his face green with bile, he went about the room looking for pistols and hunting-knives, resolved at least to sell his life dear. Master Nardo and those few house-servants who had remained faithful out of necessity, recommended their souls to God. At last Baron Mendola succeeded in making them open the little side-door to him. Don Gesualdo, posted at the window with a gun, nearly caused a disaster.

"Eh?" yelled Mendola, entering done-up. "You want to shoot me dead, if you please! This is my reward!"

The other wouldn't hear reason. He was trembling from head to foot with rage.

"Ah? so that's it! That's what we've come to, that a gentleman isn't safe even in his own house? and his own things aren't his own? Here I am! But Samson will fall along with the Philistines, mark you! Even the wolf, when you get him cornered—"

Zacco and two or three others of the well-disposed, having arrived in the meantime, worked themselves into a sweat trying to persuade him, shouting all at once:

"What do you think you can do? Against a whole village! You're out of your mind. They'll burn everything down! They're starting their Massacre of the Innocents here! You'll get yourself murdered and everybody else."

He, infuriated, with his hair bristling:

"So, if it's like that!—If they reckon they're going to put their hand in my pocket by force!—If this is how they're going to repay me!—I've been good to them—I've fed the whole village—Now they can eat powder, and I'll start with the first that comes up—"

Actually! He was determined to make a slaughter of it. Thank goodness, canon-priest Lupi burst into the room and flung himself upon him without minding risks, pushing him and wrestling with him round the room till he succeeded in wresting the gun from his hands.

"What the devil! You don't play with firearms!"

He was gasping for breath, his cranium was red and bald, smoking like when he was young, and he stammered in a broken voice:

"Oh, holy devils!—Lord, forgive me! You make me swear like a pig, Don Jackass! We're here to save your life, though you're not worth it! Do you want them to start sacking and burning the whole village?

I don't care about you, fool that you are! But there are some things that we mustn't let start even in fun, you understand. Nay, not even against a mortal enemy! If that lot who have got no further than shouting, so far, if they once lay their hands on other people's possessions, we're done for!"

The canon-priest was properly beside himself. Then the others all started again on that pig-headed fool of a Mastro-don Gesualdo who was risking compromising them all; they abused him for ingratitude; they simply stunned him. Baron Zacco even went so far as to put his arm round his neck, in confidence, confessing in his ear that he was with him, on his side against all the rabble; but for the moment you had to be prudent, let things take their course, and give in.

"Say yes—everything they want, now—There's no lawyer to put your promises on paper—A bit of management, a bit of money—Better your purse should suffer than your belly—"

Don Gesualdo, seated on a chair wiping away his sweat with his shirt-sleeve, did not say a word, dazed. Down before the great door meanwhile Baron Rubiera, Don Nicolino, Neri's son were all striving and struggling with all their might to calm the most riotous spirits.

"Gentlemen—you are right—Everything you want shall be done—We can swallow all the lot of them in one bite—Hurray! Hurrah!—All brothers!—One hand washes the other—To-morrow—by daylight. Anybody who's in want come here to us—Now it's late, and we're all one colour,—rogues and gentlemen —Hey! Hey! I say—!"

Don Nicolino had to catch by the collar a fellow who was slipping through the partly opened door,

profiting by the confusion and press which had arisen
around a woman who was screaming and pleading:

"Nunzio! Gesualdo! My sons!—What are they
making you do!—Nunzio—Ah, holy Madonna!—"

It was Diodata, who had heard that her boys were
among the mob, shouting for death and destruction
against Don Gesualdo, along with the rest, and she
had come running with her hands in her hair.

"Holy Madonna!—What are they making you do!"

Meanwhile Zacco and Master Nardo brought down
little barrels full of wine, and helped to make peace
by pouring out drink for whoever wanted it, while the
canon-priest preached from above:

"To-morrow! Come back to-morrow, whoever
wants anything.—There's nobody at home now—Don
Gesualdo is away in the country—but in his heart he
also is here, along with us—helping us.—Every man
is to have his own loaf of bread and his own piece of
land—We'll make it right—Come back to-morrow—"

"To-morrow be damned!" Don Gesualdo grumbled
inside himself. "It looks to me as if your honour
wanted to pay for everything out of my pocket,
Canon!"

"Will you keep quiet! Do you want to make me
look a liar?—Haven't I said you're not here, to save
your skin—"

But Don Gesualdo still rebelled.

"Why? What have I done? I'm in my own
house!—"

"What you've done is that you're as rich as a pig!—"
the canon-priest bawled in his ear at last, losing patience. Then all the others attacked him at once,
with fair words and foul, saying that if the revolu-
tionaries only found him there, they wouldn't leave one

stone of the house upon another; they'd take everything; they wouldn't even leave him his eyes to weep
his losses. So at last they induced him to flee by the
side door. Mendola ran to knock at Uncle Limòli's.

Hearing the uproar in the village, the marchese
by this time as deaf as a mole, had thrown a mantle
over his shoulders and stood at his balcony window
looking down; he was in his shirt, with his bare feet
in heel-less slippers, and a little earthenware warming-
pan in his hands, when this new shot took him in the
wind. They had a rare job making him understand
what they wanted with him at that hour, Mastro-don
Gesualdo more dead than alive, the others shouting
at the top of their voices in the old man's ear:

"They want to play the deuce with him—with
your nephew Don Gesualdo.—You must hide him—"

He winked with his flabby, dropping eyelids, nodding yes, and showing a malicious smile.

"Ah?—play the deuce?—with Don Gesualdo?—
Quite right! Your time has come, my dear man—
You are the sample of the goods—"

But at last, when he realised that they actually did
want to do for him, he changed his tone, pretending
to be anxious, in his cracked voice:

"What?—Him himself! But what do they want
then?—What's going to become of us, at this rate?"

Mendola explained to him that Don Gesualdo was
just the pretext for falling upon the richest people
in the village but there at the marchese's they'd never
come to look for riches. The old man shook his
head, agreeing that they naturally wouldn't, looking
round his rooms with that sour little smile on his
toothless mouth.

They were two little rooms that had grown old

along with him, and on which his every habit had left its mark; the patch of grease behind the chair in which he nodded off after dinner; the floor-tiles worked loose in that short track between door and window, the plaster rubbed off the wall by the bed where he struck a light. And in that squalor the Marchese lived like a prince, spitting his poverty in everybody's face.

"Excuse me, gentlemen, if I receive you in this rat-hole—It isn't good enough for you, Don Gesualdo—The fine lot of relations you've got now, eh?—"

On the old sofa with its back against the wall, after they had propped it steady with pieces of the above-mentioned broken tiles, they made up a bed for Don Gesualdo, who could not keep up any more, while the Marchese grumbled on:

"Look you now what's come to pass!—I've seen a good many things! But this I didn't expect!"

However he offered to share with him the basin of milk in which he had put his crusts to soak.

"I've come back to pap, you see. I've nothing else to offer you for supper. Meat won't do for my teeth any more—neither for my purse.—You're used to different fare, my friend.—Well, it can't be helped! The world turns round for all of us, my dear Don Gesualdo!"

"Ah!" replied the latter. "It isn't that, Marchese, sir. It's that my stomach won't let me. It's full of poison. I've got a mad dog in my belly."

"All right," said the others. "You can thank God. Here nobody will touch you."

It was a tremendous blow for Mastro-don Gesualdo. The agitation, the bile, the sickness he had upon him —The night passed as best it might. But the day after, at Ave Maria, Mendola came again muffled up in his cloak, with his hat down on his eyes, looking carefully around before entering the door.

"Now something else!" he exclaimed, entering. "They've set spies on to you, Don Gesualdo! And they want to dig you out even from here, to make you keep all those promises which the canon-priest made.—Ciolla in person—I saw him just down there, standing sentinel—"

The marchese, who had become lively again and gay amid all this upset, sharpening his ears and poking in between people to catch a word of what was said, now ran to the balcony.

"That's right! There he is in his blouse like a little boy.—That's a sign that everybody is growing backwards!—"

Don Gesualdo had risen gasping, shouting that it was better to make an end of it, that he would run down and pay Ciolla, pay him all the promises, full on the spot! And that if they were looking for him, there he was, quite ready to receive them!—

"Of course, of course," repeated the marchese. "If they're looking for you it means they need you. They don't come looking for me, you bet. They want to make you shout Death! and Hurrah! along with them. Well then go along! Hurrah for you if you've got something to make them shout with."

"No! I know what they want!" returned Don Gesualdo, who was becoming stupefied.

"Excuse me, but it's not a question of you only," observed Mendola. "It's that after you there's the whole village, me and everybody!"

Arrived the canon-priest, scratching his head, perplexed by the turn things had taken. The spree was still going on. A fine look-out for some folks! Those rascals had fastened on to those words of peace which he had let fall, and now they were waiting in the market-place expecting the manna to drop from heaven:—"You've got me into a fine mess, you have, Don Gesualdo!"

At this new departure from the canon-priest arose a new squabbling between the two of them.

"I, eh?—I?—It was I who promised them earth and air and sea?"

"To keep them quiet, in God's name! Words of the moment, of course. I'd have like to see you stuck in front of all their infernal faces."

The marchese was quite amused:

"Just hark! hark now! Look! Look!"

"Anyhow," concluded Mendola, "this sort of talk is no good, and we've got to gain time! So meanwhile you'll take yourself off, *causa causarum!* At the bottom of a cistern, in a hole, where the devil you like, but you can't go on putting so many fathers of families into danger, just for your sake!"

"In the Trao house!" suggested the canon-priest. "Your brother-in-law will receive you open-armed. Everybody's forgotten that he's still alive, and they won't come looking for you there."

The marchese also approved of this.

"Splendid! It's a splendid idea! Dog and cat shut up together!—"

Don Gesualdo was obstinately against it.

"Then," exclaimed the canon-priest, "I wash my hands of it, like Pilate. Then I'll go and call Ciolla and all the lot of them, if that's what you want."

Don Gesualdo was reduced to such a state that they did as they liked with him. Two hours after dark, through certain back streets, they went to wake Grazia who had the keys of the street door, and then in the darkness, cautiously, they arrived at Don Ferdinando's door.

"Who is it?" they heard an asthmatic voice bleating from within. "Grazia, who is it?"

"It's us, Don Gesualdo, your brother-in-law——"

No answer. Then they heard a stir in the darkness. And all at once Don Ferdinando bolted himself in, and began to pile tables and chairs in front of the door, screaming continually:

"Grazia! Grazia!"

"Devil and all!" exclaimed Mendola. "This is worse than ever! That fool will bring all the village." The canon-priest was smiling under his nose, shaking his head. Meanwhile Grazia had lighted a stump of candle, and was looking first one and then the other in the face, bewildered, blinking her eyes.

"What do you want to do, gentlemen?" she hazarded timidly. Don Gesualdo, who really could not stand, pale and broken, broke forth in a desperate tone:

"I want to go back to my own house!—no matter what happens—I'm determined on it!—"

"No sir!" interrupted the canon-priest. "This is your own house as well. There's your wife's share in it. Why, good Lord! You've borne till now— Now enough!—There, in Donna Bianca's room. The bed is there same as ever."

Mendola regained his good humour while they were making the bed. He rummaged round everywhere. He went to poke his nose into the dark passage behind the door. He made jokes, recalling old stories.— What changes! What things had happened!—Who could ever have told, eh, Don Gesualdo?—

Even the canon-priest himself let slip a little smile.

"While you're here you can meditate all you wish upon life and death, to pass the time away. What a comedy it is, this dirty world! *Vanitas vanitatum!*

Don Gesualdo gave him a black look, but did not reply. He still had strength of stomach enough to shut his troubles and misfortunes inside himself, without amusing his friends by sharing with them. He threw himself down on the bed and was left alone with his pains, stifling his laments and swallowing down the bitterness that every memory brought up into his throat. Only one thing troubled him, that he might die there where he was, without his daughter ever knowing. And there in the fever there passed before his darkened eyes Bianca, Diodata, Master Nunzio, and others, and then his own second self that slaved and toiled in sun and wind, always with a sullen face, and which spat in his face with words like:

"Fool! Fool! What have you done! You look well!"

With the day returned Grazio who came to help him a bit, spent as she was, panting if she moved a chair, stopping every moment full in front of him with her hands on her enormous stomach, to start again her complaints against Don Ferdinando's relations, who left him there on her hands, poor thing, begrudging him even his bread and wine.

"Yessir, they've every one forgotten him, there in his corner like a sick dog!—But my heart won't let me!—We've always been neighbours—good servants of the family—a great family—My heart won't let me, it won't!"

In her wake came a swarm of children turning everything upside-down. Then arrived Speranza

screaming that she wanted to see her brother, as if
he was on the point of death.

"Let me come in! He's my own flesh and blood,
when all's said and done. Now he is as he is I don't
think of anything but that I'm his sister."

She, her husband and children. They set all the
neighbourhood in an uproar. Don Gesualdo got up
out of bed gasping. Chains wouldn't have kept him
in it.

"I want to go to my own house! What am I doing
here? Anyhow, everybody knows—"

With great effort they persuaded him to wait till
evening. And then after Ave Maria, quietly and secretly, Burgio and all his relations accompanied him
home. Speranza wanted to stop and look after her
brother, since he was so ill, and for a miracle they
hadn't put everything to sack and pillage that night.

"It's no good saying we've fallen out. In time of
need folks show their heart. Money is one thing, love
is another. We have quarrelled and we shall quarrel
till the Judgment Day, but we are children of the
same father, we are one blood!"

She protested that she'd cherish him like the apple
of her eye, him and all that belonged to him. She
arrayed in front of him her husband and her children,
who kept looking around with greedy looks, and she
repeated:

"These are your own kith and kin! These won't
betray you!"

And he, beaten, weary, disheartened, hadn't even the
strength to rebel.

So, bit by bit, they all foisted themselves on him.
His nephews roving round the house and gardens,
playing the master, laying hands on everything. His

sister, with the keys at her waist, rummaging, ran-
sacking, sending her husband here and there, to fetch
remedies, to look for healing herbs. As Farmer Fortunato grumbled that he hadn't the legs of a man of
twenty to run round in this fashion, she yelled at him:
"What do you want? Don't you do it for love
of your brother-in-law? Prison, sickness and necessity call for an amnesty."

She wasn't frightened of Ciolla nor any of that
tribe. Once when Vito Orlando thought he would
come and do a bit of showing off, with his pistol in
his pocket, to settle certain debts with Don Gesualdo,
she followed him down the stairs throwing a pot of
dirty water over him. Even Canon-priest Lupi himself had had to put his tail between his legs, and
couldn't try being generous with other people's things
any more, now that Ciolla and the most scoundrelly
members had gone off to seek fortune in the city,
with banners and trumpets. The canon-priest, in
order to quiet the rest, had had to resort to the
expedient of going out in procession, with the scourge
and the crown of thorns; and so the others let off their
steam in festivals and holidays, while he went round
preaching brotherhood and love of one's neighbour.

"He doesn't fork out a farthing, for all that,"
bawled Gossip Speranza.—"And all right then. But
if he comes trying it on again here at this house, playing
the camorrista, I'll receive him as he deserves—like
Vito Orlando."

In the meantime Don Gesualdo's house was being
sacked and pillaged all the same. Wine, oil, cheese,
pieces of cloth also, disappeared in the twinkling of an
eye. From the Canziria farm and from Mangalavite
appeared farm-managers and peasants laying com-

plaints against the sons of Farmer Fortunato Burgio
who came ruling with a high hand, and sacked the
fields and orchards of their uncle as if the place was
already masterless. He, poor wretch, fast in bed,
fretted in silence; he dared not rebel against his sister
and her husband; he thought of his own troubles. He
had a dog, there in his belly, which devoured his liver,
the mad dog of Saint Vito the Martyr, which martyred
him also. In vain did Speranza lovingly seek for herbs
and medicines, and consult Zanni and others who had
secrets for all ills. Each one brought a new remedy,
decoction, ointments, even the relic and the image of
the blessed saint, which Don Luca wanted to try with
his own hands. It was all no good. The sick man
insisted:

"It's nothing—a touch of colic. I've had so much
to trouble me. To-morrow I shall get up—"

But even he didn't believe it, and he never got up.
He was reduced almost to a skeleton, skin and bone;
only his belly swollen like a water-sack. In the village
they began to say he was done for; the hand of God
was upon him destroying him in the midst of his riches.
His noble son-in-law wrote from Palermo for precise
information. He also spoke of affairs which he had
to regulate, and moneys which were falling due, and
which he had to pay. In the postscript were two
unhappy lines from Isabella, who had not recovered
from the blow she had received a little while before.
Speranza, who was present just when her brother
was feeling touched by the letter, spat out her venom:

"There you are! Now you'll make yourself worse,
and all! If you don't look out you'll be gone to the
next world—alone and abandoned like one who doesn't
own a thing!—Who have you found ready at your

side in time of need, tell me that! Your daughter may
send you pretty words—But her husband knows what
he's after—"

Don Gesualdo did not answer. But when he was
alone he turned to the wall and lay and cried, softly,
unseen. He seemed to have become a child again.
You wouldn't have recognised him. When Diodata
heard that he was so ill, and wanted to go and ask
his pardon for the breach of respect her boys had
committed, on the night of the rising, she was petrified
at seeing him such a wreck, smelling of the grave, with
eyes that became so lustrous at every new face.

"Don Gesualdo, sir—I came to see you because they
told me you were so bad.—You must forgive them—
those scamps who offended you like that—Boys who
didn't understand—They let themselves be led on,
without knowing what they were doing.—You must
forgive them for my sake, Don Gesualdo sir!"

Any one saw she spoke sincerely, poor thing, with
her pitiful face, trying to swallow down and hide the
tears that came to her eyes at every word, trying to
take his hand to kiss it. He made a vague gesture,
and shook his head, as if to say it didn't matter, now.
Whereupon arrived Speranza and took upon herself
to abuse the brazen hussy who had come to tempt her
brother on his death-bed, to get something out of him,
to strip him to the last shred. A blood-sucker! She
had fattened upon him already! Wasn't it enough?
The crows were flying, now they smelt carrion. The
sick man closed his eyes to escape the torture, and
writhed in his bed as if he had another attack of
colic. So that Diodata left without being able to say
good-bye to him, her head hanging, clutching herself

together in her mantle. Speranza came back to her brother all loving and smiling.

"You've got us here now to help you—We won't leave you by yourself, don't you worry—Everything you want—You've only to speak. What do you want with that witch now? She'd eat you up body and soul. You couldn't even take the viaticum with that scandal in the house!"

As for her, she attended to him better than a servant, looked after him with love, sparing neither trouble nor expense. But seeing that nothing did him any good, she went so far as to call in the son of Tavuso, who had just returned raw and fresh from Naples, with a doctor-of-medicine degree—a young fellow without a hair on his chin yet, who made you pay as if he was a prince.—However, Don Gesualdo spoke his mind when he saw him putting pen to paper to write the usual fraud.

"Don Margheritino, I saw you born. Do you want to write me a prescription? What do you take me for, my dear chap?"

"All right then!" returned the little doctor, infuriated. "All right then, let the vet. cure you. What did you send for me for?" And he took his hat and marched off.

But since the sick man suffered all the tortures of the damned, in the hope that somebody might still find a cure for him, and to shut the mouths of the neighbours, who accused him of avarice, he had to bow his head once more, bow his head to doctors and medicaments. Tavuso's son, and Bomma, and all the upstarts in the village, they all passed before Don Gesualdo's bed. They came, they looked, they touched and poked, they bandied among themselves a lot of

nasty outlandish words that made your flesh creep, and
they all left their say each one on a bit of paper—
bits of scribble like leeches. Don Gesualdo, terrified,
didn't say a word, but tried to catch whatever they
meant; watching their hands suspiciously as they wrote.
Only, so as not to throw his money away too freely,
he took Don Margheritino aside and showed him
that he'd got a cupboardful of little pots and bottles,
bought for his wife, poor soul.

"I spared no expense, Doctor. And I've got them
all there, just as they are. If you think they might
be any good now—"

But they took no notice of him even when he kept
stammering, frightened by those serious faces:

"I feel better. To-morrow I'm going to get up.
Send me into the country and I shall be better in
twenty-four hours."

They said yes, to please him, like a child.

"To-morrow! The day after to-morrow—"

But they kept him there, to milk him, doctors, relations, and druggists. They turned him over, and they
turned him back again, they tapped him on the stomach
with two fingers, they made him drink a thousand
dirty mixtures, they smeared him with stuff that raised
blisters on his abdomen. Once more there was an
arsenal of medicines on the chest of drawers, just
as in the last days of Bianca, rest her soul. He grumbled, wagging his head:

"We've come to the medicines that cost a lot. That
means there's no more hope."

Money in streams, a come and go, a turmoil throughout the house, the table spread the whole day long.
Burgio, who wasn't used to it, ran to show his tongue
to the doctors, when they came to visit his brother-in-

law; Santo never stirred out of the house any more, not even to go to the tavern; and the nephews, when they came in from the land, tore each other's hair, quarrels and contentions amongst them as to who could lay hold of most, rows which even reached the sick man's chamber, so that he listened for all he was worth, crazy to know what they were doing with his things, till he even began to shout from his bed:

"Let me go to Mangalavite. All my things are going to rack and ruin. Here I eat my heart out. Let me go, else I shall die."

He'd got a ball of lead in his stomach, which weighed on him, and wanted to come out, always hurting him; from time to time it contracted, it got red hot, it throbbed like a hammer, and danced in his throat till it made him scream like one in hell, and bite everything that was near him. Then he was left spent, panting, with the vague terror of another attack in his starting eyes. Everything that he made himself swallow, to keep him alive, the most delicate tit-bits, that he never asked what they cost, just turned to poison inside him; they came back again like hell-stuff, blacker than ink, bitter, God-cursed. And the pains and the swelling increased; a paunch that his legs couldn't support any more. Bomma tapping on it one day, said:

"There's something here!"

"What did you say, your honour?" stammered Don Gesualdo, bouncing up into a sitting posture on the bed, in a cold sweat.

Bomma looked him full in the face, drew up his chair, turned this way and that to see if they were alone.

"Don Gesualdo, you are a man—you're not a child, are you?—"

P

"Yessir," he replied with a firm voice, all at once calm, showing the courage which he had always had upon necessity. "Yessir, speak out."

"Very well, you ought to have a consultation. You haven't just got a prickly-pear thorn in your stomach! It's something really serious, you know! It's not a thing for the wise beard of Don Margheritino or one of that sort—let me say it without offence to them, here in confidence. Fetch the best doctors you can find, from a distance, Don Vincenzo Capra, Doctor Muscio from Caltagirone, whom you like—You're not short of money—"

At these words Don Gesualdo went into a rage.

"Money!—You can none of you take your eyes off the money I've earned!—What good is it to me—if I can't buy even my health?—A lot of bitterness it's brought me—always!—"

But nevertheless he wanted to hear the rest of what Bomma had to say. You never can tell—He let him finish, keeping still, holding his chin, thinking of his own case. At last he wanted to know:

"A consultation? What will a consultation do for me?"

Bomma lost his stirrups.

"What will it do for you? Be hanged! It'll do what it can for you—at least folks won't be able to say you died without proper attention. I speak for your own sake. It won't put anything in my pocket— I'm just a druggist.—It's not my affair—I don't understand those things. I've attended you for friendship's sake—"

But as the other shook his head, diffident, a sly smile on his livid lips, the apothecary put aside every respect.

"You're a dead man, Don Sillyface! I tell you straight."

Then Don Gesualdo looked around slowly and tenaciously, blew his nose, and sank down on to the bed. After a while, looking up at the ceiling, he added with a sigh:

"All right. We'll have the consultation."

He didn't sleep a wink at night. Tormented by a new anxiety, with shivers that seized him from time to time, and cold sweats, fears which made him suddenly sit up in bed with his hair on end, looking around in the shadows, always seeing the menacing face of Bomma, feeling himself, stifling his pain, trying to delude himself. He really did think he felt better. He wanted to take care of himself, since it was a serious matter. He wanted to get better. He repeated the very words of the apothecary: he wasn't short of money; he had worn out his life for it; he hadn't earned it all to please his noble son-in-law; why should ungrateful folks enjoy it, when they left him to die without coming near him; out of sight out of mind! That's how the world is made, everybody turns the water to his own mill. And his own mill, for his part, was to get his health back again, with his own money. There were good doctors in the world, who might cure him if he paid them. Then he wiped away his sweat of agony, and tried to sleep. He wanted the strange doctors who were coming the next day to find him in better form; he counted the hours; it seemed a thousand years to him, till he could see them there before his bed. The very light of dawn encouraged him. Then, when he heard the bells of the litter which carried Doctor Muscio and Don Vincenzo Capra, he felt his heart expand I can't say how much. He drew himself lightly up to sit on the bed like one who really feels better. He greeted these good folk with a fine smile which would reassure even them, the moment he saw them enter.

But they hardly looked at him. They were all ears for Don Margheritino, who was telling the story of the illness with a great amount of personification of abstract things; and they nodded their heads from time to time; they only glanced now and then abstractedly at the sick man, whose face was becoming more and more perturbed, seeing those grave countenances, and those grimaces, and hearing the trilling of the bit of a doctor who seemed as if he was reciting the funeral oration. After this youngster had finished chattering, the other doctors rose one after the other, and began feeling and questioning the sick man, shaking their heads, with a certain sententious blinking, and certain glances from one to another that absolutely stopped his breathing. There was one of the strangers particularly who stood there frowning and pensive, going every moment "Uhm! Uhm!" without opening his mouth. The relations, the servants, even some neighbours crowded round the doorway out of curiosity, waiting for the sentence, while the doctors confabulated together in low voices in a corner. At a sign from the apothecary, Burgio and his wife also went to hear, on tiptoe.

"Speak out, gentlemen!" then exclaimed the poor man, who was pale as death. "I'm the one who's bad, I believe. I want to know where I stand."

The Muscio fellow started a smile that made him look uglier than ever. And Don Vincenzo Capra, in proper style, began to expound the diagnosis of the illness: *Pylori Cancer,* the *pyrosis* of the Greeks.

There were as yet no symptoms of ulceration; even
the adhesion of the tumour to the vital organs was
not certain; but the degeneration of the tissues was
already shown by certain pathological symptoms. Don
Gesualdo, after having listened attentively, replied:

"That is all very fine. But tell me if you can cure
me, your honour. Without thinking about money—
paying you according to your merit—"

At first Capra wouldn't answer, and shrugged his
shoulders.

"Eh, eh—cure you—of course—that's what we're
here for, to try and cure you."

But the Muscio fellow who was more brutal blabbed
straight out the only thing that there was left to try,
the extirpation of the tumour, a rare job, a surgical
operation that would do anybody credit.—He explained the way how it should be done, getting quite
heated over the proposition, accompanying his words
with gestures, already smelling blood, his eyes kindling
in his fat face that went quite purple, as if he was
just going to roll up his sleeves and set to work; so
that the patient opened his eyes and mouth, and shrank
instinctively away; and the women, overcome, broke
out into moans and sobs.

"Madonna of the Perils!" Speranza began to scream.
"They want to kill my brother for me—cut him up
and quarter him alive like a pig!"

"Be quiet," said he, passing the hem of the sheet
over his face that was dripping drops of sweat. The
other physicians were silent, and agreed more or less
with Doctor Muscio, out of courtesy. Don Gesualdo,
seeing that nobody uttered a sound, repeated again:

"Be quiet!—It's *my* skin that they're talking about
—so I can say what I think.—Gentlemen—I am a

man—I am not a child. If you say it is necessary, this operation—If you say it is necessary—yessir—we'll have it done.——But let me say what I think—"

"That's right, you say."

"Well then—one thing only.—I want to know first if you really guarantee to save my life.—We are gentlemen—and I trust you.—It's not a bargain to be made with your eyes shut. I want to see my way clearly—"

"What are you talking about!" interrupted the Muscio man, bouncing on his chair. "I am a surgeon, my friend. I practise my own profession, and don't set out to make quack's promises! Do you think you're dealing with Zanni, at the fair?"

"Then we'll have nothing to do with it," replied Don Gesualdo. And he turned his back on them. "Look here, Bomma, you gave me a fine bit of advice!"

Speranza, most anxious, saw that the time had come to turn to the saints, and she rushed round trying to procure relics and blessed images. Neri thought that they ought to warn the daughter and son-in-law at once of the danger Don Gesualdo was in. But *he* wouldn't hear anything. He said he'd got a heap of saints and relics already, there in Bianca's cupboard, along with the other medicines. He didn't want to see anybody. Since he was condemned, he wanted to die in peace, without any operations, away from all his worries, in his own country place. He clung to life with might and main, desperate. He had gone through other stress before this, and he had always helped himself, when he was in a tight fix. He'd got courage and a thick skin. He ate and drank; he persisted that he was better; he got up for two or three hours a day; he trailed himself through the rooms, from one piece of furniture to another. At last he had himself carried to Mangalavite, gasping for breath, Master Nardo on one side and Masi on the other, holding him up on the mule;—a journey that took three hours, and made him say a hundred times: "Throw me in the ditch, that's the best."

But once there, among his own possessions, he realised that it was actually all over, that every hope was lost, for nothing mattered to him any more. The vines were already coming into leaf, the young corn was high, the olives in flower, the sumachs green, and over everything a mist was spread, a gloom, a black veil. The house itself, with its windows shut, and the terrace where Bianca and his daughter used to sit and work, the deserted avenue, even his own country people who were afraid of bothering him and kept at a distance, there in the courtyard or under the shed, everything wrung his heart; everything said to him: "What are you doing? What do you want?"— All the things that belonged to him, there, the pigeons that circled in flocks above his head, the geese and the turkeys that cackled in front of him—You could hear the voices and singing of labourers working in the fields. Along the little road from Licodia, in the near distance, people passed on foot and on horseback. The world still went its way, while there was no more hope for him, gnawed by a worm like a rotten apple that must fall from the bough, not having strength to take a stride, nor even the will to swallow an egg. Then, in despair that he must die, he began to beat the ducks and turkeys, to break down the buds and the young plants. He would have liked to destroy with one blow all the wealth and substance he had got together bit by bit. He wanted his possessions to

go along with him, desperate as he was. Master
Nardo and the man-servant had to carry him back
to the village again more dead than alive.

A few days after arrived the Duca di Leyra, summoned by express courier, and he took possession of
his father-in-law and of the house, saying that he
wanted to take him to Palermo to have him attended
to by the best doctors. The poor wretch, now only
a shadow of himself, let them do as they liked; yet
he opened his heart again to hope; he was softened
by the anxiety of his son-in-law and of his daughter,
who was awaiting him with open arms. He fancied
his strength was already coming back. He couldn't
wait to be gone, as if he thought he would leave all
his ills behind him, there in that house and in those
fields that had cost him so much sweat, and which
now weighed on him like a burden. His son-in-law
busied himself with the procurator getting his affairs
in order. As soon as Don Gesualdo was fit to travel,
they put him in a litter and set off for the city. It
was a rainy day. The houses of note, and the faces of
his acquaintances, which hardly turned to look at him,
passed by the windows of the litter. Speranza and her
lot, angry because the duke had come to turn them
out, did not put in an appearance. Master Nardo had
wanted to accompany his master as far as the last
houses in the village. In the Street of the Masera
they heard somebody shouting: "Stop! Stop!"—And
Diodata appeared, wanting to say good-bye to her
master for the last time, there in front of her own
door. And then, when she came near him she hadn't
a word to say, and she stood with her hands on the
window-ledge nodding her head.

"Ah Diodata—you've come to wish me a good journey?—" said he.

She nodded yes, yes, trying to smile, her eyes filling with tears.

"Poor Diodata! You're the only one that remembers your master—"

He looked out of the window, perhaps expecting somebody else, but as it was raining he drew in quickly again.

"Now you mind yourself—out in the rain—and nothing on your head!—It's your old bad ways!—You remember, don't you, you remember?"

"Yessir," she replied simply, and she kept on nodding her head to her words. "Yessir, have a good journey, your honour!"

Then slowly, slowly she drew back from the litter, as if unwillingly, and she went back into her house, closing the door, humble and very sad. Then Don Gesualdo remembered Master Nardo who had come with him so far, and he put his hand in his pocket to give him a few pence.

"—I'm sorry, Master Nardo!—I haven't got anything.—It'll have to be another time, if we see one another again, eh?—if we see one another again—"

And he threw himself back, with his heart swollen because of all the things he was leaving behind him, the muddy road he had traversed so often, the church-tower lost in the mist, the cactus plants striped with the rain which threaded down on either side of the litter.

V

It seemed to Don Gesualdo as if he had come into another world, when he found himself in his daughter's house. It was a great palace so vast that you lost yourself inside it. Everywhere curtains and carpets till you didn't know where to put your foot;—even on the marble staircase;—and the door-keeper, a proper grand somebody, with such whiskers and such a tail-coat on him, stared you up and down, scowling, if by ill luck you had a face he didn't take to, and he shouted at you out of his cage:

"There's a scraper to wipe your shoes on!"

An army of lazy rascals, lackeys and chambermen, yawning with their mouths shut, walking on tiptoe, and serving you without saying a word or taking one extra step, and so very condescending that they fairly made you feel you hadn't a will of your own. Everything regulated by a bell ringing, with as much ceremony as high mass—to get a glass of water, or to go to your daughter's room. And the duke dressing himself up at meal-times as if he was going to his wedding. Poor Don Gesualdo kept his courage up for the first few days, to please his daughter, and dressed himself to come to table, trussed and shackled, with a roaring in his ears, his throat tight with all that paraphernalia, with the waiter who counted every mouthful he ate, behind his back, and whose cotton glove appeared every moment under his nose, reaching out treacherously to snatch away his food from in front of him. His son-in-law's white cravat also intimidated

432

him, as did the side-boards high and glittering like al-
tars, and the exquisite table-linen, so that he was always
terrified of dropping something on it.   And so he was
scheming to get his daughter to himself for a while,
so that he could say what he had on his mind.   The
duke, luckily, got him out of the difficulty by saying
to Isabella, after coffee, with his cigar in his mouth
and his head leaning on the back of his big arm-chair:

"My dear, I think it would be better to have your
father's meals served in his own rooms, after to-day.
He no doubt has his own hours and his own habits—
I don't want to put him out—And then with the special
régime that his state of health demands—"

"Yes, yes," stammered Don Gesualdo.   "I was just
going to tell you—I should like it better myself—I
don't want to be in your way—"

"No.   I don't mean that.   It is a pleasure to us to
have you, always, my dear sir."

He behaved like a real good son to his father-in-
law; he encouraged him to smoke a cigar; he assured
him that he found him looking better, since he had come
to Palermo, and that the change of air and the careful
attention would quite cure him in the end.   And then
he tried the business touch.   He showed himself
shrewd; he wished by every manner of means to secure
himself the pleasure of his father-in-law's company in
his house, without having to fear that the latter's
affairs would go to rack and ruin;—a general power
of attorney—a sort of *alter ego*.—Don Gesualdo felt
his smile die on his lips.   There was nothing to be
done.   This son-in-law, even when he wanted to be
amiable and as nice as possible to you, had something
in his face, in his words, even in the tone of his voice,
which seemed to thrust you backwards, and made your

arms fall to your side even when you were just wanting
to fling them round his neck, like a real son, and say to
him:

"Eh bless you, that's enough said! Never mind
the rest! Do as you like—"

So that Don Gesualdo didn't often come down to
see his daughter. He felt uneasy with his noble son-
in-law; he was always afraid lest he might start on
that tune of *alter ego* again. He felt he couldn't
breathe, there among so many idle-jacks. He had
almost to ask leave of the servant who was posted in
the antechamber if he so much as wanted to see his
daughter, and he had to flee if a visitor arrived. They
had put him in a wing on the upper floor, a few rooms
that were called the guest apartment, where Isabella
came to see him every morning, in her dressing-gown,
often not even staying to sit down, loving and thoughtful for him, it's true, but somehow she seemed to the
poor man a real stranger. Sometimes she was so pale,
she looked as if she too had not slept a wink. She
had a fold between her brows, and something in her
eyes which was to him, old and used to the world as he
was, by no means pleasant to see. He would have
liked to take her too between his arms, and hold her
fast, fast, and ask her softly in her ear:

"Why what's amiss?—tell me then!—You can tell
it to me, for I've had so many troubles myself, I
shan't betray you."

But she drew in her horns like a snail. She kept
herself close, spoke very rarely even of her mother,
as if the nail was driven right in, fixed;—showing the
proud stomach of the Traos, who closed their rancour
and their diffidence against you, implacable.

And so he had to keep back his kind words, and even

his tears, which swelled his heart big inside him, and he had to keep his own troubles to himself. He passed melancholy days at the window, watching the horses being groomed and the carriages being washed, in that courtyard as big as a market-place. Stablemen in their shirt-sleeves and with bare feet in their wooden pattens, sang, shouted, bandied jokes and chatted with the house-servants who were wasting their time at the windows, with their big aprons up to their necks, or in red waist-coats, carelessly trailing a duster in their rough hands, making coarse jokes, so that their quizzing rascally faces, so well-shaven and carefully combed, seemed now to turn into masks. Then the coachmen, other grand gentlemen, stood looking on with cigars in their mouths and their hands in the pockets of their smart coats, talking now and then with the concierge who came out of his little house for a smoke also, making signs and shouting snatches of vulgar song to the servant-maids whom they saw passing behind the windows of the balcony, maids who for their part peeped out provokingly to shout down ugly words and laughter of loose women, from their Madonna faces. Meanwhile Don Gesualdo was thinking how much good money must be slipping through these hands; all that host eating and drinking at his daughter's expense, devouring the dowry he had given her, Alia and Donninga, the good land which he had brooded over with his eye for so long, night and day, and measured out with his desire, and dreamed of in his sleep, and won at last rood by rood, day by day, denying himself the very bread from his mouth; the poor bare earth that had need of ploughing and sowing; the mills, the houses, the store-barns he had built with so much effort, so much sacrifice, one stone upon another. Canziria, Mangalavite, the house, everything, everything would slip through those hands. Who would be there to defend his property after his death?—alas, poor property! Who knew what it had cost? The noble duke, he, when he went out of the house with his head high and a cigar in his mouth and the head of his little cane in the pocket of his great-coat, the moment he stopped to glance at his horses, everything was obsequiousness like before the Holy Sacrament, the windows shut in a hurry, everybody ran to his post, all with their hats in their hands, the concierge holding low his gold-laced cap, erect in front of his window, the stablemen motionless by the crupper of their horses, the currycomb resting against their thighs, the first coachman, a grand gentleman, bending double while the review lasted, and while he received his orders: a comedy that lasted for five minutes.—Afterwards, hardly had he turned his back than the row and chatter started again, from the windows, from the arcade of the portico that led to the stables, from the kitchen which smoked and flamed under the roof, full of scullions dressed in white, as if the palace was abandoned to a starving horde, paid on purpose to squander everything until the sound of the bell announced some visitor—and then another solemnity.—On certain days the duchess prepared herself in greater state than ever to receive visits, like a soul in purgatory. From time to time arrived a flaming carriage; it passed like a flash of lightning before the concierge, who had hardly time to shove his pipe in his pocket and hang on to the bell; ladies and footmen in fine array exploded hastily out into the high vestibule, and ten minutes later back they came, to set off full speed for somewhere else; really like folks who had been hired by the day to do it. And he, alas, spent his time counting the tiles opposite, and calculating, with all the love and solicitude of his old trade, how much the carved windows had cost, and the massive pillars, the marble steps, the sumptuous furniture, all that stuff and velvet, those people, those horses which ate and swallowed money as the earth swallows seed, as it drinks up rain, but without giving anything back, without bringing forth fruit, always more hungry, more devouring, like the illness which devoured his own bowels. What couldn't have been done with all that money! How many good strokes of the hoe, how much labourers' sweat would it not have paid for! Farms, whole villages it might have built—land sown, as far as you could see—and an army of harvesters in June, mountains of corn to bring in, money in streams to put in your pocket!—And then his heart swelled to see the sparrows squabbling on the tiles, the sun dying on the cornice without ever coming as low as his windows. He thought of the dusty roads, the fine fields gold and green, the twittering along the hedges, the beautiful mornings when the furrows steamed!—And now!—And now!—

Now he was shut up between four walls, with the rumble of the city always in his ears, the clanging of so many churches beating on his head, as he was slowly consumed by the fever, gnawed by pains that made him bite his pillow, sometimes, so as not to disturb the servant who was yawning in the next room. During the first days, the change, the different air, perhaps also some medicine they had hit upon, by mistake, had performed the miracle and made him believe in the possibility of cure. Then he went back and was worse than before. Not even the best physicians had been

able to find any help for that accursed disease! no
better than the ignorant doctors of his own village, and
they cost more, as goes without saying! They came
one after the other, grand doctors who kept their carriage and made you pay even for the servant they left
in the antechamber. They examined him, they felt him,
as if they were handling a child or a peasant. They
showed him to their apprentices as the quack at the
fair shows the cock with horns, or the sheep with two
tails, expounding the case in mysterious words. They
hardly answered him, speaking from their lips, if the
poor devil took the liberty of enquiring what disease it
was he was nursing inside him, as if he had nothing to
do with it, nothing to do with his own vitals! And this
lot as well had made him buy a whole druggist's shop;
mixtures which you counted by the drop, like gold, ointments which you smeared on with a fine brush, and
which opened raw places on you, poisons which gave you
colic worse than ever, and left the taste of copper in
your mouth, baths and sudorifics which left him exhausted, without the strength even to move his head,
seeing the shadow of death already spread over everywhere.

"Gentlemen, what are we playing at?" he wanted to
say. "All right then, if it's always the same old game,
I'll go back to my own village."

At least they respected him for his money, down
there in his own place, and they let him speak, if he
wanted to know how much they were spending for the
sake of his health. Whereas here he seemed to be at
the hospital, cured out of charity. And he had to stand
in awe even of his son-in-law, who came up to accompany the grand gentlemen who were called in to a consultation. They spoke in an undertone among them-

selves, turning their back on him, without caring in the least about him who was waiting open-mouthed for the word of life or death. Or else they charitably gave him an answer which meant nothing, or a little smile which very plainly meant: "Good-bye, my good man. See you again in Paradise."—And there were even some of them who turned their backs on him as if they considered themselves offended by him. He guessed that it must be something serious, by the faces which these doctors made, and their discouraging shrugs of the shoulders, at their long stay with his son-in-aw, and by the long murmuring which they kept up among themselves in the antechamber. At last he could restrain himself no longer. One day when these gentry were playing the same pantomime over again, he seized one of them by the coat-tails before he could get away.

"Doctor, sir, just let me know. It's I who am ill, after all! I'm not a child. I want to know what it really is, since it's my own life that's in danger."

But the doctor fellow began making a scene, almost as if he had received an insult in his house. And it took heaven knows what to calm him down, and prevent him from throwing over the patient and the disease, once and for all. Don Gesualdo heard them saying to him in an undertone:

"Bear with him—He doesn't know how to behave— He is a primitive man—in the state of nature—"

So that the poor man had to put up with everything, and turn to his daughter to try and learn something from her.

"What do the doctors say?—Tell me the truth!— It's a serious disease, isn't it?"

And when he saw her eyes fill with tears, in spite of her effort to keep them back, he became furious. He didn't want to die. He felt a desperate energy come over him, to arise and depart from that accursed house. "I don't mean you—You've done all you could.—I don't want for anything.—But I'm not used to it, you see.—I seem as if I'm stifling inside myself—"

But neither was she happy in that house. The poor father knew it in his heart. They seemed to be in perfect accord, husband and wife; they talked courteously to one another, before the servants; the duke almost always passed half an hour in his wife's little sitting-room after dinner; he went to bid her good morning every day before breakfast; and on All Souls' Day, and at Christmas, for the feast of Saint Rosalia, and on the occasion of her name-day or of the anniversary of their wedding he gave her jewels which she showed to her father for him to admire, in proof of how fond her husband was of her.

"Ah, ah—I know—they must have cost a rare lot!— But you're not happy, for all that—one can see plain enough that you're not happy—"

He read in the depths of her eyes another secret, another mortal anxiety, which would not leave her even when she was with him, but which made her start if she heard an unexpected step, or if the bell that announced the duke rang at an unusual hour; and which gave her a deathly pallor, and certain rapid glances in which he seemed to read a reproof. Several times he had seen her arrive running, pale, trembling like a leaf, stammering excuses. One night late, when he was in bed with his sufferings, he heard an unusual disturbance downstairs, doors banging, the voice of the chamber-maid screaming almost as if she was crying for help, a voice that made him sit up terrified in bed. But the next day his daughter wouldn't tell him anything; it seemed moreover as if his questions annoyed her. They seemed, moreover, as if his questions annoyed her. They even counted their words and their sighs in that house, each one keeping his own troubles to himself, the duke with his cold smile, Isabella with the good grace they had taught her in college. The curtains and carpets suffocated everything. And yet, when you saw them together, husband and wife, so calm, so that no on would ever have suspected what was lurking underneath, it sent a shiver down your spine.

And then, what could he do, anyhow? He had enough of his own troubles. Worse off than anybody was he who had got death on his shoulders. When he was gone all the others would be at peace, just as he had found a certain peace after his father's death, and his wife's. Everybody leads the water to his own mill. He had given plenty of water to turn other people's mills! Speranza, Diodata, all the rest—a real river. And there as well, in that lavish palace, everything was of his earning; and yet he found no rest between the fine linen sheets and on the down pillows; he was stifled by the curtains and the fine silk stuffs that shut out the sun. All the money he spent to keep the show going, the noises in the courtyard, the servant who watched over him behind the door and counted his sighs, even to the cook who prepared him his insipid broths which he couldn't get down, everything was like poison to him; he didn't even digest the choicest morsels, they were like so many nails in his flesh.

"They're starving me to death, they are," he complained to his daughter, occasionally, his eyes kindled with despair. "It's not out of meanness—I believe it's good stuff.—But my stomach isn't used to it. Send me back home. I want to die there where I was born."

The thought of death now never left him; it revealed itself in his insidious questions, in his looks full of suspicion, even in his anxious efforts to conceal it in various ways. He had no fear of anybody now, and he stopped anybody who came near him with the request:

"I want to know the truth, dear sirs.—To put my affairs in order—my business affairs—"

And if they tried to reassure him, telling him it was nothing urgent—nothing serious—for the moment, he kept on insisting, watching with a sharp eye, cunningly, to see through them.

"You see I've got such a lot to do, down there in my own village, gentlemen!—I really can't stop here wasting my time!—I must think of everything, if I don't it spells ruin."

Then he explained whence this disease had come upon him.

"It's all the troubles I've had!—all the bitter things! —and I've had a lot!—You see, it's left the yeast here in my inside—!"

He had become cunning. He was afraid that they couldn't wait to get rid of him, to save his expenses and lay hold of what he possessed. He tried to reassure them all, with an affable smile:

"Never mind the expense—I can pay.—My son-in-law knows it.—Everything that's needed—It won't be money thrown away.—If I live I shall make more, plenty more money—"

With shining eyes, he tried even to ingratiate his own daughter. He knew that money, alas, made hell between father and children. He talked to her. He stammered, caressing her just as when she was a child, watching her furtively all the time, with his heart in his throat:

"What do I lack here? I've got everything I can have, to cure me. We'll buy everything that's needed, won't we?"

But the disease conquered him and took away every illusion. And in those moments of discouragement the poor man thought aloud:

"What use is it to me?—What good is it all?—It was never any use to your mother either!"

One day the duke's manager came to see him, officious, and, like his master, all kindness when he was getting ready for an attack. He enquired about his health; he condoled with him about the illness which had lasted so long. He could well understand, being himself a business man like Don Gesualdo—how much disorder—how many losses—the consequences—such a vast property—without anybody really to look after it.—In the end he offered to take the responsibility of it upon himself—for the sake of the interests of the house, which he had at heart—and for Her Grace the Duchess' sake. He had been a good servant of the noble duke for so many years—So that he had Don Gesualdo's welfare also at heart. He proposed to relieve him of every burden—until he was well again; —if he thought—by giving him a power of attorney—

And in proportion as he went on spitting out his poison, Don Gesualdo became more and more disconcerted. He hardly breathed, but listened with his eyes wide open, ruminating meanwhile how he should get out of the mess. All at once he began to cry and throw himself about as if he was seized once more by the colic, as if his last hour had arrived, and he could neither hear nor speak any more. He only stammered, raving:

"Fetch my daughter! I want to see my daughter!"

But no sooner had she arrived, terrified, than he became silent. He closed up inside himself to think out how he should extricate himself from the evil situation, sullen, suspicious, turning his back so that he should not let escape any look which might betray him. Only he fixed a long look on that gentleman who went away rather smaller than he had come. Then, bit by bit, he pretended to grow calmer. He had to use all his cunning to get out of those clutches. He began to nod yes, yes, fixing his eyes lovingly on the dismayed face of his daughter, with a paternal smile and a kindly manner:

"Yes—I want to put everything I've got into your hands—to relieve myself of the burden.—I shall be only too glad—seeing the state I'm in.—I want to give away everything—I haven't long to live.—Send me back home to make the procuration—the deed of gift —everything you wish.—I know the lawyer there—I know where to put my hand on everything.—But first send me back home.—And then I'll do everything you want!"

"Oh, father, father!" exclaimed Isabella, tears in her eyes.

But he felt he was dying from day to day. He couldn't move any more. It seemed to him as if he hadn't the strength to get up from the bed and go away, because they were taking from him his money, and the blood from his veins, to keep him a prisoner on the quiet. He bluffed, he raved, he howled with pain and rage. And then he fell back exhausted, threatening, foam at his mouth, suspicious of everything, keeping his eye on the hands of the servant if he drank a glass of water, looking everybody in the eyes to read the truth, to read his own sentence, forced to resort to artifice to find out something about the very things that concerned him most.

"Fetch that man that came the other time.—Bring me the papers to sign.—It's all right, I've thought about it. I've got to let somebody take the responsibility for my affairs, till I get better—"

But now they were in no hurry; they kept on promising him, from day to day. The duke himself shrugged his shoulders, as if to say it was no good now. A greater, closer terror, the fear of death, took hold on him, seeing their indifference. He insisted, he wanted to dispose of his possessions, as if to hold on to life in that way, to perform an act of energy and will. He wanted to make his will, to show himself that he was still master. At last the duke, to quiet him, told him there was no need, since there were no other heirs— Isabella was the only child—

"Ah?" replied he. "There's no need—she's the only child?"

And he lay down again, lugubrious. He would have liked to answer him that there were heirs, born before her, blood of his blood. And with his bile remorse arose. He had bad dreams, ugly pale angry faces appeared to him in the night; voices, shocks which woke him up with a start, bathed in sweat, his heart hammering hard. So many thoughts came to him now, so many memories, so many people filed before him: Bianca, Diodata, and others still: they would never have left him to die helpless! He wanted another consultation, the best doctors. There must be special doctors for his disease, if you knew how to find them, and paid them well. That's what he had earned his money for, in fact! In his own village they had given him to believe that if he would consent to have his inside opened—All right, he would, he would!

He awaited the consultation on the appointed day, from the early morning, sitting up in bed, shaved and combed smooth, his face the colour of earth, but firm and resolved. Now he wanted to see clearly into this matter.

"Speak freely, gentlemen. Everything that needs to be done shall be done!"

His heart beat rather fast. He felt a creeping sensation among the roots of his hair, in a spasm of anticipation. But he was ready for everything: he almost uncovered his abdomen to let them do as they liked with it. If a tree has canker on it, what does it amount to? You cut off the bough! But now the doctors wouldn't even operate on him. They had scruples, buts and ifs. They looked at one another and mumbled half-words. One was afraid of the responsibility; another observed that it wasn't necessary—now—The oldest of them, with such an ill-omened face that it made you die before your time, as God's above, had already started to comfort the family, telling them that it would never have been any good even earlier, with a disease of that sort—

"Ah—" replied Don Gesualdo, become hoarse all at once. "Ah—I understand—"

And he let himself slide very slowly down, stretched in the bed, overcome. And for the time being he said no more. He kept still and let them finish what they had to say. Only he wanted to know if the moment had come when he must think of settling his affairs. It was no use joking now! He had such a lot of serious business to get into order.

"Be still! Be still!" he muttered, turning to his daughter who was weeping at his side. With a cadaverous face, and eyes like two nails sunk in their livid sockets, he waited for the answer they would give him, at last.

"—No, no—There is time.—Such illnesses last for years and years.—But yet—yes—to be ready—to get your affairs in order in good time—it wouldn't be a bad idea—"

"I see what you mean," said Don Gesualdo, with his nose among the coverlets. "I thank you, gentlemen."

A cloud descended on his face and stayed there. A sort of rancour, something which made his hands and his voice shake, and which leaked out through his half-shut eyes. He signed to his son-in-law to stay behind; he called him to his bed to speak to him quite alone.

"Well, now, this lawyer—will he come, or won't he? I must make my will—I've got some scruples of conscience.—Yessir!—Am I master or aren't I?—Ah—ah—you're there listening as well, are you?"

Isabella threw herself on her knees at the foot of the bed, her face buried in the mattresses, sobbing in despair. The son-in-law for his part did his best to calm him.

"Why yes, why yes, whenever you wish, and just as you wish. There is no need to make scenes.—Look how you have upset your daughter—"

"All right," he kept muttering. "All right! I know!"

And he turned his back on them as his father had done, rest his soul. As soon as he was alone he began to moan like an ox, with his nose to the wall. But then if people came he kept quiet. He nursed his disease and his bitterness inside himself. He let the days go by. He thought to spin them out, maybe, to win at least those few, one after another, taking them as they came, and patience! While there's breath there's life.

And in proportion as his breath failed him, little by little, he gave himself up to his sufferings; he even got used to them. He had a broad back, and would hold out for a long time, thanks to his tough constitution. Sometimes he felt a certain satisfaction inside himself, under the sheet, thinking at the face my lord the duke would make, and all the others, seeing what a tough constitution he had. He had even come to be fond of his pains, he listened to them, caressed them, wanted to feel them there with him, to go forward with them. And his relations had got used to it as well; they had learnt that that disease lasted years and years, and they took it calmly now. That is how the world is, alas; when the first excitement is over everybody goes his own way and minds his own business. He didn't complain either; he said nothing, like the sly peasant he was, so as not to waste his breath, and not to let out what he didn't want to say; only he let some very significant glances escape him from time to time, seeing his daughter come to him with that desolate face of hers, and afterwards he turned on the husband, who kept him prisoned there under his eyes, pretending to be fond of him, to cherish him, for fear he should play him some trick in the will. He divined that she had other hidden troubles, and that sometimes her mind was straying elsewhere, while her father was lying there with death upon him. He fretted himself away inside, as he grew physically worse; his blood had every bit turned to poison; he became more and more sullen, taciturn, implacable, with his face to the wall, replying only in grunts.

At last he made up his mind that his time had come, and he prepard himself to die like a good Christian. Isabella had come at once to be with him. He put all his strength into his elbows and raised himself to a sitting posture on the bed.

"Listen," he said to her, "listen here—"

His face was troubled, but he spoke calmly. He kept his eyes fixed on his daughter, and nodded his head. She took his hand and burst into sobs.

"Be still," he resumed. "Leave off. If we start like that we shall get nowhere."

He panted because he was short of breath, and also with emotion. He looked around suspiciously, and kept on nodding his head in silence, out of breath. And she turned her eyes full of tears towards the door. Don Gesualdo lifted his wasted hand and made the sign of the cross in the air, to signify that it was over, and that he forgave everything, before going.

"Listen—I've something to say to you—while we're alone—"

She threw her arms round him, desperate, weeping, sobbing No, no, her hands wandering caressing him. And he slowly stroked her hair, slowly, without speaking. After a while he resumed:

"Yes, I say. I'm not a child—Don't let us lose time uselessly—"

And then he suddenly softened.

"You're sorry, eh?—You're sorry, aren't you!"

Her voice was also softened, her eyes, gloomy as they were, had become sweeter, and something trembled on her lips.

"I've been fond of you—I have—as much as I could. —And when a man has done what he could—"

Then he drew her slowly to him, almost hesitating, looking at her closely to see if she wanted it too, and he clasped her close, close, putting his rough cheek on her fine hair.

"I don't hurt you, do I?—like when you were a child!"

And then other things rose at the same time on to his lips, waves of bitterness and passion, those odious suspicions which scoundrels had tried to put in his mind, for his money's sake. He passed his hand over his brow, to drive them back, and changed his manner.

"Let us speak about our business. We won't waste ourselves in useless talk, now—"

She didn't want to, she went raving round the room, she thrust her hands in her hair, she said he was breaking her heart, that it was like an ill-omen, as if her father was going to close his eyes for ever.

"But no, let us talk!" insisted he. "There are serious things to say. I've no time to lose now—" His face was going darker, the old rancour glittered in his eyes. "You mean then that you don't care— that you're like your husband—"

Then seeing her resigning herself to listen, sitting with her head bent, beside the bed, he began to talk about all the heart-aches she had given him, she and her husband, with all those debts—He begged her to look after her property, to protect it and defend it— "Rather have your hand cut off, look you—when your husband starts asking you again to sign papers!—He doesn't know what it means!—"

He explained all that they had cost him, those fields and groves, the Alia, Canziria, he lingered over them with loving resignation; he recalled how they had come to him, one after the other, little by little, the arable lands, the pastures, the vineyards; he described them minutely, furrow by furrow, and their quality, good or bad. His voice trembled, his hands trembled, all his blood flamed in his face, tears came to his eyes.

"Mangalavite, you know—you know it yourself—you were there with your mother.—Forty square furlongs of land all with trees!—you remember—the splendid oranges?—your mother, poor thing, used to refresh her mouth with them in her last days!—three hundred thousand a year, they gave! Nearly three hundred guineas! And Salonia—corn-land worth its weight in gold—miraculous crops—blessed by your grandfather, whose bones lie buried there!—"

Till at last he began to cry like a child, with emotion.

"Enough," he said then. "I've got something else to say to you.—Listen—"

He looked fixedly into her eyes that were full of tears, to see what effect his will would have made on her. He made her a sign to come closer, to lean over him as he lay stretched out, hesitating, fumbling for his words.

"Listen!—I've got scruples of conscience.—I would like to leave a legacy to some people towards whom I've got obligations—just a little—It won't be much for you who are so rich—you can think of it as a present which your father asks of you—on his deathbed—if I have done something for you—"

"Oh father, father!—What are you saying?" sobbed Isabella.

"You'll do it, will you? You'll do it?—even if your husband isn't willing?—"

He took her temples between his hands and lifted her face to read in her eyes whether she would obey him, to make her understand that it really was important to him, and that he had that secret on his mind. And as he looked at her like that, he seemed to read in her that other secret, that hidden pain there in the depths of his daughter's eyes. And he wanted to say more to her, he wanted to ask her other questions, at that point, to open her heart as if to her confessor, and to read in his own. But she bent her head again as if she had guessed, with the obstinate frown of the Traos between her brows, drawing back, closing inside herself, haughty, with her sufferings and her secret. And he felt himself become a Motta again, as she was a Trao, suspicious, hostile, another flesh. He slackened his arms and said no more.

"Now fetch me a priest," he said in a changed tone of voice. "I want to make my accounts with the Lord God."

He lingered for a day or two still, alternating between better and worse. He even seemed to be reviving a little, when all at once, one night, he got rapidly worse. The servant whom they had ordered to sleep in the next room heard him restless and raving before dawn. But since he was used to these goings on, he turned over, pretending not to hear. Then, irritated by that song, which didn't come to an end, he went sleepily to see what was amiss.

"My daughter!" muttered Don Gesualdo, in a voice not like his own. "Fetch my daughter!"

"Ah, yessir! I'll go and fetch her now," replied the man-servant, and he went to lie down again.

But that miserable creature didn't let him sleep. Now he was high and shrill, now he was worse than a deep bass in his snoring. Hardly had the servant closed his eyes than he heard a strange sound that made him jump up in bed; raucous squeakings, like one who was puffing and panting, a sort of rattling that worried you and made your skin creep. So that at last he had really to get up again, furious, mumbling curses and abuse.

"What's up? Has he got a heat on him now? Is he up to some trick? What's he after?"

Don Gesualdo did not reply; he continued to gasp as he lay supine. The servant took off the lampshade to look at his face. Then he started rubbing his eyes hard, and the desire to go back to sleep left him all at once.

"Ohee! Ohee! What are we up to now?"—he stammered, scratching his head.

He remained a moment watching, with the lamp in his hand, wondering whether it was better to wait a bit or to go down at once and wake the mistress and upset all the house. Don Gesualdo meanwhile grew calmer, breathing shorter, seized by a tremor, only making a grimace with his mouth from time to time, his eyes always fixed wide open. All at once he went stiff and was quite still. The window began to whiten. The first bells were ringing. In the courtyard horses were heard stamping, and curry-combs rattling on the pavement. The servant went to get dressed, then came back to straighten the room. He drew the curtains of the bed, opened wide the windows, and stood to take a breath of air, smoking.

The stableman who was leading a sick horse up and down, lifted his head towards the window.

"Morning, eh, Don Leopoldo?"

"Night as well!" replied the chamber-man yawning. —"This nice job has had to fall to me!"

The other shook his head as if to ask what had happened, and Don Leopoldo made a sign to say that the old man had gone, thank God.

"Ah—so—slipped off quiet, like?" observed the concierge who was dragging the broom and his slippers along the corridor.

Other servants had appeared meanwhile, and they wanted to go and look. So that in a few minutes the death-chamber was filled with people in shirt-sleeves and pipe in mouth. The maid who attended to the wardrobe, seeing all those men at the window opposite, came as well to peep from the next room.

"What an honour, Donna Carmelina! Pray come in; we certainly shan't eat you. Nor will he either— he will never lay hands on you again, that's a fact—"

"Be quiet, irreligious creature!—No, I'm frightened of him, poor thing. He has ended his sufferings—"

"So have I," added Don Leopoldo.

And so, to the group of them, he told all the bother which that Christian there had been to him—a man who turned night into day, and you never knew how to take him, and he was never satisfied.

"Bad enough to wait on those who were really born better than we—But there, we won't speak ill of the dead."

"You can see how he was born," observed the first coachman gravely. "Look what hands!"

"Ay, they're the hands that have made the pudding! —See what it is to be born lucky—You die in fine linen like a prince!—"

"Well then," said the concierge, "am I to go down and shut the great door?"

"Why of course! He's one of the family. Now we've got to warn the duchess' maid."

THE END

PRINTED BY BUTLER AND TANNER LTD., FROME AND LONDON